"First and foremost," the man said without any preamble after getting everyone's attention, "we don't want anyone to panic. . . .

"There's a medical emergency in progress at the Somerset Medical Center. The hospital is now under quarantine, and I've been told by the CDC to instruct all students and staff to remain indoors for the time being."

"The CDC?" someone called out.

"The Centers for Disease Control and Prevention," the man explained. "There's been an exposure to a toxic, possibly lethal substance on campus. We hope to have the situation contained by morning."

"Contained?" someone said.

"Why can't you tell us what it is?" someone else shouted.

"Is it terrorists?"

"I don't even live in this dorm."

"Please . . . just listen," the man shouted back, raising his arms as though physically trying to hold back the mob. "We'll notify you about what's going on as soon as we can. For now this building is considered secure. I've been ordered to post guards at all exits, so just try to relax and wait until we get an all clear. At this point, that's all I can tell you."

"This isn't fair!"

"Do we still live in America, or what?"

Several students started booing as the dark-suited man and his police escort turned and walked quickly out of the dorm. As the glass doors swung shut behind them, Yoshiko noticed for the first time the two police officers who had taken up positions on the steps on either side of the front door.

Both of them had rifles in their hands.

Body of Evidence thrillers
by Christopher Golden

Body Bags
Thief of Hearts
Soul Survivor
Meets the Eye
Head Games

with Rick Hautala
Brain Trust
Last Breath
Throat Culture

christopher golden
and rick hautala
THROAT CULTURE

A *Body of Evidence*
thriller starring Jenna Blake

SIMON PULSE
New York London Toronto Sydney

For my compadre, Rick Hautala, godfather to Jenna.
We've raised the girl right, amigo.
—C. G.

For Chris Golden, for inviting me to share Jenna's world
and, more importantly, for friendship "above and beyond"
over the years. Thanks, Chris. . . . When they ask me "Who
dah man?" you know I'm gonna say it's you.
—R. H.

SIMON PULSE
An imprint of Simon & Schuster Children's Publishing Division
1230 Avenue of the Americas, New York, NY 10020
Copyright © 2005 by Christopher Golden
All rights reserved, including the right of reproduction in whole or in part in any form.
SIMON PULSE and colophon are registered trademarks of Simon & Schuster, Inc.
Designed by Kamil Vojnar
The text of this book was set in Dante MT.
Manufactured in the United States of America
First Simon Pulse edition April 2005
10 9 8 7 6 5 4 3 2 1
Library of Congress Control Number 2004114618
ISBN 0-689-86527-9

Eternal gratitude to my wife, Connie, and to our children, who give me hope. Thanks to my editor, Michelle Nagler, and to Lisa Clancy, without whom Jenna would never have been born. Thanks, as always, to Tom Sniegoski, Jose Nieto, Amber Benson, Bob Tomko, Allie Costa, and Ashleigh Bergh. And special thanks to Dr. Maria Carlini for her always helpful insight and expertise.

—C. G.

I would like to thank my enkeli, Holly, for being incredibly supporting and loving during these times when "there's always something." I also want to express my love and appreciation to my sons, Aaron, Jesse, and Matti, for being who they are . . . relentlessly.

—R. H.

PROLOGUE

Sometimes hell is other people. John knew he'd read that somewhere, and in recent times he had come to believe it. His life was tainted by other people now, poisoned by them, and the crowning achievement of his damnation was the time he had spent over the past two weeks listening to the chatter of tourists and breathing in the greasy, fried-food air inside Oceana's by the Sea.

No, it's purgatory, not hell, John thought as he hefted the tray full of appetizers and balanced the edge on his right shoulder. *Because it's going to be over soon.* Not soon enough to suit him, but his time in this restaurant of purgatory was a necessary evil. He just had to deal with it.

The busy sounds of food preparation in the kitchen—the shouted orders and idle chatter of the staff; the clash of dishes, pots, and pans; the hissing spray of the automatic dishwasher—grated on his nerves. Even

1

the sounds of the customers' conversations out in the dining area were an annoyance to him. Here it was, the middle of July. He'd been working here less than two weeks, and already he couldn't stand it. It was bad enough that he had to humiliate himself by working in a place like this. Worse, though, was putting up with the incessant demands of the staff and the customers.

Who do they think they're dealing with, anyway?

He shook his head and snorted softly as he started toward the double swinging doors that led out into the dining area. He wasn't working as a waiter at Oceana's all the way up in Ogunquit, Maine, because he *liked* the job. And he certainly wasn't here because the money was good. What both irritated and amused him was that none of them—not a single one of the people he worked with or the people he waited on—could see that a menial job like this was far beneath his dignity and station in life. The summer tourists, the irritating families with their whining children and demanding adults, the honeymooners and loving couples of all persuasions—*none* of them saw how out of place he was here, or realized how easy it would be for him to make them pay attention.

Today, for instance, he would change a handful of lives forever.

Call it an experiment.

All he had to do was choose.

And what am I waiting for?

"Pickup for Number Three," shouted Benny, one of the chefs—the fat one who was always bossing him around.

John caught Benny's eye, indicating with a quick nod of the head that he would deliver this order and be right back for the next one. Benny curled his upper lip into a slight sneer just before he turned away to tend to the meals he was preparing.

Don't think I didn't see that, John thought as he shouldered the swinging door open and walked out to deliver the food. Before he went to the customers' table, though, he paused at the wait station, carefully placing the tray down as though to adjust it. He kept his face perfectly expressionless as he reached into the pocket of his clean white waiter's jacket and opened the plastic bag he had there. The piece of shrimp felt warm and oily in his fingers as he withdrew it and casually arranged it as though it was part of the shrimp cocktail on the tray.

Nothing like a field test to see how things work, he thought, fighting back the smile that threatened to spread across his lips as he raised the tray, adjusted it on his shoulder, and walked quickly over to the table where his customers were seated by the window, looking out on a gorgeous view of the Atlantic Ocean. The sun was setting, and the ocean was a slate blue against the darkening sky. A bright point of light—*probably Venus,* John thought—was low on the horizon.

"Here you go," he said, wondering if either of them detected the faint note of excitement and anticipation in his voice.

It won't pay to give it all away, he told himself. *Not before we see the results.*

"You had the Caesar salad, correct?" he said, addressing the man. "And here's your shrimp cocktail," he said to the woman as he slid the plate in front of her. He couldn't help but glance out the window at the beach and ocean and think that this beautiful view was the last thing one of them would ever see.

"I'll be back when your entrées are ready," he said, sliding the tray under his arm and bowing slightly before turning and walking away.

He smiled broadly as he walked back into the kitchen and picked up the next order for "Number Three." *He probably doesn't even know I have a name,* he thought as he glared at Benny's back.

John delivered the order and just kept right on working as though nothing was different, but he felt a thrill, knowing that the test had begun. In spite of himself, he couldn't help but glance over at his customers by the window whenever he was on the floor. Anyone who saw him do that would simply assume he was being attentive to see if they needed anything, but he was waiting.

Despite his anticipation he was surprised and even a bit taken aback when the commotion began. He was heading back into the kitchen for another order when the woman screamed. There was an earsplitting crash as dishes and glasses shattered on the floor. The man at the table shouted his wife's name.

"Alice!"

Everyone in the immediate area reacted. Several of the waitstaff rushed out from the kitchen to see what the problem was.

Faster than I expected, John thought as he joined the throng and moved toward the couple at the table by the window. Only now they weren't sitting there so pleasantly. The man was down on the floor on one knee, and the woman was flat on her back. Her legs were under the table. A sudden rush of blood had colored her flabby cheeks a brilliant red, and her tongue protruded from her mouth, looking like the tail end of a huge purple slug she was trying to swallow. A thin trail of vomit ran down her chin and her fingers twitched as though she were trying to move her arms but found herself incapable of doing so.

Mark Hamilton, the maître d', rushed over, his face pale with shock in spite of his summer tan. Other staff members gathered nearby. Someone told Mark that they had already called 911.

This is much better than I could have hoped, John thought. He had to cover his mouth with his hand to hide a grin.

The woman was lying rigidly on the floor. Her lips were moving, and she was making sounds, but it was nothing coherent. Her breathing came in short, sharp gasps, and she winced as though in pain.

"What the hell is happening?" her husband yelled as he looked up at the people ringed around him.

"Did she choke on something?" Mark asked, kneeling down and leaning over the stricken woman. Already, far away outside, the sound of an approaching ambulance wailed louder and louder.

"No. She just started bloating, and then she had

this . . . this fit," the husband said. His face was almost as red as his wife's.

The woman on the floor convulsed so hard her foot kicked the leg of the table and pushed it back a foot or two. Her husband's chair tipped and crashed to the floor. He and Mark leaned over her, but it was obvious that neither one of them had any idea what to do.

The woman's breathing came in shorter and shorter gasps. Her eyes widened and bulged. She took a breath, and a watery, gagging sound came from deep in her chest. Her eyes rolled back and she twitched once, and then she let out a long gasp and lay still.

Bingo, John thought.

While everyone was focused on the woman on the floor, he drew back toward the doors leading into the kitchen. He didn't want to be anywhere near the dead woman when the emergency medical crew arrived.

It works.

chapter 1

Jenna Blake sat in the back of her Gross Anatomy class and tried not to fall asleep. Two massive problems had presented themselves to her since the fall semester had begun, and both plagued her during this particular class. The first was that it was one of those rare classrooms in the center of a building, and so there were no windows. Every time she entered the room, she thought of prison. If that wasn't bad enough, it was already the end of October, the Monday before Halloween, and Professor Booth had yet to tell the class a single thing she did not already know.

Sleep beckoned, and Jenna resisted with all her might.

Several times during the lecture her chin began to dip toward her chest, and she had to sit up straight, forcing her eyes to stay open. She even pinched her leg under the desk. Her blue jeans were crisp and new, but even through the denim it hurt enough to give her a jolt. An image swam into her mind of reaching down and giving her belly button piercing a twist. She smiled and cringed at the same time at the thought. But it helped her wake up a bit.

For a while.

Professor Booth droned on and on. Jenna's eyelids felt heavier, like they were lined with sand. Her laptop was open in front of her, and her fingers tapped the keys without any purpose, writing gibberish instead of notes, and then she stopped altogether.

"Jenna?"

It was too warm in the room. She felt flushed. An old Liz Phair song played in her mind. Halfway down in her chair, the sound of her voice was enough only to get her to raise her brows without opening her eyes.

"Hmm?"

"Jenna!"

She snapped awake. Every face in the room was turned toward her, her classmates laughing and smiling. There was no malice in their reaction. Hell, if it had been anyone else, she would've been just as amused. Jenna's cheeks flushed as she sat up, shooting an apologetic look at Professor Booth, who did not seem at all in a forgiving mood.

"Can you answer my question, Jenna? I'm sure you can, given how hard you were concentrating on it just now."

Oh yes, bring on the mockery, she thought. *If only I could slip on a banana peel and then maybe split the seat of my jeans, it'd be my best day ever.*

Jenna tucked a lock of her shoulder-length auburn

hair behind her ear. "I . . . I'm sorry, Professor. I didn't get the question."

Bob Booth sighed and nodded. For a moment he tapped his pencil on the lectern before him, and then he nodded again.

"The question, Jenna, was 'In cases of severe third degree burns, damage to what organ is likely to cause the death of the patient?'"

She frowned, knitting her brows. Before she could stop herself, she blurted out the words forming in her mind. "But that's a trick question."

Professor Booth arched an eyebrow. "Is it?"

Good one, Blake. Fall asleep in the guy's class and then challenge him in front of his students. The wise thing to do would certainly have been just to answer the question the way Booth clearly wanted it answered, but Jenna had never been the kind of person to hide what she knew or who she was.

"Yes. It is." She sat up a bit straighter and lowered the screen on her laptop. The rest of the class glanced at her, then the professor, and then back to her, like spectators at a tennis match.

"Explain please," the professor said, slightly pompous, crossing his arms. "I'm intrigued."

"Well, what you want me to say is that damage to the skin is the cause of death in cases of severe third degree burns. Most people don't realize that the skin is an organ, so simply asking what organ is responsible wouldn't typically make you think of the skin. But beyond that, it's also not necessarily true."

Booth looked confused and not a little aggravated. "Of course it is."

Jenna shook her head. "I'm sorry, Professor, but no. Certainly there are a lot of ways in which the damage to the skin is the cause of death in a case like that, though then you're usually talking about skin infection or, I guess, in a situation where you had massive third degree chest burns and the docs hadn't had time to make eschers cuts to relieve the tension, the tightening of the burned skin could cut off respiration, suffocating the victim. But that's really stretching it."

She paused a moment, wishing she hadn't started, but now she had to finish.

"In a case with serious third degree burns, the victim might have inhaled enough superheated air or even flame itself to cook the lungs. Or the airways might be scorched enough to cut off breathing, a lack of oxygen leading to brain death and cardiac arrest. Never mind the damage to other organs that could take place. Kidneys often fail in a situation like that. Actually, if the patient survived all that, pneumonia might develop and, if the victim is weak enough, that could be fatal."

Jenna stopped. The grins on the faces of her classmates had disappeared, but they were all still staring at her. Some of them seemed repulsed by what she had said; others seemed surprised. She saw one or two of them roll their eyes.

Crap, she thought. All she had been doing was providing information, answering the question honestly. Only now did she realize that doing so could make her seem like she was showing off or sucking up.

Professor Booth was scrutinizing her as though he had just seen her for the first time. His eyes were wide, and for several seconds he seemed incapable of replying.

Those seconds seemed to stretch out forever. Jenna slid lower in her chair and raised the screen on her laptop again, wishing she could hide behind it. *Great. So now I'm either a suck-up or show-off or a freak.*

The professor smiled and chuckled softly. "Yes, well, you're absolutely right on all counts, Jenna. And maybe I was oversimplifying a bit, but we're focusing on anatomy here. As you correctly pointed out, I was leading into a discussion of the skin as an organ, rather than a dissertation on cause of death in burn victims. I do thank you for your insights, however."

He seemed bemused now, and Jenna was grateful for that at least. It was far better than annoyed.

"So," he went on, leaning over the lectern, the sole point of interest in an otherwise featureless room. "You've done some studying, I take it. A hobby?"

His tone suggested what a gruesome hobby he would consider it.

Jenna shrugged, shrinking down further. "Something like that."

Her classmates who knew about her job already thought she was a freak. She felt no urge to spread that impression around. There were enough people who treated her as though she were some kind of intruder on campus, like she didn't belong there. The truth was, she often felt like that might not be so far from the truth.

A focus on partying and studying was enough of a life for most college students. But her life was just a little more full than that. In a lot of ways, though she wasn't even halfway through her college career, she had moved on already to the concerns and responsibilities of life after college. Her job put her not only in the real world, but in the midst of the grimmest aspects of human nature and civilization. She dealt with life and death— well, mostly death—nearly every day. In that light, the things that were vital to most other students at Somerset University didn't seem all that big a deal to her.

By the way Professor Booth and the other students were looking at her, she could see that this wasn't going to go away so easily. She had to offer some explanation.

"My mother's a surgeon," she announced.

A lot of her classmates nodded. That made sense to them. It had the added bonus of being true. Her mother, April, was a doctor back home in Natick. But that wasn't where Jenna had come by her knowledge of biology and forensics. In fact, before she had arrived at Somerset the previous fall, she had been the type to faint at the sight of blood. Her job had helped her get over that. Blood from a dead patient didn't alarm her because, after all, the patient was already dead.

Professor Booth grunted in interest. "Well, there you go," he said, as if the words meant something. "Maybe she can prescribe something to help keep you awake in class."

A ripple of laughter went through the classroom, and Jenna joined in, grateful that the focus was shifting away from her. Professor Booth opened his mouth to continue his lecture on the skin, but then he stopped and glanced at Jenna again, curiosity lining his forehead.

"Wait. Jenna Blake." He smiled. "I'm surprised I didn't make the connection before. I've certainly heard your name often enough. You work for Dr. Slikowski, don't you?"

Jenna smiled. Slick was her friend and her mentor. She might not want to be looked at as a freak by people whose ignorance caused them to be weirded out by her job, but she wasn't going to lie about it either.

"That's me," she piped up, once again tucking a lock of her hair behind her ear.

"Sorry, what? You mean the medical examiner?" said a guy in the front whom Jenna had appreciated from the first day of class. Not that she had any interest in him. He was just eye candy, with his chiseled features, dark hair, and olive skin. Jenna thought he was Eastern European, based on the accent. Or possibly Russian.

"Yes," she said curtly.

"You've been a pathology assistant there for over a year," Professor Booth said. "Walter's spoken very highly of you. Do you even need this class?"

Jenna smiled apologetically. "It's required for my major."

The professor nodded sagely. "Of course it is. Well, now I know who to get to sub for me if I ever have to call in sick."

13

There was some grumbling among the other students, but several of them actually shot her admiring looks. Jenna liked that. Premed was about as cutthroat a course of study as existed on the planet, but she thought maybe not everyone who wanted to be a doctor was so petty. Some of them had to be doing it because they were good people who wanted to help.

Of course, that didn't mean she wasn't glad that her work with Dr. Slikowski—whom some of his friends called Slick, though usually not to his face—gave her an advantage.

Class ended shortly thereafter, and she was thrilled to be released from that windowless cell, that prison of heat and boredom. Outside, it was a beautiful autumn day. The leaves were turning red and orange and yellow, and the air had a clean snap that she found refreshing. The sun shone brightly as she walked across the green lawns of Somerset's campus, but as the wind whispered through the trees, it carried just a hint of winter's chill, a promise of things to come.

Jenna loved it. Fall was her favorite time of year. October, especially. Sweaters and sweatshirts and leather jackets, warm and soft and comfortable clothing, fireplaces and jack-o'-lanterns and kids in costumes, ghost stories and all of it. Just . . . all of it.

The scene in Professor Booth's class had left her strangely happy, and the fallen leaves and October breeze erased any trace of awkwardness or embarrassment she had felt.

As she marched across campus toward her room in

Whitney House, Jenna soaked up the sun, and she sang softly under her breath, that same Liz Phair tune she had been dreaming about in class.

"Average, everyday, sane/psycho supergoddess . . ."

Somerset University had begun in the early nineteenth century as a single building atop a hill from which the distant skyline of Boston was a beautiful panorama. Jenna often wondered what the skyline had looked like in those days to the handful of young men who had made up the first graduating class. Could they even see Boston, or were there too many trees in the way? Over the decades the university had grown organically, spreading first across the hill before spilling down its sides and out into the surrounding city. Most of the students at Somerset lived in traditional dormitories, separated in a strange kind of rivalry between "uphill" and "downhill."

But on the outskirts of the campus proper, there were other housing options. Fraternity and sorority houses existed side by side with the Arts House, the all-female Richardson House, and the African-American Center. All of those options required special applications, however. More common was nondormitory student housing that the university handled as part of the overall housing lottery. Old houses in the city of Somerset had been purchased by the university and converted for student living.

On the western edge of the campus, past the tennis courts and the rugby field and at the end of a long row of fraternities, Whitney House stood on the corner of Carpenter Street and Sterling Lane. It was an enormous, sprawling house that appeared to have begun as a Colonial and then had new wings added to it over the course of many years. Yet despite its size, Jenna thought it was cozy in comparison to the dorms. There was a huge central common area just inside the front door with a large masonry fireplace and comfortable chairs and sofas all around. The residents of the house often gathered there to study or socialize or a little bit of both. The communal air of the place felt more intimate and somehow safer to her than Sparrow Hall, the dorm she had lived in "uphill" during her freshman year.

When Jenna opened the door, a gust of chilly fall air breezing in with her, she was greeted by a song. A dozen or so residents were gathered around the common area as Martin Crowther strummed his fat-bellied acoustic guitar and sang a Jason Mraz song in a sweet baritone voice. When he spotted her, Martin smiled and gave her an upward tilt of his chin in greeting as he played.

Jenna shifted her shoulder bag and responded with a little wave. Martin was gruffly handsome, with too-long sandy blond hair and the constant need of a shave. But he could get away with being a bit scruffy because he was British. Somehow, the accent went quite well with that just-rolled-out-of-bed ersatz-hippie look.

She stood and listened for a minute or two. Martin was one of the new friends she had made in her sophomore year, and it was always nice to talk to him and listen to him play. Right now, though, Jenna wanted to get back to the room and see what Yoshiko had planned for dinner. She headed toward the rear of the house and then down the stairs to the basement hall and to the room they shared. Yoshiko Kitsuta had been her roommate freshman year as well, and the two girls had become the best of friends. Though the room was in the basement, they felt they had found one of the best-kept secrets on campus. Their room in Whitney House was the biggest double either of them had ever seen, and it had the added benefit of having its own bathroom, complete with shower.

They had absolutely lucked out.

Jenna fished her keys out of her pocket and unlocked the door. As she stepped into the room, slipping her bag to the floor, Yoshiko glanced up in surprise from her computer. Without a smile, she closed whatever it was she was working on.

"Hey," she said, turning in her chair to face Jenna.

There was an odd tension in her expression, and Jenna's mood dipped immediately. Yoshiko was still her best friend at Somerset, at least as far as she was concerned. But ever since the fall semester had begun, she'd started to wonder if her roommate still felt that way in return. Most of the time she was her old self, but there were times—entire days, even—when she was distant and even a bit chilly. It wasn't like her at all. At least, not like the Yoshiko Jenna knew or thought she had known.

"Hey," Jenna replied halfheartedly.

Yoshiko hesitated as if there were somewhere else she would rather have been. After a moment, though, she took a deep breath, and her features changed entirely, as if suddenly she remembered who it was she was talking to.

"Something wrong?" she asked. "Bad day?"

Not up until now, Jenna wanted to say. But she had already brought up Yoshiko's preoccupation several times since they had moved into Whitney House, and she didn't want to badger the girl. It seemed to Jenna that something was weighing on her friend, but if Yoshiko didn't want to talk to her about it—as much as that hurt her—that was her roommate's prerogative. Jenna didn't want to harp on it. She only hoped that whatever was bothering Yoshiko, it wasn't anything to do with her.

"Nah, not really," she said, cringing inwardly at the lie. Then she hit on a plausible explanation for her own obvious mood shift. "Just something that happened in class." She quickly described the events in Gross Anatomy and the way the other students had looked at her.

Yoshiko smiled and waved a hand as if to brush her concerns away like they were unseen cobwebs. "Hey, you know the story there. For better or for worse, and sometimes maybe for both, you *aren't* like them. Your life is different. It's like when that actress from that show, *Eighth Wonder* or whatever . . . she went to MIT. You've got a whole 'nother world, and sometimes you have to dial it back down to our speed, put yourself on the wavelength of people your age while you're on campus. That can't be easy."

"No," Jenna agreed. "Sometimes it's not."

"Which is why I think we need to have a party."

One eyebrow shot up, and Jenna stared at her. "A party. Us?"

Yoshiko grinned. "Sure. Why not? Saturday night. A little pre-Halloween bash. The common area down here in our basement dungeon is almost as big as the one on the first floor. Less noise to bring the police. And even if they do show up, we can just slip into our room and shut the door. End of party. Come on. Now that we're settled into the daily grind of school, let's *really* get the semester rolling."

Stunned, Jenna shook her head in amazement. When she had walked into the room, Yoshiko had seemed a bit gloomy, even cold. Now the girl who had once been quiet and demure wanted to throw a party and was even talking about the police having to break it up.

"Yeah . . . all right," Jenna said, smiling broadly and thinking that perhaps this was exactly what they both needed. "I'm in."

But even after that, the conversation left Jenna wondering if the distance she had been sensing from her roommate was Yoshiko's fault or her own.

Tuesday was Jenna's lightest course load of the week. The morning started at 8:50 with Developmental Bio, but she was happy to get that out of the way early. Women in America to 1900 began at 11:10, and it was already her favorite class. Aili Heikkinen, a recent addition to the faculty, was one of the most dynamic women she had ever met, and every session felt like a window into the secret history of the country. Jenna's father, Frank Logan, was a professor of criminology at Somerset, and she had almost taken one of his classes instead of Women in America. While she still planned to take criminology in the spring, she was very happy that she had chosen to put it off another semester.

Not that there wasn't a certain trepidation in taking one of her father's classes to begin with. But she didn't have to worry about that for a few more months.

She had lunch in Keates Hall, the largest and grandest of the uphill dormitories with its domed roof and the facade columns that made it look like a government building. Jenna saw plenty of people she recognized, but she needed to get to work, so she chose to eat alone, hurrying through her meal.

From the back of Keates it was simply a matter of crossing Carpenter Street, and then she was on the grounds of Somerset Medical Center. The hospital complex was like a mini-city unto itself, comprised of several enormous buildings, one of which housed the medical school associated with the university. It was another beautiful autumn day, and it seemed a shame for her to spend the afternoon indoors.

Good thing I love this job, she thought as she strode quickly along the tree-lined path to the main entrance to SMC. From her pocket she retrieved her ID badge and showed it to the security guard at the front entrance; then she went through the lobby. The morgue and the autopsy room were downstairs, but the medical examiner's office was on the fifth floor. Jenna made her way along a corridor and then rode the elevator up with several people who were there to visit patients. It was always fascinating for her to study their faces, which revealed so much about the reason for their visit. In many cases she could tell how sick or injured their loved ones were just by looking at them.

The fifth floor was mostly offices, and so it was always quieter than the rest of the medical center. It also lacked the antiseptic smell of the patient floors and surgical areas.

Another corridor brought her to a short side hallway where the medical examiner's office was tucked away. Jenna still held her ID badge in her hand because it doubled as a key card to let her into the office. She had last worked on Tuesday, and she knew there were likely to be several audiotapes for her to transcribe. Dr. Slikowski—Slick—had grudgingly installed a digital recorder, but he didn't like it. The man was only in his mid-forties, but there was something very old-fashioned about him. He didn't always trust the new technology, worried that it might fail him. Dr. Albert Dyson, the pathology resident who worked with Slick, would use the digital recorder whenever possible, but he and Jenna were still trying to convince Slick that the tech was trustworthy.

There would be reports to send to various police departments in the county, documents to file, and phones to answer. And, if Dyson was unavailable or they had a particularly interesting case that Slick wanted

Jenna to see, she might be asked to assist with an autopsy. She had already decided that this was what she wanted to do with her life, and Slick saw in her a mind much like his own. She was grateful that he had the patience to let her learn from him. There was a long way to go—the rest of undergrad, then med school and beyond—but Jenna was focused.

If that meant answering phones and e-mailing autopsy reports to police departments, she could do that.

As she arrived at the door, it swung inward. She looked up, startled, even as Slick emerged from the office, gently propelling his wheelchair into the hall. Dyson was behind him, followed by Audrey Gaines, a homicide detective with the Somerset police department.

"Jenna," Slick said, nodding a curt greeting. He removed his round wireless glasses and wiped them off before returning them to the bridge of his nose. "Your timing is impeccable. Dr. Dyson and I have a subject waiting downstairs. I know you have plenty of work waiting for you, but would you mind locating the autopsy report on Anthony Zemek and making a copy for Detective Gaines? She's as impatient as always."

Audrey caught Jenna's attention and, smiling thinly, rolled her eyes. Dyson muttered a subdued hello as Jenna nodded to Slick, and then the two doctors were moving down the hall, leaving Jenna standing there in the open doorway with Audrey.

"I'll take care of it," Jenna called after them. "Are you sure you don't need my help?"

"'Thank you," Slick replied, not slowing, barely glancing back. "But I'd hate to be responsible for getting you any further behind in your work."

"Oh," she said with a tiny shrug. "Okay."

She watched as they turned the corner, and then remembered that the detective was waiting for her. Audrey was watching her curiously, and Jenna smiled at her, feeling a bit awkward.

"Let me get that report for you," she said, moving over to her desk and booting up her computer. A screen came up asking for her password, and she typed it in. As the computer verified it, Jenna looked up at Audrey. "So how are things going?"

The detective looked tired. Her skin was soft, the color of chocolate, but lately there was a gray tint to her face that spoke of how much stress she'd had in her life recently. At the end of the summer her partner, Danny Mariano, had been suspended after shooting a suspect in the middle of an attempted murder. The suspect had died, and now there was an investigation, and Danny was sidelined without pay until the investigation was concluded.

"As well as can be expected."

Jenna studied her screen for a moment, clicking open folders until she found the file she was looking for. She double-clicked on it to open it, and then hit PRINT. The printer began to hum.

"And how are you doing?" Audrey asked.

The autopsy report was already printing, but Jenna kept her eyes on the screen. She had spent a lot of time since the summer not thinking about the situation with Danny. In the past year they had become friends and almost more than that. But the difference in their ages—nearly fifteen years—had forced them both to realize that they would have to be satisfied, at least for now, with friendship. Even so, Jenna wondered if that might change, given time. She thought maybe Danny wondered too. She cared deeply for Danny, and the horror of what had happened to him pained her. Even after all this time, the ache still resonated. Particularly because Jenna had been the victim Terri Yurkich was trying to murder when Danny stepped in and shot her.

Sometimes she snapped awake at night from nightmares of drowning, staring up through the water at the blurry face of her killer as she gulped down mouthfuls of chlorinated pool water. Darkness would start to sweep over her, filling her with dread for her impending death, and then there would come a pop, and blood would float like a shroud of fog upon the water. Red fog. The dreams were terrible, so Jenna always found herself grateful to be awake.

"Me?" Jenna replied, unused to sympathy from the detective. "I'm all right, I guess. I can't erase my memories, but I'm making new ones. So far the semester's going really well. New dorm, new classes, some new friends. My dad's wedding was last weekend, and that was a blast. It's all good. I'll be okay. I'm really more worried about Danny."

Audrey smiled. "Yeah. And I'm sure he's more worried about you than he is about himself."

Jenna glanced away from her, staring at the printer as the last of the pages dropped into the tray.

"What is it?" Audrey asked.

"Huh? Oh, nothing."

A firm hand landed on her shoulder. Audrey was trying to comfort her, but it made Jenna jump a little.

"Hey," the detective said. "I know I can be a bit of a hardass, but we're past that, aren't we?"

Audrey fell short of saying they were friends. That would be too unprofessional for her. But Jenna knew what she meant, and she agreed, nodding.

"Then what is it?"

Jenna shrugged. "I'd like to talk to him. If he's worried about me, then he has a funny way of showing it. Not that I care. I mean, I don't need him to be worrying about me or anything. I do all right taking care of myself. But it's killing me, knowing what he's going through because he saved my life. I want to be there for him, Audrey, but he doesn't return my calls."

The detective shook her head. "Idiot," she muttered. Then she smiled. "No. Idiot's too strong a word, but he probably thinks he's doing you a favor keeping you at a distance. Truth is, he's not doing very well. The investigation isn't looking good for him. We all know if he hadn't shot Yurkich you'd probably be dead now, but the *probably* is the problem. He can't prove that. Nobody can. It could really go either way. There's a disciplinary hearing coming up, and it all comes down to what the board decides to do with him. I think Danny figures you've had enough trouble lately."

"Maybe," Jenna said, but she had her own theories. She thought that maybe Danny was upset enough that he didn't care about logic, that maybe he resented her, blamed her a little for what happened. But she wasn't going to argue about it with Audrey.

"Here you go," she said, handing the autopsy report to the detective.

Audrey took it, thanked her, and turned to go. At the door she paused and looked back at Jenna.

"And listen. Maybe you're hurting because Danny's not returning your calls, and maybe you're still a little raw after what Yurkich did to you. So just in case you're feeling sensitive . . ." She gestured out into the hallway. "The way Slick and Dyson brushed you off just now?"

Jenna nodded, not admitting that it had irked her but not denying it either.

"They look out for you, Jenna. That's all. You've got a lot of people in your corner. The docs didn't want you coming down to the autopsy because the vic they've got on the table is a seven-year-old boy. Maybe you're a part of their team and you've proved you can handle things like a professional, but they didn't want you in there for this one. Don't be too hard on them."

Jenna felt a wave of sadness for the little boy and his parents, and a churning revulsion in her stomach as she wondered about his cause of death. She wanted Slick to think of her as a professional, but the truth was, she wasn't yet. Ultimately, she was glad they hadn't invited her to take part.

"I won't," she finally said. As the detective started out the door, Jenna called to her. "Audrey?"

The statuesque woman shot her a curious glance.

"Thank you."

"You just worry about Jenna for a while, 'kay? Go to class. Study. Hang with your friends. Have a party. Have a life. This stuff will all work itself out in the end."

"But you'll keep me posted?"

Audrey nodded. "Of course I will."

Then she was gone, and for a while Jenna only stared at her computer screen, her eyes seeing nothing.

Have a party, Audrey had said. And Yoshiko had suggested the same thing the night before. It was starting to sound better and better every time it came up.

Jenna couldn't remember ever needing a party more.

chapter 2

On Wednesday morning Frank Logan stood in his bedroom staring at his reflection in the full-length mirror on the door. He couldn't stop wondering why he wasn't able to get his fingers to do what he wanted them to do.

This isn't difficult, he told himself, but he simply couldn't get his fingers to cooperate. Heaving a heavy sigh of frustration, he tore the necktie from under his collar and shook it out violently.

"Blasted thing," he snapped.

"Is something the matter, hon?" Shayna, his wife, called from the bathroom.

They had gotten married the previous Saturday in Magnolia, on the North Shore. Following the ceremony at the local Episcopalian Church, they'd held the reception at King's Grant, an elegant seaside restaurant with a gorgeous view of the Atlantic Ocean. It had been a full moon the night of the wedding, and the view had been spectacular. Because both Frank and Shayna taught at Somerset—he in the Criminology Department and she in the English Department—they'd had to postpone their honeymoon until the winter semester break. Frank told himself that it didn't matter. After all, they had just spent last spring semester on sabbatical in Europe, so another vacation would have to wait.

But so far married life suited Frank just fine. He was much happier with Shayna than he had been with either of his previous wives. Maybe it was just that he was older and wiser, more experienced; but if he was older and wiser, then why was he having such a deuce of a time trying to tie his necktie?

"It's just this tie," Frank said, flapping it angrily and cracking it like a whip. "I've tied one of these things scores if not hundreds of times, and I never seem to get it right."

"Here. Let me see," Shayna said.

Frank watched her in the reflection as she opened the bathroom door and walked up behind him. She had a large bath towel wrapped around her. Her dark hair clung to her forehead in damp ringlets, and her skin was still beaded with moisture from the shower. Her face usually tended to be pale, but it still held traces of the tan she had gotten during the spring and summer. She looked much healthier and happier than she ever had, as far as he was concerned.

Shayna turned Frank away from the mirror so he was facing her and reached up to place the tie around his neck. She smiled as she carefully threaded it underneath his collar. Her breath was warm on his face, and Frank's first impulse was to lean forward and kiss her, but he stayed right where he was, allowing her to tie it quickly and expertly into a perfect knot.

"There. All set," she said, smiling with satisfaction as she patted him on the chest.

Frank turned back to the mirror to inspect her work. It was perfect—better than he could ever have done on his own.

"How'd you do that?" he asked as he shifted the tie back and forth until it was comfortable on his neck . . . at least as comfortable as it was ever going to get. Before she answered him, he turned around again and gave her a big hug.

"Oh, I have my secret ways," Shayna said as she looked up at him with a warm smile. Standing on tiptoe, she planted a warm, wet kiss on his mouth.

After they broke off the kiss, Frank shook his head and said, "Wouldn't you really rather be heading out to the airport to catch a plane to the Caribbean?"

Shayna considered his question for a moment before answering, and Frank realized that this was one of the many things he admired about her: She never answered a question—even a simple one—quickly. She always considered before giving a truthful answer.

"Not really," she finally said. "I mean—sure, I'd love to be off on another trip, especially with you, but I happen to enjoy the fall, and we'll appreciate the Caribbean a lot more in January."

"True . . . true," Frank said as he slid his hands up her

arms and clasped her by the shoulders. "But anywhere is fine . . . as long as I'm with you."

"Even this reception today?" Shayna asked.

There was a mischievous twinkle in her eyes that Frank couldn't miss. She knew how uncomfortable he was about where they were going. Frank had told her too many times to count that he didn't want anyone making such a big thing about them getting married, but the truth was, they both were important members of the Somerset faculty, and today's faculty reception in their honor was supposed to be fun.

"What's wrong with this picture?" he asked, still holding her tightly.

Shayna frowned and shook her head.

"I'm not sure I know what you mean," she said.

Frank chuckled. "Here I am, all dressed up and ready to go, and you've just stepped out of the shower."

Shayna smiled and shrugged. The motion loosened the towel, and it would have fallen away if she hadn't grabbed it quickly.

"I just wanted to make sure you had plenty of time to get that tie on correctly," she said.

Frank smiled, but then he thought of something else that made his expression drop. Shayna caught it immediately and reached up to caress his cheek.

"What is it, sweetie?"

Frank started to speak but then fell silent. He looked at his wife and saw the love and concern in her eyes.

"It's nothing," he said.

"Oh, it's something, all right," Shayna said, "and

you're going to tell me what it is even if I have to beat it out of you."

Frank considered for a moment, then cleared his throat.

"It's just . . . Jenna," he said, his voice dropping low.

"What about her?"

Frank shrugged. "Well, I know I'm the one who told her not to worry about coming to this thing. I mean, there won't be any other students there, it's just faculty, she'd be bored. But it's sort of odd to be celebrating like this with her just across campus."

"She was there for the wedding, honey, not to mention the embarrassingly big reception at the hotel afterward," Shayna said. "And you're right. She would be bored."

Frank nodded and said, "I know, I know, but still . . . it's just—" He heaved another sigh, but this one was not from frustration but from longing. "She's growing up so fast. I feel like in some ways my life is just careening past me, and I . . . I worry about her."

"I don't see why," Shayna said with a sympathetic smile. "She's a great kid. I'd say you and April did a great job raising her. You should be very proud."

"I am," Frank replied, "but I . . . she's still my little girl."

"Uh-uh. I beg to differ," Shayna said, shaking her head. "She's not a little girl at all."

"You just said she was a great kid," Frank said, feeling unaccountably a little defensive.

Shayna hesitated for a moment before speaking.

"Yes, I did, but that's a relative term. Jenna's more responsible than some adults I know, and you're going to have to accept that she's growing up. You're going to have to start dealing with her like she's an adult."

Frank was a little taken aback by his wife's directness, but he knew that she was saying exactly what she meant. That was a part of Shayna's nature that he admired so much.

"I know, but it—sometimes it's so damned difficult."

"Of course it is," Shayna said with an impish grin. "That's why they call it life."

Frank studied her for several seconds in silence, feeling totally confounded.

"Wait a second," he said, frowning at her. "That's why they call it life? That doesn't even make sense."

Shayna wheeled around and, smiling at him over her shoulder, walked back into the bathroom and closed the door.

"Think about it," she called out from behind the door. A second later the high-pitched buzzing sound of the blow dryer filled Frank's ears. He stood there for a while, just staring at the door as what Shayna had said about Jenna sank in. And he realized that Shayna was absolutely right. Jenna would always be his little girl, but he was going to have to get used to the woman she had become.

"Maybe I am getting a little wiser along with the older," he muttered to his reflection in the mirror as he readjusted the tie, loosening it just a bit more so he could swallow.

"So," Hunter LaChance said, dragging the word out with his slow Southern drawl, "are you planning this as a Halloween costume party?"

Jenna had run into him after her morning class and they had wandered up onto the roof of the library. Now they stood gazing toward the distant Boston skyline. The air was unseasonably warm and perfectly clear, not a cloud in sight, making the city look much closer than it usually did. The sunlight gave Hunter's face a rich, golden glow and highlighted his blond hair, making it look almost white.

"I'm not sure," Jenna replied with a quick shrug. "Probably not. I don't think we'll be able to pull it together fast enough, and I don't want it to be lame. Besides, we're doing it Saturday night because we don't want to compete with Halloween night on Sunday. Who'd want to compete with the Sparrow Hall Halloween Run?"

Every Halloween it was traditional for the residents of Sparrow Hall—at least those who dared to and wanted to—to run around the outside of the dorm naked at midnight. Other students could join in, but the tradition had begun with Sparrow.

"You running this year?" Hunter asked. One side of his mouth twitched up into a smile.

"I'd only do it if you and Yoshiko did," Jenna replied. "And even then . . . I don't know."

"So did you invite Damon?"

"Of course I did," Jenna replied, perhaps a bit too quickly, she thought. "We invited him and Ant and all the other guys." She paused and glanced at Hunter. He was looking straight at her, and she stared for a moment into his bright blue eyes. She could sense the unspoken question. "I don't have any hard feelings about what happened between me and Damon."

"Really?" Hunter asked.

"Yes . . . really. I'm over it."

Hunter leaned back against the cement wall, squinting as he gazed at the Boston skyline. "But he was two-timing you. I mean—maybe *you* don't carry a grudge or anything—but I kind of do *for* you. He hurt you, Jenna, and . . . and . . ." He chuckled and, leaning forward, shook his head. "And I should probably just keep my nose out of your business, right?"

"No, you shouldn't," Jenna said, smiling. "I'm glad you care."

A warm rush of affection filled her as she reached out and gently touched Hunter's arm. He looked at her. The touch had no romantic undertones to it. He was like the brother she'd never had, especially since she and her half brother, Pierce, weren't very good about staying in touch.

And Jenna was happy that Hunter and Yoshiko were a couple. They were perfect for each other, and she could see how each of them was good for the other. They had both blossomed so much since hooking up in the beginning of freshman year. Even if Jenna had found Hunter overwhelmingly attractive, she knew she would have steered clear of him if only out of respect for her roommate.

The funny thing was, ever since they had returned to school this year, Jenna had felt much closer to Hunter in some ways than she did to Yoshiko. The distance she sensed between her and her roommate bothered her even though it was understandable—at least to her. Over the summer break, Yoshiko had gone back home to Hawaii and, while there, had spent some time with Tony Maleko, an old high school friend. Tony was the boy Yoshiko had had a crush on all through high school, but he had never noticed her . . . until this past summer. Jenna still didn't know what—if anything—had happened between them, and she wasn't sure she wanted to know. But that, no doubt, had to be contributing to the feeling of distance between her and Yoshiko.

Most of all, it bothered her that—at least as far as she knew—Yoshiko hadn't said a word about it to Hunter. It made her wonder if something more had gone on . . . something Yoshiko hadn't admitted even to her.

But then again, that was between Hunter and Yoshiko, and—like Hunter had just said—maybe she should keep her nose out of her friends' business.

"You don't have to carry any grudges for me, though, Hunter," Jenna said, tightening her grip on his arm for emphasis. "I'm fine by myself."

She smiled when he turned and looked directly at her again. It was good to realize just how close they had grown since first meeting a little over a year ago. Freshman year seemed like a lifetime ago. Jenna honestly felt as though she wouldn't even recognize herself if she could somehow go back in time. So much had happened to her and her friends. She had been feeling a bit melancholy today, and she suddenly realized one possible reason. It had been almost exactly a year since her first and closest friend at college, Melody LaChance—Hunter's sister—had been murdered.

"So you're gonna come, right?" Jenna asked.

Hunter shrugged. "Sure. It's just that . . ."

He was quiet for a long time.

"You okay?" she asked, already knowing the answer to the question.

"Yeah, it's just that . . . you know, I've sort of been avoiding coming to visit you guys. Melody was rooming in Whitney House last year before she . . ."

"I know." Jenna rubbed his arm to comfort him.

"It's kinda hard, you know, to think that you and Yoshiko have a room in the basement just down the hall from her old room."

"I'm sorry. I know it can't be easy," Jenna said, "and I find myself thinking about her . . . a lot."

She turned away. Bright yellow and red leaves rose like flames among the green maples. The air seemed suddenly colder, and she hugged herself as she shivered.

"It's been a whole year, you know?" she said, her voice husky with emotion. "And the angle of light, the chill in the air . . . I'm sure it triggers memories of . . . of what happened."

She looked at Hunter and saw that his eyes had grown damp and red with unshed tears of grief.

"I—I'm really glad you got to know her," Hunter said. His voice was thick with emotion. "I'm glad you were her friend because you know what I—" His voice choked off, but he forced himself to keep talking. "You know what I lost."

"She was an amazing person," Jenna said, fighting her own tears.

"I just think it might be hard to come to a party at Whitney House."

"Maybe," Jenna said, smiling sadly. "But you know Melody wouldn't have stood for us mourning all the time. She'd kick our asses, telling us to have fun, enjoy ourselves while we're still alive."

"I know," Hunter said. "But I gotta tell ya . . . It's only because of you and Yoshiko that I was even able to make it through last year. You're a good friend, Jenna. I don't know what I'd ever do without you."

"Me either." Jenna shivered so hard her teeth chattered, and Hunter turned and looked at her.

"You're freezing," he said. "How 'bout I buy you a cup of coffee?"

"Sounds good," Jenna said as she stood and brushed the grit from the seat of her pants. "But as I recall, you paid the last few times, so it's my treat."

Early afternoon sunlight was slanting in through the high vaulted windows of the Emerson Room, giving the wood-paneled walls and hardwood floor a rich butterscotch glow. The high-backed chairs usually scattered about the faculty lounge were pushed against the walls, which were lined with an array of dark oak bookcases that held antique volumes and rare books relating to Somerset's history. Higher up on the walls hung oil portraits of past presidents of the university, along with various administrators and deans who had served the school since it was founded in 1847.

This afternoon the room was packed with faculty. A round of polite applause went up the instant Frank and Shayna entered, walking arm in arm. Various friends and colleagues offered their congratulations. Many of them seemed to be a bit underdressed for the occasion. Either that, or else Frank and Shayna were seriously overdressed in gown and tuxedo, but it didn't matter to them.

This was *their* reception, and they were going to do things *their* way.

Set up to one side, below the windows, was a long buffet table that ran more than half the length of the room. It was overflowing with every kind of treat imaginable—sandwiches of every variety, salads, fruit, raw vegetables and dips, desserts, punch, wine, and an assortment of quality domestic beers and ales.

"Whatever happens," Shayna said, leaning close to Frank, "do *not* let me near any of those desserts."

Frank chuckled and whispered, "I've learned a great many things over the years, and one of them is *never* to get between a woman and her chocolate."

"You're a very wise man," Shayna said with a mock-serious nod as she poked him playfully in the ribs. They both straightened to attention when they noticed Craig Havelock, the dean of the College of Arts and Sciences, standing at the back of the room not far from where his portrait, showing him much younger, glared down on the proceedings. As soon as he saw them, the dean cleared his throat and, speaking in a rich baritone voice, commanded everyone's attention.

"Here they are now," he announced, raising his wineglass up high. "Ladies and gentlemen of the faculty of Somerset University, may I present to you Mr. and Mrs. Frank Logan."

When the room exploded with applause, Frank felt a sudden rush of embarrassment. Holding hands, he and Shayna nodded in several directions while he wedged his forefinger underneath his necktie to loosen it a bit more. He felt a little like he was choking, and he could feel his face flushing.

"Doesn't he know that I kept my maiden name?" Shayna whispered to Frank.

"Please," Frank said, speaking out of one side of his mouth. "You know how traditional Dean Havelock is. I think he's been at the university since it was founded."

"At least," Shayna said.

Dean Havelock did, indeed, look like he was a relic from another century. He was a large, bald-headed man with full, flushed cheeks, a severe double chin, and a florid face that made him look like his head was overinflated and about to pop. He always wore a dark suit with a white shirt and dark tie, usually navy blue with the Somerset crest in the pattern. The thick lenses of his eyeglasses distorted his eyes, giving him an odd buglike appearance. He was smiling and had his right hand extended as he walked over to greet Frank and Shayna.

"Congratulations to both of you," he said warmly as

he first shook Frank's hand and then leaned forward to give Shayna a hug and a quick kiss on the cheek.

"Thank you, Dean Havelock. Thank you very much," Frank said, bowing stiffly and then looking around to acknowledge everyone else in the room. "This is quite the festive occasion."

Frank didn't usually enjoy formal gatherings, but he knew how much this meant to Shayna, and for some reason the formality of the occasion touched him deeply. When he glanced at Shayna, he saw that she was almost overcome with emotion.

"Perhaps you'd like to say a few words to your colleagues," Dean Havelock said.

"Maybe in a little while," Frank said.

He didn't like being in the spotlight like this, and he was anxious to get something to eat if only to settle his queasy stomach. After making small talk with the dean for a few minutes, he and Shayna excused themselves and drifted away. They chatted with friends and accepted their congratulations as they made their way to the buffet table. It took them better than fifteen minutes to get there, but finally they were moving down the length of the table, filling up their plates.

"Ooh, look. Real china plates," Shayna noted. "And university silverware."

"Nothing but the best," Frank said.

He started down the line, inspecting the food as he went. When he got to a stack of finger sandwiches on a crystal platter, he frowned when he read the handwritten sign. "That doesn't look like ham," he said. "It looks like—" He picked up a sandwich, sniffed it, and then took a tentative bite, grimacing at the taste. "This is seafood. I think they got the signs mixed up."

Shayna picked up two sandwiches from the same plate and took a bite of one, smiling as she chewed. "Whatever they call it," she said, "it's delicious."

"I'm not all that big on seafood," Frank said with a quick shake of his head. He moved down the line to another plate that was labeled SEAFOOD and picked up a wedge of sandwich. After inspecting it carefully, he tasted it and nodded. "Ahh—yes. This is the ham." He glanced around, looking for one of the servers, but the nearest one was helping another guest. "We should tell the caterer that they've mislabeled these."

"Who's going to notice?" Shayna said as she continued to heap food onto her plate.

The sunlight dimmed and faded as evening came on, and someone switched on the overhead lights. Faculty and staff drifted in and out of the lounge. Frank was hoping that the dean had forgotten all about asking him and Shayna to say a few words to the people, but suddenly the sound of someone tapping a piece of silverware against a glass filled the room. Everyone stopped talking and turned their attention to Dean Havelock, who was, once again, standing beneath his portrait.

"Your attention . . . Your attention, please," he said, his voice bellowing as he raised his wineglass. "We here at Somerset are a very special family, and we're gathered here this evening to celebrate a very special—"

Without warning the dean's voice cut off sharply.

The room fell silent, and people looked momentarily confused. The expression on the dean's face appeared to be frozen. His mouth was still open, and his eyes were wide and staring as though he had just seen something that horrified him. For a second or two no sound came from him, but then, very faintly, he started making an odd grunting noise.

Everyone in the room froze, looking stunned as they watched the dean's face suddenly turn bright red. The veins on his forehead seemed to inflate, and his tongue protruded from his mouth, looking like a large foreign object he'd been unable to swallow and was now spitting out. Frothy yellowish foam gathered in the corners of his mouth and spilled from his lips, running in thick streams down to his chin. The gagging sound grew steadily louder, and his eyes bugged out even more.

"Oh, my God!" someone at the back of the room said, and a wave of panic ran through the crowd.

"What's the matter?" someone else shouted, and then a chorus of panicked voices filled the room.

Dean Havelock took a few steps forward, but then he stopped as though he had walked into an invisible barrier. His legs folded up underneath him, and he dropped to the floor, spinning in a lazy half-circle as he fell. It sounded like someone had punched a watermelon when his head thumped against the hardwood floor. It hit hard enough to knock his glasses off, and he lay there, his eyes wide open and staring up at the ceiling.

"Someone call 911. Now!" Frank shouted as he rushed forward and knelt down beside the dean.

Convulsions racked the man's body so hard his head and feet kept thumping on the floor with an odd, drum-like sound. His complexion quickly turned a violent purple, and his throat made strange clicking sounds whenever he inhaled.

"Just relax, Craig," Frank said, thinking how foolish he must sound. "Help is on the way."

Knowing this was serious, Frank looked over his shoulder at Shayna, who was standing close beside him. Her face was ashen, and Frank thought she looked like she might be about to pass out. Before he could say anything, someone at the opposite end of the room let out a piercing shriek. There was a sudden bustle of activity.

"What's going on?" Frank shouted.

Shayna's face was creased with concern as she shook her head in confusion.

"I don't know," she said, her voice thin and wavering. "I think someone else might have fallen down."

"Has someone called for an ambulance?" Frank shouted to no one in particular. "Shayna. Do you have your cell with you?"

Shayna shook her head no. She opened her mouth, about to speak, but her lower lip was trembling, and her face was drained of color.

"Shayna?" Frank said, shifting his eyes back and forth between his wife and the fallen dean. "Is something the matter?"

The faculty lounge was in chaos. People were screaming and crying out. There was a bustle of activity as two more people staggered and then fell to the floor.

Glancing to his left, Frank saw Peter Tauber, one of the physics professors, down on the floor, his body shaking as violently as Dean Havelock's.

"What the hell is going on?" he muttered as he stared down at the dean. Frank's hands were shaking as he loosened the man's tie to allow him to breathe, but something told him it was a futile gesture. Dean Havelock's face was as purple as a plum. His eyes had a distant, glassy glaze, and Frank was positive that the man couldn't see him as he looked up from the floor.

"Shayna," Frank said. "I need you to—"

He never finished what he had been about to say because even as the words were leaving his mouth, they blended into a terrified shout as he watched Shayna stagger backwards. She raised her hands to her throat as though she were trying to tear away unseen hands that were choking her. She took several steps backward, and then her left leg buckled and she went down. She landed hard on her butt on the floor and then keeled over onto her back.

Frank forgot all about the stricken dean as he scrambled over to his wife's side.

"Shayna! What is it? What's the matter?"

Shayna tried to speak, but her throat was closed off. The tendons in her thin neck stood out like pencils beneath her skin. Her breath came in short, sharp gasps that made her wince.

Frank shifted around so he could cradle her head in his lap as he looked up at the crowd that had gathered around them.

"Is there an ambulance on the way?" he cried out. His own throat felt constricted, and his vision blurred with tears as he looked back down at Shayna. Her body was rigid in his arms, but he could feel a tremor deep within her. Her mouth kept moving, but her lips seemed oddly rigid, making it impossible for her to form words.

"Shayna," Frank murmured, not even sure she could hear him above the panicked din in the lounge. "I'm right here with you. Don't worry, sweetie. I'm right here with you. You're going to be all right."

But as he looked into his wife's glazed eyes, he had trouble believing his own words. He could see that the gleam in her eyes was getting dimmer, and she struggled to take even the smallest breath.

"Did someone call for an ambulance?" he called out again, but he was so lost in worry and fear for Shayna that he didn't even know if anyone answered him or not.

The café in the Campus Center was never empty, but now that the lunch crowd had thinned out, there were only a few occupied tables, mostly couples or groups of friends taking a study break. Jenna and Yoshiko were seated in a padded booth at the far end of the room. Because she hadn't had a chance to eat earlier, Jenna had ordered a veggie burger, salad, and soda, but her stomach was in such a knot that she didn't think she could eat.

She didn't like feeling so awkward around her best friend, and she couldn't help but wonder if Yoshiko felt the strain like she did. If they were such good friends, wouldn't Yoshiko come out and tell her if something was bothering her?

Or is it just me? Jenna wondered. *Am I just making all of this up?*

"I—uh, I saw Hunter a little while ago," Jenna said, searching for a way to bring up what was bugging her.

47

"We were talking about the party. Going over some of the people we should invite."

Yoshiko's expression remained neutral as she nodded, but she didn't say anything. She didn't even ask how Hunter was. She just sat there, staring blankly at the cup of coffee she was gripping with both hands.

"Are you guys getting together tonight to study?" Jenna asked.

Yoshiko shrugged and shook her head, her dark hair brushing against her shoulders.

"I'm not sure. I haven't really talked to him today. I've been pretty busy with classes and all."

Jenna smiled tightly and nodded as she took a tiny bite of her veggie burger and chewed it. It was dry and gritty in her mouth, and her throat made a funny gulping sound when she swallowed. She hoped Yoshiko didn't notice.

"He was asking if we'd do the Halloween Run with him this year."

Jenna was hoping to lighten the mood because she knew that, in spite of the many ways Yoshiko had changed since freshman year, she was still a modest person. Convincing her to get her navel pierced at the beginning of the summer had been a major accomplishment, and Jenna wasn't surprised that her roommate hadn't kept the piercing over the summer.

Yoshiko's expression shifted to a slight scowl, but that quickly faded as she took a sip of her coffee.

"I thought the run was exclusively for residents of Sparrow Hall," she said.

"It is," Jenna said, "but I don't think anyone'd complain . . . especially since you and Hunter are a couple."

Yoshiko seemed not to give it even a moment's thought. She shook her head again, more firmly, and said, "I think our party will be more than enough excitement for one weekend, don't you?"

"Yeah. You're probably right," Jenna said with a small sigh.

"Is something bothering you?" Yoshiko asked. The scowl had returned.

Jenna told herself she should back off. Since the events of the summer, she had vowed to focus more on her own life and let other people do whatever they did. She thought she'd been doing pretty well, too . . . until now. *Keep your distance, Blake,* she cautioned herself, *especially when it's your best friends.*

An awkward silence settled between them. Yoshiko took another sip of her coffee, but Jenna could see that her roommate was clearly upset about something. Jenna was still hungry, but she couldn't bring herself to eat.

"What is it, Jenna?" Yoshiko finally asked.

She couldn't let it drop. She had to say *something*.

"All right. Here it is. I don't think you're being fair to Hunter."

"What?"

The word burst out of Yoshiko so suddenly that even she looked surprised. People at nearby tables stopped talking for a moment and glanced over at them. Jenna squirmed under the sudden scrutiny, and she leaned forward, lowering her voice. "You haven't been at all honest with him about what happened between you and Tony over the summer."

Yoshiko was silent for a moment, her eyes flicking nervously back and forth. "That's because nothing happened," she finally said. Her eyes practically gave off sparks as she glared at Jenna.

Jenna had never seen her roommate angry like this, and it upset her.

"Yes, it did," Jenna said. "Something *did* happen. When you called me just before we got back to school, you told me about it, and you said that you were tempted. Even if that's all it was, don't you think you have an obligation to tell Hunter about it?"

For a long time, Yoshiko didn't say anything.

"He has a right to know what's in your heart," Jenna said, pressing her point.

Finally Yoshiko took a deep breath and leaned back in the booth. Her eyes were blinking rapidly as she stared up at the ceiling for a moment or two.

"I love Hunter," she finally said, lowering her gaze and looking straight at Jenna. There was still a distance in her eyes and expression. Jenna felt as though an unseen wall had gone up between them. "*Nothing* happened between me and Tony this summer . . . and . . . and even if it did, what good would it do to tell Hunter about it? Why would I want to hurt him and ruin what we've got?"

"Why? Because you told me you think Hunter's a great guy and that he deserves nothing but honesty. Because just now you told me that you love him. That's why."

"I do love him, and he does deserve honesty," Yoshiko said, but Jenna could hear the flatness in her voice, and she felt the distance between them widen. The temperature in the café seemed to have dropped several degrees. Jenna shivered and hugged herself, feeling absolutely desolate inside.

Damn you! Now you've gone and done it, she chided herself, and she found herself wishing that she had never said a word.

"Yoshiko, you know that I—"

Before she could finish, her cell phone rang. She hated leaving their conversation hanging like this, but when she glanced at the caller ID and saw Slick's cell phone number, she knew she had to answer it.

"Dr. Slikowski," she said after flipping the phone open.

"Hello, Jenna," Slick said.

There wasn't a trace of warmth in his voice; he was keeping this call on a strictly professional level. That told Jenna immediately that something was wrong. Slick continued before she could say anything.

"I'm afraid I have some very bad news for you."

Ice shot through Jenna's veins as she glanced at Yoshiko. Her mind filled with dozens of horrible things that could have happened.

"What . . . what is it?" she asked, hearing the tremor in her voice.

"Your father has just taken Shayna to the Medical Center," Slick said. "They were at the faculty reception, and several guests—including Shayna—fell ill."

"Is she all right?" Jenna asked, knowing before Slick answered that it had to be serious if she'd been taken to the Medical Center.

"She and several other guests are experiencing various degrees of paralysis that seem consistent with some type of food poisoning, possibly shellfish. I think you should get to the hospital immediately."

"Yes . . . yeah, I will. Thank you for calling," Jenna said.

As she turned off her phone and slid it into her pocket, Jenna felt a shudder go through her. She glanced over at Yoshiko, who was obviously still angry with her and was making a point of looking away from her like she was insulted that Jenna had interrupted their conversation to take the call.

"I, uh—I'm sorry, but I have to go," she said as she scrambled to get up from the booth. She didn't like that there was still so much misunderstanding and miscommunication between them, but she picked up the veggie burger and salad and turned toward the nearest trash can. Her knees felt rubbery, and she was so distracted that she had to pause for a moment to collect herself.

"Are you all right?" Yoshiko said, coming out of her snit enough to register that something was wrong.

"My father's wife . . . Shayna's in the hospital. I—I have to go."

The pique on Yoshiko's face instantly melted away. She stood up and took the plate and salad bowl from Jenna.

"I'll take care of that for you," she said. Jenna nodded

her thanks as she pulled her coat on and started for the door.

"I don't know how long I'll be," she called back over her shoulder, but before Yoshiko could answer, she was out the door and racing across the darkened campus toward the medical center.

"Dad!" Jenna entered the hospital room and rushed to her father, who looked up at her, his face stricken. Shayna was lying perfectly motionless in the bed. Her face was drained of all color, and she looked thin and frail. An oxygen mask was strapped to her face, and an array of monitors beeped softly at her bedside.

Frank Logan put his arms around his daughter, and Jenna could feel him trembling. His breath was warm on the back of her neck, and when he tried to speak, all he could manage to say was, "Oh, Jenna . . . Jenna."

"What happened?"

Her father shook his head and held her all the closer.

"They're not sure," he said, his voice sounding raw. "No one knows for sure yet."

"I—I'm sure she'll be all right, Dad," Jenna said soothingly, hearing the hollow uncertainty in her own voice. She held her father for a few seconds more, then eased back.

"So, tell me. What happened?"

Frank shivered. Letting his shoulders drop, he stared blankly at her and shook his head. His face was gaunt with worry. His eyes were bloodshot. In a halting voice, he told Jenna about the reception and what had happened to Dean Havelock and more than a dozen other guests, including Shayna. Jenna listened quietly, trying her best to absorb it all.

"They think it's some kind of food poisoning," he said once he was finished. "They're running tests on everything that was served at the reception, but they think it was the seafood. These shrimp sandwiches."

Jenna blinked in amazement. "I can't believe food poisoning would hit so many people so hard, so fast. How many people ended up hospitalized?"

"I have no idea. I left in the ambulance with Shayna."

"Have you heard anything? Is everyone else all right?"

Frank shook his head. "I'm afraid not. Dr. Slikowski stopped by. He left right after he called you, but he said he'd come by again in a little while, but—no. Not everyone's doing well. A lot of people are sick and, well, Dean Havelock is dead, Jenna."

"Oh, my God! That's terrible!"

Her father's words hit Jenna hard. As she glanced past him at Shayna, lying peacefully in the bed, she couldn't help but think the worst.

"Have the doctors given you any prognosis?" she asked, mentally bracing herself for the worst possible news. "Will Shayna be all right?"

"She's stable for the time being," her father said, "but all we know for now is that the paralysis is quite severe. They have to figure out what caused it before they can determine if it will be permanent or not. It was interfering with her breathing, which leads them to think it might be some sort of shellfish poisoning. She was in and out of consciousness but now . . . I don't know. For now, they have her on the oxygen. But if she—" His voice wavered and almost broke. "Oh, Jenna, if she—"

He covered his mouth with both hands. Feeling absolutely helpless, Jenna watched the panic and pain of possibly losing his wife so soon after their wedding spread across her father's face.

"We have to trust the medical staff here," she said. She cringed, hearing how hollow her voice sounded. "They have some of the best doctors in the world."

Frank stared back at her blankly and nodded. Then, after giving her another bracing hug, he went back to sit in the chair beside Shayna's bed. Taking her motionless hand in his, he cupped it gently and patted the back of her wrist as he leaned forward and kissed her forehead. The muscles in Shayna's face appeared to be slightly tensed. They pulled her mouth down, making it look like she was angry about something.

Jenna and her father sat for several minutes without speaking, the silence broken only by the constant hissing of the oxygen tank and the steady beeping monitors. It was a good sign, she told herself, that Shayna's vitals were steady and appeared to be strong. After a short while they heard a light knocking at the door, and both turned to see Dr. Slikowski as he propelled his wheelchair into the room. Jenna greeted him with a somber nod.

"Any change in her condition?" Slick asked, his voice low and full of concern.

Frank shook his head. "Still the same."

"I checked with Dr. Kilburn," Slick said. "He informed me that all of the other patients are stable as well. That's a good thing. They're conducting some tests now, but—" He glanced over at Jenna. "The test to determine if it's food poisoning is called a mouse bioassay. Basically, they prepare the suspected food and feed it to mice, using a control group. Unfortunately, it takes several days before you get definitive results."

"Even for something that hit everybody so fast?" Jenna asked.

"Good point," Slick said. "That's why Dyson is downstairs even as we speak, prepping Dean Havelock for an autopsy."

"Do you think that will do any good?" Frank Logan asked without shifting his eyes away from Shayna. Jenna didn't like the note of utter hopelessness she heard in her father's voice.

"It certainly appears to be some type of food poisoning, but they're trying to determine exactly what," Slick said. "What's unusual, as Jenna said, is for it to act so quickly. Usually, PSP—that's paralytic shellfish poisoning—takes upwards of an hour or two to hit. The staff is interviewing the patients who are conscious, asking them for precise details about the symptoms to see if they're consistent with PSP. However, I think we might be able to get more immediate results from an autopsy."

"Do you need me to assist?" Jenna asked.

Her father and Slick exchanged a brief glance, then Slick shook his head firmly. "It might be better if you stayed here with your father . . . at least until we have some idea what the cause is."

Jenna wanted to tell Dr. Slikowski that this wasn't like most cases, where she wanted to be involved simply because she was fascinated. This involved Shayna, and right now, she needed to keep busy. The best way for her to do that was to help in the autopsy room. Before she could say anything, though, her father cleared his throat.

"I'll be all right here." He looked at Jenna, his face still creased with concern, and added, "I called your mother. She's on her way over right now."

"Really?" Jenna was unable to mask her surprise. Ever since their divorce, her parents got along fairly well; at least they were civil to each other. But Jenna had assumed that her mother might be feeling a bit awkward now that her father was remarried. Apparently that wasn't the case.

Her father nodded. "She's a doctor," he said. "I guess we can't get enough of those right now. And she probably knows me better than anyone else." He sighed, still holding Shayna's hand with one hand. "It—it'll be good to have her here with me if I . . . if Shayna . . ."

His voice faltered and cut off, and he took a deep, shuddering breath. Jenna could see that once again, he was contemplating the unthinkable. She wished there was something she could do or say.

And there was.

She had to be in the autopsy room to help Slick and Dyson try to determine the cause and—hopefully—the cure.

"Don't worry, Dad. Shayna's going to be fine," she said. "And if you're *sure* you'll be all right for now—" She turned and looked at Slick. "I want to help. I want to feel like I'm doing something."

Slick started to protest again, but after another quick glance at Frank, he nodded his agreement. Jenna went over to her father and gave him another tight hug and a kiss on the cheek.

"Shayna's going to be all right," she said. "I'll come back as soon as we're done."

She walked over to the door and held it open for Slick as he wheeled out into the corridor. After taking one last, lingering look at her father and Shayna, she followed Dr. Slikowski down the hallway to the elevator that would take them to the basement of the hospital.

Jenna's lips were set in a grim line behind her surgical mask as she entered the autopsy room a few steps behind Dr. Slikowski. Both of them were wearing surgical gowns, gloves, and masks. Dyson was already hard at work. He had completed the preliminary external examination and photographing of the body, and was now preparing to make the initial Y incision into Dean Havelock's chest and abdomen so they could study and then remove, examine, weigh, and dissect the dead man's internal organs.

What if this was Shayna? Jenna thought as she approached the body on the table.

Of course, there was no possibility of mistaking Dean Havelock for Shayna, but an icy ball filled the pit of her stomach when she considered that it very well could have been—

And still might be!

—her stepmother, lying here on the autopsy table.

Without a word Jenna stepped close to the table, prepared to assist. She wondered why the doctors didn't simply remove the dead man's stomach and examine that. If this was a case of food poisoning, then the toxicological exam of the stomach and its contents would provide the most important findings.

But she had worked with Dr. Slikowski long enough to know that he wouldn't skip over any steps of the examination. The most important lesson she had learned from him was that it never paid to hurry things or jump to conclusions. If they rushed, it would be all too easy to miss a hint or clue, and Dr. Slikowski never rushed.

"I noted the contusion on the back of his head where he impacted on the floor when he fell," Dyson said. He was speaking to Slick, but he pronounced each word distinctly so the tape recorder would pick up his observations. "My conclusion is that it wasn't severe enough to be the cause of death, but we will examine the skull for any intracranial bleeding or subdural hematoma."

"That's the first of our concerns," Slick said, glancing quickly at Jenna before he started working on the body. "We have to determine if the food poisoning is what killed him, or if his death was the result of something else—perhaps an injury he suffered as a result of the food poisoning."

"I've spoken to Tercotte in the ER. This subject is the only fatality thus far," Dyson went on. "But all of the patients who were admitted to the hospital from that reception today have suffered varying degrees of paralysis." He glanced at Jenna, sadness in his eyes. "Some worse than others. The symptoms covered the range of classic food poisoning—tingling, burning, numbness, drowsiness, incoherent speech, and respiratory paralysis. There's a possibility he was asphyxiated, unable to breathe because the paralysis affected his chest muscles. We also have to determine whether or not he had a cardiac event."

"Being overweight certainly didn't help him," Slick said as he leaned close and watched Dyson slice across the top of the dead man's chest from shoulder to shoulder and then cut a line down the center and across his abdomen, all the way to the pubic bone. "I've been telling him for years—*years*—that he should lose some weight."

Dyson didn't say anything as he worked to spread the incision open. Jenna also was silent, but she stayed close, watching everything intently and handing Dyson whatever surgical instruments he needed—scalpels, bone cutters, and spreaders—whenever he needed them. Working carefully, he finally got through the rib cage and started to open it up.

An autopsy was a slow and methodical process. Jenna had learned that on her first day on the job. It was an investigation. Before they removed the dead man's internal organs for analysis, Dyson inspected the man's heart and lungs and checked the body cavity for blood or any other fluids.

"Uh-oh. This doesn't look good," he said, glancing over at Slick.

Slick repositioned his wheelchair closer to the table so he could get a better look.

"Torn heart tissue and evidence of bleeding in the left ventricle," Dyson said loudly, for the benefit of the audio recording. "This indicates that the subject may have suffered a heart attack."

"We'll check the protein levels of his blood to determine if that's in fact what happened," Slick said. "But—" He cleared his throat and spoke distinctly for the record. "A tear and a quantity of blood in the left ventricle indicates that the subject may have suffered a myocardial infarction, which in all likelihood was the immediate cause of death."

"So the food poisoning didn't kill him?" Jenna asked.

"We can't determine that at the moment," Slick said. "Even if Dean Havelock did die of a heart attack, there's no telling whether or not the poisoning would have killed him eventually. We have to determine exactly what it was so we can predict what course it will run."

"This isn't exactly the healthiest-looking heart I've ever seen," Dyson said, shaking his head sadly. "If I wasn't already exercising, this certainly would convince me."

Jenna looked into the dead man's chest cavity and was astounded by what she saw. The heart looked gray and flabby, and it was riddled with a sickly yellow material that she knew was globs of fat. The interior of the artery Dyson had cut open was as narrow as a pencil and contained a thick mass of lumpy yellow tissue.

"That's what years of eating improperly and getting little to no exercise will do to you," Dyson said, glancing at Jenna.

"Let's get the stomach and other organs out so we can get some samples of the contents and lining to analyze," Slick said. "I'm also curious to find out what the fluid in the stomach contains. What we're looking for is evidence of saxitoxin, most likely domoic acid, which is most commonly associated with PSP."

"So you're convinced it's some kind of shellfish toxin?" Dyson asked.

Slick nodded. "From all we've been told and discovered thus far, that seems likely, but I'm not familiar with anything that strikes so quickly."

"Is there a way to counteract it?" Jenna asked. She knew it was unprofessional of her to let her worry for Shayna show, but she felt confident Slick and Dyson would understand because of what was at stake.

"We can only hope," Slick said as he watched Dyson remove the block of internal organs and place them on the lab bench beside the corpse. Then, as if realizing his comment had been too cold and clinical, he turned to her. His eyes narrowed as he looked at her above the edge of his surgical mask.

"It's impossible not to worry, I know, but it isn't time for panic yet, Jenna," he said, sounding much warmer and more concerned now.

She took a deep breath, trying to let some of her fear go with it as she exhaled. "You'll let me know when it *is* time to panic?"

Slick nodded without a trace of humor.

"Absolutely."

chapter 4

When the elevator door opened on the third floor of Somerset Medical Center and Jenna stepped out, she felt as though she was in another world. It was only just after five o'clock, but it felt much later to her. Nothing seemed real. Her skin tingled like she had just stepped from the shower, freshly scrubbed. During the autopsy she had pinned her hair back, though it was much shorter now than it had once been, and she had left the clips in. She was aware that it probably looked silly, but she was unconcerned.

Such a petty thing. How could it matter?

There was an odd numbness in her feet and her fingers, as if her extremities had fallen asleep or as if she herself had been poisoned. But Jenna had lived through enough trauma to know by now that it was nothing physical. It was the weight on her heart that made her feel so weak and disconnected.

But she did not let it slow her down. Her arms swinging at her sides, she strode like a martinet along the corridor. A portly nurse, emerging from a patient's room with a clipboard, gave her an appraising glance. Jenna paid her no mind. She wore her SMC ID clipped to her shirt, and even if she hadn't had one, visitors were common in these halls. But Jenna wasn't here only as Shayna's stepdaughter.

Stepdaughter. I was just starting to get used to the idea.

She pushed the pessimistic tone of that thought away, unwilling to pursue it. Shayna was going to be fine. She had to be.

Jenna's father had not always been good to her. Not that he had been cruel . . . it was that after her parents divorced, he had not made an effort to be much of a father to her. Often she would see him only three or four times a year. Though he would be wonderful company, funny and kind, she did not really know him beyond those visits. Frank had not been a stranger to Jenna growing up, but he had not been a *parent* to her either. She was old enough to understand that he had had his own issues to deal with, a life to work out. It had taken her enrollment at Somerset University for the two of them to really get to know one another, and she would be forever grateful for that. He was a sweet man who had never been lucky in love.

Everyone believed that Shayna was going to be the one to change all of that. Jenna had never seen her father so happy.

And now this.

It just isn't fair.

She knew what her friends would say, or her mother. *Life isn't fair. Who ever told you it was?* But sometimes that point was hammered home with just a little too much ferocity. Jenna had changed a lot since her freshman year at Somerset, and right now, the most important part of that change was that she had learned self-reliance above all things. Not that she could not depend on others, but that what was important was her own intentions, her own determination. She had learned that her actions could affect the world around her.

That had never seemed more vital to her than right now. If fate had decided to be cruel, she wasn't going to just let it happen, just let it flow. She was going to fight back.

The soles of her shoes squeaked on the linoleum as she hurried down the corridor toward Shayna's room. It seemed to her that she was somehow a little more real than the rest of the world, that the air rippled with her passing. The anger and frustration and sadness in her gave her a furious strength, as though she might reach out and grab hold of the fabric of the world and force it into submission. As crazy as that seemed and as silly as she knew it was, the truth was not so far off.

Jenna had no intention of just waiting for someone else to help Shayna. Not when she had watched the bliss dance in her father's eyes at their wedding, or seen the yearning ache in him when she had first arrived at the hospital room before Dean Havelock's autopsy.

She had long since grown used to the smells of the

hospital, the way the antiseptic odors of the cleaning products only masked the odors of waste and disease that permeated everything, even the walls and people. Today, though, it churned her stomach to think of Shayna as one of the patients whose illness was the source of that smell.

The thought disturbed her so much that her step faltered, and she paused there in the corridor, veering off toward the wall.

Quit it. Just stop.

Jenna took several deep breaths and then nodded in determination. Yes, Shayna was in bad shape, and Jenna had just helped autopsy a man who was dead because of exposure to the same toxins. But it wasn't going to end up with Shayna's body down on a slab in the cold room, waiting for autopsy. She wasn't going to end up in some drawer in the morgue.

It's not going to happen.

A familiar voice drifted to her from down the hall, and she glanced up to see her mother emerging from Shayna's hospital room. April Blake was a beautiful woman whose face revealed too much of her heart. Even from fifteen feet away, Jenna saw tragedy in her mother's expression. She hurried to close the distance between them.

". . . long as she's stable, we have to remain optimistic," April was saying.

"Mom?"

April turned and saw her daughter. A sad smile spread across her face. "Jenna," she said, and opened her arms.

As Jenna went to her mother, she saw her dad standing just inside Shayna's room; but in that moment it was just the two of them. Mother and daughter, the way it had been for so many years growing up when her father wasn't around. Dad and Shayna might be her family too, but April was the only one who had ever really been her parent. Her mother was everything to her. An errant thought skittered across Jenna's mind that she was glad it was Shayna in that room and not her mother. It made her cringe inwardly with guilt, and she chided herself for it, but that didn't make it any less true. She liked Shayna very much and wanted her father to be happy, of course. But what was happening made her very aware of how much she loved her mother, and so when they hugged, Jenna held her very tightly.

"Hey," April whispered. "It's going to be all right."

"Yeah," Jenna said. "I hope so."

Then she pulled back and regarded her parents carefully, taking a deep breath. "But that's the mom talking. And I think from here on out, I need to talk to the doctor."

April nodded. Then she gestured toward her ex-husband. "I was just saying to your father that Shayna's stable. The doctors are in there with her right now. I spoke with them for a few minutes. At the moment, anyway, she doesn't seem to have any additional symptoms. The paralysis is alarming. It's far more radical than anything I've seen or even heard of with shellfish poisoning . . . assuming that's what we're dealing with. The speed and totality of it is frightening. But as long as she remains stable, they'll keep monitoring her for improvements."

Frank moved over to Jenna and slid his arm around his daughter. She leaned in against him. "What kind of window are we looking at, April? Be honest. What are we looking for?"

Jenna's mother started to say something, then hesitated. She reached up to tuck a lock of auburn hair behind her ear and glanced away briefly, her eyes blinking rapidly. Then she turned and met Frank's gaze steadily. They knew each other all too well, these two. Marriage and divorce, Jenna had observed, seemed to teach people more about each other than they had ever wanted to know.

"We're going to want to see some movement in forty-eight to seventy-two hours," April said. "Anything could happen. If there's no improvement by then, it won't mean the paralysis is permanent. But her odds are much better if we have something by then."

Jenna sighed and reached up to press her fingers against her eyes. She was not especially sleepy, but she felt exhausted. Absolutely drained. Low voices came from Shayna's room—the doctors, examining her again—and she glanced inside. The slender form beneath the hospital sheets seemed so small. So frighteningly still.

"So what do we do now?" she said, without turning around.

"Go home," her father said.

Jenna turned, her brows knitted, and stared at him. "What? I'm not going to just—"

"Shayna's stable," he said. "I appreciate your mother and you coming out here. I know you're worried. I'm . . . I don't even know what to do with myself. Yes, I want company, 'cause I'm not leaving. But you have work and school to attend to, and nothing's changing right this minute. So go. Study if you need to. See your friends if you need to. Get your mind on something else for a while, and come back to visit when you can. Maybe later tonight. Your staff ID will get you in whenever you want, right?"

She nodded. "Well, yeah, but . . ."

"I'll be all right. Honest," Frank said, putting a hand on her shoulder. "I do want you around. I need to see your smile once in a while. But I also need to know that you're tending to other things. Shayna certainly wouldn't want you to screw up the semester because of this. And hey, who knows? Maybe she'll surprise us all and be up in time for a late dinner."

The word hit a terribly sour note after the circumstances of Shayna's affliction, and her father looked as though he regretted it the moment it came out of his mouth.

"All right," Jenna replied, pushing past it. "I guess. I mean—I'll come back tonight. Maybe there'll be more news by then. Slick and Dyson have the techs running about a dozen different tests."

"Any guesses so far?" Frank asked.

Jenna grimaced and shook her head. "Dr. Slikowski doesn't guess. Ever."

"All right," her mother said. "Anything useful, then?"

"He said pretty much what you and Shayna's doctors have said. That it's probably food poisoning. Probably paralytic shellfish poisoning. But that the tests will tell one way or the other. They need to isolate the toxin to see why it's so virulent, what exactly it's doing to those who get infected, and if there's an obvious anti-toxin."

Something in her father just quit then. He muttered under his breath, and all of his fear for his new wife bloomed on his face once more. He ran a hand over his salt-and-pepper beard and seemed for the first time in Jenna's life to be totally lost. Her mother took his hand and squeezed it, lending him her strength and support. Jenna hesitated only a moment, and then she joined her hands with theirs, clutching them tightly.

"Do you have any idea when the tests will be complete?" her father asked.

"I'm not sure," Jenna admitted. "But I do know this. Slick will haunt those lab guys like a demon until they get the results back to him. He'll be on them constantly."

"He's a good man," Frank said idly, his attention drifting back toward Shayna's room as the doctors began to emerge.

April smiled wanly at Jenna and then put a comforting hand on her ex-husband's shoulder. "So are you, Frank. So are you."

Jenna felt like she'd been electrocuted. It had not been easy to hold it together in front of her parents, and when she left the hospital, there was simply no way she was going back to Whitney House. It was only half past five. What would she do there? Her father wanted her to study and focus on her own life. That was a joke. *This* was her life.

Shayna wasn't her mother. It had not been all that long since Jenna had started to adjust to not calling her Professor Emerson. But it still haunted her to see her lying there in the hospital bed, completely helpless.

You spend almost as much time cutting up dead people as you do studying, she thought. *What the hell is wrong with you?*

But it was a rhetorical question. She knew the answer. Every corpse had a story, and every autopsy was its own mystery. People died. No one liked to think about that terrible, simple fact. Everyone just hoped that their own end could be put off as long as possible. And when death finally claimed someone they loved, they were torn between grief and the dreadful question of when it was their turn. What the M.E. did was help ease that process. To provide answers when there were questions, and maybe a little peace of mind. As much as anyone ever got.

It was good being able to help, to shed some light in the darkness.

But sometimes the darkness came too close. Jenna had almost died herself not very long ago, and it felt to her now that the shadow of that close call draped around her like a shroud. Still, she had pushed too far too many times on this job, put herself in harm's way. It was her own fault. Dyson had done the same thing. And

Danny . . . hell, Danny was a homicide detective. He lived every day in harm's way.

Shayna was a college professor. A relatively young woman. A newlywed. The closest she should ever come to an autopsy room was watching some police procedural on television. But today she had come all too close, and that thought cut into Jenna with a sharpness that made her chest ache. Her memories of her own near drowning were still too fresh. So were her recollections of Melody LaChance's murder.

It had gotten dark by the time Jenna left the hospital. Instead of walking down to Whitney House, she cut diagonally across campus, through the quad, and then down the library steps to Sterling Lane. In the back of her mind, she knew where she was headed, but her conscious mind didn't dwell on it. Her instinct in the past year had been to confront things head-on.

Now, though, she paused on the sidewalk in front of Richardson House and leaned against a parking meter. The metal was cold against her hands, and the ache in her chest sharpened as she paused, taking a deep breath and pressing her eyes tightly shut.

Would the image ever leave her of that day, just a year ago, when she had walked into the autopsy room and seen that familiar face, now cold and pale, tinted blue . . . when she had seen her best friend Melody on that steel table with her ribcage splayed open, her heart torn out?

Never, Jenna thought, and it was half a certainty and half a vow. She would never forget. Danger to herself frightened her, but not nearly as much as danger to the people she loved.

A trio of students walked by, heading toward the Campus Center. The girl nearest Jenna gave her an odd look as her two friends babbled on about one of their classes. Jenna forced a smile that was meant to be amiable, but she thought it probably came off as a little freaky, since the girl glanced away quickly.

The incident was a tiny thing, but it was enough to force her to shake off her thoughts of the past and focus on the present. She started down Sterling Lane again. The road sloped gently down to the right, and there were dozens of tall, old maples and oaks and evergreens behind the buildings, most of them private homes that had been converted into administration offices. Past the trees was Hawthorne Hall, a grand old building with a gothic-looking exterior. It housed the alumni center, the development office, and career services. Today it had been the scene of something awful.

Several police cars were parked at odd angles in front of the building. Ambulances had long since departed, but the police presence was still obvious. Yellow crime scene tape was stretched across the arched brick entryways at the front of Hawthorne Hall, and three campus cops were standing sentry there with a single police officer in the uniform of the Somerset PD. Jenna figured there would be other Somerset cops inside, but not a single campus officer. The Somerset detectives thought very little of the campus police and wouldn't allow them to participate in anything more than busting up a frat party or ticketing students parked in the faculty parking lots.

Jenna strode past the police cars, shivering a little as a cold evening breeze kicked up. As she approached the scene, the police continued talking, but one by one they all noticed her arrival and tracked her. When it was obvious that she was not going away, their conversation faltered.

"Can we help you with something?" asked one of the campus cops.

Jenna ignored him. The one guy there in a Somerset uniform was Vin Delmonico, a short, dark-eyed cop with an intelligent face. She had met him many times, and she knew that Danny and Audrey thought he was a good cop with a promising future.

"Hello, Officer Delmonico," she said.

Vin nodded. "Jenna."

"Who caught this one?" she asked, lapsing into "cop shop" talk without missing a beat.

"Gaines and Ross."

She flinched. It ought to have been Gaines and Mariano and would have been if Danny hadn't been suspended. But now wasn't the time for her to think about that. She had stressed enough over Danny for the time being.

"I'd like to talk to Audrey. Do you want to check with her first?"

The campus cops were all watching this exchange with great interest, unable to make sense of what some cute little coed was doing talking to Vin Delmonico as if she was on the job, and likely getting more respect from the officer than they ever had.

Vin considered her request for a moment, then shook his head. "Go on in. If she gets annoyed, I'll say you snuck by."

Jenna smiled and nodded her thanks. Officer Delmonico was no fool. He wasn't going to break protocol for some civilian. But regardless of her status as a student, he had seen the way the M.E. and detectives from various police departments treated her, and he obviously considered her a member of the club.

"Thanks." She started to push up the yellow crime scene tape, but as she ducked underneath it, one of the university cops called after her.

"Hold on there!"

Jenna paused and turned to face him.

Vin Delmonico scowled and glared at the cop. "You have something to say, Honan?"

The campus cop hesitated, then shook his head. As Jenna went up the stairs to the front door, she heard the police officers arguing quietly among themselves. She had no doubt that Delmonico was about to let them know just what was and wasn't their business.

The only person in the foyer was Chomsky, the head crime scene tech. Of course, it wasn't technically a crime scene, but someone had died, and it had to be treated as such for the time being while they gathered evidence and interviewed witnesses and victims. Chomsky glanced up curiously from a table he'd set up with his kit. He and his crew must have been having a grand day collecting samples of the food that had been served and the vomit that had been regurgitated onto the floor. *Good, clean fun,* Jenna thought dryly.

"Hey," Chomsky said as Jenna went through the foyer.

"Just what you wanted tonight, huh?" she asked.

His smile was thin, resigned. "Beats another shooting. I'm up for a little variety now and then."

Jenna shook her head in amazement. These were the things that made life interesting for people in this line of work. The most disturbing part of it was that she understood exactly what he meant.

She walked down the main corridor of Hawthorne Hall and found the broad double doors to the Emerson Room, where the faculty reception for her father and stepmother had been held. It was a beautiful room of the sort that she always had in her mind when she read Sherlock Holmes stories. Tall windows with heavy velvet drapes, all dark wood and ominous portraits and bookcases on the walls. *Opulent* was the word that sprang to mind.

Right now, though, the room was buzzing with cops.

Jenna stood frozen in the open doorway, watching them work. There were tables set up with white tablecloths and chairs arranged around them, like a small wedding all on its own. Food that had been served was still sitting out on plates, half-eaten. Several of Chomsky's staff members were working in the room, barely noticed by the police. Four Somerset uniforms had corralled some of the guests and members of the kitchen staff from the luncheon. The ones who had gotten sick were at the hospital, but Audrey Gaines and Detective Dwight Ross, a large, older man with a thick white walrus mustache and very little hair, were here interviewing the others one by one in a far corner. Ross and Audrey didn't like each other very much, but being friends wasn't part of the job.

On the wood floor was a chalk outline that had been made around the dean's corpse before they had hauled it away. It was like the residue left behind when his ghost vacated the premises.

Jenna had no idea how long she stood there before someone called her presence to Audrey's attention. She felt numb as Audrey whispered something to Ross and crossed the room toward her, sliding her notepad into her back pocket.

"What's going on?" Audrey asked, frowning.

"I figured you'd tell me."

The detective gazed balefully at her for a moment and then sighed. She ran a hand over her face in frustration. When she focused on Jenna again, any trace of their friendship was gone. She was all cop.

"You're close to this thing, Jenna. I understand that. But you don't have any reason to be here. Not professionally. The vic is already over at SMC."

"The autopsy is already done," Jenna admitted.

Audrey shrugged. "Then you don't belong here."

"I just wanted to see it." Jenna glanced away, a little embarrassed. "It didn't seem completely real to me. It's so . . . I was having a hard time getting my head around it."

A glint of understanding lit Audrey's eyes, but a moment later her expression hardened once again. "And now you've seen it. Go home. Or go back to the hospital and be with your father. This thing . . . it's tragic, but there's no one to blame."

Jenna drew a long breath and nodded. She turned to go, but Audrey called after her. "I hope your stepmother's all right."

"Yeah. So do I."

Danny Mariano lay on the couch in his living room watching *Dog Soldiers,* a little film about a platoon of soldiers stranded in a forest and the not-so-friendly werewolves who lived nearby. It looked like it had been made for about ten dollars, but it was a lot better than the budget would have suggested.

A diversion.

Lately he had been spending a lot of his days searching for diversions, watching movies and reading books, going to the gym, and taking walks. Solitary diversions. His family and friends wanted to help, but he had little patience with their sympathy. It was the last thing he wanted, really. If he hung around with the people who cared about him, it was a constant reminder of the bizarre limbo he found himself in at the moment.

On suspension, just for saving someone's life.

If he could have gone back and put a second bullet into the body of Terri Yurkich, the serial killer cop who had tried to drown Jenna, he would have done it in a heartbeat.

All Danny wanted was not to think about it. His sister called him constantly. He figured she had seen too many cop movies and expected him to be sitting around in his underwear, drinking beer and surrounded by old pizza boxes, maybe spinning his service revolver around with one finger, the chamber loaded with just one bullet. But drinking was the one thing he had no interest in doing alone, and although he hadn't shaved in days, he did manage to shower and dress every morning. As for pizza boxes? One of the solitary occupations he used to distract himself was cooking.

His stomach rumbled at the thought. The movie was only halfway through, but he was considering watching the rest of it later so he could make himself some dinner. He had two other movies lined up to watch tonight—*The Usual Suspects* and *Open Range*. It had become his custom to stay up until he could no longer keep his eyes open. If he let his mind rest, he would inevitably dwell on the charges against him.

As he reached for the remote control, the doorbell rang.

Danny frowned. There wasn't anyone he wanted to see.

He paused the DVD as he got up from the couch and went to the door in bare feet. He wore a Somerset PD T-shirt and dark blue sweats spattered with two-year-old dried paint from the time he had painted his bedroom.

Danny Mariano was a homicide detective. He had been wounded in the line of duty before. His hand flexed as though looking for his gun, but he'd had to turn it in when he'd gotten suspended. Still, he was trained to be cautious, so he stepped back as he opened the door, ready to defend himself if necessary.

Jenna Blake was standing on his doorstep, wearing blue jeans and a battered brown leather jacket. She wore no makeup, and her shoulder-length auburn hair curtained her face on one side and was tucked behind her ear on the other side. Though she tried her best to smile, behind it he could see loss and sadness that reached inside Danny and took hold of every protective instinct he had.

"Hey," she said, her eyes forming a question her lips seemed unwilling to ask.

"Look what the cat dragged in," he said. Then he stepped back from the door. "Come on in."

Jenna hesitated a moment, like she had something she wanted to say first, but then she crossed the threshold. Danny closed the door quietly behind her.

"I'm sorry I haven't been very good about calling you back," he said, hearing how lame the words sounded even as he spoke them. "I really haven't been calling anyone back. It's sort of a stressful time and I—"

"I know," she said. "I understand."

Her hazel eyes narrowed with some unspoken pain just before she turned away. She walked around his living room as though touring a museum, studying his home, looking at everything but Danny. "I mean—I'm the cause of all of this, right? I don't blame you for not wanting to be reminded."

"Hell, no," he protested. "Cut it out."

Jenna turned to face him but said nothing.

Shit, Danny thought. *I really didn't need this tonight.*

And yet a part of him was ridiculously grateful that Jenna had come, and he realized it might be exactly what he needed. To be with someone who cared. He might not really be able to spell out to his family or his friends in the department how he felt, but he didn't have to explain anything to Jenna. She didn't want explanations. All she wanted was to see him.

"You can't blame yourself. I don't blame you. I did what I . . ." He let the words trail off when he saw the way her eyes glazed over as though he was just saying these words to make her feel better. Danny went over to her then and took her by the shoulders. He ducked his head, forcing her to meet his gaze.

"And I'd do it again," he said, his voice low. "No matter what the consequences end up being, don't ever doubt that. I'd do it again. I didn't have a choice."

She gnawed her lower lip the way she sometimes did, and his pulse quickened.

God, she's beautiful.

It plagued him that the most amazing woman he'd ever met wasn't even twenty years old yet. Where was the justice in that?

Then he saw that her eyes were tearing up, and she started to shake her head slowly from side to side as though denying something.

"What is it, Jenna? What's wrong?"

"My . . . the faculty had a thing for my dad and Shayna today. A bunch of people . . . a bunch of people got food poisoning."

"Oh, God," Danny whispered. "Is your father—"

"Shayna's practically comatose. She—she's paralyzed. They don't know if she'll come out of it." Jenna stiffened, her nostrils flaring, forcing herself not to cry. "One of the deans died. I just . . . I think about that it could have been my dad and I—I just needed to see someone.

"I needed to see you."

Her lower lip trembled a little, and he could hear it in her voice, the doubt she felt, wondering if she was welcome or not, if he really wanted to see her.

Danny slipped his arms around her waist and pulled her close. She shook a little as she let out a long breath of relief, as though she had been holding it in forever and needed very badly to let it out.

"I'm so scared for him. And for Shayna. I don't know what he'll do if she—"

Her voice broke off, and she could not continue. Danny held her tighter and kissed the top of her head, wanting so badly to protect her, to make all of her fears and sorrow go away.

"Ssshh," he whispered to her, cradling her, kissing her head again. "Shayna'll be all right. The docs at Somerset will make sure of that. And your dad's okay. That's the important thing. It's all going to be all right, Jenna."

She was very still in his arms for several moments, giving herself up to his comforting embrace. Jenna nodded as he spoke those consoling words. Then she reached up and slid her fingers behind his neck, tilted her face upward and drew him down.

When their lips brushed together, Danny felt as though he were falling into her, a rush of heat moving through him, a wave of emotion crashing down upon him.

The kiss deepened, and all reason departed.

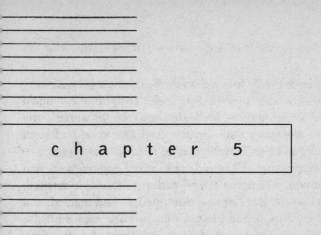

chapter 5

Audrey was tired and cranky and not at all pleased to be partnered with Dwight Ross. Interviewing witnesses or—in this case, anyway—victims, was always a stressful part of the job, and already it had been a long, crappy day. She and Ross were working a series of burglaries that appeared to be connected, but it was awkward not having her real partner around. Audrey couldn't put Danny out of her mind. She was always mentally comparing how Ross handled situations and how Danny would have handled them.

When they'd gotten a call from an informant who apparently had a lead on the burglaries, she had been more than happy to see Dwight Ross take off to investigate. And for his part, Ross looked happy to be going. The two of them had never gotten along. Now, though, she wished they could swap cases. If it weren't for her feeling that she owed it to Jenna to stay close to this one,

CHRISTOPHER GOLDEN AND RICK HAUTALA

she'd have gladly focused on the burglaries. Interviewing witnesses was annoying as hell. Despite what she'd heard some suggest, well-educated people weren't any better witnesses than anyone else. Everyone had been looking at Dean Havelock as he tried to make a toast to the happy couple. The old man started gagging and then fell down. Moments later—within seconds, it seemed, based on the interviews—other people had reacted, and total confusion had broken out. No one had a precise and accurate memory of what had happened after that. Like many cases where there were multiple witnesses, there were conflicting reports and observations.

Audrey had just finished up questioning Professor Douglas Claggart, who taught in the Sociology Department. Like everyone else, he had a very selective memory of what he had seen and heard. Audrey thanked him for his time and dismissed him, anxious to interview her final witness of the night—an economics professor named Joyce Kimball.

Professor Kimball was an attractive Caucasian woman who was new on campus this academic year. Audrey thought she looked entirely too young to be teaching at the university, more like a coed. Her long blond hair framed a thin, pale face with flawless skin, and her blue eyes were so light-colored they appeared almost gray. She wore an attractive gray suit that emphasized her complexion and slender figure.

"Are you feeling all right?" Audrey asked, trying to keep the edge out of her voice as she pulled a chair out from the table and motioned for Professor Kimball to have a seat. She noticed that the woman's nose looked chafed and red, and she was clutching a wad of Kleenex.

Professor Kimball sniffed and said, "This isn't from the food poisoning. I'm just getting over a little bout with the flu."

"That's bad stuff," Audrey said. "I appreciate you sticking around to talk to me."

"It's been quite an ordeal," Professor Kimball said wearily as she sat down. "But what choice did I have?" She folded her hands on her lap demurely and lowered her gaze.

Audrey turned to a new page in her notepad and held her pen, ready to write.

"So," she said, "I understand that you also may have eaten some of the seafood that's suspect."

She felt a sympathetic tiredness when she saw how drawn and worried Professor Kimball looked. She wanted to conclude this interview as quickly as possible, but she cautioned herself against going too fast. Take it a step at a time. Hurrying could make her miss something that might be important later.

Professor Kimball shivered slightly and then, raising her head, looked straight at Audrey. Her pale blue eyes widened a little, and her lower lip twitched.

"I—I'm going to be all right, aren't I?" she asked, her voice twisting with thinly disguised worry.

Audrey nodded reassuringly. She knew that only a thorough medical examination could accurately determine if the woman was or would be affected by the food poisoning.

"I'm no doctor," she said, "but given how fast everyone else was affected, I think you would have experienced some reaction before now."

Professor Kimball nodded and looked down, focusing her eyes on her hands, which she kept clenched in her lap. Her eyes blinked rapidly as though she were fighting back tears, but Audrey found that she didn't have a whole lot of sympathy or patience left after the day she'd had.

"Do you remember what you ate?"

Professor Kimball cocked her head to one side and squinted in thought for a moment. "Well, I did have some of those little shrimp sandwiches, or whatever they were. Macaroni salad. Stuffed mushrooms. I think that's it."

"You're the only person who had the shrimp but didn't get sick," Audrey said, nodding as she jotted the woman's response down on her notepad. "Does that strike you as odd?"

"Absolutely. Or lucky."

"Yes, very lucky," Audrey said. "Or maybe you have a natural immunity to the toxin. If I were you, though, I'd check with my family doctor just in case."

"In case of what, detective?" Professor Kimball said, a bit snappily. "How will my doctor know what to check for if nobody knows what caused this? I just . . . I can't believe all of this. I was just starting to move down the food line when Dean Havelock had his . . . when he fell down." She took a deep breath and hugged herself when she shivered. "I—I can't believe that he—that he just died like that."

There was an edge of real fear in the professor's voice, but much as she felt for the woman, Audrey didn't have the time or patience right now to play nursemaid.

"Believe it," Audrey said, not even bothering to chastise herself for sounding so uncaring.

As far as she was concerned this was an open and shut case, and the department was wasting her time, having her take statements like this. She should be running down human suspects, not platters of tainted food. The lab would test all of the buffet foods to determine what the toxin was and if there was an antidote. No doubt a lawsuit or two against the university would result, but this wasn't a matter for the police. The bottom line for Audrey was, she'd already had enough of a day. Even if Danny were here with her, it wouldn't make it any better. She'd just be wasting his time too.

"If you don't mind, I'd like to go home now," Professor Kimball said.

You and me both, Audrey thought.

"I'd like to call my husband and ask him to come and get me. He's quite concerned about what has transpired."

"Just one last thing," Audrey said with a curt nod. She kept her pen poised above her notepad. "Could you give me your home address? I doubt I'll have to follow up, but I might have some more questions later."

"I live at 121 Allen Avenue, here in Somerset," Professor Kimball said as she fished her cell phone out of her purse. "We just moved in this August."

Audrey jotted down the address in her notepad,

closed it, and slid it into her jacket pocket. As she watched Professor Kimball dial a number, she felt a twinge of guilt for being so abrupt with her. It wasn't like she didn't have her reasons, but still . . .

"No sense having your husband drive over to campus," she said. "I drive right past your street on my way back to the station. I can drop you off, if you'd like."

Professor Kimball hesitated for an instant, then nodded as she canceled the call and put her cell back into her purse.

"Yes. Thank you. That's very kind."

"No problem." Audrey slid her chair back and stood up. She stifled a yawn as she stretched her arms above her head. "I'm parked right out front."

Audrey was grateful that Joyce Kimball didn't make small talk as she and the professor walked outside, crossing the police line on their way to her car. But something was nagging at the back of her mind. The more she thought about it, the more it bothered her.

Why didn't she get sick?

It was a short drive from campus to the house on Allen Avenue. Neither Audrey nor Professor Kimball spoke until they slowed to a stop in front of the house. As Audrey shifted into park, the front door of the house opened and a tall, thin man with hawklike features came out onto the stoop.

"Thanks for the ride," Professor Kimball said as she opened the passenger door and stepped out onto the curb.

"No problem," Audrey said with a wave of the hand, but she found it a bit curious that the woman's husband, who she said was so concerned, didn't come down the walkway to greet her.

Professor Kimball swung the car door shut and, without a backward glance, walked quickly up to the front steps. Before Audrey drove away, she noticed that the husband and wife didn't embrace when they met on the doorstep. They simply went inside, closing the door behind them. A second later the entryway light winked out.

"Curious," Audrey said as she sat there behind the steering wheel, drumming her fingers on the steering wheel and staring up at the house.

A couple of things didn't quite fit.

For one thing, Professor Kimball's husband didn't seem at all demonstrative about seeing his wife returned home safely. Maybe he was just a low-key kind of guy, but Audrey sensed some kind of tension. More than that, though, she still found it curious that Professor Kimball had acknowledged eating the tainted food but hadn't gotten sick. Not even a mild reaction that might have required immediate medical attention.

"Is that possible?" she asked herself out loud, still gazing up at the house.

If Audrey knew anything, it was that if something didn't make sense, if it didn't feel right, she should follow it up. More often than not, these little hunches led nowhere, but every now and then, they paid off. Another thing she knew was that if there was anything medical that didn't add up, there was one person she could count on for an answer. Keeping her eyes on the lighted windows of Professor Kimball's house, she picked up her cell phone and dialed a number. After three rings the person at the other end of the line answered.

"Hello."

"Hello, Dr. Slikowski? This is Detective Gaines. You're still at the office?"

"I am," Slick said.

"I wonder if I could swing by," Audrey said. "I have a few questions I think you might be able to help me clear up."

"I'm waiting on some test results," Slick said. "I'll be here until eight-thirty at least."

"Be there in five."

What the hell are you doing? . . . This is wrong. . . . This is absolutely, totally crazy. . . .

No, this is right. . . . This is soooo right.

Jenna tried hard to ignore the voices in her head and lose herself in the moment as she wrapped her arms around Danny and pulled him close. His body was warm and strong, and his scent—an intoxicating mixture of soap, deodorant, and just his natural smell—filled her head, making her dizzy.

Danny's lips brushed against hers, making them tingle as the kiss lengthened. She thrilled when he ran his hands down from her shoulders to the small of her back. She could feel the muscles in his arms tense as he pulled her against him hard, his mouth covering hers, his tongue darting playfully between her lips.

Jenna opened her mouth wider, inhaling his breath like it was incense. She moaned softly and ran her hands up and down his back, feeling the interplay of muscles beneath his thin T-shirt. Stepping back, she leaned against the wall, reveling in the pressure of his body against hers.

I don't want this kiss to end . . . ever, she thought, but she knew it would have to eventually because of what she wanted to have happen next.

She wanted Danny to sweep her off her feet and carry her into the bedroom. She wanted to lose herself in his arms. All the yearning and pent-up emotions she felt for him rose up inside her like a groundswell, like the heavy lift of an ocean wave that was going to carry them away.

Yes . . . oh, God—yes, Jenna thought. *This is so good.*

She was so lost in passion that it took her a moment to realize that Danny had broken off the kiss and pulled away from her. Feeling suddenly bereft, she opened her eyes and looked at him, dazed.

"Danny," she whispered, her voice husky with emotion as she stared into his dark eyes.

"Jenna, I—" Danny turned away from her.

She reached out for him, catching him by the elbow to turn him around, but he yanked his arm away from her, breaking her grip as he avoided her eyes.

"Danny. What is it?"

For several heart-stopping seconds, he didn't say a

word as Jenna stared at him. She was filled with a power-ful longing for him, but an icy ball of panic had begun to form in the pit of her stomach.

She took a few quick steps toward him and wrapped her arms around him, trying to pull him close, but his body was stiff and unyielding, as though he had sud-denly turned to stone.

"I—I don't understand," Jenna whispered. She reached out and touched his cheek, running her finger-tips over his dark, olive-toned skin down to his jawline.

Finally he turned back to her and looked her straight in the eyes. Taking a deep breath, he said, "No. This isn't . . . I can't—"

"Yes, you can," Jenna said heatedly, feeling her heart swell inside her. "We can. You know it's what we both want and need."

Danny's mouth turned into a thin, hard line as he stared back at her and firmly shook his head from side to side.

"I'm sorry, Jenna," he said in a broken whisper. "But it's not—I just can't. It's not right." He sniffed and shook his head as though trying to clear water from inside his ear.

"Yes, it is," Jenna said, trying to mask the desperation in her voice. Even as she said it, the coldness in her stomach spread up to her chest, and she knew that what-ever had been started had already ended.

Danny bit down on his lower lip as he looked at her and shook his head even more firmly.

"No, Jenna," he said. "I . . . I don't want to hurt you or

anything, but I . . ." He took a deep breath, held it, then exhaled slowly. "I haven't been entirely honest with you."

"What do you mean?"

His expression was grave. "I just . . . I mean, I know we talked about the feelings we have for each other, and the attraction between us, and we agreed it was too complicated, but the truth is . . . and I don't want to hurt you saying this . . . but the truth is, no matter how I really feel about you, your age is a bigger deal than you think it is. You're maybe the most amazing girl I've ever known, but you're still a girl."

Jenna took a step back, letting her shoulders sag. Her face flushed with embarrassment, and a tight, trembling chill ran through her. The backs of her legs felt suddenly too weak to support her, and she reached out to put her hand against the wall to steady herself.

"I care about you," Danny said. "I really do. But it's wrong—"

"Not if we say it isn't," Jenna said, her voice cracking on nearly every syllable.

"Yes, it is. Even then. For me, it's just wrong. You start up something real with me, at your age, and it's like you're just skipping a whole part of your life that you've got to live through first."

Jenna's face flushed even hotter, and she clenched her fists so tightly her wrists began to ache.

"Maybe I just want you, Danny. Just for now. With no strings."

Danny glanced away. "You know that isn't what you want."

A hot sourness churned like bile in her stomach, and her eyes began to sting as tears gathered. He was right. The last thing she wanted with him was some one-night stand.

Danny reached out to her, but she darted away from his grasp. "You mean the world to me, Jenna, and if we were closer in age, I would definitely want to be with you, but I can't do it. Not like this. The thought that I was taking advantage of you would always be in my mind."

Jenna closed her eyes to keep herself from crying. They were silent for a long stretch, and as much as she wanted to reach out and hold him and let him know that everything would be all right, she knew she would start shouting if he so much as touched her.

"You're just thinking about yourself," Jenna said, once she was able to speak. She opened her eyes and looked at him, fighting the urge to slap him across the face. Without another word she spun around on one foot and headed for the door.

"Jenna . . . please," Danny said, but her hands were already fumbling with the doorknob.

"Don't even talk to me, you selfish asshole," she said quietly.

She flung the door open and stepped out into the hallway. A chill gripped her.

"I'm thinking about you," Danny said, shaking his head, confused and pained by her words.

"Maybe you think you are. But I figure all you can think about is what other people would say, how it would complicate your life. Funny thing is, I think *I'm* mature enough to handle it. Obviously, you aren't."

Jenna slammed the door behind her. She heard the security chain bounce and rattle on the other side.

She cringed as she waited to hear the apartment door open behind her, because she expected Danny to chase after her, but she was out the front door of the building and heading down the street with no sign that he was following. She was both relieved and devastated.

The moon was low in the sky, and a cold wind blew through the bare branches of the maple trees that lined the street. But that chill was nothing compared to the steely cold that filled her, because she knew—as much as she wished and wanted things to be some other way—that her relationship with Danny would never be the same.

"It's over," she whispered to herself, her breath coming out a white cloud that lingered in the air for a moment and then faded away on the cold night breeze.

"It is *so* over!"

It was going on nine o'clock. Audrey had been in Dr. Slikowski's office for more than half an hour, listening to him review everything he and the staff at Somerset Medical Center knew so far about the food poisoning case. It wasn't much, Audrey thought, but they were making steady progress.

"We have determined that the cause of death in Dean Havelock's case was cardiac arrest," Slick said. "With a man his age and weight, his system couldn't handle the sudden panic and the strain of the paralysis when it set in."

"He was scared to death, in other words," Audrey offered.

Dr. Slikowski shook his head. "No. We can't determine what his psychological state was, but the people who were nearest to him said he gave no indication that he knew what was happening or was reacting to it. The physiological strain alone was simply too much for his heart to bear. Judging by the condition of his heart, I would speculate that it was inevitable. Even if he hadn't had a heart attack, the paralysis would most likely have killed him simply because of the stress it put on his body."

"I see," Audrey said, nodding.

"What I'm mostly concerned about is Professor Emerson's condition," Slick continued, his face darkening with concern. "None of the other patients have been so adversely affected. Many of them have already recovered fully and been discharged. But the professor . . . she's stable for the time being, but the longer she's paralyzed, the greater the risk that she will incur serious and possibly permanent physical damage."

"So this hit her body pretty hard too," Audrey said. "Neither she nor any of the other victims had a cardiac event, but could it still kill them?"

Slick shrugged. "At this point, there's no way of telling. Until the lab determines the exact type of toxin, we're completely in the dark as far as an antidote is concerned. For the time being, she's on a respirator. We can keep her alive indefinitely, but we're helpless unless or until the paralysis abates . . . if it ever does."

"So tell me, can there be different levels of reaction to the toxin?" Audrey asked. "I mean, would the reaction be based on the amount of toxin in a patient's system, or would it be a matter of their sensitivity to it?"

Again, Slick shrugged. "It could be either or both, or it could be something else entirely. Certainly somebody could be more or less susceptible to the toxin than someone else. There's the famous anecdote about how Rasputin, the Mad Monk of Russia, took daily doses of strychnine in order to develop a tolerance to poison.

"My concern is that Shayna is clearly more susceptible to the effects of this toxin than most of the other patients. Perhaps a basic shellfish allergy added to her reaction. I'm surprised she didn't know of it before this happened. The lab will have more answers for us soon."

"That doesn't sound too promising," Audrey said.

"No," Slick said. "It doesn't, but where there's life there's hope."

"Did the reactions people had depend in any way on the amount of tainted food each of them ate?" Audrey asked.

"Again, we can't be sure until we know what the toxin is," Slick said. "But in many cases of food poisoning, the amount ingested and the reactions vary only slightly. A lot or a little will give you essentially the same reaction. There could be a slight differential, but in most cases it's not significant."

Audrey was tempted to take out her pad and jot down a few notes, but this was all just background information. It wasn't like she was investigating a crime. It was just an unfortunate event.

"One more question, and then I'll leave you alone," Audrey said. "There was at least one guest there today who ate the tainted shrimp but had no adverse reaction. Is that probable?"

"Not really," Slick said. "Possible, but not likely. He could—"

"It was a woman—Professor Joyce Kimball."

"Well, Professor Kimball could have a natural immunity to the toxin. I'll mention that to the doctors here. Maybe they have a bit more insight into it than I do. But she should consider herself a very lucky woman."

"I'm sure she does," Audrey said with a quick nod. "The crime scene techs are running their own tests on the remainder of the food, so maybe they'll come up with something that will answer more of our questions."

"For Shayna's sake, I hope so," Slick said. He glanced past her to the clock on the wall. "I was going to head upstairs to visit with Shayna and Frank." He exhaled loudly, puffing out his cheeks. "It's been one hell of a day."

"Tell me about it," Audrey said as she got up from her chair and headed for the door.

"And it isn't over," Slick said as he rolled his wheelchair back from his desk. "After I go upstairs, it's back to the lab. It's going to be a long night, I'm afraid."

"Not for me," Audrey said as she rubbed her eyes. "I'm done, but make sure you give Frank my best, okay?"

"I will," Slick said with a nod.

Audrey thanked him for his help and then headed out, riding the elevator down to the main floor and then pushing out through the main doors of Somerset Medical Center. As she cut across the parking lot to her car, she felt exhausted. She couldn't stifle a big yawn as she unlocked the door and slid in behind the steering wheel. There was only one thing on her mind right now—the nice, hot bath she had promised herself.

c h a p t e r   6

"How you doin'?"

"I'm doing all right. How you doin'?"

"A lot better if I could buy you a drink."

The young woman cocked her head to one side as she considered his offer, then nodded her agreement. Benjamin didn't know her name, but he had seen her around campus quite a bit this semester. She was pretty, with long, dark hair that draped over her shoulders. Her eyes were dark in the dim lighting of the bar, and Benjamin could see that she was already a little tipsy, even though it was early in the evening. The Bramhall Pub, a cozy bar within easy walking distance of campus, was generally crowded on Thursday nights. The clientele consisted mostly of graduate students with a few upperclassmen mixed in. It was a great place to meet women, and Benjamin spent a lot of his weekends here, looking for another conquest.

"So what are you drinking?" Benjamin asked, indicating the young woman's empty glass.

"It's called an Apple Knocker," she said, slurring the words just a little.

"Really?" Benjamin said. He placed one hand on the bar and turned to look at her straight on. "I've never heard of that. What's it made with?"

"Mostly vodka, thankfully," the woman said. It was obvious she had had more than the one she was just finishing. "And there's some apple cider and lemon juice in it, and some strawberry daiquiri."

"Sounds intriguing," Benjamin said. "Do you mind if I have one with you?"

Without waiting for a reply, Benjamin raised his hand. Catching the bartender's attention, he indicated the young woman's empty glass and held up two fingers. The bartender nodded and turned to prepare the drinks.

"Is this seat occupied?" Benjamin asked.

"Only by my invisible friend," she said, chuckling softly at her own joke.

"My name's Benjamin . . . Benjamin Hall," Benjamin said as he sat down and extended his hand for the young woman to shake.

"Katie Mullion," the young woman said as she swung her hips around on the barstool so she was facing him.

She had a strong handshake. He held on to her hand a little longer than necessary, and Katie Mullion definitely got the message. Her eyes widened with surprise, and she smiled as she looked at him with a little more careful interest.

CHRISTOPHER GOLDEN AND RICK HAUTALA

"You go to Somerset?" Benjamin said, half-statement, half-question. "I think I've seen you around campus."

"Oh, really?" Katie said, her smile widening. "So you've been stalking me. Is that it?"

"No, no," Benjamin said, wagging his forefinger at her as though he were scolding her. "Nothing of the sort, but I do tend to notice beauty when I see it."

For the first time since he'd started speaking to her, Katie appeared genuinely flustered. She glanced away, seeming grateful for the interruption when the bartender approached them and slid two fresh drinks onto the bar in front of her.

"Thanks," she said, tipping her head down in an exaggerated nod. Her eyes appeared unfocused, and Benjamin thought she might be drunker than he had first assumed.

Like shooting fish in a barrel, he thought, smiling smugly to himself as he picked up one of the drinks. He had no doubt that she was his already. He knew this because when she lifted her glass to sip, she turned back to him and gave him a low, sultry look.

"Well . . . cheers," he said as he took a sip. He smiled as he swallowed, then nodded. "That's very good." He smacked his lips, savoring the taste. "The apple cider gives it a nice autumnal zing."

"Autumnal?" Katie said. "You *must* be an English major."

When she smiled at him, her teeth gleamed dully in the dim light. Benjamin couldn't help but notice how lush and full her lips were, and he found himself filled with the anticipation of their first kiss. It was just a matter of time.

"Is it that obvious?"

"I like a man who has a way with words," Katie said as she lowered her glass, still staring at him. "So tell me a little bit about yourself, Mr. Benjamin Hall."

"Well, you're a very intuitive person, for one thing," Benjamin said. "I am an English major—I'm a senior. Mostly I'm studying modern British poetry."

"Wow," Katie said, and she sounded as though she really meant it.

During the next hour or so, Benjamin and Katie consumed several more Apple Knockers. As they talked, practically shouting to hear each other above the din in the bar, Benjamin kept moving closer to her until their knees were touching. Several times during their conversation, whenever he wanted to emphasize a point, he would put his hand on her arm or shoulder. Before long, those touches lingered much longer than necessary. Finally the moment of truth had arrived, and Benjamin knew he was going to have to play his hand.

"It's going to be last call soon," he said, putting his mouth close to her ear so he wouldn't have to shout. "What do you say we get out of here? Go someplace where we don't have to yell to talk."

Katie thought about it for a moment. He could see that she was making the necessary mental calculations, as best as she could, trying to decide if he really was an okay guy who could be trusted. Finally she leaned close to him and, placing her hand on his shoulder, her fingertips grazing the side of his neck, simply nodded.

Benjamin paid the tab, leaving a hefty tip for the bartender, and they slipped on their coats and went outside. It was past midnight, and the wind was blowing, giving the October air a ferocious bite. It seemed entirely natural for Benjamin to put his arm around her, if only to help keep her warm. But he had other plans for tonight, and it looked as though—just like so many other nights before—he was going to get lucky.

No, he thought, repressing a wicked smile. *Luck doesn't have anything to do with it.*

"My apartment's near Lafford Square," Katie said, slurring her words. "I don't have any apple cider, so I can't offer you any more Apple Knockers." She giggled and shook her head. "But maybe you'd like to come upstairs for a glass of wine or beer . . . or whatever."

"Whatever sounds good to me," Ben said, and his smile widened even more as he gave her a more bracing hug.

Bingo, he thought.

Side by side, they staggered down the sidewalk, passing several closed shops and parked cars. Off in the distance, the wailing sound of a police siren rose and fell. As they rounded the corner onto Haven Court, a small side road off University Avenue, Katie tripped on the uneven sidewalk and would have fallen if Benjamin hadn't been holding her so tightly.

"Oops," she said, sniffing with laughter. "I'm so clumsy. Maybe I had a lee-tle too much to drink."

"Me too," Benjamin said. "I'm a little under the alfluence of inchohol myself."

They both laughed and then paused on the street

again. When Katie turned and looked at him, he could see in her eyes that she was reconsidering what they both knew was going on here. The streetlight on the corner illuminated her eyes, making them look like two deep pools of ink. Benjamin swallowed hard as he reached out and brushed away a strand of hair that had fallen across one of her eyes. Then, before she could say or do anything to stop him or reverse the course they were on, he leaned forward and kissed her softly on the mouth.

There was a moment of hesitation, but then Katie leaned against him, practically melting into his arms as the kiss lengthened. Benjamin ran his hands up and down her back, crushing her to him. He could taste the apple cider and strawberry on her breath as passion flooded him, making him want her all the more. If Katie had had any doubts before, Benjamin could see that they had evaporated in alcohol fumes. She looked a little unfocused as she smiled up at him, moaning softly as she drew his face down to hers for another, longer kiss. A sudden gust of wind made them both shiver.

"C'mon," Katie said. "It's much warmer at my place."

"Do you have any roommates?" Benjamin asked.

"Don't you worry about that," Katie said, and her laughter rang out like a bell in the cold night. "Both of them are away for the weekend." A wicked glow lit up her eyes as she ran her fingers along the edge of his jaw. "We'll have the whole place to ourselves."

The heavy window shades blocked out the Friday morning sun, and Benjamin was surprised—and a little irked—when he realized he had slept later than usual. He rolled over and grimaced when he saw the alarm clock by the bed. It was already after nine o'clock.

Damn! he thought. *I should have gotten up earlier.*

Whenever he ended up at his "date's" place, he *always* made it his policy to wake up before she did and hurry off with some lame excuse about having to get to work or needing time to study for an upcoming exam. He never stayed for breakfast, although after a night of drinking and partying, he was usually famished. But sticking around might send the wrong message . . . like that he might want this to be something more than a one-nighter.

Which he *never* did.

One night was just right. Or one afternoon. Even one morning. There were too many available women out there to commit to just one, no matter how good it was.

But even after a few hours' sleep, he was still tired. He and Katie had stayed up until three or four in the morning. He'd been sleeping soundly until . . . something had awakened him. He was trying to remember what when Katie uttered a low, grunting sound that made him jump.

"Hey—," he said, rolling over to look at her, but he never got to speak the words he was going to say next.

Katie was lying on her back, her arms rigidly at her side and her legs straight out. Her eyes were wide open, staring at the ceiling. They were glazed and staring, like she had caught sight of something horrible. Her mouth was clenched tightly shut, making her lips a thin, pale line.

"Jesus, Katie," he whispered, thinking he was lucky even to remember her name. "What's the—"

His first thought was that she had epilepsy and was having a seizure, but he was pretty sure that if it was a seizure, she'd be shaking and twitching. Katie didn't look anything like that. She appeared to be frozen.

"Are you all right?" Benjamin asked, his voice trembling. "Katie?"

Katie didn't move her head, but she squinted as she looked up at him. It was obvious she was struggling, having a hard time focusing on him. The light in the bedroom wasn't very bright, but her face looked drained of blood.

Maybe she's having a reaction to so much alcohol, he thought.

"Katie . . . ?" he said again, his voice winding up an octave or two.

Her eyes were unusually reflective in the dim light. They looked like the silver backing of a mirror. She moved her mouth, struggling to say something, but the only sound she made was a low, barely audible clicking. If she was breathing at all, it was only in tiny sips of air that made her throat click.

A wave of nausea washed over Benjamin. He eased himself slowly out of the bed, moving mechanically, unable to take his eyes off her. Leaning over her, he grabbed her by the shoulders. Her skin was cool, almost icy to the touch. He shivered as he tried to lift her, but her body was stiff, unyielding. She felt so brittle he was afraid her spine might snap if he tried to get her into a sitting position.

Okay, don't panic . . . do not panic, he told himself, but he couldn't help it. This wasn't just from drinking. Something was seriously wrong with her. The muscles in her body were so tensed they felt like stone. Her back seemed to arch, as though she were flexing, and a tremor ran through her.

"Wha—what's the matter?" Benjamin asked.

He could see that she was trying to speak, but she had no control of her body. A low, wavering groan came from deep inside her chest.

"Do you need a drink of water or something?" he asked, knowing how stupid he must sound. Katie seemed not even to hear him. Her breath came in quick, labored hitches that made her eyes bulge. Somehow she managed to raise one hand to her neck and scratch feebly at her throat. It looked as though she were trying to remove a rope that was choking her. Benjamin stepped back, horrified, when he saw that her face was starting to turn a rich plum color. Her eyes bulged so much from their sockets that he could see red-rimmed whites all the way around.

"I—I have to get help," Benjamin said as his panic rose even higher. "Do you—Where's the—"

Then he remembered that he had his cell phone. He picked his khaki pants up off the floor and fumbled with the pockets until he found his phone. His hands were shaking so badly he almost dropped it as he tried to dial 911. On the third ring, the emergency dispatcher answered.

"Please state the nature of your emergency," the woman's voice said in a calm, professional tone that was absolutely devoid of emotion.

"My—I'm at a friend's house . . . and she—she's having some kind of seizure. She can't breathe or move, and I—I don't know what to do."

"Just calm down, sir, and tell me the address where you are," the dispatcher said.

"I—"

Benjamin suddenly realized to his horror that he didn't know where he was. He had never bothered to ask Katie her address. What did it matter? He was going to be in and out of there in one night and never come back.

"I—I'm not sure," he said, his voice still cracking with panic. "It's somewhere near Lafford Square on . . ." He closed his eyes, trying to remember the street sign where they had turned last night. "Something Court, I think. . . . It's something Court right off Lafford Square."

"I'm sorry, sir, but I need more information than that," the dispatcher said. "I need a street address and number if I'm going to send an ambulance."

Benjamin moved away from the bed and went over to the desk that Katie had set up near the window. It was a mess of papers and books, but he fished around until he found an envelope under a stack of papers. It was addressed to Katie.

"Apartment 2-B in thirteen . . . thirteen Haven Court," he said, his voice wavering as he practically shouted into the phone. "Haven Court! You got that? Get over here right away!"

"We'll have someone there within a few minutes, sir, but can you tell me the nature of—"

Before the dispatcher could finish her question, Benjamin broke the connection. He couldn't tear his eyes away from Katie, who was now absolutely motionless on the bed. Her eyes, wide and watery, were still wide open, and she was staring at him. Benjamin shrank under her steady, unblinking gaze, but knowing he had to get out of there, he moved quickly to the bed and picked up his clothes from the floor. He was shaking so badly he had difficulty getting dressed, and he was still zipping up his pants and tucking in his shirt as he slipped his feet into his unlaced sneakers and raced for the door.

Leave the door open, he told himself as he ran down the stairs. *That's the least you can do to help her out.*

He leaped down the steps onto the sidewalk and started walking away. As he rounded the corner, heading back toward campus, he heard the distant wailing of a siren and knew help was on the way.

All he could do was hope that it wasn't too late.

It was a gorgeous Friday afternoon with the sun shining through the brilliant foliage, but Jenna couldn't enjoy it. She sat in the chair by the window in the hospital and stared at Shayna, who was lying motionless in the bed. Her father had kept constant vigil since Wednesday afternoon, but at her insistence he had gone down to the hospital cafeteria to get something to eat. He looked so worn out and worried that Jenna was growing concerned about his health as well. Lost in her own thoughts, she jumped when the door opened.

"Mom," she shouted, unable to mask her surprise.

She practically jumped out of the chair and went quickly to hug her mother.

"Where's your father?" April asked, looking around.

"I sent him downstairs to get some lunch," Jenna replied. "He hadn't eaten since yesterday afternoon."

Her mother nodded her approval as she approached the foot of the bed and stared at Shayna.

"There hasn't been any change," Jenna said. "No improvement, but no worse, either."

Again, her mother nodded but said nothing. Jenna began to wonder if she had spoken to the doctors and knew something she didn't want or dare to tell her.

"Well," April said, "I've just been talking to Dr. Nixon, who's in charge, and he told me that three of the patients who were admitted Wednesday had only a limited reaction to the toxin. They've already recovered and are going to be released tomorrow morning, after another day for observation."

"Did he have any news on Shayna?" Jenna asked.

Her mother pursed her lips and shook her head. "Nothing. They have no idea what's going to happen with her. For now they're still taking a wait-and-see approach."

"Dad hadn't heard anything, but does Dr. Slikowski have any more results from the autopsy?"

"I haven't heard either, but I'm sure he's working on it." April exhaled and shook her head. "You know Walter. Once he gets going on something, absolutely nothing is going to stop him." She paused and looked at Jenna, the admiration she felt for her daughter obvious in her expression. "A little like someone else I know."

Jenna shifted her gaze to Shayna as a wave of utter frustration and defeat swept over her. "I just wish there was more I could do for her," she said, talking to herself as much as to her mother. "I don't like this wait-and-see approach. It never worked for me."

"It never did the whole time you were growing up," her mother said, "but you have to have patience. I'm sure they'll have an answer soon."

"I hope so."

"You don't look like you've had much sleep," her mother said. "It won't do you or Shayna or anyone else any good if you let this run you down."

"I know, but—"

"It's out of your hands, Jenna."

Her mother moved closer to her and placed a hand reassuringly on her shoulder. The touch filled Jenna with sadness . . . sadness edged with frustration. As frightening and sad as this whole situation was, as scary as it was to contemplate that her father's new wife might actually die, it was a puzzle, and Jenna—just like her boss, Dr. Slikowski—couldn't rest until she found some way to solve it.

"I'm not going to ask if you've been going to class, Jenna. I understand it must be difficult to focus right now. But why don't you go back to your dorm and get some sleep or do some studying . . . anything to get your mind off this."

Jenna started to protest but knew it was futile. She nodded and then gave her mother another hug. After looking at Shayna one last time, she kissed her mother on the cheek and left. The temptation was strong to go down to the office and see if any new reports had come in, but she understood what her father had been saying to her last night, and her mother this morning. She had other obligations. If there was something to be done for Shayna, she would do it. But they had no idea how long the coma and paralysis would last, and for everyone else the world kept spinning, not caring that for her father it had come to a crashing halt.

She tried not to dwell on what was happening as she walked back to Whitney House. She stared at the bright flames of color in the trees that lined the walkway as she cut across campus, but she couldn't stop thinking that there had to be something she could do to help.

When she got back to her room, she found a note on her bed. It was from Yoshiko, informing her that she and Hunter had plans for tonight to see Bob Marley, a stand-up comedian from Maine, who was performing at the Campus Center. The show started at eight o'clock, and Yoshiko wanted to know if Jenna would come.

She folded the paper up and placed it carefully on her desk, then glanced at the clock. The last of her Friday classes was just about over. She still had plenty of time to get some studying done. She was a little behind in her reading for the American Women class. Maybe she'd stroll on up to the library, try to put her worries about Shayna out of her mind, and get some work done. She had her cell phone with her, so her father or mother or someone could call and let her know if there was any change in Shayna's condition.

Some down time with Hunter and Yoshiko was exactly what she needed right now.

"Weird," she muttered to herself, shaking her head as she grabbed the books she'd need and tucked them into her backpack. It was so odd having to move between these two worlds—one so grim and filled with autopsies and criminal investigations, and the other so comparatively carefree.

I'm lucky to have friends like this, she told herself as she hefted her backpack and went out the door.

chapter 7

Somerset University's Campus Center was an enormous pagodalike building with a walkway that zig-zagged across its face and along the jutting corners of its perimeter. It was an attractive enough structure, but architecturally it was completely out of place among the dormitories, ivy-covered academic centers, and turn-of-the-century houses that surrounded it. Audrey thought that was probably why she liked it so much. It had its own dignity.

She went through the Sterling Lane entrance and paused in the large vaulted foyer inside before walking to a wooden railing. Below her the main function of the building played out, with faculty, administration, and visitors to the school eating at various tables. The Campus Center was set into the hill so that in the back—downstairs in the dining area—tall glass windows along the entire wall looked out on a stretch of lawn and the road and university buildings beyond. It was as nice a setting as any for the building. Students could use their dining cards there, but visitors could pay cash. Audrey had had the misfortune of eating there once with Dr. Slikowksi, proving that campus food didn't taste any better when you had to pay for it.

The lower level also had a separate nightclub-type area, but Audrey had never seen anyone in there. Any time she'd been in the building, those doors had been locked and the lights dark.

Why she was scanning the crowd now, she couldn't have said. She was a police detective, and there was something decidedly *off* on campus at the moment. That was reason enough.

After a moment she turned away from the railing and weaved her way through a group of students who had gathered in front of an ATM machine. There was a girl—maybe a grad student—at the information kiosk, but Audrey didn't need to ask. She knew exactly where she was headed. She passed a stack of *Somerset Daily* newspapers and noticed a headline about the death of the dean the day before, but she didn't bother to pick it up. Student reporters meant well, but they generally wrote what was said, not what they discovered themselves.

She took the stairs to the upper level two at a time. There were a number of administrative offices on that floor as well as the offices of the Student Senate and the Campus Food Services manager. The latter was her destination.

The door was open, and when she arrived, the manager was seated behind his desk looking at his computer screen as though it were a puzzle he couldn't solve. He was stocky, perhaps forty, with brown hair in need of a trim. Pleasant looking, but only just.

"Mr. Kirk?" she asked, knocking lightly on the open door.

His eyebrows arched. "You're the detective who called?"

Audrey nodded, not waiting for an invitation to enter the office. As she walked across to him, Kirk stood to shake her hand. "Audrey Gaines, Mr. Kirk," she said, showing him her badge and ID.

"Call me Jim. And feel free to get any *Star Trek* jokes out of the way early."

"I'm sorry?" She opened her hands to indicate that she didn't understand the reference.

Kirk smiled. "James T. Kirk. Captain Kirk. *Star Trek*."

"Oh, yeah. Right. Never seen it. Sorry."

"Don't apologize! I've spent most of my life with people making jokes about my name. I'm happy to meet someone who doesn't want to talk about how cruel my parents were, giving me that name."

Audrey took out a notepad and a pen. "I don't spend a lot of time being funny."

The manager seemed a bit put off by her focus on business.

What the hell, she thought, *this isn't a social call.* But even so, she wished Danny were off suspension and back on the job with her. He was much better at putting people at ease. It came naturally to him. Audrey, on the other hand, simply didn't give a shit.

"What can I do for you, detective?"

She narrowed her eyes. What sort of question was that?

"I believe I explained that to you already, Mr. Kirk. I need a list of all of the food services employees who were working the reception in the Emerson Room when Dean Havelock died. Prep cooks. Chefs. Waiters. Cleaning staff. Everyone. Names and contact information."

Kirk bristled a bit, glancing away from her. He scratched the back of his head and took a few steps toward his desk, then leaned against it. "I can't say I'm entirely comfortable with that. I mean, it isn't like you're investigating a murder or anything. These people have a right to their privacy."

Audrey slipped her pad and pencil back into her pocket. She had been planning to make this as easy as possible for Kirk. The guy certainly must have other things to attend to—talking about how his parents ruined his life by naming him after some idiot from *Star Trek,* for instance. Now, though, she was less inclined to accommodate him.

"Mr. Kirk, let me disabuse you of a couple of notions. First, Dean Havelock is dead. Under some fairly odd circumstances. We don't assume something like this is murder, but homicide handles it until we're convinced it wasn't. Evidence is handled properly that way. The right tests get done. The right avenues are pursued. Just in case. That's my job."

She took a breath and wished once again that Danny were here to handle this part.

"Your job, sir," she continued, "is to follow the instructions of your employer. And Somerset University is very concerned about the death of Dean Havelock and the health of its students and employees, even if you aren't. The administration is cooperating fully. I somehow doubt they'd appreciate you wasting my time when what I'm trying to do is make sure no one else gets sick or dies from whatever killed the dean."

Jim Kirk shook his head, nostrils flaring, mouth contorted in protest. "Now, just a minute!"

Audrey spotted a comfortable-looking chair in the corner of the office, strode over, and sat down. "I'll just wait right here while you print me out a list of names, addresses, and telephone numbers. I'll also want length of employment stats."

The manager's face flushed, and he started to protest again, but Audrey closed her eyes and tilted her head back, resting it against the wall. After a moment she heard him sigh and walk around to his desk, and then he began to type at his computer keyboard.

Less than twenty minutes later she was walking along the zigzag brick path away from the Campus Center. Her car was parked at the curb. As she opened the door to climb in, her cell phone rang. Audrey slid behind the wheel, thumbing the button to answer it.

"Hello?"

"It's me."

Danny.

"How's it going?" she asked automatically.

He sighed. "Best as it can, I guess. My union rep tells me I should have word about my suspension in a few days. But my lawyer says it might be sooner. How about you? How's your day?"

Audrey thought of telling him about her conversation with the food services manager and how she'd been thinking how well they worked as a team. But she knew Danny. It would be meant to cheer him up, but it would only make him more depressed. She thought he had not always been that way, that maybe she'd carved that cynical streak into him, and she regretted it.

"I'm partnered with Dwight. How the hell do you think it's going?" she said.

Audrey started her car and pulled away from the curb. She always glared at motorists she saw talking on their cell phones while driving, but sometimes it couldn't be avoided. Danny hadn't reached out to her much since his suspension, and she wanted to talk to him, but she had to get rolling back to the station house.

"We caught a case yesterday, a drive-by. Dwight's on that, thankfully. I'll have to join him soon enough. Right now I'm following up on all the employees who were working the reception Wednesday. Making sure none of them have gotten sick after the fact. Seems a little odd, don't you think? All those people getting so sick so fast from eating the food, but nobody who touched it during the prep process getting so much as the sniffles."

"Yeah. It does sound kinda strange," Danny agreed.

But he seemed off. Distant. Preoccupied with something that had nothing to do with his suspension. This was different from the way he'd been in recent weeks.

"So what's on your mind, Danny?"

She heard a sigh over her phone that could have been static, but she knew it wasn't. But he had called her to talk, and Audrey knew he wasn't the type to pretend nothing was bothering him.

"Jenna came by Wednesday night."

Audrey tapped the brake even as she drew a short breath. "Oh, boy."

"No—no. Nothing happened," he added quickly, then paused. "Well. Not nothing, exactly. Things started to happen. She's having a hard time right now with her stepmother being in the hospital, and she needed someone to talk to. I'm sure you know how that song and dance goes."

"Boy, do I."

"Anyway, we were getting . . . closer. Jesus, Audrey, in so many ways she's the perfect girl for me."

"You love her," Audrey said. It wasn't a question. She had discouraged the sparks she saw between Jenna and Danny from the beginning. Jenna was pretty remarkable, but at the end of the day, she was still a college girl, and Danny was a homicide detective, set in his ways.

"Maybe . . . maybe I do. But when it started to happen between us, I . . . I had to stop it. Even if she was out of college, in med school or something. But I just couldn't get it out of my head that early last year she was in high school. High school, Aud."

The car rolled slowly, without Audrey even realizing

CHRISTOPHER GOLDEN AND RICK HAUTALA

it. She was in no rush to get back to the station. Not while Danny needed to talk to her.

"How'd she take it?"

"Not well. Not well at all. I never should have let it get started. Never should have gone so long without telling her that her age was *always* going to be an issue for me. Jesus, I'm such a shit."

Audrey laughed softly. "Yeah. Yeah, you are."

"What? Hey, you don't need to agree so quickly."

"But I do. It was a shitty thing to do, Danny. You can't have it both ways. You're almost fifteen years older than she is. You're supposed to be the grown-up. You should have made a clear choice a long time ago, partner. Keep her at arm's length or just go for it, dive right into the whole Michael Douglas, Catherine Zeta-whatever thing head on. But you care about her, and you liked the idea of something between the two of you. The idea, but not the reality. You owe her an apology."

Audrey drove a block and a half before he answered. "I know," he finally said. "I know I do. I just don't know if she'll accept it."

"Neither do I. You're on your own there."

Jenna came back from the library early and spent the rest of the afternoon studying in her room. She wanted to at least make the attempt so she wouldn't have to lie to her father if he asked her about it. He wanted her to focus on her classwork, but that had never been more difficult. With Shayna still paralyzed, and after what had happened with Danny Wednesday night, it was nearly impossible for her to concentrate on school. Which was all the more reason why that was exactly what she needed to do.

There were people she could have talked to about the things that were troubling her, but she made a conscious decision to deal with this on her own for a while. Ever since she had met Danny, she had expected him to be more focused in his life, more mature about his feelings than guys her own age. Now that he'd proven he didn't know any better what he wanted than anyone else, she found she could not really be angry with him. Still, the disappointment was bitter and deep.

She still planned to meet Hunter and Yoshiko at the Campus Center tonight, but until then, she wished she could just lose herself in her reading. The afternoon went by with excruciating slowness, and Yoshiko did not come home. At dinnertime Jenna fished her soft, brown leather jacket out of her closet and traipsed over to Morrissey Dining Hall. She ran into a couple of girls she knew from her freshman year rooming at Sparrow Hall, and they all caught up over something resembling chicken. It was all mindless chatter, but Jenna discovered it was just what she needed at the moment.

By a quarter to seven, when she left Morrissey and started up the street toward the Campus Center, her heart didn't feel quite so heavy. Improv comedy could cut both ways. Sometimes it was painfully funny, and sometimes it was just painful. But Jenna was looking forward to having an excuse to laugh. This guy from Maine, Bob Marley—in spite of the unfortunate coincidence of having the same name as the reggae singer—was supposed to be very funny. He'd even been in a couple of movies recently.

The night was cold, the wind brisk, and Jenna zipped her jacket and turned up her collar. It was an early taste of winter, just a hint of what was to come. *Should've gone to college in Florida*, she thought, shivering. When she was little, winters in New England had been magical. Head-high snow, bright blue skies, icicles hanging from the roof, cozy evenings by the fireplace. There were still some beautiful days that brought a trace of the magic back, but for the most part, she could do without ice and snow.

Autumn, though.

She took a deep breath of the crisp, clean air and smiled, despite the chilly wind. She *loved* autumn.

She walked up the steps between the Campus Center and the university bookstore. People passed her, going in both directions, laughing girls and swaggering guys, headed to parties or into Cambridge, or just back to their dorms to watch movies. An afternoon alone had been enough, though. She was glad she'd come out tonight.

There was a small cluster of people around the main entrance to the Campus Center. Jenna spotted a heavy-set guy smoking a cigarette in the crowd and frowned. She would never understand how anyone could smoke, knowing what it did to them. It was just plain stupid. The guy saw her looking at him and interpreted it the wrong way. He gave her a flirty smile, raising one eyebrow.

Jenna rolled her eyes and moved along, making her way toward the front door.

It swung open, and several people emerged. Jenna stepped out of the way, pushing in among the crowd, and almost didn't notice that one of the people leaving the Campus Center was Hunter. His face was flushed pink and twisted up in fury, and he strode away hurriedly, his hands shoved into his pockets.

"Hunter!"

"Hey, watch it!" a girl shouted as Jenna bumped past her.

"Sorry!"

She jogged after Hunter, leaving the zigzag brick path to cut across the grass. Apparently he had not heard her call his name—or he was avoiding her—but she finally caught up with him.

"Hey, Hunter," she said, a flutter of concern going through her. "What's the matter? What going on?"

Hunter paused on the sidewalk along Sterling Lane, shaking his head as he turned to face her. He started to say something, then shook his head again and began to walk away.

Jenna's heart sank. She had a terrible feeling that she knew exactly what was going on.

"Hey." She caught up with him, reached out, and snagged his hand, making him stop and meet her gaze. "Talk to me."

Hunter took a long breath, steadying himself. They stood there in the chilly night until—finally—he gestured up the hill with a sharp nod. "Take a walk with me?"

Jenna felt a wave of sadness sweep through her even as she linked her arm with his as though they were following the Yellow Brick Road. They crossed the street together, and anyone watching would have guessed they were a couple. They walked through the black wrought iron gate and started up the asphalt path that separated the lawn behind the president's house from the library. Dying leaves had blown into drifts along the path, and there were people about, but none close enough to overhear them.

"It's Yoshiko, right?" Jenna said.

Hunter drew to a halt on the path and regarded her carefully. His eyes were wide and moist. "You knew?"

"Some. But I have a feeling not all. Talk to me, and I'll explain."

They kept walking.

"While she was home over the summer," Hunter began. "You know about this guy, this Tony Maleko? They were hanging out a lot. I knew that. I mean, they're old friends, y'know? Thoughts cross your mind, but you try not to act like a jealous fool. Girl likes to be trusted, doesn't she?"

The ache in his voice was almost too much for her to bear. Jenna sighed as they started up the concrete stairs beside the library. The windows of the chapel at the top of the hill were lit up beautifully, yet there was something lonely and melancholy about them tonight.

"Yes. Yeah, of course she does."

"So I tried to bite my tongue, you know? And *this* is what I get."

Jenna glanced up at him as they walked. "She cheated on you?" The words were so hard for her to get out they almost caught in her throat.

Hunter blinked his eyes rapidly as he looked up at the sky, somehow managing to keep moving up the wide stairs. In the glow of the lampposts, she could see that he was crying. "Yoshiko doesn't call it that. 'Fooled around a little.' That's how she put it. They didn't do *it*, I guess. But they did something. Isn't something enough? To be called cheating?"

Jenna gritted her teeth together, furious at Yoshiko. Her cheeks flushed with emotion, with sadness for Hunter and for herself. She knew that Yoshiko had been torn, and she had understood. But to just lie like that . . . Jenna could not understand that part. Everyone made mistakes. What was important was how you dealt with them.

"It must have been burnin' in her. The guilt," Hunter went on, his New Orleans accent growing thicker with his emotions. "She mentioned him, and I teased her about it a little. Hell, one look at her face right then, and I just knew. She started tellin' me, clarifying things. Well, I don't need to know any more, do I?"

They reached the top of the steps between the chapel and an enormous oak tree. Jenna turned to face Hunter. Once upon a time, she had seen him as not much more than a kid, still a little boy. But that had been a year ago, and since then, he had dealt with his sister's murder, his mother's battle with alcoholism, and now this. He didn't seem like such a little boy anymore.

"I'm so sorry, Hunter. I can't believe she did that to

you." Jenna put her arms around him, and he crushed her tightly against his chest, clinging to her as though he were afraid someone would try to steal her away.

"So how much did you know?" he asked, his voice quaking as he stepped back, hands sliding back into his pockets.

Jenna tasted something bitter in the back of her throat. She shook her head. "Yoshiko told me there was some flirting going on. That she was tempted. But she told me nothing happened."

"Then she lied," Hunter said, his voice barely above a whisper.

"Yeah. And that really sucks."

They were quiet together for a while. Several people passed them going up or down the stairs. Then he gave her his arm, and she took it. They started to walk once more, passing the chapel as they went out onto the academic quad.

"Did she say anything else?" Jenna asked.

"I didn't really want to talk about it there. But she started in on how after it happened, she was just losing her mind, and that's why she came back early, why she came to New Orleans."

They passed Bailey Hall, then cut across the quad on a diagonal path that led up toward the front of Sparrow Hall, where all three of them had lived the previous year. Its gothic peaks and high windows made it the most interesting bit of architecture on campus. Jenna missed it, especially now.

"So what are you going to do?"

Hunter took a long breath and shook his head as he let it out slowly. They turned left in front of Sparrow. "We're done. Kaput. Maybe that's a little harsh. Another guy might be able to deal with that bullshit, a more confident guy. But I'm not him. I can't look at her the same way now."

Jenna nodded. Yoshiko was her best friend, but after this—after the way she'd hurt Hunter—it was going to take time for her to figure out how this would affect their friendship. They were roommates, still. But Yoshiko had cheated on Hunter and lied about it to him and to her, and then she'd gone on like nothing had happened. *I feel like I don't even know her,* she thought. Jenna knew Yoshiko must be hurting too, but she didn't feel very sympathetic at the moment.

"It's going to be—," she began.

"Jenna, what's that about?"

Hunter was pointing straight ahead. A pair of ambulances and a police car were parked in front of Carter Hall, on the south side of the residential quad.

"Good question," she said, picking up her pace.

They crossed Fletcher Avenue at a jog. Jenna's thoughts had already shifted from student to Somerset Medical Center employee. SMC was just beyond Keates Hall on the other side of Carpenter Street. If Keates hadn't been in the way, they could have seen it from here. Whatever had happened, a fight, a suicide attempt, an accident, the victim wouldn't have far to go.

As they arrived at the front of the dorm where several dozen students had gathered in silence to watch the proceedings, a pair of EMTs brought a girl out on a stretcher and headed straight for the nearest ambulance. The Somerset police car was parked at an angle on the road that circled the residential quad, its blue lights flashing. One officer must have been inside the building, but the other stood on the steps watching the crowd and making sure nobody got in the way of the EMTs doing their job.

Jenna recognized the cop, a young guy with a thick neck and a buzzcut who looked like he'd either just left the army or not made the NFL draft. Blake something, but she couldn't remember his last name.

"Stay here," she told Hunter, and she pushed through the crowd and trotted up the steps. At the Campus Center she had tried to slip through unnoticed, not wanting to bother anyone. This was different.

"Miss, can you please—," the cop began.

"What happened?" Jenna said, cutting him off. "What's going on?"

The cop's brows knitted. "I know you, right?"

"Yeah. Jenna Blake," she said, nodding. "From the M.E.'s office. I was just passing by and—"

"Yeah, right." The cop snapped his fingers and pointed at her. "Jenna." He smiled for a second, but then it faded. He glanced up at the building as though he could see through the walls at the scene that was unfolding inside. "Then you must know about the food poisoning thing the other day, right? When the guy—some dean or whatever—died?"

Jenna winced at his casual callousness. "Yes."

"We've got two girls on the same floor of this dorm here with symptoms just like that. Throwing up. One of the EMTs said both are partly paralyzed. And there was another one early this morning. Some nasty stuff, huh?"

Jenna shivered and hugged herself and stared at the ambulance even as the driver shut the door, closing one of the girls inside.

"Yeah," she whispered to herself. "That's some nasty stuff."

c h a p t e r 8

"They say as people get older they don't change, but you definitely have."

Frank, who had been sitting with his elbows on his knees, his chin resting in his hands, grunted and raised his head to look over at his ex-wife, April. She was standing at the foot of Shayna's bed. Bars of light from the streetlight outside, sliced by the Levolor blinds, rippled across the floor, but her face and shoulders were muted by shadow. He thought she looked beautiful in the mellow glow, and he remembered one of the many reasons he had fallen in love with her and married her. It seemed so long ago . . . almost like another lifetime.

"Thanks," he said listlessly.

He shifted his gaze over to the motionless form of his new wife, lying in the bed. Her hair looked thin, spread out against the pillow. Her eyes were closed, and the expression on her face appeared frozen. The hiss of the respirator and the spiked green lines on the monitors were the only indications that she was still alive. Sadness cut deep, and Frank found himself wondering—as he had so many times since this horrible thing happened—how he would cope if Shayna died.

"You have to have faith," April said, as if she were reading his mind. Her voice was barely above a whisper, but it made him jump. April was more religious than he was. As far as he knew, she still attended church every Sunday, just as she had when they were married.

"I know I do . . . but I—it's hard."

His voice faded away, and he shook his head as a deep shudder ran through him. He hunched his shoulders forward as though he were crying without shedding any tears. Maybe he had already cried all he could, but he knew that if Shayna didn't survive this there would be many more tears. He tried to push such horrible thoughts from his mind, but that was all he could think. The doctors had told him that each passing hour she was in the coma, the more possibility there was of permanent physical and mental damage.

And now she's going to die . . . before we even had a chance to have a life together.

April stepped up close beside him and rested her hand lightly on his shoulder. Frank looked up at her.

"Thanks for being here, April. I know we haven't always been—"

She raised a hand to shush him. "That's all in the past. We've both grown a lot since then. And anyway, we must have done something right because we have a

CHRISTOPHER GOLDEN AND RICK HAUTALA

wonderful daughter." April smiled at him with a warmth he hadn't felt from her in so long he had almost forgotten it even existed.

"You got that right. Jenna is an amazing kid, isn't she?"

April shook her head and smiled. "Yes, but she's not a kid. She's an amazing young woman who's finding her way in life just the way we did."

Frank sniffed with laughter and reached up to wipe the tears that were gathering in his eyes. "I have a feeling . . . and it's just a feeling, but I think she's doing a hell of a lot better job at it than we—certainly better than I did at her age."

"We have every right to be proud of her," April said, "but I want you to know something else. I wish you nothing but good things in your life." She took a deep breath. "Even after all the upset and turmoil we went through, I can honestly say I'm glad to call you my friend."

Frank stared at her. Feeling absolutely drained of all emotion, he stood up slowly, turned to her, and enfolded her in his arms. They hugged, clinging to each other with near desperation. He could feel her trembling in his arms, and he knew that she was struggling not to cry.

"Thank you," he whispered.

They kept hugging until April finally broke it off and stepped back, looking a bit flustered. She smoothed her clothes and ran her fingers through her hair.

"Look, I have to get going," she said, her voice straining with emotion. "I'm on call tomorrow. But don't worry. Things are going to work out just fine. I know it. We just have to have faith."

Frank nodded. A crushing load of grief and worry dropped onto him when he turned and looked at Shayna in the bed. He wished he could believe April and the doctors when they told him that it was just a matter of time before the toxin worked its way through her system. But it didn't bode well that everyone else who had been afflicted had already recovered and was going to be released from the hospital in the morning. His fear was that there might be a serious weakness in Shayna's system, something in her biochemistry that wasn't going to flush this poison out of her.

"I'll be praying for you—for both of you," April said as she started to back away, moving toward the door.

Frank smiled at her, grateful beyond words that she had been there for him when he needed the support of a true friend, someone who really knew him. There was no way he could express his gratitude.

"I'll come by tomorrow afternoon after work," April said, "but I mean it." She wagged a finger at him. "If you need someone to talk to, any time, day or night, you call me."

"I will. Thanks," Frank said, his voice low and husky with emotion. "I . . . you have no idea what your being here means to me."

"What are you talking about?" April said, looking genuinely bewildered. "Of course I'm here for you."

"I know. But what you said just now . . . it . . . I really appreciate it."

"Well, it's been needing to be said for a long time. I'm just sorry it took something like this to make it happen. But I'm glad we can still talk like this."

"Me too."

Frank watched as his ex-wife walked out, closing the door quietly behind her. Then tears filled his eyes once again as a wave of emotion swept through him. His legs almost buckled underneath him as he walked back to his chair and sat down by his wife's bedside.

"Please . . . *please* come back to me, Shayna," he whispered as he folded his hands together tightly and bowed his head.

"This just doesn't make sense," Dyson said, shaking his head in bewilderment as he walked into Dr. Slikowski's office.

"What doesn't make sense?" Slick asked. He sounded a bit irritable as he looked up from the paperwork he was shuffling around on his desk. He looked drawn and tired.

"I've been reviewing both lab reports, from the hospital and from the Somerset PD CSI unit." Dyson held up the two manila folders he'd been studying for the past half hour or so. "The findings just don't add up."

"What do you mean? They found different results?"

"Oh, no. They identified the same thing, but according to them, there wasn't any shellfish toxin present in any of the samples."

Slick arched one eyebrow as he looked at the resident.

"What they did find was a virus. It was present in every sample they tested."

Slick was silent for a moment as he sat thinking and stroking his chin.

"The reactions everyone got, to a greater or lesser degree, are indicative of shellfish poisoning," Slick said. "Those toxins are all relatively common. They all act in similar fashion, blocking the sodium ion movement in nerve and muscle cell membranes. That's what causes the paralysis and, at least in Dean Havelock's case, his cardiac arrest. It would take a specialized lab to identify the exact toxin we're dealing with, but there's no effective treatment for any of them, regardless. In any case, much as you know I hate to leap to conclusions, it seemed fairly obvious what was happening here. I don't understand how they could not have found shellfish toxins. I don't know of any virus that would cause something like this, and certainly not something that would spread so quickly."

"Then it's one we don't know about," Dyson said. "I've checked and double-checked. They did the tests properly. No shellfish toxin, but something that mimics the effects. Both labs have identified this virus as the active agent."

Slick narrowed his eyes, his expression darkening. "But for a virus to imitate a naturally occurring toxin so completely . . ."

"Uh-huh," Dyson nodded. "If you asked me—"

"Which I am," Slick said when Dyson hesitated.

"Well, I'd say—based on these reports, anyway—I'd

speculate that to cause such a specific response, almost like the virus is masquerading as the shellfish toxin, well, is that the sort of thing that happens naturally? Ever?"

"You think someone bioengineered this thing?" Slick stared at him, taking a deep breath and then rubbing the dark circles under his eyes. "It sounds so damned unlikely, Al. But since none of us can make sense out of what we've got so far . . . ah, hell. That would just ruin my year."

The M.E. reached for the test results. "Let me take a look at those."

Slick adjusted his glasses and held out his hand for the reports. Dyson gave them to him and then took a few steps back, waiting patiently. Slick nodded and grunted a few times as he read, and he kept shifting back and forth from one report to the other, his brow getting more and more furrowed the whole time.

Finally Dyson cleared his throat and said, "Both labs, working independently, identified the same virus as the cause, but it doesn't match any virus on record as being associated in any way with shellfish toxins."

"Curiouser and curiouser," Slick muttered as he kept reading without looking up. At last he glanced up, gaze distant with comtemplation. "It's possible this is something completely new. It could be the result of a mutation that hasn't been identified before now. On the other hand . . . you never know what the military or research labs are cooking up these days."

"True, but look at the DNA summary." Dyson shifted uncomfortably. "Doesn't it strike you as just a little too perfect?"

Slick was silent for almost a full minute as he compared the two charts in the reports. Dyson moved around behind the desk and stared at the reports over Slick's shoulder. Maybe he had been working too hard as well, and he had missed something that should have been glaringly obvious.

"We'll have to have more exacting testing performed before we can be certain. I'd like to send some samples over to Dr. Parisi at the microbiology lab at Mass General."

"That'll help," Dyson said, "but let's say, for the sake of argument, this thing *was* created. Why would someone want to mimic the effects of shellfish toxin?"

"Biological warfare, cell research, even a search for an antidote."

Dyson felt sick. "Jesus."

Slick's chair squeaked as he leaned back, slipped his glasses up onto his forehead, and massaged his eyes again.

"You should go home," Dyson said. "Get some sleep. They'll call if there's anything new."

"So should you," Slick countered.

"I will if you will." Al Dyson smiled.

The M.E. considered a moment, then nodded. "All right. You've got a deal. At least we now have some idea what we're dealing with. There's not much we can do to fight a virus, but in Shayna's case, at least the doctors can try some kind of medicinal cocktail and hope something works."

"Fine," Dyson said, "but more than that, what I want

to know is, how the hell did this virus end up in the food at the reception?"

Slick clicked his tongue softly and then said, "Ah-hah . . . that, my friend, is the million-dollar question."

"You making any progress with that food poisoning case?" Lieutenant Gonci asked when he stuck his head out of his office door and saw that Audrey was still at her desk, hunched over her computer.

Audrey pushed herself away from the desk and took a sip of her coffee, which had long since gone cold. She winced and rubbed her eyes.

"Some," she said. "You know, I've been meaning to thank you for letting me catch this one." She trusted that her boss would catch the sarcasm. "It's been absolutely fascinating."

Gonci held his hands up and shrugged like he was totally helpless.

They both had been working late, and Audrey thought he looked almost as tired as she felt. It wasn't fair, she knew, to take out her frustrations on him like this, but she'd spent the better part of the afternoon on into the evening running down names, addresses, and phone numbers for everyone who worked on food prep at the Hawthorne Hall reception. The list of employees she'd gotten from the Food Services manager at the university seemed fairly complete and accurate, but she wanted to make sure it was one hundred percent before she went out and started talking to people.

As much as she hated this assignment, she was grateful

that the lieutenant had decided to keep Ross on the drive-by and let her work this one alone.

"One thing is bugging me, though," she said, hoping to keep Gonci's attention now that she had it.

Gonci looked like he'd been about to duck back into his office, but he hesitated and asked, "What's that?"

"From what I've found so far, not a single person who handled the food got sick." Audrey took another sip of coffee, even though it tasted so bad it made her shudder. "The guests, but not the cooks or the servers. Doesn't that strike you as odd?"

"Hey. I'm a cop, not a doctor," Gonci said with a shrug.

"Yeah, but it's just . . ." She let her voice trail away because she knew there was something else she wanted to talk to her boss about. In most situations she would have just charged ahead and said what was on her mind, but she knew this matter needed to be handled delicately.

"I was talking to Danny the other day," she said, gazing at Gonci above her computer screen.

"'S'that so?"

Audrey nodded but, for one of the few times ever in her life, was at a complete loss for words. The silence stretched between them so heavy she imagined she could almost see it, distorting her vision.

"Look," Gonci finally said, "I know what you're getting at. You're dying to ask me what's going on with Internal Affairs, but I can't discuss the case with you. You know that. I appreciate your concern, and I know you want to get back to working with Mariano, but until we jump through the hoops with IA, there's not a thing I can do."

"I know, I know," Audrey said. "It's just that working with Ross isn't any day at the beach, if you catch my drift."

"It's not supposed to be a day at the beach. It's your job. Look, Audrey. Mariano's a damned good detective. There's no denying that. You know it and I know it."

Audrey nodded. "And Ross . . . ?" Gritting her teeth, she shook her head and told herself to take it down a few notches. "Well, Ross is Ross, and that's all I'll say. But even with this food poisoning situation, if I was working with Mariano, we'd have been done with the drive-by case by now."

Gonci regarded her with a cold, steady stare that bothered her, mostly because it was so unreadable. All it did was make her think that maybe things weren't going so well with Internal Affairs, and that maybe—for whatever interoffice political reasons—Danny might not be exonerated for the shooting last summer that had gotten him put on suspension.

"One Mariano is worth a hundred Rosses."

"Thank you for sharing your opinion," Gonci said, his voice perfectly neutral. "Now maybe you should get back to doing what you were doing." And with that, he ducked back into his office and closed the door.

Stung and fuming with anger, Audrey sat at her desk for almost a full minute before finally turning back to her computer. It took a great effort to go back to the mundane work of checking the list. There were only a few names left to do, but just before Gonci came out of his office, she had been stuck on one person—a man named Jack Hawkins. The contact information on his application wasn't even close to valid.

"Do they even check this stuff?" Audrey asked herself.

She was positive the address he had written down, 1153 Anderson Street in Medford, was bogus. She knew the neighboring town well enough to know that Anderson Street was too short to have street numbers much over one hundred.

Could be a typo, she thought as she picked up her phone and dialed the home phone number on the man's application. After three rings she got a recorded message.

"We're sorry. The number you have dialed is no longer in service. If you need assistance, please stay on the line, and an operator will—"

Audrey disconnected the call before the message finished playing.

"All right," she said to herself as she scratched her head.

The address and phone number were phony. The only previous work reference the man had listed on his application was a stint as a waiter over the summer at a restaurant in Ogunquit, Maine, a place called Oceana's by the Sea.

"That's it? One job?"

Audrey glanced at the date written in the space for

date of birth and with some quick mental math, figured out that Mr. Hawkins would be in his mid-forties.

"Mid-forties, and that's it for job experience?"

It didn't add up. It looked like it was time to call this restaurant in Maine and see what she could find out about the guy. As long as the phone number for the restaurant was good, and the place was still open after the summer season, she should be able to find out a little more about Mr. Jack Hawkins. She was just reaching for her phone when Gonci's office door flew open so fast it hit the wall hard enough to rattle the wire-mesh window. Startled, Audrey looked up at her boss.

"Something the matter?" she asked. Her only thought was that he was going to break some bad news about Danny.

"Just got a call from the campus cops at Somerset," Gonci said. "Looks like two students over there just came down with the same kind of food poisoning. I want you to get over there and check it out."

"Sure thing," Audrey said.

She hit SAVE on her computer and then got up. All thoughts of Jack Hawkins and his single reference for employment were forgotten as she pulled on her jacket, checked to make sure she had her revolver, and ran out the door.

chapter 9

Jenna ran across the residential quad, cutting in front of Keates Hall, only half aware that Hunter was keeping pace with her. Her heart was racing, and she could hear her own breathing—too loud—in her ears. The night had taken on a kind of super-reality. Her vision was clearer than it had ever been, and she could smell fireplace smoke from somewhere in the distance.

"Why are we running?" Hunter asked, right beside her.

"Just keep up," she said. "I'll get back to you with an answer in a minute."

She needed that minute to figure it out for herself. It was as though half of her already knew what had sent her sprinting away from the ambulance, what she suspected had set alarm bells off in her mind. But the rest of her brain was playing catch-up. There was something about it that didn't make sense at all. It was as though she had been trying to put together a puzzle with a photograph of a bouquet of flowers on the box, trying to pick out the right pieces to make that picture, and in her frustration had thrown all of the pieces onto the ground only to have them fall in a way that suggested an entirely different image. Maybe these were pieces of an entirely different puzzle.

They ran past Keates Hall, through the parking lot in back, and dodged a car that was going much too fast up Carpenter Street. The lights of Somerset Medical Center and the med school behind it were beacons, drawing her on, encouraging her to work it out.

Work it out. . . . Work it out, Jenna!

"Jenna!" Hunter said, echoing her internal voice.

She glanced over her shoulder. Hunter had started to slow down, and so she was forced to do the same.

"Come on. Seriously."

He picked up the pace a little. "Fine. But why are we running? Tell me what's going on. You're completely freaking me out."

Another time she might have smiled at the turn of phrase, something he had probably picked up from her, and she from her mother. But not tonight. Not right now.

Jenna ignored the pleasant tree-lined path that would have taken them around front to the hospital's main entrance. Instead she ran right through the parking lot, headed for the ER entrance. The first of the two ambulances had probably come and gone already, but the second ambulance—carrying the second of the two girls who had come down with the paralysis symptoms tonight—was just arriving.

"Jenna!" Hunter shouted, frantic now, maybe even a little angry. He hustled up beside her, grabbing at her arm.

"Stop," she said. "Just . . . I need to talk to Slick, okay? To Slick and to the doctors treating Shayna. This doesn't make any sense. It should've been an isolated thing, right? One batch of bad shrimp or whatever. But if these girls got sick too, then it isn't isolated at all. Two girls in the same dorm, okay? But there was that girl this morning, too. What are the chances all three girls ate the same tainted food? And even if they did . . . why only them? If there's all this tainted food in the dining halls, how come only three people got sick? At the lunch for my dad, more than a dozen people were affected. But on campus, just three girls? So what if it's something else?"

They raced toward the automatic doors that led into the emergency room, bathed in the flashing red and white lights of the ambulance that was parked there, door open. The patient had already been taken inside.

"Like what?" Hunter asked, glancing nervously at the ambulance.

Jenna finally paused to catch her breath, turning to him as they walked through those automatic doors. "Like something in the *air*. Or the water."

"Oh. Oh, damn," Hunter muttered. "I hope that's just a wild hunch that I'm going to give you tons of crap for later."

"Yeah . . . so do I."

Jenna knew she was running on a hunch. It was possible that the girls had all eaten tainted food. No matter how ridiculously improbable, it was possible that some of whatever had been served at the lunch reception had been diverted elsewhere in the campus food service system, and that only those three girls had gotten sick from it.

But what were the odds?

She couldn't even begin to calculate them.

As they hurried to the emergency room waiting area, Jenna nearly collided with her mother. As a doctor at another hospital, April always found a way to get the parking spot nearest to the ER, of course. She was reaching into her purse for her keys when Jenna and Hunter came upon her.

"Mom?"

April looked up and smiled. "Jenna. I was just going to drop by and—" Her face suddenly clouded over. "What is it? What's wrong?"

Hunter had a fretful look on his face, but he said nothing, looking back and forth between the two Blake women as he waited for Jenna to pick up the ball.

Jenna shrugged and shook her head quickly. "I don't know. Maybe nothing. Maybe I'm just panicked and freaking out. I have a tendency to do that. But maybe I'm not, which means I need to talk to Slick."

"I don't understand what you mean, honey. What's going on?" April asked, looking at Hunter now.

"There are two girls being brought in right now with the same symptoms as Professor Emerson," Hunter explained. "And there was one this morning."

April frowned. "I didn't see that coming. I'm sure they must have cleaned the hall thoroughly and disposed of any seafood that came in from the same supplier. They would have taken precautions."

"A lot of it doesn't make sense," Jenna said. She took a deep breath to calm herself. The three of them were speaking in low voices in the ER waiting room, and Jenna felt out of place. "Look, I'm probably overreacting. That's fine. But why don't you two come up to Shayna's room while I talk to Slick? Then we can all talk to Dad and Shayna's doctors."

April nodded her agreement, and they all rode the elevator up, lost in their own thoughts. Jenna could see that her mother was turning the possibilities over in her mind. Hunter rocked on the balls of his feet, agitated. As the elevator rose, Jenna began to feel silly. It was only a theory, after all. One she considered only a possibility. But the possibility was so frightening that she wanted to bring it to the doctors' attention immediately. She saw her mother and Hunter's anxiety, though, and regretted her reaction, sure she had worried them needlessly.

You're overreacting, she told herself. Between Shayna being in the hospital, her father filled with such despair, and what had happened with Danny, maybe she could be forgiven a little melodrama. Even so, something about all of this just didn't sit right with her.

They got off the elevator, and Jenna had to force herself to slow down and walk at a normal pace down the hall. At Shayna's room her mother knocked softly on the door. Jenna saw her father look up from his seat at his wife's bedside.

Frank frowned. "Is something the matter?" he asked.

"Maybe nothing," Jenna said, trying not to sound out of breath. "Probably nothing. But I'd just like Mom and Hunter to stay here a few minutes while I talk to Slick. Mom will explain." She turned to Hunter. "Ignore my rambling. Seriously. It's probably just the food. Not that that's any better. No telling how many people could get sick if it's gotten into the dining halls."

"What?" her father asked, his eyes widening.

"Mom. Explain," Jenna said, and then she was out the door, leaving them all staring after her.

Yoshiko shivered and pulled her jacket around her as she walked back to Whitney House. For a while after Hunter had left, she had just stood there, shell-shocked, barely aware of her surroundings. As her mind had begun to clear, she remembered that Jenna was supposed to come to the comedy show, and she had determined to wait for her.

That had lasted all of five minutes.

The truth was, Yoshiko did not feel like talking to Jenna. She loved her roommate, but Jenna had warned her more than once what could happen if she wasn't honest with Hunter. She might not use the words "I told you so," but Yoshiko knew she would see the accusation in Jenna's eyes. She wasn't in the mood to deal with it.

What she'd done was wrong. No doubt about it. Not just with Tony Maleko—the thought of whom still made her blush—but afterward. Rushing back to New Orleans to see Hunter, trying to pretend to herself that she hadn't done anything to be ashamed of. They hadn't had sex. She had told Hunter the truth about that. But they had done just about everything short of that. It had been two months of sexual tension, of longing looks and flirtation, and then there'd been that night with the warm breeze off the ocean and too many margaritas.

That's right, Yoshiko. Blame the margaritas. Bullshit.

She loved Hunter. But she had loved Tony first, all through high school, and had never been anything more than a friend to him. When it was obvious that he was paying more attention to her, that he was attracted to her . . . well, that was powerful stuff. All of her old emotions, things she had convinced herself she was over, had been stirred up again. She had told herself that nothing would happen, and for a long time, that had remained true.

But that one night . . .

The next day she had booked a flight to New Orleans, and she had gone directly from Louisiana to Boston. Tony had been sending her e-mail all the time, but she didn't respond. The fact that he didn't have her phone number and that her mother would never give it to him were the only things that had saved Yoshiko from having a complete breakdown up to this point.

All along she had wanted to tell Hunter the whole truth, but she just couldn't figure out how to do it. Then tonight it had just come out, and she realized she had waited too long. Guilt had delayed her, and the delay had only made things much, much worse.

"Oh, damn. Hunter," she whispered, and she reached up to wipe tears from her eyes.

Yoshiko shivered again. The night was growing colder. It felt to her as though the temperature had dropped fifteen degrees in the past hour. But that might just have been her heart.

She knew that going back to Whitney House probably meant talking to Jenna, but there wasn't really anywhere else she wanted to go. If she could just curl up under her blankets and sleep until the sun came up, then maybe in the morning she would have a better perspective. More courage and more resolve. She would give Hunter the night and call him in the morning to try to explain . . . again. She would beg him to forgive her.

The worst part was that she knew if the situation were reversed, she would never forgive him.

But Hunter's a kinder person than you are, she thought. *A better friend. He's probably better off without you.*

Eyes moist, shivering from the cold, Yoshiko trudged behind the tennis courts and across the rugby field, coming out at the intersection between Carpenter Street and Sterling Lane. She felt numb, but it wasn't from the cold. She fished her key from her purse and let herself in, passing through the lobby of Whitney House with only a wan, false smile and a polite wave to the friendly faces that greeted her in the common area.

The phone was ringing as she unlocked the door to her room. The lights were off. Jenna wasn't there. Yoshiko only stared at the phone for a moment before deciding against answering it. She couldn't think of anyone she wanted to talk to except Hunter, and he wouldn't be calling.

The answering machine picked up. "Hey, it's Jenna—" "—and Yoshiko—" "Please leave a message—" "—and if you're lucky, we'll call you back."

"Yoshi, it's me."

Hunter!

She snatched up the phone. Her chest hurt, and she could barely breathe. Her eyes burned with fresh tears. Yoshiko could not believe he would call her so soon, and she wasn't sure if that meant something good or something bad. Was he calling to talk it over with her or to tell her he never wanted to see her again? But there was only one way to find out.

"Hello?"

"Hey," Hunter said, his voice distant and a little cold. "I tried calling your cell, but you didn't answer."

"I turned it off at the show. Forgot to put it back on. I didn't stay."

There was a pause before Hunter spoke again. "Are you . . . do you feel okay?"

"No," she said, her voice hitching. "Of course not. I'm so far from okay. God, Hunter, I don't know how to—"

"Stop."

Yoshiko blinked. Caught her breath. The harshness in his voice had brought her up short.

"What is it?"

"I can't do this now. I don't want to talk to you about this right now, okay? Maybe not ever. I don't know.

What I mean is, do you feel okay physically. Are you feeling sick?"

Yoshiko barely registered his question because three words were still echoing in her mind.

Maybe not ever.

Somehow she managed a response.

"No. I—I'm not sick."

"Look, there's something going around campus. It might not be a big deal, but there's a chance it might be. And I just wanted to . . . I just think you should stay in tonight. If you've got any food in the room, that's fine. But don't eat anything from any of the dining halls or the Campus Center or . . . you didn't eat anything at the show, did you?"

As if she could've eaten anything with the way her stomach was all twisted up. But she did not tell him that. Hunter sounded worried. More than worried. He sounded a little scared.

"No."

"Don't. Seriously. Wait until you hear from . . . till you hear from Jenna, or she comes back to your room."

"God, Hunter. What's going on?"

"I wish I knew. Just don't eat anything, okay?"

"Yeah. Okay."

There was a long, painful pause. Yoshiko imagined that he was trying to figure out how to end the call. Until tonight, all of their conversations had ended with "I love you."

But not this one.

"Night, then," Hunter said. "Stay in your room."

"Okay. Good night."

As Yoshiko hung up the phone, it occurred to her that despite whatever Hunter was feeling, despite how furious he must be, how hurt he had to be feeling, he had still called her to make sure she was all right. Some kind of illness was going around campus, and his first thought was to call and check on her.

She knew for certain then that she didn't deserve Hunter LaChance. She hoped he would love her anyway, and if he did, she would never be the one to tell him that she didn't deserve it. She was a good person who had made a terrible mistake. All she wanted was an opportunity to make it up to him.

Sliding out of her coat, she walked over to her bed and, lying down, stared at the ceiling. From time to time, her gaze would shift to the small windows high up on the wall, and she would wonder what was going on out there that had Hunter so spooked, and when Jenna was going to come back to the room.

Yoshiko had changed her mind about that. Just then, she would have liked nothing more than to see Jenna coming through that door.

The moment she stepped onto the elevator, Jenna pulled out her cell phone. The signal wasn't very strong, but she thought it would be enough. She hit the memory dial for Dr. Slikowski at home. He often worked late, but she knew his schedule, and there was nothing on his agenda at the moment that would have kept him on the clock after hours. The elevator descended as the phone rang. It stopped on the second floor to let passengers on. It was nine o'clock. Visiting hours were over, and people were going home so the patients could get some sleep.

"Hello?"

"Dr. Slikowski. It's Jenna?"

He reacted to her anxious tone immediately. "What's wrong, Jenna? What's happened?"

"I—I'm not sure." As she spoke, she became all too aware of the other people around her. The elevator dinged for the first floor. "Can you hold on a second?"

Jenna let the others step out of the elevator before she did. They turned toward the lobby and the exit, and she went the opposite direction, through the sterile corridors that led to the emergency room.

"Hello?"

"Yeah, I'm here," she assured him. Glancing around to make sure she was alone, she stopped in front of a service elevator. "I'm not sure what's going on, but I've got a really bad feeling about it. Between this morning and tonight they've brought in three—at least three—new patients with the same symptoms as Professor Emerson. Two are from the same dorm, but one isn't. Sure, it's possible the girls all ate at the same place, but what if they didn't?"

"What do you mean? So you think this is spreading some way other than in the food?"

"Maybe. Unless the whole campus's food supply is contaminated, which seems unlikely. If that's the case, wouldn't we have hundreds of students down here?" She lowered her voice as a couple of nurses strode down the corridor past her.

"Your logic is sound. Everyone who ate the contaminated food at your father's lunch fell ill to a greater or lesser degree. This might only be the beginning, if the food is contaminated. But if there are only a handful of patients showing these symptoms, it's possible that they've contracted the toxin some other way. Dr. Dyson has a few theories of his own that make your news particularly grim."

"What?" Jenna asked. "Did Al find something in the tests on Dean Havelock?"

"Let's speak about that when I see you. I'll be there in twenty minutes. I'll phone Al as well. Will I find you with your father?"

"No," Jenna said. "I'm on my way to the ER right now. I want to see if they've been able to connect the patients, especially if they've eaten in the same dining hall today. I also want to find out if any more cases have come in."

"I'll meet you there."

Jenna slipped her cell into her pocket and made her way through a series of wide swinging doors. Some of the offices in the hospital were dark and locked up tight, but a handful of administrative employees were still at work. An orderly rushed past her with a wheeled bucket and a mop. Then she turned right and pushed through the double doors into the emergency room. She knew better than to disturb any of the doctors or nurses who were on their way from one task to another. They had patients to deal with. There were several empty gurneys lined up along the right-hand wall, and many of the curtains were drawn back to reveal that the cubicles were empty.

A comparatively quiet night in the ER. That was good.

Jenna walked all the way through the ER but didn't go into the waiting area. Instead she slipped behind the counter at the front window. The admitting nurse looked up sharply, her very glance a challenge.

"May I help you?"

"My name's Jenna Blake. I'm a pathology assistant for Dr. Slikowski. He's on his way here now. We're working on the case of a DOA who came in the other day, and I understand you've got several new patients with similar symptoms. I was hoping I could speak to the doc who's attending."

The nurse's tag said Helen Ford, RN. She was a thin woman, probably in her thirties, though she wore so little makeup and looked so tired she looked at least a decade older. She studied Jenna for a moment before nodding. Nurse Ford didn't even have to look at her files. She knew exactly what Jenna was talking about.

"You want to talk to Dr. Gifune," the nurse said. She rose and peeked out into the waiting room, then led Jenna back into the emergency room.

On a side corridor were half a dozen examination rooms that were more private than the curtained cubicles. Two of the doors were open, but the others were all closed. As Jenna and Nurse Ford approached, one of them opened and another nurse emerged, a tall, imposing woman with perfect dark skin.

"Valerie, is Dr. Gifune in there with a patient?"

The towering nurse nodded. "Exam room four."

"This is Jenna . . . Blake, was it?" she asked. Jenna nodded. "From the M.E.'s office. Slick's sent her down to talk to A. J. Can you take it from here? I don't want to leave the desk."

"Sure," Valerie said. She nodded to Jenna. "You just have a seat right over there, sweetie. Dr. Gifune will be out in a minute or so, and I'll make the introductions."

As Nurse Ford made a beeline back to the admitting desk, Jenna took a seat in the hardest plastic chair she had ever had the misfortune of encountering. The discomfort made her fidget while she waited anxiously. There was a clock on the wall diagonally across from her. She stared at it, and the time seemed to crawl. Eleven minutes passed before another door opened.

The man who emerged was a big, burly bear of a man, dark haired and unshaven. He had dark bags under his eyes and a stethoscope around his neck, and his white lab coat was a size too small. It only enhanced the impression of his size.

Jenna glanced around, but the last she had seen of Valerie, the woman was escorting a patient through to a cubicle, a man with his hand wrapped in bandages and a dishrag filled with ice held against it. She wasn't going to wait, just in case the doctor slipped off again.

"Dr. Gifune?" The bear turned around, eyebrows raised. Even though Jenna had stood up, he towered above her. "Sorry to disturb you. They said I could wait. I'm—"

"Jenna?"

Given the doctor's size, Jenna had only been vaguely aware of another figure emerging from the room behind him. Now she saw that it was Audrey Gaines. It was a comfort to see her here. It would make introductions easier.

"Hey, Audrey."

"What are you doing down here?" the detective asked.

Jenna glanced back and forth between the two of them, but she addressed Dr. Gifune. "I was on campus when the EMTs were taking away these two new patients that have this paralytic . . . infection, or whatever it is. And I was told there was another girl this morning. Dr. Slikowski did the autopsy on Dean Havelock, the patient who died of these symptoms. He's very concerned about the new cases and how the patients might have come into contact with the source of contamination. He's on his way down now, I suspect to compare notes. Meanwhile, I wanted to ask if you've had any other patients with the same symptoms today or just these three?"

The doctor frowned deeply. "I'm sorry, who are you again?"

"Jenna Blake."

Audrey stood beside Jenna as though to back her up. "She works for Dr. Slikowski."

"Well then, Jenna, the answer is yes. We have had one

other patient with the same symptoms, just an hour or so ago. I'll look forward to Dr. Slikowski's input. Now, if you'll excuse me, I have patients to attend to."

He moved past her, and as much as Jenna wanted to know more, she knew that she could not insist that he talk to her about his patient. Slick would be here soon enough, she thought. On the other hand, Audrey had been in with Dr. Gifune and the patient.

"What's going on, Jenna?" Audrey asked.

Jenna bit her lower lip and frowned. "What do you mean, what's going on? You're here, aren't you? Obviously something's going on, and we'd all like to know what it is. Have they figured out what made these girls sick? Do they know each other? Did they eat together?"

Audrey's eyes narrowed, her expression grim. "No. One of them, the one admitted this morning, Katherine Mullion, doesn't even live on campus, so she doesn't eat here. One of the new arrivals is a vegetarian who only eats in the Campus Center. The other two eat in the regular dining halls, but they haven't been in the same one recently."

A hard, cold knot twisted in Jenna's stomach. "Then how is it spreading? It's food poisoning, so where's the connection to the food?"

"Perhaps it's not," called a familiar voice from behind her.

Slick propelled his wheelchair through the quiet ER with Dr. Dyson walking beside him. They both greeted Audrey, but the weight of their concern was heavy on all of them.

"What are you suggesting?" Audrey asked.

The M.E. glanced at Dyson and gestured for him to answer.

"Initial tests indicate that it may not be bacterial at all. It's a virus that was in the food the people at that faculty luncheon ate. The effects are incredibly similar to paralytic shellfish poisoning, but it appears to be something else."

Jenna sagged back and let out a slow breath as she stared at the two doctors. "What does that mean? How did it happen?"

"We're working on that," Slick replied. "I'm meeting with the infectious disease staff in a few minutes."

"More importantly, how is it spreading?" Audrey asked.

"They'll have something to say about that as well," the M.E. replied. "In the meantime, perhaps you and the ER staff will be able to help with that question. We speculate that it could be airborne—"

"The students who got sick don't even know each other," Jenna told him. "They couldn't have been exposed at the same time or in the same place."

Slick nodded grimly. "Contact transmission is a possibility as well. Bodily fluids? Mononucleosis is thought to be contagious through saliva. Kissing alone can pass it along. If something this virulent could be passed that way—"

"We'll have the whole campus in here in a day or two," Audrey muttered, her eyebrows furrowing.

"That's just one possibility, though," Dyson assured them. "We still don't know what we're dealing with."

"So how do we test for it?" Jenna asked, shaking her head in disbelief. "Can we use a throat culture, like we do for strep?"

"We'll have to figure all of that out," Slick replied.

Audrey tapped Jenna on the arm, and they all turned to see Dr. Gifune moving toward them. His expression was deeply troubled.

"Dr. Slikowski," Gifune said, "you're right on time. Another one of my patients just became one of yours." His gaze shifted to Audrey and then to Jenna before returning to Slick. "Katherine Mullion just died."

chapter 10

"I was going to head back upstairs to see how Shayna's doing," Jenna said, her eyes shifting nervously back and forth between Slick and Dyson. "But my mom and Hunter are there, and I don't think I need to be there right now. Besides, if you need me to help with—"

Slick made a clicking sound with his tongue as he shook his head quickly. "No, no, Jenna. Al and I can take care of everything in the lab. You should go and see them and check on how your father's holding up."

Jenna nodded her agreement and started to leave, but she pulled up short. She couldn't remember ever feeling so torn between what she *wanted* to do and what she *needed* to do. But the truth was, Shayna's condition hadn't changed, and the doctors still had no idea when—or if— she would recover. Besides, Hunter and her mother were already up there, and Jenna knew she would be a lot more valuable helping with the autopsy on Katherine Mullion.

"Actually, on second thought, let me come down to the morgue with you first," she finally said. "I'll just help you get things started. I have to talk with Audrey about something. Then I'll be down. Give me five minutes."

Slick shot her a questioning look but then, apparently deciding not to argue with her about it, nodded and turned his wheelchair around. He left with Dyson walking beside him. Once they had passed through the swinging double doors that led out to the emergency room front desk, Jenna took a shallow breath and turned to Audrey. After looking up and down the busy corridor, she cleared her throat and said, "Is there someplace we can go to talk?"

"Is this really important?" Audrey asked, sounding a bit more abrupt than usual, even for her. "I have a few questions for Slick or Dyson, and then I have to get back to the station. There are a couple of things I have to clear up before I go home tonight."

Jenna hesitated, no longer sure that she wanted to ask Audrey what she had been about to ask. She was still stewing about what had—and hadn't—happened between her and Danny, and she had wanted to talk to Audrey about it. Maybe she could gain a little better insight into what Danny was going through. She was worried about him . . . not just about whether or not he would lose his job, but how he was doing.

Finally she lowered her gaze and, letting her breath out slowly, shook her head.

"No," she said, her voice lowered almost to a whisper.

"It—it's not that important. I can . . . we can talk some other time."

Audrey seemed to take her at her word and, without saying anything else, gave her a quick nod, turned, and started to walk away. Jenna couldn't help but feel deserted as she watched the detective walk down the corridor. Then again, she told herself, what could Audrey possibly tell her that she didn't already know? Danny was on suspension, and he wasn't handling it very well. Maybe what had happened—what had almost happened between them—had just come from the sense of desperation the two of them were both feeling.

Just leave it alone, Blake, she cautioned herself.

Standing in the middle of the hallway, she watched as the automatic doors swung shut behind Audrey. For several seconds she remained where she was, unable or unwilling to move. It was like being paralyzed. She had rarely—if ever—felt so torn, so helpless, and she was almost overwhelmed by the thought of what might lie ahead of her.

"Just get your butt in gear," she whispered to herself, but as she walked slowly down the hallway to the elevator that would take her down to the autopsy lab, she glanced over at one of the closed examination room doors. She knew that one of the girls who had been admitted was in that room, and she was suddenly curious to find out how serious the woman's condition was. Was she going to end up on the autopsy table herself in a day or two?

Jenna approached the closed door, wondering

whether or not she should intrude. She had no right to be poking around like this. The young woman had a right to privacy, but Jenna was trying to unlock the key to the puzzle this thing had become, and her curiosity drove her on.

She was trembling as she rapped lightly before opening the door and silently entering. Valerie, the nurse Jenna had spoken to earlier, was standing next to the woman's bed. Jenna was glad to see that the patient was wide-awake and alert.

"May I help you?" Valerie asked, glancing at Jenna over her shoulder. There wasn't a trace of annoyance in her voice, but Jenna was still painfully aware that she didn't belong here.

"I thought I might have left my purse in here," Jenna said, offering the first lame excuse that popped into her head.

Valerie took a glance around the room and then shook her head.

"Sorry. I don't see it." She hesitated. "I don't remember you having a purse with you when you came in."

Jenna scratched her head as though confused, but she couldn't tear her gaze away from the patient. It was the young woman's eyes that got her. They were wide open and staring off into the distance, as though she were peering into some dark, bottomless abyss. Her face was pale, her lips thin and bloodless. Her blonde hair hung in limp strands that fanned out across the pillow. Her breathing was low and regular, but suddenly she convulsed and let out a belly-deep grunt.

"Are you in any pain?" Valerie asked, turning back to her patient.

"My stomach feels . . . really tight," she said. "Like cramps, and my chest—" She took a breath that cut off sharply. "It hurts every time I inhale." She hesitated for a moment and licked her lips. "And I think it's getting worse."

As if to prove her point, she took another shallow breath, and it was cut off as a convulsion snapped her body, almost making her sit straight up in the bed. She let out a low, pained groan as she eased back onto the bed.

She's lucky she's even still conscious, Jenna thought, unable to stop herself from comparing this woman's condition to Shayna's.

Jenna glanced at the chart at the foot of the bed, but all she got was the patient's name: Lauren Cole. She tried to take it all in, but after a few awkward seconds, she started backing up toward the door. She muttered a feeble, "I'm sorry," but she wasn't even sure if the nurse or the patient heard her. She opened the door and stepped into the corridor, sighing as she eased the door closed behind her. Just before it shut, though, she heard the nurse address the young woman.

"So if you didn't know the other two women, who have you been in contact with in the last couple of days?"

Jenna heard Lauren sigh before she replied. "Just the people I told you about. I gave you everybody's name."

"Are you sure there's no one else you might have come in contact with?" Valerie asked. "This condition has affected several other people, and it hits pretty fast. It will help us stop it if we know how everyone is connected."

There was a long silence from the room, and Jenna felt suddenly nervous about getting caught eavesdropping. She had no business listening in on a nurse and her patient's private conversation.

"Well . . . I was with Ben yesterday afternoon," Lauren said. Her voice sounded strained, as though it was getting increasingly difficult for her to speak.

"Ben?" Valerie said. "What's his last name?"

"Ben Hall," Lauren said, and her voice cut off with a loud, pained grunt. "I—I met him at the Bramhall last night, and we sort of . . . you know."

"Had relations?" Valerie said.

"Uh-huh," was Lauren's reply, but Jenna didn't hear anything else. She closed the door as silently as she could and went down the hall to the banks of elevators. She pressed the button for the basement, but before the elevator arrived, she turned and walked quickly to Emergency Room Admissions. The nurse she had spoken to earlier was still there, sipping a cup of what smelled like herbal tea as she reviewed some paperwork.

"Excuse me," Jenna said, putting on a big smile. "I'm working with Dr. Slikowski on the food poisoning case, and I was wondering if you could tell me one thing."

The nurse looked up at Jenna, her expression flat, revealing and committing to nothing.

"Was a young man named Ben . . . Benjamin Hall admitted with symptoms similar to those of the four women who came in today?"

"The name doesn't ring a bell, but let me check," the nurse said. She turned to her computer and, after opening a window, typed in the name. After less than a second, the screen flashed the message NO MATCHES.

"Doesn't look like it," the admissions nurse said.

"Was anyone else—especially a male—admitted today with similar symptoms?"

The admissions nurse looked at Jenna and shook her head. "I came on duty at eight o'clock this morning, and—the answer is no. These are the only four that I know of."

Jenna was tempted to ask if there was a possibility that she wouldn't know of every case that came through, but she sensed that would be insulting, so she simply thanked the woman for her help and turned to take the elevator down to the autopsy room.

Dyson had the preliminaries for the autopsy well under way by the time Jenna got scrubbed up and into her surgical gown, mask, and gloves. Katherine Mullion was already lying on the autopsy table, and Al was taking a series of photographs. Dr. Slikowski had gone to his office to call several hospital administrators and the infectious disease specialists, but Dyson told her that the M.E. would be coming downstairs shortly to do the autopsy.

As Jenna stepped forward to help Dyson position the body on the table, the dead girl's hand slipped and hung down off the edge of the table. The fingers were curled up, but Jenna saw that there was some kind of mark on the palm of the girl's hand. Written in marker were the initials BH followed by a phone number. Jenna let out a low gasp and took a step back.

"Are you all right?" Dyson asked, catching her reaction. Jenna tried to speak, but her throat had closed off. BH. Which could stand for Benjamin Hall. *This has to be just a coincidence,* she told herself.

"What are the chances?" Jenna whispered, unaware that she had spoken out loud.

"Chances of what?" Dyson asked. His eyes narrowed with concern as he looked at her above his surgical mask.

Jenna was still trying to convince herself that this couldn't be what she thought it was. There was no way Lauren Cole's mention of Ben Hall and the initials written on Katherine Mullion's hand were connected. But something inside Jenna was telling her otherwise. Right now they were all looking for the things that connected the patients who had been infected. There had to be something. Maybe this was it. Something was telling her she'd just found another piece of the puzzle.

"Jenna," Dyson said, his voice edged with concern. "If you're not up to this, if you think you should be upstairs with your family . . ." He paused, then shook his head. "We've got things covered here."

Jenna hesitated as she mulled over the things that were coming together in her mind. Someone had to go check on Benjamin Hall. She didn't want it to be her, not with the chaos on campus and the risk of exposure to the virus if the guy had been infected and she had to try to get him back to SMC. But Slick and Al had their work to do. The doctors at the hospital were going to be putting all their efforts into figuring out what this thing really was and stopping it.

If both Lauren and Katherine had been with the same person whose initials were BH, then he had been exposed to the virus and was in danger. At the very least, someone should look him up and warn him about what was going on.

Another day she would have asked a detective to go along with her. But Audrey and the rest of the Somerset PD were going to be dealing with their investigation and, before long, with panic as well, and Danny was suspended without pay. Off the job. Not that Jenna would have gone to him tonight, no matter what. The point was, this was a medical issue, not a criminal one. With all that was happening, she couldn't ask Audrey to break off whatever else she was doing just to come with her to check up on some kid who *might* be sick.

So that leaves me.

"Dr. Martin. Walter Slikowski here." Slick glanced over at Dr. Gifune, who was seated on the other side of the desk with the extension phone to his ear. "How have you been?"

"Dr. Slikowski," replied the doctor at the Centers for Disease Control and Prevention in Atlanta. "I'm fine. Working too hard, as usual. But if you're calling me at home at quarter to ten on a Friday night, I don't suppose we have time for small talk."

As always, there was a cold distance in Pamela Martin's voice, even when it appeared as though she was trying to sound friendly. Slick eased back in his wheelchair and closed his eyes for a moment, mentally picturing the woman at the other end of the line. She was tall and lanky, with bright red hair and freckles that gave her an almost impish look. In truth, she was an attractive woman except for that haughty tone of voice she always maintained. Slick wondered how much of that was really a part of her and how much was a facade she put on to help her deal with the pressures of working at the CDC. But over the years he had worked with her on several cases, and he admired her professionalism, even if it did color her personality.

"Well, the truth is, we've got quite a problem up here. Dr. Aaron Gifune, who heads up Somerset's infectious disease unit, is here with me."

"Hello, Dr. Martin," Gifune said. "Thank you for taking our call."

"What can I do to help?" Dr. Martin said, not wasting any time on further introductions.

The leather seat back squeaked as Slick settled back in his wheelchair and started to explain the situation. He wanted to be as complete and detailed as possible so there would be no misunderstanding. Every now and again he would refer to his notes or check with Dr. Gifune just to make sure he had the entire sequence of events to date correct. Dr. Martin interrupted with some questions on a few points, but after ten minutes or so, she had the whole story.

"So that's where we stand," Slick said. "I was hoping you'd have some insight into what we might be dealing with."

The phone line was silent for several seconds. Finally Dr. Martin said, "It does sound worrisome. There's no way of knowing what's causing this without further research, but now that a second patient has died and other apparently unrelated cases are showing up on the campus, you've got to treat this like an outbreak."

"Are you suggesting a quarantine?" Slick asked.

"There's no other way to respond. We'll have to do a contact circle tracing right away to find out any and all potential exposures, but that will take time."

"So far," Slick said, "from talking with patients who have recovered and working with the local PD, we haven't found any obvious links. Of course, our initial suspicion was that it had something to do with the tainted shellfish, but none of these new cases seem to have been exposed to any contaminated seafood. Now that we've established it's viral, not bacterial, we're not sure where to look. The pieces simply aren't fitting together in any sensible pattern, and we don't have the resources to do much more than we already are."

"The CDC people will cover the contact tracing," Dr. Martin said sharply. "The way things are today, we can't rule anything out. For all we know, it could be bioterrorism. We've got a team in Boston. I can have them there in an hour to get things started, and I'll organize a full investigation and have my own team on a flight from Atlanta as quickly as possible. Meanwhile, though, we need someone on site to be our point person. That's you, Walter. Under federal authority, I want you to lock that hospital down. And I'd like you to transfer me to the hospital's head administrator."

"Are you saying—," Dr. Gifune said, but Dr. Martin cut him off.

"Your facility is the most logical spot to get locked down initially simply because of the greatest risk of widening exposure from the cases you already have. Any patients who are still sick, all of the staff, and any lab workers who have processed specimens, and all security, will have to stay put. I don't want any pickups or deliveries. The police lab should be notified too, since they handled materials as well. Any new patients with similar symptoms should still be brought into the hospital or else to another designated site adjacent or close to the hospital."

"This is going to put quite a strain on our facility and resources," Dr. Gifune said. No doubt he was feeling a little intimidated after this first experience with Dr. Martin.

"Yes, it is," Dr. Martin replied, speaking so quickly that Gifune's words were cut off as cleanly as if they'd been sliced by a razor. "We have no idea what we're dealing with, but consider the alternative. What if this were to get out into the general population?"

Dr. Gifune didn't have an answer for that. Slick glanced over at him and gave him a curt nod.

"So let's stop wasting time here. Put me in touch with your chief administrator."

Audrey had put on a surgical mask, gloves, and a gown and now she stood close to the wall, watching as Dyson proceeded to work on the body of Katherine Mullion. Slick was on the phone with the CDC, and she suspected Dyson wished he hadn't let Jenna leave in such a hurry. He sure looked like he could use some help, but Audrey wasn't qualified to step in.

"This is taking too long," he said to Audrey as he placed tissue samples in the refrigerator. His surgical mask sucked in and out of his mouth as he spoke. "They know it's a virus. They've got to reverse engineer it, figure out how to help the people who haven't made it down to the basement yet."

"Reverse engineer? Is it that easy?"

Dyson shrugged. "Probably not, but if somebody built this thing, they've got to be able to see the way it's put together."

"What do you mean, built?"

"We think it might have been custom-made."

"Custom-made? Are you saying someone might have done all of this on purpose?"

"It's a strange world out there—," Dyson said.

"And getting stranger," Audrey finished for him. "If that's what this is, do you have any idea why they're doing it?"

Dyson looked over at her, his eyes shifting back and forth over the edge of his surgical mask. He didn't say anything for several seconds, but finally he sighed and shook his head.

"I'm not paid to figure it out," he said. "And if you want to know the truth, I don't want to know."

"You mean you haven't speculated?"

Dyson shrugged. "Sure I have. There could be any number of reasons. The most likely, it seems to me, is that someone poisoned the food at the reception for Frank and Shayna on purpose."

"You mean they wanted to kill someone?"

"Or make them sick. How the hell can we know? And that very well might not even be why. We could be dealing with something experimental that got out of one of the labs nearby, or for all we know, it might be some kind of terrorist act. I'm sure the officials upstairs have already contacted the Department of Homeland Security."

Audrey didn't say a word, but she rolled her eyes, wondering how effective that would be.

"I appreciate your time," she said. "Give me a call when you have the results, will ya?"

"I sure will," Dyson said, and without another word, he turned to the table and got back to work.

In the outer room Audrey stripped off the surgical mask, gloves, and gown, tossed them into the HAZMAT container, and took the elevator up to the main floor. When she got there, she noticed a flurry of activity in the main lobby. By the time she had walked down the hallway to the back door, the hospital was in near chaos. Hospital security and several campus and local cops were swarming the hallways, setting up barriers and blocking the door, closing the hospital down. Emergency lights outside in the parking lot strobed red and blue flashes across the walls and floor.

Audrey saw Peter Heinz, a new recruit at the department, standing by the door. She smiled as she approached him.

"Hey, Heinz. What gives?" she asked.

"We've got orders to close the place off," Heinz said. He seemed a bit spooked by the notion.

"Damn," Audrey said. "All right. I'm headed back to the department, but I'll check in within the hour."

Heinz opened his mouth to protest, but she went right past him, through the panic and confusion and out the door. Audrey strode outside and cut across the short expanse of dying grass to where she had parked her car. She took a deep breath of the chilly night air.

The parking lot was crowded with emergency vehicles and police cars that were parked at all angles in front of the door. More were pulling in by the second, their sirens wailing and emergency lights flashing. Audrey forced down the surge of panic inside her, telling herself that she—like everyone else here—had a job to do. She went to her car and slid in behind the steering wheel. Her cell phone rang. She flipped it open and pressed it to her ear.

"Gaines," she said.

"Hey. Audrey. It's me," the voice said. Audrey had trouble hearing it above the sounds of sirens outside.

"Danny?" Her grip tightened on the cell phone, and

she sighed and shook her head. "Danny, I really don't have time right now."

"I just got off the phone with Gonci," Danny said, forging ahead as if he hadn't even heard her. "They're coming down with a decision Monday, and he wanted to give me a heads-up."

"I'm sure you're gonna be fine," Audrey said.

At the other end of the line, she heard the faint sniffing sound of laughter.

"You think?" Danny said. "Because Gonci told me that they found against me. I've been fired."

chapter 11

"Stupid . . . stupid . . . *stupid!*"

Yoshiko could feel herself getting angrier by the second as she paced back and forth across her dorm room floor. She wasn't really sure who or what she was more angry at—herself or Hunter or Jenna or the whole damn stupid situation. Maybe Tony Maleko was to blame.

She didn't like feeling this agitated. In general she prided herself on how cool and calm she usually remained . . . unless she was cutting loose and acting silly with her roommate or some other college friends. She almost laughed out loud when she recalled a bumper sticker she had seen some time ago. It read: IF YOU CAN KEEP YOUR HEAD WHILE OTHERS ARE LOSING THEIRS, YOU OBVIOUSLY DON'T GRASP THE SITUATION.

"And what exactly *is* the situation?" she asked herself aloud.

Why, it was nothing all *that* serious . . . except that she had just broken the heart and betrayed the trust of a truly wonderful man who genuinely loved her, and she may have damaged her relationship with her best friend in the world, possibly beyond repair.

"Naw . . . nothing too serious," she muttered as she continued to pace back and forth, back and forth across her dorm room, feeling as restless as a caged beast in a zoo.

With every pass, she would pause beside her desk and stare at her cell phone lying there next to a stack of books and notebooks.

What would be the harm if I called Hunter? she asked herself.

She could admit she was wrong.

Couldn't she?

The least she could do was ask him to forgive her so they could move on.

What's so hard about that?

She came back to her desk and hesitated again, reached out slowly to pick up the cell phone, but then stopped herself. He'd have to be a saint to forgive her.

"I could call Jenna," she said, her gaze still fixed on the silent cell phone.

The fact was, she needed to talk to *someone*. If she couldn't face Hunter just yet, then maybe Jenna was the person to talk to.

She jumped when the sudden loud wail of a police siren rose outside the dorm, piercing the night. Leaning across the heater, she pressed her face to the window so she could see the flashing red and blue emergency lights of the cruiser that was just pulling into the driveway outside Whitney House. Off in the distance in the direction of the main campus, more emergency lights strobed in the night like distant flashes of lightning.

Down on the street in front of the dorm, the police cruiser's doors opened, and two uniformed police officers along with a man wearing a dark suit stepped out. They moved quickly up the front steps to the main entrance. Yoshiko jumped and spun around quickly when someone out in the hall knocked on her door.

"Yeah? Who is it?" Yoshiko called out as she started toward the door. A low surge of panic was starting to build up inside her.

"Yoshiko? Jenna? Are you guys in there?"

"Nope. Just me," Yoshiko shouted back before she opened the door and found Sydney Woods, the RA on their floor, standing there. Sydney was wearing a tank top, threadbare pajama pants and pink bunny slippers. She had her hair pulled back in a tight bun at the top of her head, and the frightened look on her face gave Yoshiko's nervousness a jolt.

"What's going on?" Yoshiko asked, trying hard not to let her rising panic show.

"The police are upstairs," Sydney said. "They want to talk to everyone in the dorm."

"Is there a fire or something?" Yoshiko asked.

Sydney shrugged as she turned away, hurried down the hall to the next door, and started knocking.

"Dunno," she said over her shoulder. "All I know is,

I got a call from the resident director, who told me to get everyone on the floor up to the lobby as quickly as possible."

By the time Yoshiko got to the lobby, the common area was full to overflowing with students. The man wearing the rumpled dark gray suit was standing by the front door, flanked by the two cops. He didn't look anything like a campus or town cop to Yoshiko.

"First and foremost," the man said without any preamble after getting everyone's attention, "we don't want anyone to panic. I've been instructed to inform you that there's a medical emergency in progress at the Somerset Medical Center. The hospital is now under quarantine, and I've been told by the CDC to instruct all students and staff to remain indoors for the time being."

"The CDC?" someone called out.

"The Centers for Disease Control and Prevention," the man explained. Before he could say anything more, a wave of excited chatter burst from the crowd. Students expressed their dismay and outrage as a barrage of questions about what exactly was going on filled the room.

"Quiet. Please," the man said, waving his arms to silence them.

Yoshiko, who was standing at the back of the room, thought she caught a hint of barely concealed nervousness in the man's demeanor. Was it because he was inexperienced at crowd control, or did he know more than he was saying and was frightened about the situation, whatever it was?

"At this point," the man said, "we're not at liberty to

discuss the matter since it's still under investigation. But we're asking for your complete cooperation until the issue is resolved. We ask only that you remain in this building for the time being, even if you're not residents. You aren't being confined to your rooms, but—please—do not attempt to leave the premises for any reason until you receive official notification."

"You can't do this!" someone yelled. A chorus of protest immediately filled the room. The man looked genuinely threatened by the students' sudden outburst, but he waved his arms emphatically above his head until the chaos subsided.

"Please . . . please!" He had to shout to be heard above the rising chorus of complaints. "There's been an exposure to a toxic, possibly lethal substance on campus. The CDC has an investigative team en route. We're asking for your understanding and cooperation here. In all likelihood you will be confined to the dorm overnight. We hope to have the situation contained by morning."

"Contained?" someone said.

"Why can't you tell us what it is?" someone else shouted.

"Is it terrorists?"

"I don't even live in this dorm."

Once again the room erupted with a flurry of complaints and questions.

"Please . . . just listen," the man shouted back, raising his arms as though physically trying to hold back the mob. "We'll notify you about what's going on as soon as we can. For now, this building is considered secure. I've been ordered to post guards at all exits, so just try to relax and wait until we get an all-clear. At this point that's all I can tell you."

"This isn't fair!"

"Do we still live in America, or what?"

Several students started booing as the dark-suited man and his police escort turned and walked quickly out of the dorm. As the glass doors swung shut behind them, Yoshiko noticed for the first time the two police officers who had taken up positions on the steps on either side of the front door. Both of them had rifles in their hands.

Oh, my God! Yoshiko thought, totally numbed by the panic rising up inside her.

She glanced around at the sea of faces. They all looked as frightened and confused as she was. Without Hunter or Jenna here, she felt completely isolated. She had never felt so alone in her life.

Hunter was feeling more than a little awkward sitting in the room with Jenna's divorced parents and her father's new wife. Throughout their freshman year, Jenna had told him bits and pieces about her parents and how their marriage had fallen apart. Nothing brutal. Nothing bloody. It was just that one day Jenna realized her father had moved out, and later that evening, her mother told her that he wasn't coming back. Jenna had been too young at the time to comprehend the details of the marriage's ending. It was something that just happened, a natural falling apart.

Like what just happened to me and Yoshiko, he thought.

Now, being in this hospital room with both of them, Hunter had an opportunity to observe them up close for the first time. Of course, the circumstances were a little strained. The doctors still weren't sure when—or even if—Professor Emerson would recover and, if she did, whether there would be any long-term effects.

Hunter couldn't help but listen whenever Professor Logan and Dr. Blake spoke to each other. He was impressed that they could even be in the same room at the same time together.

How do they do it? he wondered, looking back and forth between Frank and April.

"Care for a cup of coffee or tea?" April Blake asked. She glanced back and forth between her ex-husband and him, so Hunter knew he was included.

Frank let his shoulders slump as he shook his head no.

"No, thanks," Hunter said with a quick nod. "I'm all set, I guess."

Feeling more than ever like an intruder, he turned away. When his gaze came to rest on Shayna, he was suddenly convinced that he saw her eyes twitch. She looked like someone who was resting who flinched when the light was suddenly turned on.

Hunter stiffened in his chair and glanced over at Frank and April, but it looked like neither of them had noticed.

"Did you—," he started to say, but then he cut himself off and shook his head, adding a feeble, "Never mind."

He was reminded of when his Gram-Gram died, and he had gone to her funeral. One of the clearest memories he had—other than how much his mother cried all that week—was how really freaky it was to look at his grandmother, lying there in the coffin at the funeral service. Time after time, he was sure as he stared at her that he had caught a glimpse of motion—that he had seen her closed eyelids twitch or her chest rise and fall ever so slightly.

It was just an illusion . . . like this, he told himself, but as he stared at Shayna, he saw it again. The corners of her eyes crinkled just a little, like she was wincing.

"Professor Logan . . . ?" he said, keeping his voice low and trying to contain his excitement.

Frank regarded him with red-rimmed eyes. He looked worn out past the point of exhaustion.

Hunter got up slowly from his chair and approached the bed. He was trembling inside and still trying to convince himself that he had just imagined it. As he moved closer to the bed and leaned over Shayna, though, he saw it again, distinctly this time.

"There! Did you see that?" he asked, pointing at Shayna's face.

In a flash Frank was on his feet and leaning over his unconscious wife.

"Shayna?" he whispered, bending close to her ear. His knuckles turned white as he gripped the bed railing.

Nothing.

Not the slightest sign of movement.

Hunter blushed with embarrassment and wished

he'd kept his mouth shut. He looked at April, who was standing by the bedside, her gaze shifting back and forth between the patient and the electronic monitors.

"There was a slight change on the EEG," she said softly. Hunter could hear the note of hope in her voice.

Frank squeezed Shayna's hand, clutching it tightly against his chest as he brought his mouth close to her ear and whispered something to her that Hunter couldn't quite make out. He had his face so close to her that he didn't notice when Shayna's eyelids twitched again, this time so noticeably that even April saw it.

"There's some eye movement," she said. "I'll go get the doctor."

She turned and walked quickly and silently from the room. Hunter stepped back and exhaled, realizing he'd been holding his breath. He felt even more like he was invading Frank and Shayna's privacy, and he wished Jenna would come back so they could leave. But he also felt an undeniable rush of joy when the corner of Professor Emerson's mouth twitched.

I can't believe this is happening, Hunter thought as a rush of relief and excitement went through him.

"Shayna . . . honey . . . please come back to me," Frank whispered.

Hunter saw Shayna's eyelids move again. It wasn't much.

But it's something, he thought.

He started to reach into his jacket for his cell phone. He wanted to call Jenna and tell her, but then he stopped himself.

Don't go butting in, he cautioned himself. *This isn't any of your business.*

Even though Professor Emerson hadn't uttered a sound, much less sat up and spoken to them, Hunter was convinced that he had just witnessed something close to a miracle. He was positive Shayna had rounded the corner and was now on the road to recovery. They would have to wait for the doctors to arrive and confirm it, but finally it looked as though there was going to be some good news.

The conference room at Somerset Medical Center was crowded with staff and security people. The department heads on duty or their assistants from every department in the hospital were present. At the head of the table Slick and Dyson sat with Dr. Harold Nolan, the hospital's chief of staff, and Dr. Gifune from the Infectious Disease Unit. The hospital's director of public relations, Allison Pranger, stood by the wall at the front of the room with Roger McMasters from Security.

So far the PR staff had been able to keep the media away, but with the hospital sealed off, everyone knew it was just a matter of time before word leaked out and they were barraged with questions. Using the authority Dr. Martin had given him, Slick had also ordered the two dorms where the most recent cases had occurred to be quarantined, and a curfew on the rest of the campus. The conference room was buzzing with whispered conversation until Slick rapped on the tabletop.

"All right. Everyone, please," he called out. "If I could have your attention for a moment."

The room instantly quieted down, and all heads turned toward him.

"I don't have to tell you how serious this situation is," Slick began. "We've had two fatalities so far—Dean Havelock and a student named Katherine Mullion. We still have four patients in the critical care unit: Professor Shayna Emerson and three students—Lauren Cole, Jennifer Hilton, and Eloise Lambert."

Before he could continue, someone's cell phone or pager started beeping. The culprit—a young woman from Gifune's staff—quickly reached into her pocket and shut it off. She looked at Slick and shrugged a silent apology.

"That reminds me of something," Slick said with a frown. "I know how difficult this will be for all of you, but we are insisting that none of you communicate with your family or friends or anyone else outside of the hospital using your cell phones. All incoming calls will be routed to the message center, and outgoing will be monitored."

A low murmur of objection went around the table.

"Until we know exactly what we're dealing with here and how to stop it, we have to keep it from the media. We certainly don't want to create a panic in the surrounding area due to idle speculation."

"But what if the disease has already spread?" one of the residents asked.

"Working with Dr. Dyson and the Infectious Diseases Unit, we have devised a test to detect the virus—"

"Excuse me, Dr. Slikowski," said one of the nurses that Slick recognized from Shayna's ward. "I was under the impression that we're dealing with food poisoning."

Slick shook his head. "So were we, but it appears to be nothing of the sort. While this virus seems to mimic certain aspects of shellfish poisoning, we have determined in lab tests that it is, in fact, viral. We've devised a simple test for the toxin that's similar to the oral swab throat culture we use to test for strep throat and will shortly begin administering it to the community at large."

More murmurs and whispered comments went through the room.

"Because this all began on campus," Slick continued, "all students, faculty, and staff will have to be tested. After I've finished bringing you all up to date, Dr. Gifune will go into more details about the test as well as some of the other steps we're taking toward treating the disease. Right now, my concern is that we're all on the same page here, and that no one—absolutely *no one*—speaks to the media. That duty will fall to Ms. Pranger, who will turn it over to the CDC team as soon as they arrive."

Roger McMasters, the head of security, straightened up and tentatively raised his hand. Slick acknowledged him with a curt nod.

"We have all of the entrances and exits barricaded," McMasters said. "A team from the Boston office of the CDC should be here soon if they aren't already. I'll check with my people downstairs in a moment. Other than CDC, though, absolutely no one is going to enter or leave the hospital until the team from Atlanta figures out what the hell's going on."

Slick nodded his agreement. "I've been in touch with Dr. Pamela Martin, and she's catching the first available flight to Boston. I expect she'll be here within three hours. Until then, I want you all to know what we're dealing with . . . at least as much as we know."

For the next several minutes Slick got everyone up to speed on the outbreak, how many people were affected, and the measures—such as they were—that they were taking to treat the disease. He was interrupted now and then by questions and had to clarify several points.

"This is a very serious matter," he went on. "We're fairly certain that no one is in danger of contamination unless they have direct physical contact with someone who is already infected. And even then, there appears to be immunity in some individuals. Further testing will help us determine how rapidly and widely—and more importantly, just *how*—this thing is spreading. Are there any questions?"

The conference room was absolutely silent for several seconds as everyone absorbed what Slick had just told them.

"Good. I'll turn the discussion over to Dr. Gifune." Slick rolled his wheelchair away from the table as Gifune rose to his feet, acknowledging him with a quick nod.

"Thank you, Dr. Slikowski. Now, as to our approach," he said. "We're administering standard antiviral therapy as a 'Hail Mary' approach to try to destroy the virus in the infected patients, but so far we haven't had any definitive results. Once CDC arrives, we'll have a lot more resources to draw on."

"I have a family who are going to be wondering why I'm not home for supper," said a nurse from the ER.

Dr. Gifune nodded sympathetically.

"I understand, but we're all just going to have to sit tight and do our jobs for now," he said. "It's going to be a long night. We're working out a schedule to rotate shifts in the event we're here for any length of time. For now, I'd say let's get back to work and see if we can lick this thing."

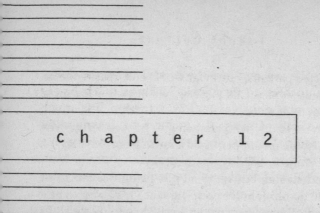

chapter 12

Talbot Hall was relatively isolated from the other dormitories. It stood at the far end of Dearborn Avenue, diagonally across the street from Coleman Auditorium. Talbot's exterior, with its peaks and angles, was slightly reminiscent of Sparrow Hall, where Jenna had lived her freshman year, but the red brick cut into any gothic flair, and Talbot was much smaller than Sparrow.

Jenna had crossed the academic quad and gone past Brunswick Chapel, then took the stairs that ran downhill past the library. A pair of police cars had blown by her on Sterling Lane without sirens, but with their lights flashing brightly, splashing blue across the street and the wrought iron gate that bordered the President's Lawn. It had taken her a moment to decide whether or not to continue on her present course or to follow the cops, just out of curiosity. A lot of really unpleasant things were going on around here, and she wanted to get to the bottom of it.

Then she realized that she needed to let the police and the doctors do their jobs. This was much bigger than just one girl. Her present intention was much more the scale of things she ought to be dealing with. In a crisis, the hospital and the authorities were going to have to deal with the things that were right in front of them. But someone had to look in on Benjamin Hall.

If he had been involved with Katherine Mullion and the other girl Jenna had heard talking at the hospital, and this thing was a virus, chances were good Hall was infected. If so, he needed to get to the hospital and get treatment.

Or he might end up like Shayna. Or, worse, like Katherine Mullion.

Jenna pushed those thoughts away. She didn't like linking Shayna to Mullion in her head. Only ugly ideas lay in that direction.

So she had kept on, taking the steps in the arcade between the Campus Center and the bookstore and emerging on Dearborn Avenue. It was strange to her that so few people were outside. She had seen a few small gatherings of people, but it almost seemed off-season, like everyone was gone for Christmas break. Only it was months too early for that.

Jenna didn't like the feeling. Everything felt off. Wrong. She shuddered, but not from the autumn chill, as she went up the front steps of Talbot Hall. The door was locked, of course. She rapped her knuckles on the thick wood, then spotted the doorbell and pressed it once, hearing the muffled electric hum and, inside the building, an old-fashioned *dingdong*.

Motion from her peripheral vision drew her attention. Even as she rang the bell again she turned to her right to see a police cruiser pulling up to the curb.

With a clank of locks, the door opened. Jenna glanced up to see a large, bearded mountainous man who might have seemed far older than she was if not for the almost childlike nature of his eyes and his smile.

"What can I do for you?"

"I'm here to visit Benjamin Hall. He's in 3F."

Any spark of friendliness in the burly guy's eyes flickered out and an odd expression crossed his face. It might have been jealousy, or possibly just boredom. "Of course you are," he said as he stepped back to let her in. "I need to see your student ID and you have to sign in . . ."

Jenna did as he instructed and as she walked to the stairs she thanked him, smiling, trying to be pleasant. But it was as though the minute he realized she was there to see Benjamin Hall she had become beneath his notice. She should have been furious at the guy for being so horribly dismissive. So why did she feel like she was the one doing something wrong, and what did that say about this Hall guy?

As she started up the steps she heard the bell ring again, then a solid, insistent knocking at the door. Apparently the police were visiting Talbot Hall also. Whatever was going on with the virus, apparently the word was spreading. She hoped that the news would save some lives, and not cause too much of a panic.

On the third floor she hurried along the corridor until she found 3F. The hardwood floor needed cleaning and there were Halloween decorations on the walls that had faded and seemed to have been there for decades. Many of the doors had some kind of message board hung on them, most of them with several different messages penned in a rainbow of erasable markers.

Benjamin Hall's door had no message board. In fact, other than the fact that the 'F' in 3F was cracked in two, the lower power dangling upside down from a screw, the only adornment on the door was the faint trace of the word ASSHOLE where someone had written it in marker and then someone else had tried their best to scrape it away.

Jenna knocked.

Immediately she heard a thump from within, as of someone bumping into a chair or desk, but then nothing further. She frowned. Either Hall didn't feel like answering the door, or he was too sick to get up.

"Hello?" she called. She knocked harder. "Benjamin? Hello?"

At first there was nothing. Then, even as she raised her hand to knock again, he replied, "Who is it?"

"You don't know me. My name's Jenna Blake, and I . . . I just need to talk to you."

After a moment the door swung inward. Benjamin stood just inside, leaning against the open door and making no effort to invite her inside. He was a handsome guy, a bit thin, but with dark hair and eyes and strong features that oozed confidence. Or they should ave. The guy didn't seem sick, but he was nervous about something. He studied her, obviously trying to figure out who she was.

"Yeah?"

"Who were you expecting?" she asked. "Jehovah's Witnesses?"

His smile was exhausted. "Just been a long couple of days," he said, but now he studied her more closely. This time it wasn't to figure out who she was, but to make a frank appraisal of her body. The way he looked at her breasts she felt more than a little like a show horse.

"So?" he prodded.

Jenna crossed her arms over her chest. "I work with . . . I work at the medical center." That would be less odd and alarming than telling him that her boss was the M.E. "We've got kind of a crisis going on. I don't know if you've heard about it. You might have heard some of . . ." she shrugged. "Some of the sirens. Your name turned up in connection to some of the patients who've been coming in showing certain symptoms and I wanted to see if you were all right. Any odd aches and pains? Stiffness? Nausea?"

A flash of alarm shot across his face but then he recovered, summoning a friendly, cocky expression that was entirely false.

"What, Somerset Medical Center makes house calls?"

Jenna did not uncross her arms. "Not exactly. Listen, does the name Lauren Cole ring a bell with you?"

He hesitated before answering. "I know Lauren, yeah."

"What about Katherine Mullion?"

Benjamin Hall tried to keep his eyes locked with Jenna's. He seemed about to say something, his face growing pale, and then he glanced down and to the left. At length, he nodded.

"I know Katie, too. Sort of."

"What's that mean, sort of?"

He frowned. "Who are you again?"

"Jenna Blake. Look, I'm only asking because we've got a bit of a health scare going on, and—"

"Christ," the guy said, his arms falling to his sides even as he leaned fully against the open door. "Is that why you're here? You think something's wrong with me?"

Jenna could have answered that question a hundred ways. She chose to be direct. There seemed no time for anything else. "It's possible, Benjamin. I think you're already scared. Why is that?"

He nodded, his gaze very far away. "I was the one who called it in. I was at Katie's apartment this morning when she had that . . . seizure or whatever it was and—" He stared at Jenna, eyes going wide. "Wait, shit, is that going to happen to me?"

At Katie's apartment. Jenna was so caught up with those words that she barely registered his fear, or his question.

"What about Lauren?"

Benjamin offered a small shrug. "That was yesterday afternoon."

Jenna stared at him. The link was clear. Benjamin had

been with both Lauren and Katie, had probably passed it from Lauren to Katie or possibly been the carrier himself and given it to both girls. Why he himself was not showing any symptoms yet was a mystery, but there was no time to solve that at the moment. That would be for SMC staff, not for her.

"But you feel healthy?"

He laughed abruptly, eyes haunted. "No. I feel like throwing up *now*. But I felt fine before you got here."

She nodded. That was obviously nerves—or at least she hoped it was—but she had to get him to SMC right away.

"All right. We've got to get you to the hospital, Benjamin. You're a part of a . . . I guess you could say a circuit. You're connected to it, and they're going to want to know how this all started. It was a food poisoning thing at the beginning. It shouldn't be able to be spread this way. But it's different somehow. It might be contagious now, and probably through contact. The docs'll be able to be more specific. Anyway, my point is, in the last few days have you had sex with anyone besides Katie and Lauren?"

Once more he could not meet her gaze.

"That's a yes," Jenna said abruptly. "We don't have time to be bashful. I'll need a name. And you'll have to answer the same question at the hospital."

She figured she could give the name to the police, have them go and pick up the other girl.

"Jennifer . . . something. I don't remember her last name."

"No," Jenna sighed in disgust. "Of course you don't." Then she remembered the other girls at the hospital. "Was it Hilton? Jennifer Hilton?"

He nodded. "That was just this morning, after my history class."

Jenna stared at him. She'd known there were guys who were players, but this was ridiculous. "Okay," she said, nodding. "I'll—"

"And Eloise. She's in my French class. That was this afternoon."

Jenna stared at him. That was four girls in two days. How did the guy ever get any studying done if he was that much of a dog? The sheer effort it must have taken him to convince that many women to have sex with him was incredible.

Half-joking, she cocked her hip and stared at him. "Is that all of them?"

Benjamin sighed and looked away.

"You have *got* to be shitting me!" Jenna snapped.

"I can't tell you about the other one," he said. "It was a couple of days ago, so it shouldn't matter."

"Don't be so sure. You'll have to tell them at the hospital, even if you won't tell me."

He shook his head emphatically. "I can't do that. I'll call her, but I can't even do that until Monday. I can't call her when she's . . . home."

"Then let me call her. Someone has to. Or she could end up dead like Katie Mullion."

Benjamin's eyes went wide. "Katie's . . . dead?"

Jenna did not like Benjamin Hall. He seemed just

about the sleaziest guy she had ever met, and his initial arrogance was the sort of thing that normally made her want to slap someone. But something was broken inside him now and she saw the fear and grief in his eyes, the utter desolation, and she felt a measure of sympathy.

But not half as much as she felt for the girls who'd slept with him.

"Yeah. Yeah, I'm sorry, but she is."

"Jesus, I've got to get to the hospital," Benjamin muttered, almost as though he'd forgotten she was there. He grabbed the jacket that was hanging over the chair in front of his desk and then started for the door. Jenna was in the way.

"The name first. Benjamin, whoever this secret girl is, if she is infected, she could die too."

He froze and stared at Jenna. "Wait, you think I'm the one spreading this?" The horror etched into his face was painful to see.

"You're the link."

"But where did I get it then?"

Jenna shook her head. "I don't know. It seems to spread pretty fast. If it is you, then you've infected these other girls in the last thirty-six hours or so. How often have—"

He blanched completely, so much so that Jenna thought he might faint. Then Benjamin swore and kicked the wall.

"Damn it! I knew it was stupid. I never should have—"

Jenna wanted to grab him to get his attention. She

even reached out a hand to do that very thing, but then she hesitated. The last thing she wanted to do was to touch Benjamin Hall. It seemed ridiculous to think she could be infected that way, but she reminded herself that it had all begun as food poisoning, and this sequence of events would have seemed impossible if she had considered it only days ago.

"Who is it?" she demanded.

Benjamin rolled his eyes. "It's Joyce Kimball, from Economics. She called me Wednesday night, said she needed to see me, needed some attention. We were only together for, like, an hour. She couldn't stay out long." He shook his head, muttering to himself. "Goddamn it, Joyce. Oh, shit, what've you done?"

"So she's in your economics class?"

The guy stared at her as though she were the thickest moron who had ever walked the Earth. Even then, it took several seconds for the meaning of that look to sink into her brain, along with the name. Joyce Kimball.

"You mean *Professor* Kimball? You're sleeping with Professor Kimball?"

Benjamin seemed to deflate. "Not anymore." He slipped his jacket on. "Look, I appreciate you coming here. Seriously, I do. It's pretty embarrassing, but I . . . anyway, can we just go?"

Jenna nodded. She stepped back while Benjamin locked his room and they went downstairs together. In the lobby of Talbot Hall was a police officer. He didn't want to let them leave, but Jenna insisted he radio in to Lieutenant Gonci and explain who Jenna was, and that

Benjamin Hall might be "patient zero" in this case and needed to be brought to SMC immediately.

After that the police were paying so much attention to Benjamin that it was not difficult—when they walked him out to a cruiser waiting at the curb—for her to slip away.

Joyce Kimball would have been at the luncheon for her father and Shayna. She had been a friend to Frank Logan for years. Jenna had no idea if the woman had eaten the infected shellfish or not, but logic dictated that she must have picked up the virus and passed it to Benjamin. Yet Jenna hadn't heard anything about Professor Kimball being among the people who'd gotten sick after the celebration. Could she have become infected without showing any symptoms herself?

Could she be contagious?

Jenna wanted to get back to the medical center, to be with her family. But Jenna and her father had once dropped Professor Kimball off at her house and she knew it was only a block and a half away. Joyce Kimball was married. Someone had to tell her what was going on, and do it in a way that protected her privacy. Not that Jenna approved of a married woman sleeping with one of her students, but if she said nothing, the woman might die.

And she didn't think it was a crime punishable by death.

Sometimes when chaos erupted it was difficult for a detective to focus on what was really important. The case. The facts. It was human nature to react to the chaos, to try to help in a more direct fashion, or to hide. Hiding was a big human instinct. But Audrey Gaines had taken a lot of hits during her life, and she had never given in to the instinct to hide.

The radio was on low, background noise for her life, as she drove through Medford Square in her unmarked cruiser. She was out of her jurisdiction, but the Medford cops weren't going to care. Detective Gaines was in the middle of a homicide investigation. She wasn't out to make an arrest, just poking around, asking questions. If matters of protocol needed to be worked out later, she would leave that to Lieutenant Gonci. Of course, Gonci had other things to worry about right now.

Like some kind of viral outbreak spreading across the campus of Somerset University.

Audrey was no fool. If this virus was spreading, it seemed damned unlikely that it was by air. Something that contagious would have already infected half the campus. Even so, she was no doctor or scientist, and so she knew there was the possibility, no matter how remote, that she could be infected. So she was in the car. And she'd stay in the car, with one small exception, and she'd do her best to avoid people, just in case, and then she'd go back and join in on the big, happy quarantine party that was even at that moment going down back at Somerset Medical Center.

But not just yet. Before things started spinning out of control—before the proverbial shit had hit the proverbial fan—she had been focused on the food poisoning at the faculty lunch in honor of Frank Logan and Shayna Emerson. All of the guests who had eaten shrimp at the event had fallen ill. Professor Emerson was still paralyzed and comatose. Dean Havelock was dead. But none of the food service staff serving the food had become sick.

None of them.

That didn't sit right with Audrey. On top of a lot of other indicators, it told her that someone had tainted the shellfish on purpose, poisoned all of those people. She had suspected it for a while, but from some of the things Slick and Dyson had said, she was sure of it now. Someone on the food service staff was a murderer.

How that related to this outbreak, which showed the same symptoms, she was not at all certain yet. It could be that the same person had dosed the girls who had been brought in, poisoned them on purpose, but that seemed entirely random. Her gut told her there was a different explanation.

For now, her focus was on the person who had started it all, the one who had introduced the virus into the campus population at that lunch. Audrey had followed up with all of the servers from that luncheon. All except for one. The man's name was Jack Hawkins. Forty-four years old, if the birth date on his job application could be believed, which Audrey doubted. In order to get the job as a waiter at Campus Food Services, Hawkins had listed only one other job—the previous summer—as a waiter at a small restaurant in southern Maine. What Audrey wanted to know was, what about the forty-three years before that? What about the fact that his phone number was bogus? What about the address he had written down—an address that as far as she knew did not exist?

She had been on the right track in this investigation and would already have followed up on Hawkins earlier in the day if not for the outbreak on campus. Now, even though her mind was full of questions, her heart laced with panic, she forced herself to focus on Jack Hawkins again. On the job.

Her window was rolled down and she enjoyed the chilly air breezing in. It felt cleansing. If there was anything wrong with her, fresh air wasn't going to be much of a cure. But it was comforting just to breathe it in. The low murmured rhythm of the radio accompanied her as she turned onto Anderson Street. A phone call would have answered her question, but Audrey was a tactile and visual person. She needed to see it for herself. To *know* it.

Anderson Street off of Governor's Avenue, a residential area. Audrey knew it well enough to know there was no way that there was an 1153 Anderson Street, but she drove it out anyway. Up the hill, past the elegant old homes, down a couple of blocks to where the Victorians and Colonials gave way to faded duplexes. The highest number was 217. At the end of the street she sat for a few moments, then pulled a U-turn and started back, moving more slowly this time.

There was no 153 Anderson Street either.

At number 53 she pulled to the curb and killed the

engine. No cars in the driveway, but she noticed the mailbox immediately. The flag was up, indicating that the owner had a letter or letters for the mail carrier to take away the next time he or she came by. Audrey climbed out of the car, glancing around the night-dark side street for evening joggers and dog walkers. It was a federal offense to tamper with the mail. Technically, Audrey needed a warrant to open that mailbox.

But people were dying.

It was possible someone would see her from a neighboring window, but already she had committed the act in her mind, and so there was no hesitation as she strode over to the mailbox and opened it. A stack of small envelopes sat inside and she withdrew them. Outgoing bills, each with a fresh stamp, each with the same return address label. George and Elaine Sacco.

Not Hawkins.

"Where are you, you son of a bitch?" she whispered as she put the bills back into the mailbox and closed it.

She strode quickly back to the car and slid into the front seat, fishing her cell phone out of her jacket pocket. In the dark, the engine ticking as it cooled, she dialed information.

"What city and state?"

"Ogunquit, Maine."

"What listing?"

"Oceana's by the Sea. It's a restaurant."

Audrey waited for the number, then let her mobile service provider connect her. If she needed the number later, she could always call back. For the moment she didn't feel like rooting around for a pen. She only hoped the place hadn't closed for the cold season yet.

"Oceana's," a female voice declared, as the phone was picked up on the fourth ring.

"You're open late," Audrey said.

"We're closed, actually. Just putting the chairs up."

"Could I speak with the manager, please?"

"May I ask who's calling?"

Audrey smiled for a moment. It was nice to get someone who had phone manners. But that was Maine. "My name is Audrey Gaines. I'm a detective with the Somerset, Massachusetts, police department."

"Oh." The girl's voice had changed. It was obvious she was curious, but after a moment's hesitation she went on. "Just hold on a minute. She'll be right with you."

In the dark silence inside the car, Audrey waited. She studied the houses around her, but there was nothing to see. This wasn't where the crisis was. There were only ordinary crimes around here, things behind closed doors that never involved the police.

"Hello?"

Audrey introduced herself again. "Who am I speaking with, please?"

"Gina Osnovich."

"You're the manager?"

"One of them. I'm the manager covering tonight."

Audrey took a breath, going over it all in her head again, making sure she was as confident as she felt that this was the key. She was. It had to be. Whoever Jack

Hawkins really was, Audrey was sure he had answers that would save lives.

"Gina, you had an employee this summer who went by the name 'Jack Hawkins.' I have reason to believe that's not his real name. I also have reason to believe he is involved in some pretty terrifying stuff down here, including being responsible for at least two people dying. Maybe more."

There was a hushing sound on the line, the noise of Gina Osnovich hissing air in through her teeth. "Oh, my God," she whispered.

"Gina, are you with me?"

"Yes."

"Did you know Jack Hawkins?"

"Yes. Not . . . not well. Jesus, what did he—"

Audrey interrupted. "Gina. Focus, please. I need to know if your file on Jack Hawkins has a photograph."

"I can check. I doubt it. I don't recall ever seeing photos in employee files. It's not the way the owner does business. But . . ."

"But?"

"Well, there's a bulletin board in the back with pictures from a Fourth of July party we had. I'm pretty sure Jack was there."

Audrey's pulse quickened. *Got you, jerk.* "Can you go and look, please? And hurry. I'll stay on the line."

The manager agreed. Audrey could hear the woman snapping at whoever was around the phone area not to hang it up. She was back in less than two minutes.

"Detective Gaines?"

"Yes?"

"I've got it here. It's not the best picture, but—"

"Can you see Hawkins's face in the photo?"

"Yeah."

Audrey slapped her palm on the steering wheel. "All right, look. Here's what I need you to do. I'll call the Ogunquit police. Can you go over there right now and give them that picture so they can scan it and send it to me?"

There was no response save a contemplative grunt.

"Gina?"

"Sorry. I was just thinking, detective. If you need it that quickly, wouldn't it be easier if I just sent it from here?"

Audrey frowned in the darkened interior of the car. "You have a scanner there at the restaurant?"

"Well, yeah. They're pretty standard now. We do everything online now, keep up the restaurant's Web site, do the staff schedule, all that stuff. Just give me your e-mail address. You'll have it in, like, five minutes."

A minute later Audrey hung up the phone. She sat for a few moments, just thanking the fates for the omnipresence of modern technology. Then her thoughts started turning back toward Somerset Medical Center and the girls there who were sick, who were slowly becoming paralyzed. To Katherine Mullion, who was dead.

Audrey reached over into the backseat and grabbed the cloth handles of the black bag in which she carried her laptop. In some larger American cities, even patrol cars were outfitted with laptops now. It was a hell of a lot easier to run plate numbers or background checks after a traffic stop if there was a computer on board with wireless Internet. Somerset didn't have that kind of budget, but over the summer they had at last given the homicide and vice detectives the tools that they needed. Audrey had used the thing only half a dozen times since she had gotten it, but now she was very happy to have it.

By the time she got the laptop booted up and downloaded her e-mail, the message from Gina Osnovich at Oceana's was already in her in-box. Audrey clicked on the attached file and it opened instantly. The photograph had been taken on rocks overlooking the ocean. There was a man with two women, all of them with drinks in their hands and wearing T-shirts advertising their employer's restaurant.

The face was familiar, but it took Audrey a few seconds to recognize the man. Then she understood why the phone number and address were false, and why he had no employment history prior to that summer. Jack Hawkins was not his real name.

"Damn," she whispered, putting the laptop aside. She didn't even bother to turn it off before she started the car. The engine roared to life, and only when she was already rolling, on her way back toward home, did she pick up her phone and dial Somerset PD. When the desk sergeant answered, Audrey steamrolled right in.

"Sarge, this is Detective Gaines."

"Oh, hey, detective, they're looking for you down at—"

"I know. Just listen. I need you to run someone down for me. A guy, last name Kimball. Wife is a professor at

Somerset U. I don't know his first name but they're on Allen Avenue. I'm rolling on that location now. What can you find on him?"

A younger cop might have made the mistake of falling back on his previous instructions, which likely came from Lieutenant Gonci, regarding Detective Gaines. Audrey was sure Gonci wanted her back at Somerset U. But to his credit, the sarge heard the urgency in her voice and reacted to it the way a veteran police officer had to.

"Give me a minute, Audrey."

She drove, not worrying overmuch about stop signs or red lights, but trying to make sure she didn't run anyone down on the way. She had barely made her way back to Medford Square when the sergeant came back on the line.

"Detective?"

"I'm here, sarge."

"Name's John Thomas Kimball. Forty-four years of age. Born in Buffalo, New York. No criminal record. No sheet at all, not even a parking ticket. Current employer is Massachusetts Institute of Technology."

"MIT. What does he do there?"

"All it says is something about him receiving a federal grant for research into biochemistry."

Icy fingers closed over Audrey's heart. She accelerated, tires gripping the road. The night seemed to have grown darker around her.

Danny Mariano sat on his sofa in the gloom of his living room, only the streetlights outside providing any illumination. Even the television was off. He had been watching a movie—one of those lame *Saturday Night Live* character spinoffs—but had grown disgusted enough that he had shut it off. He needed a laugh, but the movie wasn't going to give it to him.

Neither was the Corona beer on the coffee table, but that didn't stop him from reaching for it. The first beer he'd had, a couple of hours back, he'd taken the time to cut a wedge of lime and slide it down the neck of the bottle. It was the way you were supposed to drink Corona, and it did give it a nice flavor. Made him long for the summer. For the beach. For somewhere warm and far away from here.

Now he was on the fourth Corona, and though there were still some wedges of lime out in the kitchen, he had no motivation to go and get one. He was furious about the way things had come down. The shooting at the end of the summer had been righteous. Jenna's life had been in danger. She'd been seconds away from death; he'd seen it in her eyes. There was no question in his mind that he'd had to shoot.

All it had cost him was his job.

Bastards.

Danny had his regrets. Mostly he regretted that his superiors hadn't gone to bat for him, and that nobody had wanted to extend him the benefit of the doubt. Despite all of his history on the job, his arrest record, everything . . . they weren't going to cut him any slack at all. He regretted that he had spent so much time working for such cold, disloyal morons.

But shooting the crazy bitch who was trying to drown Jenna? He didn't regret that at all. If he hadn't done it, Jenna wouldn't be alive now. No contest. He had done the right thing.

That didn't mean he had zero regrets when it came to Jenna. In fact, he had several. He had not handled their mutual attraction very well at all. What had happened Wednesday night was just a catastrophic mess. He cared about her so much, and in spite of that he had let himself twist up her heart just because he couldn't control himself.

Now he didn't even have his job to bury himself in. He wouldn't be able to see her, even casually, to see how she was taking what had happened.

You could just call her, he thought. *She's your friend.*

But was she still? He hadn't acted like much of a friend.

Even so, he knew he had to call just to hear her voice, to assure himself that in spite of all the crap that he'd gotten himself into lately, Jenna would be all right. And though he didn't deserve her sympathy, he knew part of his motivation was the desire to talk to her about what had happened to him, about losing his job. He needed her warmth, right now.

Should have considered that before.

But that thought did not stop him. Maybe if he'd been on his first Corona instead of his fourth he would have hesitated longer.

Danny started to dial her number at the dorm, but when he glanced at the clock and saw the time he hung up and called her cell phone instead. Chances were that Jenna was not in her room, but even if she was, she would answer the cell phone. At the fourth ring, he thought she wasn't going to answer and prepared to hang up, reluctant to leave a message. What would he say?

"Hello?"

"Hey. It's Danny."

Jenna took a long pause before replying. At last, she simply said, "Hey."

"So . . . I hear there's some crazy stuff going on up there. I was . . . I was worried about you."

Once again she hesitated before speaking. "I'm all right."

"Maybe I was worried about you because of other things, too. I've been an idiot. I should've been more—"

"You were. An idiot, I mean. But I really am all right. I was being pretty stupid too. I was fooling myself thinking maybe we could be friends even with the feelings I had for you. I'm just starting to realize now that by doing that, holding out hope no matter what I told you—or told myself—I was ruining my chances of getting into anything really serious with someone else."

The words hurt him, but he knew he had no right to such emotions. Jenna was right. They both ought to have been more honest with themselves and with each other. The difference was that he'd known there was no real future for them and known that no matter what she said, she still harbored hopes, and he'd let her go on having them.

He laughed lightly, but there was no humor in it. "So you don't hate me?"

Jenna laughed as well. "Now I'm supposed to say something really cheesy like 'I could never hate you.' Even if it's true, it's so movie-romance silly that I can't say the words."

She sounded a bit out of breath.

Danny frowned. "Where are you? You sound like you're running."

"Walking fast. And actually, I've got to go. We can talk more about this another day, if you want—"

"I'd like that."

"—but right now, I've kinda reached my destination, so I can't talk. Maybe give me a call tomorrow?"

"I will."

They said their good-byes and hung up, and only after he'd set the phone down did Danny realize he had not told Jenna the outcome of his hearing, that he was off the job.

He hadn't told her that he was leaving.

chapter 13

Jenna stood in the dark on the sidewalk in front of Professor Kimball's house, and despite the chilly night her face felt flushed with heat. She knew she was blushing. Joyce Kimball was a friend of her father's. It had to be after eleven o'clock. How was she supposed to approach the woman? The professor had been having an affair with one of her students, at least according to Benjamin Hall. Jenna had never met Joyce's husband, but that didn't make it any easier.

Go back to the hospital. Have a doctor call her. Or Audrey.

But she knew she was not going to do that. Professor Kimball had been at the luncheon, but as far as Jenna knew she hadn't been among those who had gotten sick. Now, somehow, it seemed she had transmitted the virus to Benjamin, and he, slut that he was, to four other partners. Jenna could only hope that the girls Hall had been fooling around with weren't as promiscuous as he was, because whoever they'd been with was probably going to catch it too.

So either this woman was going to start showing symptoms pretty soon, or she was a carrier and was going to pass it on to her husband and who knew who else. She needed to get to SMC immediately, and the doctors and police had a crisis on their hands already. This was a small thing. Jenna just had to be mature enough to handle it.

She strode up the front walk and the three steps in front of the house, then rang the bell before she could let her doubts cause her to hesitate any longer. The second her finger pressed the button and she heard the *dingdong* inside, she wanted to run away. But she hadn't pranked anyone with ring-and-run since the age of ten, and she wasn't about to start up with it again now.

There were lights on inside, but they weren't very bright and the gauzy curtains did not allow a view within. Jenna stood for a few increasingly awkward moments, listening for any sign of response from the house. Her ears caught the drone of voices from an upstairs window, but there came a sputter of laughter and she understood that it was the television. The eleven o'clock news.

Twenty seconds or more had gone by without so much as the sound of a footfall from within or a voice calling for her to wait a moment. The doorbell glowed golden in the dark. She debated whether to press it again, but only for a few seconds. She wasn't going to go through the whole thing again. Jenna had decided on a course of action and that was that. Joyce Kimball needed to know what was happening.

She reached out to ring the bell, and just as her finger touched it the door was pulled open abruptly. The action tugged the storm door shut tightly with a muffled bang.

The man just inside the house was tall, at least six and a half feet, and he was thin enough that he would have looked almost like a scarecrow if not for his large eyes and beaklike nose. He was younger than Jenna's father, maybe only forty or so, but there was something about the way his mouth was framed that made him look old. He looked at Jenna like she was trying to sell him something he really did not want. It was very late. She couldn't blame him.

"Yes?"

"Mr. Kimball?"

He studied her more closely. "Dr. Kimball, actually. Who are you?"

Jenna really felt like running now. Her cheeks flushed even warmer and she glanced down. The man had a way of making her feel very small that had little to do with his great height.

"Sorry to disturb you so late. Really sorry. I'm Jenna Blake. You probably know my father, Frank Logan. He's a professor here at—"

"You're Frank's daughter?"

Jenna looked up, surprised at the genuine pleasure in the man's voice. "Yes."

"Why didn't you say so?" He smiled beatifically, and it

made him look like a completely different man. As though he were the one selling something door-to-door. "What can I do for you . . . Jenna, was it? It *is* awfully late."

"I know. I'm . . . it's pretty important. Actually, I was hoping I could speak to Professor Kimball. Is she in?"

Something flickered in his eyes and twitched at the corners of that wide, television evangelist's smile. Then he nodded. "Sure. Of course she is. Come in, please."

He stood aside for her to enter. Jenna drew a short little breath, hesitating a moment, wishing she hadn't come here. But it had been the right thing to do. The big problem now was going to be how to ask Professor Kimball if they could speak privately. But the woman had cheated on her husband, after all, so Jenna didn't feel too badly about her having to explain to him afterward what all the privacy was about. That was going to be Joyce Kimball's problem.

She went into the house.

Dr. Kimball closed the door behind her and locked it.

"My wife's just upstairs getting changed for bed, but she'll be down in a couple of minutes. Can I get you a soda or something? I was just about to put a pot of tea on. Would you like a cup?"

Jenna nodded. "Yeah. That would be great, actually."

The entire short drive from Medford Square and into Somerset, Audrey ran the entire thing over and over in her head. She had very few facts, but the ones she did have combined with her instincts to paint a picture of how all of this chaos and fear had begun. She couldn't be sure, of course, not until she asked the right people the right questions, but it seemed pretty obvious to her that John Kimball had come up with something in his lab, something that behaved an awful lot like paralytic shellfish poisoning, and had used it to try to kill his wife.

The man had worked as a waiter in some restaurant in Maine for just a month over the summer. He'd taken a few shifts a week, and all under a false identity. With the same identity he'd gotten a job with Campus Food Services just long enough to help prepare the food for Frank Logan and Shayna Emerson's wedding lunch.

What didn't make any sense to her was the motive. Somehow Kimball had managed to make everyone else at the event sick, but his wife had eaten the shrimp and had not suffered any illness. Had she lied? Or perhaps she wasn't the target after all. The biggest unanswered question, though, was how it had gone from a case of tampering with food to a contagious virus. That one she couldn't even begin to answer.

An old soul song by the Reverend Al Green came on the radio—the reason Audrey loved this oldies station so much—but she didn't bother to turn it up. There was no room in her mind at the moment for the simple pleasure of singing along to one of her favorite songs. In fact, as she approached the corner of the street where the Kimballs lived, she rolled the window down the rest of the way and turned the radio down.

She turned left, slowing to a crawl, watching the houses on the right side, checking the numbers.

Movement up ahead caught her eye. On the steps of a Cape house, a figure stood expectantly. Audrey slowed the car even more, practically coming to a stop. She glanced at the numbers again, confirming what she had thought.

It was the Kimballs' house.

The front door opened in that same instant. Light from within splashed out onto the stoop, illuminating the person who stood there. Female Caucasian, maybe five feet eight inches tall, auburn hair, and telltale nervous shifting of her weight from one side to the other.

Jenna Blake.

"You've got to be kidding me," Audrey whispered in the car, dropping it into park and killing the engine.

How the hell does she get herself into these things? But Audrey knew how. Jenna was incredibly smart—more intelligent even than she knew—and too clever for her own good. She wanted to be a doctor—a pathologist—but Audrey thought she'd make a hell of a cop. Somehow Jenna had figured out the connection between the virus and John Kimball. Or at least some aspect of it, something that had gotten her curiosity working and dragged her here. After what had happened at the end of the summer, Audrey was sure Jenna wouldn't knowingly walk into the home of a killer. But even if she had a lead, she should have called the police first.

Now Audrey couldn't just go right up to Kimball's front door. There was no telling what the man was capable of, and Audrey didn't want to put Jenna in jeopardy.

We're going to have a little talk, Jenna, you and me, Audrey thought, frowning deeply, her pulse racing as she saw Jenna go inside the Kimballs' house. She popped open her door and climbed out, closing it quietly, then started across the street in the darkness.

If you live through the night.

When Dr. Kimball came out of the kitchen, Jenna was standing in the living room looking at the framed pictures on the mantel over the fireplace. There was a wedding photo that made her smile, as it showed the couple surrounded by what Jenna assumed were members of their families. Everyone seemed to be having a wonderful time.

"The water's on."

She flinched, startled by his return.

"Should only take a minute or two," he added.

Jenna faced him, still feeling incredibly awkward. Was she supposed to make small talk with this guy whose wife was cheating on him with some twenty-year-old?

"Thank you," was all she could muster. Then, a few seconds later, "You have a nice house."

Dr. Kimball's expression did not change. He seemed not to have noticed her comment at all. The two of them stood there looking at one another, Jenna not feeling comfortable enough to sit down and Kimball seeming hesitant even to come further into the room.

"So, do you have my wife as a professor in any of your classes?"

Jenna forced a smile that she knew must have looked like a grimace. She tried not to worry about what he would make of it. "No. Not yet, at least. I've heard only great things about her as a professor, though. The students love her—"

She almost choked when she realized what she had said. Covering for her abrupt halt, she coughed into her hand, hoping he would think that was what had made her pause.

"So I hear," Kimball said, and his smile grew wider.

Wide enough that Jenna shivered at the falseness of it. *He knows.* She couldn't be certain, but that painful grin sure seemed to say that he knew exactly how much at least one student had been loving his wife. If he kept up asking her questions . . . God, if he asked her what she was doing there, she had no idea what she would say. Maybe just that other patients were showing up with the same symptoms that had befallen people at the lunch? That she thought maybe Professor Kimball should go in and see the doctors, just to make sure that she didn't have it in her system? Something like that would—

"And how's your stepmother?" Dr. Kimball asked. "That was terrible, everyone getting so sick like that, and Dean Havelock . . . what a tragedy."

Jenna felt herself shaking. "She's . . . I think she's doing better." *You shouldn't have come here, Jenna. The woman made her own mess. Somebody could have called her and asked her to come down. You don't have to play Mother Teresa to everyone. Why put yourself through this kind of awkwardness?*

But it was too late now. She was here. Nothing more to be done about it.

"That's good. I hope she makes a full recovery."

The words hung in the air. Jenna crossed her arms and took a few steps, looking at several pictures that hung on the wall. Half a minute went by and she glanced upward, wondering how long it was going to take Professor Kimball to come down. For that matter, she wondered why her husband had not gone upstairs to tell her she had a visitor.

"I think she might have jumped in the shower," the man said. "But no worries, I'm sure she'll be down momentarily."

Jenna nodded. But Professor Kimball wasn't taking a shower. She would have heard the sound of the water running upstairs, and there wasn't any.

"Let me check on the tea," her husband said, and he disappeared back into the kitchen.

Jenna stared at the ceiling, frowning. Definitely not taking a shower. Why had he said that? Why hadn't he gone up to tell her she had company?

Now that John Kimball was gone, the absolute quiet upstairs unnerved her. Jenna frowned and stared at the kitchen door, which had swung closed. She crossed the living room and glanced up the stairs. Past them, down a short hall, a light came from a room at the back of the house. Maybe a study or home office?

She started down the hall.

Audrey cut a silent path across the Kimballs' backyard. She had thought twice and gone back to the car just long enough to radio for backup. But Jenna was inside that house with a man who was probably responsible for at least two deaths, and there was no way to know if her life was in peril. Audrey wasn't going to just wait around.

There was a small deck behind the house. Audrey was glad to see that the house was old enough that instead of the sliding glass entrance so popular now, there was an ordinary door leading out to the deck. Four square windowpanes were set into the upper part of the door. Light from inside spilled out onto the deck in the shape of the panes.

If Kimball was as dangerous as Audrey thought he was, the last thing she wanted to do was set him off with Jenna still inside. She went quietly up the steps to the deck, pausing a moment in the shadows when a board creaked beneath her weight. When there was no response from within, no silhouette appearing at the back door, she padded across the deck and pressed herself against the house in the shadows beside the door.

The back door led, as she had suspected, into the Kimballs' kitchen. The floor was a faded linoleum and there were dishes piled in the sink. Books and papers were piled on the small, round table, and a large jacket was thrown over the back of a chair. A teakettle sat on top of the stove, steam rising from its neck without whistling.

Someone moved into the kitchen. Audrey did not flinch or jerk backward, but withdrew slightly, slowly, so as not to draw attention. From her place in the shadows she saw John Kimball go to a cabinet and draw down a pair of light blue mugs. In another he found a box of tea bags. Audrey felt herself calming down. There was nothing at all ominous about Kimball making tea for himself and his guest.

Except that there were two cups. Not three. So where was Joyce Kimball?

As Audrey pondered that question, she watched the professor's husband fix the two cups of tea. He added milk to both. Then he went to the freezer and pulled out a coffee can. Audrey frowned, inching closer, her pulse speeding up again. She knew some people kept their coffee in the freezer to keep it fresh, but what did he need with coffee if he'd just made tea? The question did not remain unanswered for long, as Kimball went to the sink and opened the can. He tipped it slightly, a dusting of coffee grounds spilling into the sink, and then he plunged his fingers in and tugged out a small plastic bag filled with a fine white powder.

Her first thought was drugs. Cocaine or heroin.

But this was nothing that simple. Even as she watched him very carefully open the plastic bag and sift perhaps a teaspoon of the powder into one of the mugs, she understood. John Kimball was a biochemist. A research scientist. He had figured out a way to poison an entire room full of Somerset University faculty with some bioengineered virus. Whatever he had just put into Jenna Blake's tea, Audrey was certain it was deadly.

An image of Danny came into her head. His voice echoed in her mind, haunting her. A scenario quite like this one had just cost her partner his job and the truth of that, the pain of it, had not had time to settle in yet. What if Kimball made it hard for her? What if she had to shoot the son of a bitch to save Jenna, even though it might cost her job?

Damn you, girl, she thought. *You put me here. You put Danny here.*

But Audrey didn't really believe that. Jenna found herself in trouble a lot, but it was always because she was trying to do the right thing, and usually two steps ahead of the cops. Audrey couldn't blame her for that. But they *were* going to have that talk.

As for the risk of violence, Audrey figured she could lower that risk by getting to Kimball while he was alone in the kitchen. She unsnapped her holster and slid her gun out. It was cold in her palm. She took a deep breath to steady herself, even as Kimball took the two mugs and started across the kitchen toward a swinging door that led into the front of the house.

Before Kimball even reached it, that door swung inward. The man was startled, spilling tea. Jenna Blake stepped into the kitchen with a fireplace poker in her hands, and without a flicker of hesitation she swung it at Kimball's face. The poker shattered the man's nose. Blood spurted from his nostrils and he dropped both mugs as he reeled away from Jenna. The mugs shattered on the floor as she followed him into the kitchen, swinging again. The poker struck his back and Kimball flinched and shouted in pain, cursing at her. He turned and reached for the poker.

Jenna broke his forearm.

Audrey braced herself, then put all of her strength into a single hard kick, right beside the doorknob. The lock tore from the frame, glass shattered in two of the windowpanes, and the door crashed open. Without pause she followed it in, taking two steps onto the linoleum, glass crunching underfoot. She leveled her gun.

"Hold it right—," she started to say.

Kimball sneered, blood streaming from his nose, and reached for Jenna. The girl backed away, dropping the poker with a clatter. Audrey catwalked toward them, training the barrel of her gun on the man.

"Do not move, Dr. Kimball. Detective Gaines, Somerset PD. Do not move, sir."

"Me? Did you see what she just did?"

"I did. And I also saw you put something in her tea that doesn't belong there."

Kimball began to speak again but then closed his mouth, perhaps thinking better of it. He was in pain, and he cradled his arm against his chest as he backed up against the refrigerator. Audrey kept her gun trained on him but glanced at Jenna out of the corner of her eye.

"You all right?"

Jenna's only response was a whimper.

When Audrey stole a quick look at her, she noticed for the first time the tears streaming down Jenna Blake's face. The girl hugged herself and stared at Kimball, twitching like a nervous bird, uncertain what to do next.

"Jenna?"

"I'm all right," Jenna said, her voice a throaty rasp.

"I'm okay. But I . . . I found Professor Kimball. His wife. She's . . ." Jenna's face crumpled, her mouth twisting in a mask of grief and shock. "She's on the floor in the room at the end of the hall.

"She's dead."

Audrey swore softly. She gritted her teeth as she stepped closer to John Kimball. The crisis he had begun was still going on and she didn't know how the doctors were going to stop it. But at least the man responsible was not going to get away with it. The thought was cold comfort, but it was all she had.

"Get on your stomach on the floor."

Jenna wept quietly as Kimball complied.

Audrey pulled out her cuffs. "You have the right to remain silent . . ."

EPILOGUE

There had been a storm the day before, a heavy, drenching rain. But that morning the sun was out, the sky was blue and perfect, and everything just seemed to sparkle.

Or, Jenna thought, as she steered her father's battered old BMW along Boston Avenue, *maybe it's just me.*

It was Halloween, now. Two days had passed since the night the CDC had descended on the Somerset campus, locking down the hospital and dormitories. Dr. John Kimball was in jail, awaiting arraignment from the medical wing of the facility as he recovered from injuries sustained during "a struggle that ensued in his home after a guest, Jenna Blake, discovered that he had murdered his wife."

Or at least that was how Audrey Gaines had written it up in her report. The police had quickly discarded any thought of charging Jenna in an assault, given the circumstances. Though Lieutenant Gonci had pulled her aside and warned her, in clear terms, that the next time she turned up at the scene of a crime he was going to find a way to charge her with *something*.

None of it mattered to Jenna. For a brief, frantic moment a crisis had arisen that had terrified everyone involved, from the doctors at SMC to the Somerset PD to the students at the university. But the staff at the hospital—Slick and Dyson included—had done their job. They had worked well, and quickly, and developed a test that would determine whether someone had been infected. And the team from the Centers for Disease Control and Prevention had taken over from there, testing everyone, taking care of those who had already been infected. Things could have been far, far worse.

A shudder went through her. *Things could have been worse, yeah. But tell that to Dean Havelock's family, or Katie Mullion's.* Jenna felt guilty about how thrilled she was, about how glorious this day seemed. No matter how beautiful, she knew that the day would be grim for the people who mourned John Kimball's victims. She felt for them. And yet she could not subdue her own elation.

Shayna was recovering.

She was already home.

Jenna had been so frightened that she would die, leaving her father broken, his heart shattered. When she had first learned that Shayna had awoken, the news had made her giddy, and the feeling had already lasted for two days.

A mindless, hip-hop thumping played low on the car radio. Her father would certainly grimace at the choice of stations next time he drove the car. Another tune played

CHRISTOPHER GOLDEN AND RICK HAUTALA

over the music, and she glanced at the seat beside her, where her cell phone lay beside the small grocery bag she had just picked up from Johnny's Foodmaster. Jenna picked up the phone and glanced at it. Hunter was calling.

"Hey," she said, clapping the phone to her ear.

"Good morning," he said. "How're you doing?"

"Okay," she assured him. "I had a good night's sleep last night. A little different from a couple of nights ago."

"I thought the guest bed at your father's place was really uncomfortable."

She laughed. "It is. Maybe I was too tired to notice. Are we still on for tonight?"

They had made a plan to drive to Vermont that evening. Jenna knew some people might find it odd for the two of them to blow off classes and go off for a couple of days of shopping and dinners and horseback riding and apple picking without any romantic intentions. But they were friends, and she and Hunter both desperately needed some time away to clear their heads, but neither one of them wanted to do it alone.

"Absolutely," Hunter said. "Your father's okay with letting us take his car?"

"He practically insisted." She paused before continuing. "I feel . . . kinda weird. Guilty weird."

"Why? I need . . . I need to get away for a little while, Jenna. So do you. You're one of my best friends in the world. These days, you *are* my best friend at Somerset."

"I wouldn't want Yoshiko to get the wrong idea."

There. She'd said it.

Hunter laughed softly. "Jenna, is it Yoshiko you're

worried about, or are you afraid *I'll* get the wrong idea?"

"No, I just . . . okay, maybe a little."

"Trust me. I don't have any ideas about anything right now. We just both needed to get out of here—"

"Big time."

"And I already told Yoshiko about it," he said, the sadness heavy in his voice.

"What did she say?"

"That she loved us both and she'd . . . she'd be here when we got back."

"What did you say?"

"Nothing. What could I say? We're done, Yoshiko and me. But you two are still friends, and I'm going to see her around, so I'll just have to deal with that as it comes. Anyway, I'll see you later, right?"

Jenna swerved slightly to go around a banged-up Toyota that stopped suddenly just ahead of her, intent upon a left turn the driver hadn't bothered to signal for. She had an odd moment of déjà vu, then shook it off.

"Absolutely. I'll let you go," she said. "I ought to pay attention to the road, anyway."

Jenna ended the call and set the phone back down on the seat, then focused on her driving and the world beyond the windows of the car. The homes and delis and mom and pop shops on the right-hand side disappeared and the ground suddenly rose up into the tree-covered hill that had become so familiar to her. At the top of the hill, over the trees and several buildings, she could see the spire of Brunswick Chapel and two of the larger dormitories.

As she guided the car along, she passed several of the academic buildings that were nearer to the street. There was a fence between the road and the university grounds, and a little ways on, it lifted up into an enormous wrought iron archway. Jenna slowed the car—several drivers beeped angrily as they passed her on the left—and she stared through the arch and up Memorial Steps, a set of granite and marble stairs that led up the hill to the main campus.

A brief smile flickered across her face. Then she sighed and it faded, and she drove on. Life was so full of contradictions that her head hurt. Just in the last week and a half she had attended the joyous celebration of her father's wedding, then stood by as his new wife had nearly died, and in the midst of all of it, two of the people closest to her had disappointed her horribly.

Jenna frowned. She didn't want to think about Yoshiko or Danny right now. It was too beautiful a day.

She navigated the streets around campus, loving the way the orange, red, and yellow leaves tumbled across lawns and sidewalks in the breeze. The window was open and she could smell the wonderful scent of smoke from a fireplace somewhere nearby. At last she turned into the driveway of her father's house.

After turning off the car and pulling out the keys, she gathered up her cell phone and the grocery bag and slid out. Jenna flipped the keys around, locating the correct one, and went inside.

"I'm back!" she called.

"We're up here!" Her father's voice came from the second floor.

Jenna went into the kitchen and fetched two spoons from a drawer, then climbed the stairs. Sunlight streamed into the second story through the tall windows and gleamed off of hardwood floors. She found her father, as she had known she would, sitting with Shayna. Jenna's stepmother lay in bed, her face still ashen but her eyes alight, the corners of her mouth turned up in a wan smile. The paralysis had been steadily thawing since she had awoken and now, though she still had a great deal of stiffness and less dexterity than she would have liked, Shayna was well on the way to a full recovery. The specialists at SMC had instructed her to rest for several days, though she was supposed to take a series of brief walks each day and do certain stretches and other exercises.

Frank sat on the edge of the bed in blue jeans and a Somerset sweatshirt. Jenna found that men his age often looked out of place dressed so casually and, in fact, she had thought that about him not very long ago. But either Frank had changed, or her perception of him had, for he looked very comfortable, very much at home, to her now.

"That was fast," Shayna said, a tired rasp lingering in her voice.

"I aim to please," Jenna replied.

She handed her father the spoons. He grinned. "You're a lifesaver."

"Or an enabler, high cholesterol man."

He feigned insult. "But it's all part of Shayna's healing process."

Jenna just shook her head. "Uh-huh." One by one she pulled out three pints of Ben & Jerry's ice cream, all different flavors. Shayna's smile grew wider with the revelation of each one and if Jenna was not imagining it, her color seemed to improve a bit just from anticipation.

Maybe it is part of the healing process, she thought.

"Have you heard anything else?" Shayna asked. "Is there any word about how it all happened?"

Jenna hesitated. She had spoken to Dyson from her cell phone, but she wasn't sure whether it was too sensitive a topic for Shayna still. Her father, though, nodded to urge her on.

"Well, the CDC is going to be investigating for a while, along with the police, of course. I mean, we know Professor Kimball's husband found out she was having an affair with Ben Hall—"

"I still can't believe that," Shayna whispered.

"—and that he had been working on synthetic toxins for years. Nobody will talk about that," Jenna said grimly. "The prevailing theory is that he was doing quiet work for the government, probably bio-warfare research for the military or something equally sinister. According to Audrey, he'd tested whatever the original virus was, but only once. That was why some people got sicker than others. He hadn't perfected it yet."

"So, in a way, we're lucky more people didn't die," her father said.

Jenna nodded. "Hard to see it as lucky, but yeah, I guess."

Shayna let out a deep breath. Her face was lined with

frustration and anger. "So this man, Kimball . . . he was willing to poison everyone at that lunch just to make sure his wife died?"

"He probably hoped that would make it look like a massive case of food poisoning. Like an accident," Jenna replied.

Frank grunted, his expression grim. "What a cosmic irony that Joyce was the only one to eat the shrimp and not get sick at all."

Jenna nodded. Kimball had been so twisted by vengeance that he'd willingly set out to poison a whole room full of people, and had been responsible for the spread of a virus that might have killed hundreds, maybe thousands more. And when Jenna got in the way, he hadn't hesitated to make an attempt on her life as well.

She prayed he would spend the rest of his life in prison.

"But if it was meant to be put into the food, to masquerade as shellfish poisoning, how did it spread?" Shayna asked.

Jenna nodded to assure her she was coming to that. "Sheer tragic coincidence, they think. I don't pretend to understand it all, but apparently Professor Kimball was recovering from the flu when she went to the faculty thing they threw for you guys. Somehow that saved her. Instead of infecting her, the lab virus traded genetic material with the flu she was carrying, and it mutated in her, became this really virulent, contagious version. She gave it to Ben, who had a stronger immunity than the girls he was with. He would have shown symptoms eventually, but who knows how many people could have been infected in the meantime?

"I think about what would have happened if the thing had a longer incubation period, if people could have been passing it on for days or weeks before they started showing symptoms . . . can you imagine?"

"I don't want to," Frank muttered.

Jenna clasped her hands together. "Anyway, they've treated Ben. The most amazing thing is that when the doctors started treating the patients with the standard antiviral therapy, they didn't really expect it to work. They were just trying whatever they could think of, and that was the first thing on their checklist. The basics. But because the flu was part of the virus, because this new strain was sort of based on the flu, that was the fastest and easiest way to deal with it."

Shayna let out a long breath. "So, they *did* get lucky?"

"I think that's their feeling, yeah."

"I can understand the impulse. Despite everything, I'm feeling pretty lucky right now myself," Shayna said.

Jenna's father offered her a spoon. "Are you sure you don't want some?"

"I'd love some. But I haven't been back to the dorm in two days, and though I appreciate you letting me use your washer and dryer, I'd actually like to wear *different* clothes. Not to mention that I have to work today."

Frank got up and hugged her. "You know you can stay here as long as you want, anytime you want."

Jenna returned the embrace fiercely. "I know. I really

do. And I'm so grateful for the both of you right now. But other than ice cream runs, I think you two can manage on your own, and I have some other things I have to deal with. Thanks for letting me borrow the car."

Her father kissed her on the head. Jenna said her good-byes and left the two of them alone with each other and their ice cream.

Jenna parked across the street from Whitney House. She was dreading the thought of seeing Yoshiko. She had been spending most of her time, day and night, at her father's. Though she had been there ostensibly to lend a hand while Shayna was recuperating, it had also been a welcome escape from the tension she knew she was going to have to come back to eventually.

Yoshiko was her friend. What had happened between her and Hunter had not changed that. But Jenna's anger and the awkwardness between them wasn't only because Yoshiko had done something Jenna could not condone, it was that she had then covered it up. Yoshiko had pretended it had never happened. She'd lied about it. Yoshiko had cheated on Hunter, and then lied to Jenna. If anyone had suggested that such a thing was possible a year ago Jenna would have laughed them out of the room. But it had happened. Jenna didn't want to come off as though she herself were perfect, that she would never make a mistake, but the truth was, it hurt. The disappointment was part of it, but worse was being lied to.

She felt like she didn't even know Yoshiko anymore.

They had been so close . . . and now there was this distance between them.

Jenna did not want to throw away her friendship with her roommate. She just wasn't sure she could live with Yoshiko anymore. And the thought of having that conversation filled her with a terrible sadness and uncertainty.

When she entered her room and found that Yoshiko was not home, she was flooded with relief that bordered on elation. Jenna knew they were going to have to talk about things, and she knew it wasn't going to be pleasant. Yoshiko had to be hurting right now, had to be feeling abandoned in spite of her own fault in causing it all.

Yet much as she didn't want Yoshiko to be hurt, Jenna could summon very little sympathy for her.

She had taken a shower at her father's before setting out for the supermarket that morning. Now she pulled out a change of clothes. Just putting on clean underwear seemed like a luxury. She dressed in a dark raspberry-colored scoop neck top with frayed bell sleeves and linen jeans in a chambray shade. Barefoot, she stood at her mirror and put on dark eyeliner, just a bit of shadow, and her favorite lipstick. At last she put on the ankle-high, black Doc Martens that had been an early birthday present from her mother.

Jenna made it a point not to rush, just in case Yoshiko came home.

When she was ready, however, she glanced at the clock and saw that she was already a few minutes late leaving for work. It was just a walk up Carpenter Street, but she was supposed to be there in less than five minutes. With a last glance around the room she grabbed her brown suede coat from the closet and went out the door.

As she left Whitney House, she saw Danny Mariano walking toward her across the street.

His eyes brightened when he saw her. Jenna hesitated on the steps, feeling the urge to go back inside. It was a foolish temptation, but she felt it nevertheless. Instead, she smiled at him and went down the path to meet him on the sidewalk.

"Jenna."

"Hi."

Danny shoved his hands in his pockets. "Sorry to just pop up like this. I wanted to talk to you and I thought it should be in person."

Her throat felt dry and her eyes burned a little, but she chalked it up to how tired she was and tried to ignore anything else she was feeling. "I heard what happened. With your hearing." Jenna glanced away a moment, taking in the blue sky through the branches of the trees above them.

"I'm really sorry, Danny. You did what you did for me. You . . ." Jenna swallowed hard, then she went to him and hugged him. Danny started to back away, but then he put his arms around her as well. After a moment Jenna broke the embrace and took a step back to a safer distance. Safer for her heart. "You saved my life. I'll never forget that."

Danny nodded. "You should know . . . I don't regret

it. Even knowing what was going to come of it, I would have done the same thing."

"I know," Jenna said, smiling. "That's the kind of guy you are."

"But there are things I *do* regret, Jenna."

They stared at each other for several seconds. Jenna could not summon the words to respond to what he was saying. Instead she moved closer to him again, reached up, and pulled his face down to hers. The kiss was short, but full of all of the emotion she had bottled up inside her where Danny was concerned. Her heart fluttered in her chest, but it pained her, full of the ache of melancholy.

"Everyone has regrets," she told him, taking another step back. This time it was Jenna who put her hands in her pockets.

He watched her, eyes studying her, lips forming silent words as though he had ten thousand things to say and did not know where to begin. Jenna smiled and shook her head.

"Audrey told me you were leaving town."

Danny glanced guiltily at the ground. "For a while, at least. See if there's a city out there where they'll look at my case differently. Or where they need cops badly enough that they'll hire one with a black mark on his career record."

Jenna felt as though she couldn't breathe. "You're really good at what you do. You'll find a place."

"Maybe." He paused a moment, then smiled. "Looks like we've both been talking to Audrey a lot. I spoke to her about you last night. We were saying we both thought maybe you should sign up for your father's criminology classes. You ought to be a detective yourself one of these days."

"Me? A cop?"

"Is that so far-fetched?"

Jenna shrugged. "Maybe not. But I like the path I'm on. I think I'll stick to it. Listen, Danny, take care of yourself, okay? I'll worry about you."

His brows knitted. "Yeah. Yeah, of course. Listen, though, I was hoping we could go get a cup of coffee, maybe talk a little more."

The sun was still warm on that perfect October day, but the chilly autumn breeze blew the leaves skittering along the street and made Jenna shiver. At least she thought it was the breeze.

"That would be nice," she said, her voice steady. "But I don't think so." She tucked a stray lock of hair behind her ear and gave him her best smile. "I've got to get to work."

Jenna turned and started up the sidewalk toward Somerset Medical Center, the leaves eddying around her feet in the breeze. Zipping her suede jacket, she passed through striations of light and darkness, the shadows cast by the branches of the trees above.

She did not look back.

about the authors

CHRISTOPHER GOLDEN is the award-winning, bestselling author of such novels as *The Boys Are Back in Town*, *Wildwood Road*, *Strangewood*, and *Of Saints and Shadows*. Working with actress/writer/director Amber Benson, he cocreated and cowrote *Ghosts of Albion*, an online animated supernatural drama for BBC, which will soon become a book series from Del Rey.

With Thomas E. Sniegoski, he is the coauthor of the new dark fantasy series The Menagerie, as well as the young readers fantasy series OutCast, both of which saw their first installments published in 2004. Golden and Sniegoski also wrote the graphic novel *BPRD: Hollow Earth*, a spinoff from the fan favorite comic book series Hellboy. Golden authored the original Hellboy novels *The Lost Army* and *The Bones of Giants*.

Golden was born and raised in Massachusetts, where he still lives with his family. He graduated from Tufts University. He is currently at work on a dark fantasy trilogy entitled The Veil. There are more than eight million copies of his books in print. Please visit him at www.christophergolden.com

Writing under his own name, RICK HAUTALA has published more than twenty-five books, including the million-copy, international bestseller *Nightstone* (Kensington) as well as *Twilight Time*, *Little Brothers*, *Beyond the Shroud*, *Cold Whisper*, and *Impulse*. Under the pseudonym A. J. Matthews, he has written two novels, *The White Room* and *Looking Glass*. He has also published over sixty short stories in a variety of national and international anthologies and magazines.

His current projects include *Occasional Demons*, a short story collection, *Follow*, another A. J. Matthews novel, and *Chills*, a screenplay currently under option.

A graduate of the University of Maine in Orono with a Master of Arts in Renaissance Drama, Rick lives in southern Maine with his son and author Holly Newstein who, with her cowriter, Ralph Bierber, publishes under the name H. R. Howland.

EL REY LEAR

WILLIAM SHAKESPEARE

El rey Lear

Traducida en el Instituto Shakespeare por
Manuel Ángel Conejero
Vicente Forés
Juan Vicente Martínez Luciano
Jenaro Talens
y dirigida por Manuel Ángel Conejero

TERCERA EDICIÓN

CATEDRA

LETRAS UNIVERSALES

Título original de la obra: *King Lear*

Diseño de cubierta: Diego Lara
Cubierta: Zeno

© M. A. Conejero Tomás, V. Forés López
J. V. Martínez Luciano y Jenaro Talens Carmona
© de la introducción y notas, M. A. Conejero
Tomás, V. Forés López, J. V. Martínez Luciano,
Purificación Rivas Traver, Ángeles Serrano
Ripol y Jenaro Talens Carmona
Ediciones Cátedra, S. A., 1992
Telémaco, 43. 28027 Madrid
Depósito legal: M. 21.966-1992
ISBN: 84-376-0596-2
Printed in Spain
Impreso en Anzos, S. A. - Fuenlabrada (Madrid)

INTRODUCCIÓN

EL esquema de acción de *El rey Lear* presenta la línea evo-
lutiva usual en los dramas históricos shakespearianos, es
decir, la pérdida de un poder inicial que, tras una etapa
de desorden, es restaurado al final de la obra. Como en los
dramas históricos, la obra comienza presentando una sociedad
gobernada por un poder establecido, que en este caso lo encarna el rey Lear, a cuya destitución sigue un periodo de luchas e
inestabilidades en todo el reino, que finalmente es controlado
y regido por un nuevo monarca. Pero aunque en líneas generales se mantiene el esquema clásico de drama histórico, se diferencia de éste por la forma en que se modifica la situación
inicial —no de manera súbita, sino progresiva—, y por el tono
de su final, contenido y desesperanzado. Normalmente un sector opuesto al poder establecido da muerte a su máximo repre-
sentante, lo cual constituye el origen de una guerra civil, que al
final es solucionada a favor de la monarquía o de la fórmula de
poder tradicional en esa sociedad. En esta obra, sin embargo,
el rey no es asesinado ni depuesto de forma violenta; su proceso de pérdida de poder y consecuente degeneración son pro-
gresivos, y él mismo inicia los acontecimientos que desencade-
nan esa pérdida de poder. Las consecuencias de sus actos afectan a todo el reino, que sigue una evolución semejante a la de
su rey, y que, como él, descubre los aspectos negativos de la
naturaleza y del hombre, y su incapacidad para modificarlos.
Es este descubrimiento, y la conciencia de que el hombre es un
ser-para-el-sufrimiento[1], que debe aprender a ser paciente y a

---

[1] Véase W. Elton, *King Lear and the Gods* (1966), pág. 283, a propósito de la

no albergar falsas ilusiones, lo que marca la nota final de la obra, diferente del espíritu de regeneración y esperanza que caracteriza a la mayoría de los dramas históricos.

En la obra se desarrollan dos argumentos, uno principal, relativo al destino de Lear, y otro secundario, cuyo protagonista es Gloucester. Ambos argumentos están íntimamente relacionados y presentan numerosas semejanzas y contrastes que contribuyen a la transmisión de varios núcleos significativos o grandes temas, presentados desde la perspectiva de los diferentes personajes que los ejemplifican en su trayectoria[2]. Tanto Lear como Gloucester modifican radicalmente, a través de su experiencia en la obra, su concepto inicial de la relación entre palabras y realidad, entre lo que se dice y las intenciones que subyacen a las manifestaciones lingüísticas, y lo hacen de la forma más impactante, dentro del núcleo familiar más próximo, al descubrir su incapacidad para interpretar las palabras de sus hijos, ignorando que también en el contexto de las relaciones paterno-filiales se emplean los esquemas de la retórica. La situación desencadenante de los acontecimientos en ambos casos tendrá como núcleo significativo la errónea interpretación por parte de Lear y Gloucester de las palabras de sus hijos, hábiles y engañosas en el caso de Gonerill y Regan —hijas de Lear—, y de Edmund —hijo bastardo de Gloucester—, y torpes, repetitivas[3], o incluso inarticuladas en el caso de Cordelia y Edgar, personajes que encarnan la bondad y el amor filial, unido a la credulidad, propia de otros personajes nobles shakespearianos, como Otelo o Brutus, cuya falta de penetración en las intenciones ajenas origina situaciones trágicas que terminan en la muerte. También las palabras iniciales intercambiadas entre los dos protagonistas y sus hijos inician una secuencia de acciones que termina con su muerte, y, en el espacio de tiempo que transcurre hasta ese momento, modifican

---

incidencia del argumento secundario en la transmisión de la idea de sufrimiento en la obra.

[2] Véase, sobre la coherencia y paralelismo existentes entre argumento principal y secundario, R. B. Heilman, «The Unity of King Lear», *Sewanee Review* (1948).

[3] Véase, del empleo de las repeticiones en Cordelia, A. C. Bradley, *Lectures on Shakespearean Tragedy* (1904), pág. 319.

su concepción inicial de la naturaleza, del mundo y de las relaciones interpersonales, y descubren su propia identidad y los elementos que configuran su ubicación en un determinado lugar de la esfera familiar y social.

Cuando empieza la obra, Lear se presenta como un monarca con autoridad y poder, rodeado de unos súbditos que le respetan y de unos signos externos de realeza, que abarcan tanto la corona que ostenta como las vestiduras. En ningún momento parece tener conciencia de que los signos externos son fundamentales para la posición que ocupa, descubrimiento que realizará progresivamente después del error de sus palabras iniciales. Cuando haya puesto todo en manos de sus hijas —corona, tierras, ejército— y éstas le nieguen un reducido séquito, primero, y la satisfacción de las necesidades mínimas —casa, vestido, comida— después, descubrirá en medio del sufrimiento físico y psíquico, vagando a merced de las inclemencias del tiempo en una noche de tormenta, que, una vez privado de todos los signos externos que acompañaban a su posición hegemónica, ha perdido la cualidad de rey, cualidad que consideraba como algo intrínseco, indisoluble de su condición humana, y, por tanto, suficiente para mantenerse, aun desprovisto de los símbolos. Pero la exposición más completa a la furia de la naturaleza le descubre que sin esos símbolos su condición es equiparable a la de las bestias, y, como consecuencia, se quita el vestido que lleva, único elemento que le queda de su situación anterior, y que, aislado, no le sirve para nada, y se enfrenta, desnudo, a la tormenta. En este momento parece que su dolor, físico y psíquico, ha alcanzado el límite, y que Lear ha sufrido una experiencia suficientemente reveladora —para Gloucester será suficiente un proceso de dolor físico y psíquico—, pero él es el rey, y sus errores de interpretación tienen consecuencias más graves que los de un súbdito; por eso experimentará una tortura mental[4] que termina en su locura, a la que contribuirán los comentarios del bufón y de Edgar disfra-

---

[4] Véase, para la importancia de la evolución que sufre la mente de Lear, como núcleo de la obra, D. A. Traversi, «King Lear», *Scrutiny*, XIX (1952-1953), y R. Ornstein, *The Moral Vision of Jacobean Tragedy* (1960), página 264.

zado de Tom Pobre, que le mostrarán lo erróneo de sus juicios pasados, de su anterior concepción del mundo[5] como un todo jerárquicamente ordenado, con él a la cabeza, del afecto de sus hijas, y de la situación del hombre frente a la naturaleza, y cuando su mente no pueda soportar más cambios en su concepción del mundo, perderá la razón, y hablará como el bufón[6], diciendo en frases de aparente sinsentido la verdad que antes estaba ausente de sus discursos lógicos. A un descubrimiento paralelo de la verdad llega también Gloucester, aunque, como personaje de rango inferior, y de caracterización menos compleja, se revela especialmente en el plano físico, en el que se manifiesta de forma simbólica una inversión de la realidad comparable a la de Lear: a su conocimiento de la verdad a través de la locura corresponde la visión del mundo de Gloucester, mediante la ceguera a que queda reducido cuando le arrancan los ojos.

El argumento secundario, que tiene a Gloucester como protagonista, contribuye a la intensificación de los núcleos significativos de la obra, aunque queda supeditado al argumento principal por la dimensión de sus personajes y por su inicio posterior y conclusión previa, dejando que sea el argumento principal el que inicie y concluya la tragedia, aunque en la restauración final del orden concurran elementos procedentes de ambos argumentos: Albany, perteneciente a la familia de Lear, y Edgar, hijo de Gloucester.

En la escena final Edgar retoma, desde una perspectiva de experiencia, el tema de la relación entre las palabras y la realidad, que aparece al principio de la obra, y expone una visión del mundo que mantiene vivo el recuerdo de la evolución de Lear y Gloucester.

Lear en la primera escena había convocado a sus tres hijas para repartir su reino entre ellas, y ponía como única condición la expresión verbal de la medida de su afecto. Las dos hi-

---

[5] Véase, respecto a la capacidad del bufón para ver la verdad, E. Welsford, *The Fool* (1935), pág. 253, y W. Empson, *The Structure of Complex Words* (1951), pág. 133.

[6] Véase, sobre el cambio de papeles entre bufón y Lear, E. Welsford, *op. cit.*, pág. 269.

jas mayores, Gonerill y Regan, habían aceptado la condición paterna sin cuestionarse la coherencia de esa petición ni la posible contradicción entre amor y cálculo matemático, y, siguiendo escrupulosamente los deseos de su padre, habían cuantificado lingüísticamente su amor[7]. Gonerill basaba su discurso en comparaciones hiperbólicas: «os amo más que... y más que... más, muchísimo más que..., no menos que... tanto como..., más allá de» (I.i.50-6), y medía su amor con elementos tan inconmensurables como «lo que las palabras pueden expresar», «vista, espacio, libertad», «lo estimado, lo precioso, lo raro», «la vida llena de dignidad, salud, belleza, honor» (I.i.50-6), y Regan, a continuación, mostraba su disposición natural a cuantificarlo todo, incluyendo los sentimientos: «estoy hecha con los mismos metales que mi hermana, y en su medida me valoro» (I.i.65). Lear, satisfecho, les entregaba los dos tercios respectivos de su reino, precediendo su entrega de una descripción en que destacaba la fertilidad de la tierra: «espesos bosques y campiñas, / ríos caudalosos y praderas extensas» (I.i.58-9), manifestando su deseo de que fuera transmitida a sus descendientes: «y que así sea para los descendientes / de Albany y de vos» (I.i.61-2), (y a Regan), «para vos y los vuestros en herencia» (I.i.74). Habían respondido a su concepción de la naturaleza[8] como algo ordenado, y su respuesta había sido la entrega de tierras fértiles, deseándoles descendencia, deseo muy distinto del que expresaría más tarde, al conocer la ingratitud de sus hijas, maldiciendo a Gonerill:

> Escucha, Naturaleza, diosa venerada, ¡óyeme!
> Revoca tu propósito, si era tu intención
> hacer fecunda a esta criatura.
> Llena su útero de esterilidad,
> quede yermo su vientre,
> que de su cuerpo degradado nunca surja

---

[7] Véase a este respecto la relación etimológica de la palabra «love» con los campos semánticos de la valoración y del amor, y su posible influencia en esta escena, T. Hawkes, «"Love" in *King Lear*», *Review of English Studies* (1959).

[8] Véase S. L. Bethell, *Shakespeare and the Popular Dramatic Tradition* (1944) y J. Danby, *Shakespeare's Doctrine of Nature: A Study of King Lear* (1949), en que, junto a la concepción tradicional que tiene Lear de la Naturaleza, se comenta la concepción contraria, de los personajes que se le oponen.

un fruto que la honre. Y si ha de concebir,
sea un hijo del odio, que viva para ella
como un tormento perverso y desnaturalizado.

(I.iv.259-67)

En unos términos positivos, semejantes a los dirigidos a
Gonerill y Regan al entregarles su herencia, iniciaba Lear, al
comienzo de la obra, su alocución a Cordelia, la más querida,
«cuyo amor juvenil / enfrenta, interesados, los pastos de Borgoña / y las vides de Francia» (I.i.78-80), pero su negativa a
hablar como sus hermanas, señalando la contradicción de la
exigencia de su padre, había provocado la ira de éste, y la pérdida de la herencia y de su amor. A la armonía señalada por
Lear entre la naturaleza y sus hijas mayores al comienzo, oponía la actitud de Cordelia, interpretada por él como contraria a
sus leyes: «camino... innoble, / que la naturaleza se avergüenza
de reconocer / como suyo» (I.i.206-8).

Lear progresivamente descubriría el error de su concepción
de la naturaleza y de la relación entre ella y sus hijas, de modo
semejante a como haría Gloucester, también engañado al principio por la retórica convincente de su hijo Edmund, experto
adulador, que originaba, como en el caso de Cordelia, el exilio
y la pérdida de herencia de su hijo Edgar, encarnación de la
virtud y de la sinceridad, e igualmente incapaz de sospechar de
las intenciones verdaderas de su hermano Edmund. Al final de
la obra, sin embargo, Edgar reivindica la necesidad de que las
relaciones se basen en el intercambio de palabras sinceras:

Diremos lo que nos dicte el corazón, no lo que deberíamos decir

(V.iii.322)

pero su visión del mundo no es idealizada, como tampoco lo
es la de Albany, futuro gobernante, con Edgar, del reino. Han
asistido a los procesos de sufrimiento y revelación de Lear y
Gloucester, que mueren cuando su capacidad de soportar alcanza el límite, precedido en ambos casos de un breve momento de alivio —cuando recuperan a Cordelia y Edgar respectivamente— en que la tensión se relaja como preparación a su
muerte, entre el extremo de la alegría y del dolor por la recuperación de Edgar, en el caso de Gloucester, y en una situa-

ción más compleja en el caso de Lear, que tiene a Cordelia muerta en los brazos y lucha hasta el final, negándose a admitir que haya muerto[9]. Edgar, que ha sido espectador privilegiado de los procesos de sufrimiento de Lear y de Gloucester, y que ha sufrido, asimismo, la dureza de la naturaleza, disfrazado de Tom Pobre, la injusticia de su padre, y la traición de su hermano, expone en sus palabras finales una actitud realista y desencantada ante ese mundo que debe gobernar y que ha aprendido a conocer:

Nosotros llevaremos todo el peso de estos tiempos tan tristes,

(...) Los más viejos han soportado más. Nosotros que posee-
[mos juventud,

nunca veremos tanto, ni viviremos tanto tiempo

(V.iii.321, 323-4)

ESTRUCTURA DRAMÁTICA

Quizá el rasgo estructural más destacado de *El rey Lear* sea el cuidadoso desarrollo del argumento secundario de la obra, inexistente en las fuentes, cuya calidad, elaboración y relación con el argumento principal ha sido tema de polémica durante muchos años, aunque en la actualidad se reconoce su pertinencia, del mismo modo que se consideran elementos primordiales la figura del bufón y la locura de Lear, igualmente ausentes de las fuentes, y suprimidas en las representaciones, desde la adaptación de Tate en 1681 hasta la recuperación de Macready en 1838, y aun entonces, debido a las frecuentes omisiones de texto, con una interpretación muy alejada de las que recibe hoy.

A comienzos del siglo xx todavía existían reticencias hacia el argumento secundario, y A. C. Bradley[10] manifestaba su opinión de que este argumento, analizado aisladamente y en su

---

[9] Véase a este respecto J. Stampfer, «The Catharsis of *King Lear*», *Shakespeare Survey*, 13 (1960), pág. 2, y J. K. Walton, *Shakespeare Survey*, 13 (1960), pág. 17.
[10] *Lectures on Shakespearean Tragedy* (1904), págs. 256 y ss.

relación con toda la obra, acumulaba un gran número de defectos estructurales: la dimensión de sus personajes, la rapidez de los acontecimientos, la escasez de detalles relativos a las acciones y a los personajes que aumentaban el número total de los principales y de escenas de gran intensidad, lo cual, según él, podía confundir al lector y agotarlo emocionalmente, además de dar como resultado un final donde unas situaciones se precipitaban sobre otras.

Pero hoy parece existir acuerdo en señalar que lo que Bradley vio como defectos estructurales fue diseñado por Shakespeare deliberadamente de ese modo: expresamente dejó esbozados los personajes, sin extenderse en proporcionar detalles minuciosos para evitar que una excesiva elaboración de las figuras dispersara la atención del público, desviándola del núcleo principal, Lear[11], y se limitó a esbozarlos, también, para que de ese modo el mensaje comunicado por la obra fuera de aplicación universal, al suprimir los detalles que habrían dificultado la asimilación de las ideas generales por parte de un público amplio. Deliberadamente también hizo que los acontecimientos se precipitaran a gran velocidad, en parte para que, al aumentar este efecto en el argumento secundario, la rapidez la acción principal quedara atenuada. Finalmente, hay que señalar, como respuesta a Bradley, que los acontecimientos no se acumulan al final de la obra porque el argumento secundario se cierra antes que el principal, dejándole toda la escena libre para la expresión de su final.

El argumento secundario no sólo no interfiere con el principal, sino que lo complementa, ya que presenta situaciones similares y opuestas, que sirven de eco y de contraste[12], y no interfiere, además, porque desempeña en muchas ocasiones la función de coro que hace innecesarias explicaciones en el argumento principal, y porque, como resultado global, contribuye a extender al ser humano las experiencias básicas de la

---

[11] Los personajes del argumento secundario, y muy especialmente Gloucester, hacen todo lo contrario, contribuyendo al desarrollo del personaje Lear. Véase L. C. Knights, «The Question of Character in Shakespeare», *More Talking of Shakespeare* (1959), pág. 66.

[12] Véase la nota 2.

obra[13]. En ambos planos tenemos la relación entre un padre y sus hijos, que se dividen en buenos y malos, engañando estos últimos, hábiles oradores, a sus padres, que, como consecuencia, rechazan a los primeros, los cuales se mantienen fieles a pesar de todo a lo largo del proceso de sufrimiento que se inicia a continuación. Después de un prolongado proceso de purificación alcanzan un breve momento de alegría, mezclada con vergüenza, al encontrar a sus hijos fieles, alegría tan intensa, que provoca su muerte casi inmediata. Hasta aquí las semejanzas de sus situaciones paralelas, pero junto a ellas aparecen las diferencias entre sus protagonistas, que dan lugar a una visión más amplia y generalizada de sus experiencias como seres humanos. La diferencia de su carácter se pone de relieve en sus primeras intervenciones: activa en el caso de Lear, que toma la iniciativa y pregunta directamente a sus hijas la medida de su amor, y pasiva en el caso de Gloucester, que escucha las acusaciones que Edmund hace de su hermano, aunque en ambos casos los dos personajes están en disposición de creer sus hábiles palabras. Esta diferencia de temperamento se manifiesta a lo largo de la obra hasta su muerte, y, frente a la lucha incesante de Lear con sus hijas y con los elementos de la naturaleza, aparece la figura hundida de Gloucester que busca la solución en un suicidio infructuoso.

A Lear, como rey, le asigna Shakespeare la ira como característica predominante, cuya manifestación extrema, según la opinión renacentista[14], era la locura. A Gloucester, súbdito de rango inferior, le adjudica la concupiscencia como peculiaridad definitoria, que aparece revelada en sus primeras intervenciones, y que en el Renacimiento solía estar castigada con la ceguera. Sin embargo, aunque estas son sus características fundamentales, no son exclusivas, y Gloucester, por ejemplo, es capaz de tener arrebatos de ira contra su hijo Edgar. Otra nota

---

[13] Véase, a propósito de la función universalizadora del argumento secundario de Lear, Schlegel, *Lectures on Dramatic Art* (1808).

[14] Cfr. Du Vair, *The Moral Philosophie of the Stoicks*, pág. 62. Sobre el tratamiento en la obra de temas renacentistas véase T. Spencer, *Shakespeare and the Nature of Man* (1942), y R. A. Fraser, *Shakespeare's Poetics in relation to King Lear* (1962).

que los diferencia, derivada de su personalidad respectiva, es la participación en una filosofía concreta: el estoicismo en el caso de Lear, y el epicureísmo en el de Gloucester, pero tampoco lo hacen en estado puro; por eso Gloucester, a pesar de aceptar el epicureísmo, filosofía que desdeña las indicaciones de los astros, les presta la misma atención que los estoicos, para los que sí tenían validez[15].

También las personalidades de los hijos ofrecen semejanzas y diferencias en relación a la caracterización y comportamiento de sus padres, semejanzas porque encarnan diversos aspectos suyos, y diferencias por las características propias de cada uno de ellos: Gonerill y Regan muestran el aspecto calculador de Lear y su capacidad para tomar decisiones inflexibles, que en él guardan un equilibrio precario con su capacidad para amar y para la ternura, encarnadas en su hija Cordelia, que, a su vez, las posee en exceso, y que refleja, igualmente, errores de evaluación similares a algunas actuaciones de su padre en las que se muestra incapaz de sospechar falsedad detrás de manifestaciones externas de amor, o de tomar decisiones prácticas. Los hijos de Gloucester también poseen de forma unilateral rasgos de su padre: Edmund[16], hijo bastardo, engendrado de forma ilegítima, no respeta las leyes ni el orden establecidos, y, como las hijas mayores de Lear, atenta contra su padre y contra el rey, aunque con la diferencia de que él, careciendo de un padre que le brinde la oportunidad de rebelarse, debe tomar la iniciativa. Edgar, por su parte, encarna la bondad de Gloucester, y, como en el caso de Cordelia, la falta de perspicacia o de recursos para defenderse.

La existencia del argumento secundario permite, además, profundizar en temas clave como la cuestión de la identidad, así como intensificar la sensación de grotesco[17] en el ser humano por la posibilidad que brinda de mostrarlo en diferentes personajes, multiplicados al incluir la acción secundaria. Cambios deliberados en su identidad hacen los personajes «malva-

---

[15] Cfr. A. Willet, *Thesaurus ecclesiae* (1604), págs. 24-25.

[16] Véase a este respecto Ch. Marowitz, «Lear Log», *Encore*, X (1963), página 22.

[17] Véase a este respecto G. W. Knight, *«King Lear* and the Comedy of the Grotesque», *The Wheel of Fire* (1930), págs. 160 y ss.

dos»: Gonerill y Regan, a través de un lenguaje que oculta su verdadera naturaleza cuando Lear les pide que se la descubran, y Edmund en su alocución a Gloucester, después de tomar la resolución de usurpar las cualidades asociadas al nombre de su hermano, distantes de su calificativo, «bastardo». Los personajes «buenos», al contrario, deben proporcionarse un disfraz para no ser descubiertos una vez condenados por actuar con franqueza, y la función del disfraz no es sino la de acompañar a sus propios jueces, y seguir prestándoles su servicio en todo momento, cosa que hacen Kent —único que había salido en defensa de Cordelia— y Edgar, disfrazados de hombres próximos a la naturaleza, para acompañar a Lear y Gloucester, respectivamente, en su camino de descubrimiento de su propia identidad y de la del mundo. Los personajes «buenos» o purificados después de un periodo de sufrimiento aparecen en situaciones grotescas, como Kent y Edgar bajo los disfraces que eligen; Gloucester en su intento de suicidarse saltando desde una roca, convencido de hallarse junto a un profundo acantilado, y Lear proclamando la vida de su hija muerta, en sus brazos. No comparten esta cualidad de grotesco las muertes de los «malvados»: Gonerill, Regan y Edmund, que son trágicas, pero consecuencia lógica de unos comportamientos. El hecho de que los «malos» sean castigados parece aportar una sensación dramática de alivio y justicia a la obra, pero el hecho de que los personajes «buenos» sufran una muerte inmerecida o atraviesen situaciones inexplicables, incluso ridículas, deja en la obra una ambigüedad deliberada, a la que contribuye de forma notable la existencia de un argumento secundario.

SÍMBOLOS Y TEMAS RECURRENTES

El rey Lear funciona más por acumulación que linealmente, y su lenguaje está cargado de símbolos y metáforas que llaman la atención poderosamente sobre los temas centrales de la obra, repetidos desde distintos ángulos de vista. Los símbolos[18] que más importancia cobran son los relacionados con la

---

[18] Véase sobre la simbología en la obra y su importancia como elemento de

naturaleza, el mundo animal, la desnudez, la ceguera, y la locura. Todos ellos guardan relación con la concepción que se tiene de la naturaleza en la obra, que desencadena comportamientos opuestos, y, como consecuencia, la negación de una concepción previa, estática, de la naturaleza, mostrada plásticamente a través de distintos símbolos.

La concepción estática e idealizada de la naturaleza es la que tienen Lear y Gloucester, que la consideran la quintaesencia del orden y de la armonía a todos los niveles de la vida: personal, familiar, nacional y cósmico. A la sabia ordenación de la naturaleza responde el equilibrio interno personal, el amor y afecto entre padres e hijos, la jerarquización social que pone a la cabeza al monarca, la sumisión de la mujer al marido, la fertilidad, e, incluso, el paso de las estaciones y fenómenos atmosféricos que las acompañan. Pero existe otra concepción de la naturaleza opuesta a ésta[19]: es la que hacen propia Edmund, Gonerill y Regan, y que en un comportamiento acorde supone la destrucción de la idea de Lear, ya que actuar de acuerdo con la naturaleza significa para ellos seguir ciegamente sus instintos, atenten éstos contra las relaciones paterno-filiales, matrimoniales, o contra la misma monarquía[20].

Los seres que, siguiendo los dictados de la «naturaleza», niegan cobijo a sus padres, les degradan progresivamente hasta originar su muerte, olvidan sus compromisos conyugales, y atentan contra la misma vida del rey, son representados frecuentemente mediante alusiones a animales[21], que reflejan su pérdida absoluta de control racional y su abandono a los instintos más primarios. Las comparaciones más frecuentes con animales, en este sentido, son las dirigidas a Gonerill, procedentes de su padre, que inciden en su ingratitud; las que se aplican a Regan, en menor número; las que hacen referencia a

cohesión los estudios de R. B. Heilman, *This Great Stage* (1948), y de W. Clemen, *The Development of Shakespeare's Imagery* (1951).

[19] Véase la nota 8.

[20] Véase, a propósito de la oposición entre valores nuevos y tradicionales en la obra, E. Muir, *The Politics of King Lear* (1947).

[21] Véase, a este respecto, A. C. Bradley, *op. cit.*, pág. 266; C. Spurgeon, *Shakespeare's Imagery* (1935), pág. 342; R. B. Heilman, *op. cit.*, págs. 92 y ss., 105 y ss., y 255-253; G. W. Knight, *The Wheel of Fire* (1949), págs. 185 y ss.; W. Clemen, *op. cit.*, págs. 133-53.

ambas hermanas, procedentes de distintos personajes, y alguna alusiva a Edmund. De Gonerill dice Lear:

Ingratitud, demonio con corazón de mármol,
más horrendo que el monstruo marino,
cuando te manifiestas en los hijos

(I.iv.243-5)

Mentís, buitre maldito

(I.iv.246)

tu cara de lobezna

(I.iv.291)

Ha clavado
el afilado pico de la ingratitud, como un buitre

(II.iv.128-129)

me ha herido con su lengua de serpiente

(II.iv.155)

De Regan dice Albany:

serpiente de oro

(V.iii.86)

De ambas hermanas:

(LEAR) hijas ingratas... crías de pelícano

(III.iv.66-71)

(LEAR) Ni la puta, ni el fogoso caballo van a ello
con apetito más desenfrenado.
De cintura para abajo son centauros,
aunque mujeres por arriba

(IV.vi.118-121)

(GLOUCESTER) ...no quiero ver cómo vuestras crueles garras
le arrancan sus cansados ojos de anciano, ni a vuestra feroz
[hermana
hundir sus colmillos de jabalí en su carne ungida...

(III.vii.53-5)

(KENT) ...dos hijas con corazón de perro

(IV.iii.45)

[21]

(ALBANY) tigres, ya que no hijas

(IV.ii.40)

(EDMUND) entre sí desconfían, como quien de una víbora
sufrió la mordedura

(V.i.56-57)

Albany llega a afirmar que su crueldad supera a la de los animales:

un padre, un digno anciano
a quien, con reverencia, hasta el oso enfurecido lamería.
¡Salvajes y degeneradas!

(IV.ii.41-43)

En cuanto a Edmund, su hermano Edgar le llama

traidor con piel de sapo

(V.iii.135)

y Edgar dice de sí mismo que antes de disfrazarse de Tom Pobre era

como el cerdo, perezoso; astuto, como el zorro; voraz
como el lobo; rabioso como el perro; como el león con su presa

(III.iv.87-9)

Pero no es esta la única función de simbolismo animal: también se emplea para referirse a los personajes que, privados de
todo signo externo de civilización (vestidos, ceremonias, relaciones con familiares y amigos) quedan reducidos al estado
más puro de la naturaleza, al de los animales, como afirman
Edgar y Lear de su propia situación. Lear dice:

no permitáis a la Naturaleza más de lo que la Naturaleza necesita,
y la vida del hombre será tan insignificante como lo es la de las
[bestias

(II.iv.261-262)

o Edgar en el mismo sentido:

...he pensado
adoptar el aspecto más pobre y vil
de cuantos tiene la penuria para, menospreciando al hombre,
acercarlo a las bestias

(II.iii.6-9)

y cuando se encuentran, dice Lear de él:

el hombre puro no es más que un pobre animal, desnudo
y erguido como tú. ¡Fuera, harapos! ¡Ven, desnúdame!

(III.iv.99-100)

Cuando la situación alcanza un punto límite las comparaciones presentan a los seres humanos por debajo del nivel de los animales. Lear dirá de sí mismo:

Hasta los mismo perros... / vedlo, me ladran

(III.vi.57-8)

un caballero, aludiendo a la situación de Lear la noche de la tempestad:

esta noche en que la osa que cría yace en el cubil,
y el león y el lobo hambriento
guardan seco su pelaje, sin cubrirse, corre
conjurando a quien con todo acabará.

(III.i.12-15)

Gloucester dice:

Si los lobos hubiesen aullado a tu puerta en esta hora terrible
habrías dicho: «Abre, guardián,
ya es suficiente crueldad»

(III.vii.60-2)

y luego Cordelia, refiriéndose a la misma noche:

Hasta los perros de mis enemigos,
aun habiéndome mordido, habrían pasado aquella noche
junto a mi fuego; ¿y os visteis obligado, pobre padre,
a refugiaros con los cerdos y desesperados...?

(IV.vii.36-39)

[23]

En esta situación de hombre abandonado a sus propias fuerzas, degradado y privado de todo, hasta igualarse o situarse por debajo del nivel de las bestias, se representa también simbólicamente mediante la desnudez[22] que comparten Edgar, disfrazado de Tom Pobre, y Lear, abandonando sus vestiduras y exponiéndose al rigor de la tormenta en que le dejan sus hijas al negarle protección. Esa tormenta se hace eco de la que Lear sufre interiormente como consecuencia de la ingratitud de sus hijas y de las humillaciones que soporta, y, cuando su capacidad de sufrimiento rebasa los límites, Lear pierde la razón, momento en que, viendo la sinrazón de su orden, de su antigua concepción de la naturaleza y de las relaciones entre los seres que la pueblan, hablará como el bufón, construyendo juegos de palabras y frases sin sentido, reflejando en su lenguaje la inversión de los valores que el mundo acepta como lógicos. Será en este momento cuando el bufón lo abandone porque su misión de crítico de la realidad ya no será necesaria, y sus locuras aparentes tendrán como sustitutivo una locura real. Esta locura cederá de forma pasajera cuando Lear encuentre a Cordelia y recupere la ilusión de volver a vivir con cariño y dignidad, pero su consuelo será muy breve, y cuando den muerte a su hija perderá definitivamente la razón, y, poco después, la vida. Sus últimas palabras en que se acumulan las negaciones como expresión desesperada ante la pérdida de lo que más amaba[23]:

> ¡No, no, más vida no!
> ...Nunca más volverás,
> ¡Nunca, nunca, nunca, nunca, nunca!
>
> (V.iii.303-6)

y su reacción final en que llama la atención sobre ella, resistiéndose a creer que no tenga vida, cierran el ciclo iniciado en

---

22 Véase a este respecto R. B. Heilman, *op. cit.*, págs. 67 y ss.

23 Véase, a propósito del lenguaje de Lear en situaciones de emoción, N. Nowottny, «Some Aspects of the Style of *King Lear*», *Shakespeare Survey*, 13, 1960, 51. Y sobre los distintos registros lingüísticos de Lear (ritualista y realista) W. B. C. Watkins, «The Two Techniques in *King Lear*», *Review of English Studies*, XVIII (1942), págs. 1-26.

la primera escena, en que, a la negativa de Cordelia a hablar, sigue un proceso de sufrimiento en Lear que recibe su culminación en el último silencio de su hija, silencio también definitivo para Lear.

El proceso de negación marca toda la obra[24], y afecta tanto a personajes con autoridad e iniciativa —Lear al comienzo de la obra, Edmund, Gonerill y Regan en respuesta inmediata a Lear— como a personajes débiles, fácilmente manipulables, como Edgar y Gloucester. Si los hijos ingratos no reciben la negación de sus actos hasta el final, los demás lo experimentan continuamente a lo largo de la obra: Cordelia se queda sin palabras, sin herencia, sin hermanas, sin padre, y sin vida; Lear, sin soldados, sin techo, sin ropas, sin reino, sin hijas, sin razón, y sin vida; Gloucester, sin hijos, sin vista, sin ánimo y sin vida; y Edgar, sin ropas, sin hermano, sin padre, sin dignidad, y sin nombre, aunque sobrevive y recupera el nombre y la dignidad, y la capacidad de ver, y de desear, aunque con pocas esperanzas, que el lenguaje entre los hombres sea sincero y la retórica engañosa se abandone. Sus últimas palabras son de resignación, propias de un hombre cansado, que ha pasado por experiencias extremas, y que ha descubierto que siempre cabe un grado más de sufrimiento.

NOTAS PARA UNA HISTORIA DE LAS REPRESENTACIONES
Y DE LA CRÍTICA

Aunque hoy existe unanimidad en la valoración positiva de *El rey Lear* dentro de una pluralidad de aproximaciones e interpretaciones de la obra, ésta ha pasado por etapas de muy variada suerte, a juzgar por los datos que se conservan en los registros de las representaciones, y por las opiniones vertidas sobre éstas y el texto a lo largo de cuatro siglos.

Aparece registrada la obra por primera vez el 26 de noviembre de 1607 en el *Stationer's Register*, y se hace mención a una representación que tuvo lugar en la corte «uppon S. Stephans

---

[24] Véase, a este respecto, N. Brooke, *Shakespeare: King Lear* (1963), páginas 59-60.

night at Christmas last», es decir, el 26 de diciembre de 1606, a la que probablemente precedieron y siguieron otras actuaciones en el teatro público del *Globe*. En cualquier caso, la escasa documentación que se conserva del siglo XVII coincide en reflejar la pequeña incidencia de la obra durante los primeros setenta y cinco años, como pone de relieve su reducida presencia en *The Shakespeare Allusion Book* hasta 1700. Los registros conservados apenas la mencionan con posterioridad a la Restauración de Carlos II: Downes, del Theatre Royal, alude a dos representaciones entre 1662 y 1665, a cargo de la compañía de Davenant, y se sabe por una copia conservada que se representó en Dublín a comienzos de la década de los 80.

En 1681 tuvo lugar la famosa adaptación de Nahum Tate, que introdujo importantes modificaciones en respuesta a cambios en la concepción del teatro y de la vida. El final trágico de Shakespeare fue sustituido por un final feliz donde los personajes más nobles restauraban el orden, la paz y la justicia, comportamiento lógico para una época convencida de que bajo la apariencia de las cosas existía un orden justo que el arte debía mostrar, nunca ocultar.

En la versión de Tate se introduce una historia de amor entre Cordelia y Edgar, que sirve para justificar acciones y comportamientos que en el original no quedaban explicados: aporta una razón a la negativa de Cordelia a obedecer a su padre al comienzo de la obra y Edgar constituye su agente salvador cuando intentan ahorcarla. A la misma función explicativa responde el desarrollo de la intriga de Edmund y su relación con Gonerill y Regan, que en Shakespeare aparece sólo esbozada, sin explicitación de los detalles de su evolución.

El espacio se reduce, respondiendo a las unidades de lugar, y la invasión extranjera dirigida por France y Cordelia es sustituida por una revuelta de campesinos en protesta por los impuestos exigidos por Gonerill y Regan. Finalmente, la figura del bufón se suprime por considerar que atenta contra los principios del decoro.

La versión de Tate tuvo un gran éxito escénico durante 157 años[25] —hasta que en 1838 Macready recuperó casi en su to-

---

[25] Véase, a este respecto, D. N. Smith, *Shakespeare in the Eighteenth Century* (1928), págs. 20-25.

talidad el texto original—, y recibió diversas críticas, en su mayoría positivas, entre las que cabe destacar, como máximo exponente, al doctor Johnson, que lamentaba la dureza del texto original, especialmente la muerte de Cordelia:

> I was many years ago so shocked by Cordelia's death that I know not whether I ever endured to read again the last scenes of the play till I undertook to revise them as an editor[26]

y comentaba lo positivo de las transformaciones de Tate:

> In the present case the public has decided, and Cordelia, from the time of Tate, has always retired with victory and felicity

Entre las críticas negativas resultan de interés los comentarios de Addison, que, en 1711, criticó la adaptación de Tate, por considerar que había perdido «la mitad de la belleza del original»[27].

En cuanto a la participación de los actores en la obra, se sabe que la versión de Tate sirvió de base para la interpretación de George Powell, Robert Wilkes, Barton Booth, Anthony Boheme, James Quin, Spranger Barry, John Kemble, y Garrick[28], entre otros, aunque este último, sin apartarse sustancialmente del texto de Tate, introdujo algunos fragmentos de Shakespeare, con la intención de recuperar parcialmente su intensidad poética.

Además de la versión de Tate, surgieron otras en el siglo XVIII, como reacción contra ella, entre las que merece especial atención la de George Colman, de 1768, que se aleja tanto de Tate como del original shakespeariano, ya que, aunque suprime la historia de amor que Tate había introducido, elimina igualmente el argumento secundario de Gloucester, fundamental en Shakespeare, y que Tate había conservado. De

---

[26] Cfr. *Samuel Johnson on Shakespeare* (ed. W. K. Wimsatt Jr., 1960), pág. 98.

[27] Cfr. *The Spectator,* 17 de abril de 1711.

[28] Véase a propósito de su interpretación el comentario de G. W. Stone, «Garrick's Production on *King Lear:* A Study in the Temper of the Eighteenth Century Mind», *Studies in Philology,* XLV (1948), 91, y A. C. Sprague, *Shakespearean Players and Performances* (1953), págs. 21-40.

Shakespeare recupera el final trágico, pero no se atreve a incorporar la figura del bufón por temor a su no aceptación por las convenciones escénicas de sus contemporáneos. No tuvo que esperar mucho para conocer sus reacciones airadas porque la restauración del final trágico atentaba severamente contra la sensibilidad y el gusto de la época. En *The Theatrical Review* de 1772 se comentaba así la nueva versión:

> We have only to observe here, that Mr. Colman has made several very judicious alterations, at the same time that we think his having restored the original distressed catastrophe is a circumstance not greatly in favour of humanity or delicacy of feeling, since it is now rather too shocking to be borne; and the rejecting, the Episode of the loves of Edgar and Cordelia so happily conceived by Tate, has beyond all doubt, greatly weakened the Peice[29]...

En el siglo xix surgieron numerosas críticas en defensa de la recuperación de los valores poéticos del texto original de Shakespeare, aunque se manifestaron al mismo tiempo las dificultades de representar escénicamente la obra. Fueron importantes las contribuciones de Keats, Coleridge y Shelley en el primer sentido, enfatizando sobre todo la intensidad y la fuerza poética de la obra escrita por Shakespeare. La siguiente afirmación de Keats resulta muy distinta de los comentarios habituales en el siglo xviii:

> The excellence of every art is in its intensity, capable of making all disagreeables evaporate, from their being in close relationship with Beauty and Truth. Examine *King Lear* and you will find this exemplified throughout[30].

La definición que hace Shelley de *King Lear*, aunque más breve, es igualmente contundente:

> the most perfect specimen of dramatic poetry existing in the world[31].

---

[29] Pág. 334.
[30] Cfr. *Letters*, ed. M. B. Forman (1948), pág. 71.
[31] Cfr. *A Defence of Poetry* (1909), pág. 134.

afirmación próxima a la de Coleridge:

> the most tremendous effort of Shakespeare as a poet[32]

aunque Coleridge, reconociendo el valor poético de la obra, oponía problemas estructurales, como la supuesta improbabilidad de la escena inicial, en su opinión, elemento debilitador de la unidad estructural.

Este tipo de problemas y otros de carácter interpretativo eran recogidos por Hazlitt y Lamb, que, reivindicando la aproximación a Shakespeare, sobre todo en la recuperación del final trágico, sin embargo aún mantenían la convicción de que la obra presentaba enormes dificultades de interpretación. Son conocidas las palabras de Charles Lamb ridiculizando la tradición que favorecía el final feliz adoptado por Tate:

> A happy ending! —as if the living martyrdom that Lear had gone through... did not make a fair dismissal from the stage the only decorous thing for him... as if at his years and with his experience, anything was left but to die[33]

pero tampoco hay que olvidar los problemas que veía en la representación de la obra, especialmente en la interpretación de Lear:

> they might more easily propose to personate the Satan of Milton upon a stage, or one of Michael Angelo's terrible figures[34].

Ideas semejantes expresaba Hazlitt en sus comentarios:

> there are pieces of ancient granite that turn the edge of any modern chisel: so perhaps the genius of no living actor can be expected to cope with Lear[35]

Las condiciones sociales nuevas, las grandes dimensiones de

---

[32] Cfr. *Table Talk*, 29 de diciembre de 1822.
[33] Cfr. *Works*, ed. W. Macdonald, III, pág. 33.
[34] Cfr. «On the Tragedies of Shakespeare», *The Life, Letters and Writings of Charles Lamb* (1808), IV, 205.
[35] Cfr. *London Magazine*, I (1820), 687.

los teatros, el incremento de una clase media sentimental, y la influencia del gusto femenino, determinaron unas representaciones igualmente alejadas de Shakespeare que de Tate, en las que se tomaron en cuenta las opiniones de Lamb y Hazlitt.

La representación más influyente fue la de Kean, de 1823, en que se recuperó el final trágico shakespeariano, pero manteniendo las escenas de amor, y excluyendo todavía la figura del bufón.

Quince años más tarde, en 1838, Macready ya incorporaba al bufón, aunque privado de toda su fuerza crítica y de su carácter grotesco, presentándolo como un ser frágil y hermoso[36]. Esta versión ofrecía el texto más próximo al original de Shakespeare desde 1681, aunque con importantes omisiones, y distanciado de su espíritu por los condicionantes propios de la época, influida todavía por la tradición sentimental del siglo XVIII, y, sobre todo, determinada por un fuerte espíritu historicista de las representaciones. Este afán historicista ya había llevado a Charles Kean a ubicar la acción de *King Lear* en un espacio histórico concreto: el mundo anglosajón del siglo VIII. Más tarde llevó a Macready a interpretarla con círculos druidas, y, posteriormente, a Irving a situarla en el siglo V, momento inmediatamente posterior al abandono romano de Inglaterra. La consecuencia de estas y otras representaciones del siglo XIX fue la pérdida del carácter intemporal de la obra[37], y el distanciamiento de la crueldad, justificada como elemento propio de épocas con escasa civilización, sumado a la debilitación del diseño inicial con argumento principal y secundario, fruto de las importantes omisiones que fueron práctica generalizada durante todo el siglo XIX, a lo largo del cual cobraron gran fama las interpretaciones de los actores Irving, Terry, Phelps y Booth.

En el siglo XX la situación se ha dirigido hacia una revalorización progresiva del texto original, unido a un redescubrimiento de las condiciones interpretativas del teatro isabelino, en el que la obra carecía de los problemas surgidos con poste-

---

[36] Cfr. *Diaries of William Charles Macready*, ed. W. Toynbee (1912), I, 438.

[37] A propósito de la relevancia de este carácter intemporal y universal de la obra, véase Knights, *Some Shakespearean Themes* (1959), pág. 89.

rioridad, al evolucionar las convenciones escénicas, la disposición de los teatros, y el tipo y gustos del público. En cuanto a los aspectos calificados de crueles y excesivos durante los siglos XVIII y XIX, no sólo no se consideran un defecto en el siglo XX, sino que se acentúan, dando lugar a representaciones como la de Peter Brook[38], de 1962, inspirada en interpretaciones de Jan Kott[39], y próxima en algunos aspectos al grado de absurdo de *Waiting for Godot* o *Endgame*, de S. Beckett. Otras representaciones especialmente polémicas han sido las de Giorgio Strehler, de 1972[40], y P. Zadek, de 1974. También han sido interesantes las representaciones de Glen Byam Shaw, dirigida en 1959, que prestaba una especial atención a la ambientación, vestuario y decorados, comentada por Muriel St. Clare en «King Lear at Stratford-upon-Avon»[41]; la producción de Trevor Nunn, de 1968, que intensificaba el carácter humano de Lear, al tiempo que reducía su carácter intelectual; la adaptación de Buzz Goodbody, de 1974, en que enfatizaba el sentido de las relaciones entre Edmund y Gonerill y Regan; o la versión de Trevor Nunn, de 1976, comentada por Richard David en *Shakespeare in the Theatre*[42], y sobre la que se publicó una entrevista con Donald Sinden, actor que interpretó el papel de Lear[43].

Además de Donald Sinden han sido muchos los que se han puesto a prueba en la interpretación de *El rey Lear,* destacando, entre otros, John Gielgud, William Devlin, Randall Ayrton, Donald Wolfit, Laurence Olivier, Eric Porter, Stephen Murray, Michael Redgrave, Tony Church, Charles Laughton y Paul Scofield.

La relevancia cobrada por la obra ha llevado a realizar versiones para el cine, entre las que destacan la de Peter Brook,

---

[38] Véase el comentario, a esta representación, de J. L. Styan, *The Shakespeare Revolution* (1977), págs. 217-23.

[39] Véase J. Kott, «*King Lear* or *Endgame*», *Shakespeare Our Contemporary* (1964).

[40] Véase la reflexión, sobre esta versión, de M. A. Conejero, *La escena, el sueño, la palabra: apunte shakespeariano* (1983), págs. 63-96.

[41] *Shakespeare Quarterly,* II (1960).

[42] (1978), págs. 95-105.

[43] «Playing *King Lear*», *Shakespeare Survey,* 33.

de 1971, en que Paul Scofield interpretaba el papel de Lear, comentada por Jack J. Jorgens en *Shakespeare on Film*[44], y la versión de Grigori Kozintsev, de 1970, comentada también por J. Jorgens en la misma obra.

Si han sido variadas las formas de interpretar *El rey Lear* en el siglo xx, no menos variadas han sido las opiniones vertidas por los críticos sobre la obra, aunque quizá se haya alcanzado un nivel de acuerdo inexistente hasta entonces, el de la valoración unánimemente positiva de la obra como globalidad, y aunque las discusiones sobre aspectos concretos, valorados positiva o negativamente según los críticos, se extiendan hasta hoy[45].

Resultan de gran interés las reflexiones de conjunto realizadas por G. R. Hibbard en «*King Lear*: A Retrospect, 1939-79»[46], donde se refiere a las contribuciones más importantes de esos treinta años, encuadrándolas entre el extremo de la tendencia sentimental, cuyo máximo exponente sería Paul N. Siegel[47], que llega a pensar en la reunión de Lear y Cordelia en el cielo, y la interpretación nihilista de Jan Kott. Hace hincapié en la revalorización de los símbolos y del lenguaje llevada a cabo durante este siglo, tan intensa, que ha llegado a provocar protestas de algunos críticos que consideraban excesivos los análisis realizados, como en el caso de W. R.

---

[44] (1977).

[45] Resultan especialmente interesantes para el estudio de esta obra los comentarios detallados de N. Brooke, *Shakespeare: King Lear* (1963); M. Mack, *King Lear in Our Time* (1965), y H. Gardner, *King Lear* (1967); los volúmenes 13 y 33 de *Shakespeare Survey*, por sus contribuciones críticas a la obra, así como las recopilaciones de artículos realizadas por F. Kermode (ed.), en *Shakespeare: King Lear* (1969); R. L. Colie y E. T. Flahiff (eds.), en *Some Facets of King Lear* (1974), o K. Muir y S. Wells, en *Aspects of King Lear* (1982).
Entre las contribuciones críticas al estudio de *King Lear* en el siglo xx destaca la labor desarrollada por la crítica textual. Véase a este respecto las conclusiones de J. V. Martínez Luciano, *Shakespeare en la crítica bibliotextual* (1984), páginas 75-81.
Para una aproximación bibliográfica a la obra puede consultarse el capítulo elaborado por K. Muir dedicado a *King Lear*, en *Shakespeare: Select Bibliographical Guides*, editado por S. Wells (1973).

[46] *Aspects of King Lear* (1982), reimpresión de *Shakespeare Survey*.

[47] *Shakespearean Tragedy and the Elizabethan Compromise* (1957).

Keast[48], o el de Paul J. Alper[49], pero, de cualquier modo, ha sido incorporada y aceptada en líneas generales por la crítica posterior. Alude Hibbard también a la preocupación por la interpretación de la obra y su relación con un trasfondo moral, claramente cristiano en la década de los 40[50], que recibió dentro de la misma década algunas críticas[51], intensificadas en los años 50[52], y continuadas todavía en los 60[53], a pesar de lo cual, todavía se escuchaban voces en esos años interpretando la obra como una alegoría cristiana o descubriendo detrás de ella la participación de la providencia divina[54], voces que se redujeron a alguna manifestación esporádica[55] después del detenido estudio de William Elton, *King Lear and the Gods*[56], en que relacionaba a los diferentes personajes de la obra con actitudes distintas frente a la providencia, perfectamente codificadas, y concluía que no podían hacerse afirmaciones simplistas, conclusión que constituye el denominador común de la mayor parte de la crítica posterior, donde se manifiesta una desconfianza hacia toda fórmula que intente reducir la obra a una definición[57].

---

[48] «Imagery and Meaning in the interpretation of *King Lear*», *Modern Philology*, 47 (1949), pág. 45.

[49] *«King Lear* and the Theory of the "sight patterns"»*, In Defense of Reading* (1962).

[50] J. Danby, *op. cit.*, pág. 125; R. W. Chambers, *King Lear* (1940), páginas 48-49; S. L. Bethell, *op. cit.;* J. C. Maxwell, «The Technique of Invocation in *King Lear*», *Modern Language Review*, 45 (1950).

[51] F. P. Wilson, *Elizabethan and Jacobean* (1945), pág. 121; G. Orwell, «Lear, Tolstoy and the Fool», *Shooting an Elephant* (1945).

[52] C. Leech, *Shakespeare's Tragedies and Other Studies in Seventeenth Century Drama* (1950), pág. 18; D. G. James, *The Dream of Learning* (1951), págs. 92-93; A. Sewell, *Character and Society in Shakespeare* (1951).

[53] B. Everett, «The New *King Lear*», *Critical Quarterly*, 2 (1960), y R. Ornstein, *op. cit.*, pág. 273.

[54] G. I. Duthie, introducción a la edición *New Cambridge*, pág. xx; I. Ribner, *Patterns of Shakespearean Tragedy* (1960), pág. 117; V. Whitaker, *The Mirror Up to Nature* (1965), pág. 227.

[55] R. Battenhouse, *Shakespearean Tragedy: Its Art and its Christian Premises* (1969), pág. 301, en defensa de la interpretación cristiana; R. G. Hunter, *Shakespeare and the Mystery of God's Judgment* (1976), concluyendo que la obra demuestra la inexistencia de Dios.

[56] (1966).

[57] Véase a este respecto H. A. Mason, *Shakespeare's Tragedies of Love* (1970), o M. Rosenberg, *The Masks of King Lear* (1972).

Las fuentes de «King Lear»*

La que podría considerarse primera versión de la historia del rey Lear y sus tres hijas se encuentra en la *Historia Regum Britanniae,* escrita por el clérigo Geoffrey de Monmouth, en el siglo XII, si bien un amplio sector de la crítica opina que Shakespeare no tomó la historia directamente de Monmouth, sino que la conoció a través de las llamadas fuentes intermedias, aparecidas con posterioridad, y en las que el tema, con ligeras variantes, fue tratado por otros autores.

La primera de estas fuentes intermedias es, sin duda alguna, «The Historie of England», una de las partes de *The Chronicles of England, Scotland and Ireland,* de R. Holinshed, publicada en 1577, y que, al parecer, Shakespeare utilizaba frecuentemente para la obtención de materiales históricos e incluso trágicos —*Macbeth,* por ejemplo—, que después incluía en sus obras. Otra de las probables fuentes utilizadas por Shakespeare para la composición de *King Lear* es, probablemente, *The Mirror for Magistrates,* recopilación de narrativa en verso, publicada por varios autores en 1559. En una de las ediciones posteriores de esta obra —la de 1574—, se encuentra una sección escrita por John Higgins que trata de los «desafortunados príncipes» *(unfortunate Princes)* de Inglaterra, entre los que se encuentra también el rey Lear.

Una tercera referencia importante a tener en cuenta es *The Fairie Queene,* de Edmund Spenser, poema épico incompleto dedicado por el poeta a la reina Isabel I, en el que, de manera hasta cierto punto histórica, pretende glorificar la historia de Gran Bretaña. Los libros I-III de la serie se publicaron en 1590, y los IV-VI —el poema, en su totalidad, debía haber estado compuesto de 12 libros— fueron añadidos cuando se publicó la segunda edición en 1596. En el libro II, el «Canto X» nos

---

* Notas extraídas, fundamentalmente, de K. Muir, *The Sources of Shakespeare's Plays,* Londres, 1977; y G. Bullough, *Narrative and Dramatic Sources of Shakespeare,* Londres, 1978.

ofrece «A Chronicle of Briton Kings» en el que, entre las estrofas 27 a 32, se nos presenta la historia de Lear.

Cabría citar, también, la obra dramática anónima *The True Chronicle History of King Leir,* escrita probablemente entre 1590 y 1600, pero que no aparece publicada hasta 1605, para —según un amplio sector de la crítica— aprovechar la posibilidad de hacerla pasar por el *Lear* de Shakespeare, y beneficiarse así del éxito obtenido por esta última. De cualquier modo, es más que probable que Shakespeare conociera el texto de *King Leir* antes de escribir su tragedia, puesto que son muchos y diversos los fragmentos o efectos dramáticos que parecen haber tenido influencia directa en su versión de la tragedia.

En ninguna de las fuentes intermedias o directas mencionadas existe referencia alguna a la *locura* de Lear como resultado de sus sufrimientos. Uno de los críticos más prestigiosos en lo que se refiere al estudio de las fuentes, G. Bullough, plantea un notable paralelismo entre la historia de Lear, tal y como la desarrolla Shakespeare, y la de la familia Annesley: una conocida historia de disputas familiares muy cercana en el tiempo a la fecha de composición de *Lear,* y con la que Shakespeare habría estado, probablemente, familiarizado. H. H. Furness, además, cita en su edición *New Variorum* una colección de baladas, publicada en 1726, entre las que se incluye *A Lamentable Song of the Death of King Lear and his Three Daughters.* Existen aún hoy dudas entre los críticos sobre si la balada es anterior a la composición de *Lear* —y, por tanto, Shakespeare se habría inspirado en ella— o si, por el contrario, el compositor de la canción se inspiró en la tragedia de Shakespeare.

Por último, y por lo que se refiere al argumento paralelo de la historia de Gloucester —incluyendo el tema de la ceguera (metafórica y física)—, los críticos coinciden en afirmar que se basa en la suerte similar que corre el rey de la Paphlagonia, tal y como se describe en el «Libro II» de *The Countesse of Pembrokes Arcadia,* romance en prosa escrito por Sir Philip Sidney, publicado en 1590.

Vemos, por tanto, que es posible rastrear —en ésta, como en todas las obras dramáticas de Shakespeare— las fuentes de las que el autor se vale. No hemos de olvidar, sin embargo, que estas fuentes son sólo las génesis —algo así como la excusa— a partir de la cual el autor construye la obra dramática. Y, de cualquier modo, los elementos que conforman estas fuentes —y que, directamente o transformados, componen el argumento de la tragedia— pertenecen, de alguna manera, a la cultura oral o escrita de la sociedad, y Shakespeare no hace sino utilizar esos elementos para componer su *Lear,* una de las más grandes tragedias en la historia del teatro universal.

Fecha de composición de «King Lear»

La obra de Samuel Harsnett, *Declaration of Egregious Popish Impostures,* aparece inscrita en el *Stationers' Register* (registro legal de publicaciones) el 16 de marzo de 1603, y, puesto que Shakespeare hace uso de este texto para la composición de su *Lear* —tal y como se advierte en las notas que acompañan a esta traducción—, podemos asegurar que la tragedia no pudo haber sido escrita antes de esa fecha. También en el *Stationers' Register,* encontramos, el 26 de noviembre de 1607, la inscripción de *King Lear* en la que se menciona que fue representada ante el rey el 26 de diciembre de 1606 («*...as it was played before the Kings Maiestie at Whitehall upon S. Stephans night at Christmas Last*»). Basándonos en estos datos, podemos afirmar, por tanto, que la tragedia fue escrita entre marzo de 1603 y diciembre de 1606.

En 1605 se publica una dramatización anónima —que mencionábamos ya en el apartado anterior— de la historia de Lear y sus hijas: *The True Chronicle History of King Leir, and his Three Daughters,* que —como apuntábamos— es considerada por los críticos como un intento fraudulento, por parte de sus editores, de explotar la popularidad de la obra de Shakespeare sobre el mismo tema. Este hecho, junto a una serie de sucesos turbulentos —tanto físicos como políticos— que se reflejan no sólo en el tono trágico de *Lear,* sino que además son explicitados por Gloucester —véase acto I, escena ii, líneas 94 y ss.—, nos permite aproximar la fecha de composición de *King Lear* a finales de 1605 o comienzos de 1606.

Las palabras de Gloucester —«motín», «discordia», «traición»— parecen ser una alusión, fácil de identificar, al suceso político más importante de 1605: la conjura de la pólvora *(Gunpowder Plot)*, mediante la cual Guy Fawkes y otros conjurados intentaban volar el Parlamento, el 5 de noviembre de 1605, mientras éste se hallaba en sesión presidida por el rey. Este suceso político quedó inevitablemente unido a los eclipses de luna y sol, de septiembre y octubre de 1605, considerados como presagio de grandes calamidades.

Parece obvio, por tanto, concluir que *King Lear* fue escrita en los últimos meses de 1605 o primeros de 1606, lo que nos permitiría colocarla en la secuencia cronológica de las otras grandes tragedias shakespearianas: después de *Hamlet* (1600), y *Othello* (1604), inmediatamente antes —o quizá al mismo tiempo— que *Macbeth* (1606), y un año o dos antes que *Antony and Cleopatra* (1607).

El texto de «King Lear»

Convendría mencionar, antes de hablar directamente del texto de *Lear,* el hecho de que no se conserva ningún texto original manuscrito de Shakespeare, si se exceptúan unos fragmentos de *Sir Thomas More* —que forman un total aproximado de 147 líneas—, obra que no apareció impresa hasta 1844. Resulta, por tanto, evidente que uno de los problemas fundamentales con que nos enfrentamos —antes de abordar la traducción de la obra— es el de conformar una edición en inglés, tarea que se debe realizar a partir de las primera ediciones existentes —cercanas, al menos en el tiempo, al dramaturgo—, y teniendo en cuenta ediciones posteriores realizadas por especialistas en el campo de la bibliotextualidad o en el de la propia edición que, lógicamente, incorporan a sus trabajos los resultados de investigaciones llevadas a cabo a lo largo de siglos.

Cabría recordar, además, que Shakespeare nunca tuvo, aparentemente, relación alguna con la publicación de sus obras —aunque éstas aparecieran editadas en vida del autor—, por lo que las ediciones que se ha dado en llamar «originales» —ediciones *in Quarto* e *in Folio,* que más adelante mencionaremos con referencia a *King Lear,* en particular— están, en muchas ocasiones, llenas de problemas, lagunas e inexactitudes. Si a ello añadimos, por una parte, que lo que normalmente entendemos por corrección gramatical no es una de las características más notables de Shakespeare, y, por otra, que la lengua inglesa es especialmente apta para la anfibología —por sus ambivalencias y dobles sentidos—, se comprenderá por qué la tarea de depuración y fijación definitiva del texto ha sido y, de hecho, continúa siendo de primordial importancia como paso previo a la edición.

La primera edición impresa de *King Lear* aparece en 1608, en una edición *in Quarto*, publicada por Nathaniel Butter que el 26 de noviembre de 1607 la había inscrito en el *Stationers' Register*, asegurándose así el derecho a publicarla. De esta edición, conocida como *«Pied Bull» Quarto* —puesto que en la portada anuncia: *«...and are to be sold at his shop in Pauls Churchyard at the signe of the* Pide Bull *neere St. Austins Gate»*—, se conservan sólo doce copias, dándose el curioso caso de que éstas se encuentran en diez estados de composición diferentes, ya que se ha podido demostrar, mediante los pertinentes estudios bibliotextuales, que la corrección de pruebas y la impresión se llevaron a cabo al mismo tiempo, haciéndose así correcciones en algunas hojas que, posteriormente, fueron mezcladas con otras no corregidas.

La segunda edición del texto de *Lear*, y a pesar de la información que aparece en la portada —*«Printed for Nathaniel Butter. 1608»*—, fue impresa en 1619, a partir de una copia del primer *Quarto*, y se conoce como el *Second Quarto* o *«Nathaniel Butter» Quarto*, conservándose en la actualidad un total de treinta y dos copias. Los dos textos *in Quarto* son sustancialmente iguales, y no plantean problemas a la hora de elegir lecciones procedentes de uno u otro. No siempre se ha pensado así, sin embargo, y, de hecho, se puede afirmar que, hasta la aparición en 1866 del octavo volumen de la edición *Cambridge Shakespeare*, el estudio de los problemas textuales referido a ambos *Quartos* era realmente caótico. Baste mencionar, como ejemplo, las notas hechas a la edición *Variorum* de 1821, realizadas por Boswell, que son un modelo perfecto de contradicción en lo que concierne a las referencias textuales. Esto cambió, como decíamos, con la edición *Cambridge*, llevada a cabo por los profesores Clark y Wright, si bien también ellos cometieron el error de considerar el *Second Quarto* (de 1619) como el primero en orden cronológico, y el de 1608 como el segundo; error que sería corregido por el propio Wright, en 1875, en la edición que preparó para la Clarendon Press, conocida como *Clarendon Shakespeare.*

La edición del *First Folio* de 1623 marca la tercera aparición de *King Lear* en letra impresa, y en él la obra ocupa las páginas 283 a 309, ambas inclusive, de la sección correspondiente a las «Tragedias», entre *Hamlet* y *Othello*, compartiendo con *Macbeth*, *Othello* y *Cymbeline* el rasgo de estar dividida en actos y escenas. Si bien en un primer momento —sobre todo desde que P. A. Daniel publicó su «Introducción» al facsímil *Praetorius* del primer *Quarto*— se mantuvo la teoría de que el texto del *Folio* había sido impreso a partir de una copia del *Quarto*, actualmente no existe duda alguna de que el texto del *Folio* es muy superior, en general, al de los *Quartos*, y que fue impreso a partir de un manuscrito distinto a éstos. Sin embargo, y a pesar de esta autoridad, el editor de *Lear* no puede pasar por alto el texto del *Quarto*, debido fundamentalmente a la diferencia en longitud entre ambos textos: los *Quartos* sobrepasan al *Folio* en 175 líneas, puesto que hay unas 220 líneas en los *Quartos* que no aparecen en el *Folio*, y éste, a su vez, contiene unas 50 que no aparecen en *Quarto*, fragmentos estos que aparecerán oportunamente reseñados en las notas.

Existe, también —y sin prácticamente ningún valor textual—, otra edición *in Quarto* de 1655 (conocida como el *«Jane Bell» Quarto*), además de las ediciones *in Folio* de 1632, 1663 y 1685, reimpresiones con ligerísimas variantes de la colección mencionada de 1623. De entre las ediciones más modernas cabría destacar, por su autoridad crítica, tanto para el texto como en los comentarios, las siguientes: W. G. Clark y W. A. Wright *(Cambridge*, 1866); H. H. Furness *(New Variorum*, 1880); W. A. Wright *(Clarendon*, 1886); W. J. Craig *(Arden*, 1901); K. Muir *(New Arden*, 1952; edición corregida, 1972); G. I. Duthie y J. D. Wilson *(New Cambridge*, 1960); G. K. Hunter *(New Penguin*, 1972).

ESTA EDICIÓN

La edición de *King Lear* en que nos hemos basado para esta traducción ha sido realizada a partir de las ediciones *in Quarto* —de 1608 y 1619— e *in Folio* —de 1623—, mencionadas en el apartado anterior, teniendo en cuenta, además, ediciones autorizadas posteriores; este texto inglés habría acompañado a la traducción de haber sido esta una edición bilingüe. En numerosas ocasiones hemos tenido que decidir entre las diferentes lecciones posibles que los originales ofrecían, no sólo en lo que se refiere a palabras determinadas o frases completas —de lo que ofrecemos varios ejemplos en las notas—, sino también al problema singular que plantean las acotaciones escénicas. Efectivamente, en este último caso, ha habido que reconsiderar el sistema utilizado en las ediciones de origen, en las autorizadas de los siglos XVIII, XIX y XX y, además, en las diferentes versiones aparecidas en el resto de Europa —Italia, Francia, Alemania y España, principalmente—, a lo largo de los dos últimos siglos. En nuestra opinión, un texto para la escena es por naturaleza versátil, y el uso excesivo de información escénica podría limitar, de forma negativa, su espontaneidad. Por ello, nuestro punto de referencia han sido siempre las ediciones originales, *Quartos* y *Folio,* escuetas en información, necesitadas a veces de ligeros retoques que, lejos de oscurecer el texto, ayudasen a una mejor comprensión.

Durante muchos años se han venido realizando numerosos estudios bibliotextuales, así como innumerables ediciones, de la obra de Shakespeare, por lo que podemos afirmar que el texto de las diferentes obras está ya relativamente fijado. En el caso que nos ocupa —la edición de *King Lear*—, la tónica ge-

neral es la de considerar el texto del *Folio* como superior dramáticamente al de *Quarto,* aunque —y así lo consideran la
mayoría de los especialistas consultados— sin olvidar algunas
de las lecciones de *Quarto,* proponiendo, de esta forma, una solución editorial que recoja las diferentes cualidades de uno y
otro texto, siendo, en muchas ocasiones, la pura intuición dramática la que lleva —al menos a nosotros— a escoger una entre varias opciones posibles.

En nuestro caso, además, se aborda la edición con una perspectiva diferente de la del editor anglosajón, por cuanto añadimos el punto de vista de la traducción, del trasvase de esas posibles opciones a otra lengua. Teniendo en cuenta estos aspectos que mencionamos, resulta evidente que nuestra edición del
texto se aparta muy poco de cualquiera de las otras ediciones al
uso, y, aunque el texto inglés no acompañe a la traducción, hemos creído conveniente añadir algunas notas que podrían resultar significativas para entender momentos, situaciones dramáticas o actitudes determinadas de la obra. Así, por ejemplo,
hemos considerado oportuno anotar las omisiones que los textos originales presentan porque creemos que puede resultar interesante que el lector las conozca y decida sobre su posible
importancia o significado en determinados momentos de la
tragedia.

Entre los textos originales autorizados —*Quartos* de 1608
y 1619, y *Folio* de 1623— existen un total de 1141 variantes sus-
tanciales, la mayoría de las cuales no afectan al proceso de traducción, sino al de la edición del texto en inglés, por lo que
—en las notas que acompañan al texto— sólo hemos incluido
aquellas variantes, u omisiones de alguno de los textos, que
pudieran resultar significativas. En este sentido, las principales
líneas generales de edición para la edición y traducción de *King
Lear* han sido las siguientes:

I) Variantes «Quarto-Folio»

De entre todas las variantes arriba mencionadas, no se incluyen en las notas todas aquellas que pudieran ser incluidas
en los apartados que, a continuación, se exponen, por causas
fácilmente comprensibles para el lector:

a) *Sustituciones léxicas o sinónimos*

Se trata de casos en los que los textos del *Quarto* y del *Folio* se diferencian en el uso de una palabra que, en uno u otro aparece, sustituida por un sinónimo. Ejemplos:

I.i.30:
> *Quarto:* «I shall, my *Leige*»
> *Folio:* «I shall, my *Lord*»
> *Sí, Majestad.*

I.i.60:
> *Quarto:* «...with *shady* forests and with champains...
> *Folio:* «...with *shadowy* forests and with champains
> *...llenos de espesos bosques y campiñas...*

I.i.81-2:
> *Quarto:* «What can you say to *win* a third...»
> *Folio:* «What can you say to *draw* a third...»
> *¿Qué haréis para obtener un tercio...*

I.i.178:
> *Quarto:* «The gods to their *protection* take thee...»
> *Folio:* «The gods to their *dear shelter* take thee...»
> *Que los dioses te tomen bajo su protección...*

b) *Sustituciones ortográficas*

Se trata de aquellas variantes en las que lo que varía, de un texto a otro, son las diferentes formas de deletrear una misma palabra, por lo que, como es obvio, tampoco se han reseñado en las notas. Ejemplos:

I.i.186:
> *Quarto:* «We first adress *towards* you...»
> *Folio:* We first adress *toward* you...»
> *A vos nos dirigimos en primer lugar...*

I.i.138-9:
> *Quarto:* «...this coronet part *betwixt* you.»
> *Folio:* «...this coronet part *between* you.»
> *...dividid esta corona entre los dos.*

[42]

Obsérvese, sin embargo, y con relación a estos dos mismos términos, el ejemplo siguiente:

I.i.166-7
Quarto: «...to come *betweene* our sentence...»
Folio: «...to come *betwixt* our sentence...»
...a interponerte entre nuestras sentencias...

c) *Sustituciones sintácticas*

Son aquellas diferencias entre ambos textos que, a pesar de la distinta configuración sintáctica, tampoco afectan a la traducción. Ejemplos:

I.i.101:
Quarto: «But goes *this with thy heart?*»
Folio: «But goes *thy heart with this?*»
¿Es eso lo que dice vuestro corazón?

I.ii.56-7:
Quarto: «When came *this to you?*»
Folio: «When came *you to this?*»
¿Cuando os ha llegado?

I.ii.67:
Quarto: «But I have *often heard him...*»
Folio: «But I have *heard him oft...*»
Mas le he oído a menudo...

I.iii.22:
Quarto: «Remember what *I tell you.*»
Folio: «Remember what *I have said.*»
Recordad lo que he dicho.

Resulta evidente que este último ejemplo podría haber sido incluido en el apartado primero referente a sustituciones léxicas.

d) *Variaciones singular/plural*

Gran parte de las diferencias entre los textos del *Quarto* y del *Folio* corresponden a las variaciones en número que, en la

[43]

mayor parte de las ocasiones, tampoco afectan a la traducción. Ejemplos:

I.i.3:
> *Quarto:* «But now, in the division of the *kingdomes*...»
> *Folio:* «But now, in the division of the *kingdom*...»
> *Pero ahora, con la escisión del reino...*

I.i.31:
> *Quarto:* «Meantime, we shall express our darker *purposes.*»
> *Folio:* «Meantime, we shall express our darker *purpose.*»
> *Desvelaremos, entretanto, el más penoso de nuestros proyectos.*

I.i.51:
> *Quarto:* «I love you more than *words* can wield the matter.»
> *Folio:* «I love you more than *word* can wield the matter.»
> *Os amo más de lo que las palabras pueden expresar*

I.i.62-3:
> *Quarto:* «To thine and Albany's *issue* be this perpetual.»
> *Folio:* «To thine and Albany's *issues* be this perpetual.»
> *Y que así sea para los descendientes de Albany y de vos.*

I.i.131-2:
> *Quarto:* «...the name and all *th'additions* to a king.»
> *Folio:* «...the name and all *th'addition* to a king.»
> *El nombre y todo aquello que comporta el ser rey.*

e) *Hábitos y errores compositoriales*

Existen también, entre ambos textos, notables diferencias que hemos de atribuir a los hábitos de los especialistas que componían los textos en las imprentas, y a los posibles errores cometidos en este proceso. En algunas ocasiones, estos hábitos o errores pueden influir en el significado, si bien en la mayoría de las ocasiones no lo alteran en absoluto. Ejemplos:

I.ii.122:
> *Quarto:* «...with a *sith* like Tom o'Bedlam.»
> *Folio:* «...with a *sigh* like Tom o'Bedlam.»
> *...con suspiros como de Tom de Beldlam.*

[44]

I.iv.242:
Quarto: «Detested kite, thou *list!*»
Folio: «Detested kite, thou *liest!*»
¡Mentís, buitre maldito!
II.i.122:
Quarto: «...which I best *thought* it fit to answer...»
Folio: «...which I best *though* it fit to answer...»
...a las que he creído preferible responder...

Además de los ejemplos reseñados, cabría resaltar, en este apartado, las diferencias ortográficas entre ambos textos derivadas de los hábitos compositoriales. Así, es fácil encontrar ejemplos como los que siguen, en ambos textos: *theeves* y *thieves; has* y *hath; does* y *doth; happly* y *happily; would* y *wouldst; makes* y *mak'st;* etc.

II) División en actos y escenas

En esta edición hemos mantenido la división tradicional en actos y escenas que coincide, sustancialmente, con la que aparece en el *First Folio* de 1623 (recordemos que los *Quartos* de 1608 y 1619 no señalan división alguna), con algunas salvedades de las que damos cumplida información en las notas correspondientes, y que afectan, principalmente, a los actos II —escena tercera— y IV —también, escena tercera.

III) Acotaciones escénicas

Los textos originales, *Quarto* y *Folio,* son bastante parcos en lo que se refiere a la información escénica, por cuanto ésta se incorpora normalmente al texto:

II.ii.1: *Feliz alba tengáis. ¿Sois de la casa?*
III.i.1: *¿Quién va con este tiempo de tormenta?*

Nuestra opinión, contraria a la de alguno de los editores consultados —muy explícitos en sus comentarios y anotaciones—, es la de conservar las acotaciones de los originales siempre que sea posible, puesto que son pocos los añadidos ne-

[45]

cesarios para la comprensión total de la obra en este aspecto. Cuando se necesita algún tipo de información adicional, ésta aparece entre corchetes [ ], y, además, se refleja en la nota correspondiente a pie de página, si fuera necesario, para un mejor entendimiento. Por ejemplo:

I.i.58: CORDELIA *[Aparte]*.
IV.vii.1: Entran Cordelia, Kent [doctor] y un caballero.

En estos casos, aparece una información —entre corchetes— que consideramos necesaria, pese a no figurar en los originales.

IV) DENOMINACIÓN DE PERSONAJES

Un par de casos muy concretos presentan ciertas dificultades en este aspecto a lo largo de toda la obra: la denominación de Edmund, hijo bastardo de Gloucester, y la de Oswald, mayordomo al servicio de Gonerill. El modo de designar a ambos personajes varía, en los originales, de unas escenas a otras (por ejemplo, Edmund, en *Quarto*, aparece siempre como *Bastard*, mientras que en *Folio* es ambas cosas, *Bastard* y *Edmund*).

Nuestra opción ha sido la de unificar la forma de designar a ambos personajes y, así, cuando éstos aparecen por vez primera en una escena, hacemos constar la doble nomenclatura:

MAYORDOMO [OSWALD]. *Con vuestro permiso...*
BASTARDO [EDMUND]. *¡Naturaleza, eres mi diosa!...*

mencionando, en primer lugar, la denominación que aparece en los originales; después utilizamos el nombre entre corchetes únicamente, hasta que el personaje desaparece de escena, volviendo a utilizar la doble nomenclatura, tal y como indicábamos anteriormente, cuando el personaje aparece de nuevo.

El mismo sistema se utiliza en las acotaciones escénicas que marcan las entradas y salidas de estos personajes. Por ejemplo:

I.ii.1: Entra el bastardo [Edmund].
I.iii.1: Entran Gonerill y el mayordomo [Oswald].

V) Traducción

En otras ocasiones*, hemos venido explicando la importancia que, para nosotros, tiene la *traducción teatral*, y qué entendemos por tal. Creemos necesario recordar, sin embargo, que son diversos los aspectos a tener en cuenta para explicar nuestra traducción y cuál ha sido, en cada momento, la opción elegida como texto definitivo, no sin antes advertir que en algunas ocasiones, y cuando creíamos que la elección así lo requería, hemos introducido una nota a pie de página en la que, además de la traducción literal, se dan las razones que nos han llevado a dicha elección. En apartados anteriores, hemos explicado ya cómo los problemas textuales y de edición han podido afectar al texto final, tanto en lo que se refiere al contenido como a la propia información escénica. Hemos de añadir, sin embargo, otros aspectos que, en mayor o menor medida, han podido afectar de manera general al texto final que ahora presentamos.

a) En ocasiones, son razones de tipo léxico y semántico las que nos obligan a traducir de forma diferente un mismo término, atendiendo al contexto en que éste aparece. Así, por ejemplo, el término *curiosity* ha sido traducido de manera diferente en las tres ocasiones en las que aparece en el texto:

I.i.5: «...that *curiosity* in neither can make choice...»
   ...*que ni* la más atenta observación *podría permitir la* elección.

I.ii.4-5: «and permit the *curiosity* of nations to private me...»
   y permitir que el mundo con su arbitrariedad *me deshe-rede...*

I.iv.59: «I have rather blamed as mine own jelaous *cusriosi-ty...*»
   Que preferí atribuir a mi excesiva susceptibilidad...

---

* Véanse las traducciones de otras obras dramáticas realizadas en el Instituto Shakespeare, dirigidas por Manuel Ángel Conejero, y que se incluyen en esta misma colección, así como los estudios críticos del mismo autor mencionados en la bibliografía.

Vemos, por tanto, cómo, en el primer caso, esta palabra que significaría «exactness», «scrupulousness», en este contexto —según los glosarios especializados*—, ha sido traducida por *la más atenta observación*, mientras que en el segundo ejemplo, y atendiendo a su significado de «fastidiousness» aparece en el texto traducida como *arbitrariedad*. En el tercer caso, y por aparecer calificada por «jelous», con el mismo significado que en el primer ejemplo —es decir, «exactness», «scrupulousness»—, hemos decidido traducirla por *susceptibilidad*. Se trata, por tanto, de un mismo término que se ha traducido de manera diferente según el contexto en que aparece, y teniendo en cuenta, por supuesto, la opinión de la crítica especializada sobre su significado en dichos contextos.

En otras ocasiones, el término ha sido traducido por su equivalente castellano en lo que se refiere al significado, aunque para ello hayamos tenido que alejarnos totalmente de la literalidad. Sería el ejemplo de:

II.ii.56: «Thou whoreson *zed*, thou unnecessary letter!»
    ¡Tú, cero hijo de puta; tú, letra innecesaria!

Como se observa, hemos trasvasado el valor nulo de la letra *zeta*, en aquella época, al número *cero*, cifra cuyo valor absoluto es, también, nulo.

Algo parecido ocurre cuando se trata de traducir un proverbio o refrán que, en algunas ocasiones, ha dejado incluso de ser utilizado en inglés contemporáneo, y cuya traducción literal resultaría por tanto incomprensible y fuera de contexto. Sería el caso de:

IV.ii.29: «I have been worth the whistle.»
    En otro tiempo se me valoraba.

Se trata de una alusión irónica al refrán inglés «It is a poor dog that is not worth the whistle» (lit.: *No vale nada el perro al que nadie se molesta en silbar),* y, de haber traducido literalmente el texto original por *He merecido el silbido,* la frase habría careci-

---

* Principalmente, *The Oxford English Dictionary; A Shakespeare Glossary,* de C. T. Onions; y *Shakespeare-Lexicon,* de A. Schmidt.

do del significado que tiene en el contexto dramático en que es emitida.

b) De especial importancia, sin embargo, son aquellos casos en los que la traducción ha venido impuesta por la teatralidad del texto, puesto que no debemos olvidar, en ningún momento, que *El rey Lear* es un texto dramático, un texto elaborado por Shakespeare para ser dicho sobre el escenario. De ahí que, en muchas ocasiones, haya sido la situación dramática —no las palabras exactas— lo que se ha traducido, intentando conseguir que la traducción creara el mismo efecto dramático que provoca el original, aunque las palabras no se correspondieran literalmente. Este ha sido el caso de las diferentes intervenciones del bufón a lo largo de la obra, o el caso peculiar de las intervenciones de Edgar —disfrazado— en IV.vi.229-38.

Otros casos podrían servir de ejemplo de cómo, en ocasiones, nos hemos visto obligados a alejarnos de la literalidad para expresar la idea con frases más acordes al teatro escrito en castellano:

I.i.121: «Call France! Who stirs?»
¡Llamad a France! ¡Moveos!

Como puede observarse, hemos convertido la aparente interrogación *(¿Quién se mueve?)* en una exclamación imperativa, mucho más adecuada al contexto en que es emitida por incluir el matiz de autoridad del que carecería la interrogación.

II.i.117: «You know not why we came to visit you...»
Sabed ahora la razón de nuestra presencia aquí...

En esta ocasión, la traducción literal *(Vos no sabéis por qué hemos venido a visitaros...)* nos podría alejar del significado de la frase en el contexto dramático en que es emitida. Cornwall plantea un giro en la conversación, para pasar a interesarse por los asuntos que realmente le han llevado hasta Gloucester, e informar a éste de sus intenciones y de las razones de su visita.

III.vi.2-3: «I will not be long from you.»
No he de estar mucho tiempo lejos de vosotros.

Creemos que, al traducir de esta forma la frase de Gloucester —en lugar de la, probablemente, más literal, *No tardaré en volver*—, incidimos en la idea de que, más que una vuelta física a ese lugar en el que se encuentran Lear y sus servidores, se trata de una declaración, casi una profecía, de cuál va a ser su futuro, muy parecido al del propio rey. Se trata, por tanto, de una opción de tono dramático incluida en la traducción.

Con estos ejemplos que, en las páginas anteriores, acabamos de citar, intentamos explicar cuáles han sido las líneas que han regido nuestra traducción. Cabría resaltar, a modo de conclusión, que nos hemos basado, fundamentalmente, en la voluntad de reconstruir el espectáculo verbal, teatral, por lo que los aspectos tenidos en cuenta han sido diversos: hacer una propuesta prosódica; hacer funcionar teatralmente los cambios de prosa a verso, y viceversa; intentar recrear el ritmo del original; reconstruir el texto escénico; etc., para así llegar a éste *El rey Lear* que aquí presentamos.

A pesar de que *El rey Lear* es una de las más grandes tragedias escritas por el dramaturgo William Shakespeare, hasta el momento, es la menos traducida de todas ellas en nuestro país.

A lo largo de la historia española de traducciones shakespearianas, *El rey Lear* se ha traducido y editado en nuestro país diecisiete veces; tres de ellas —y en castellano— en el siglo XIX y el resto en el XX, teniendo en cuenta que de estas últimas traducciones realizadas en el siglo XX dos de ellas lo fueron al catalán. De estas diecisite traducciones pasamos, ahora, a comentar las que —por unos motivos u otros— consideramos importantes dentro de la historia de la traducción shakespeariana en España.

De las traducciones castellanas llevadas a cabo en el siglo XIX habría que destacar que la primera de ellas —realizada por el también editor Francisco Nacente en 1872— fue traducida directamente del francés (algo habitual en las traducciones shakespearianas españolas del siglo XIX), y como parte del primer intento de verter las *Obras Completas* a nuestro idioma.

De la traducción realizada por el británico residente en nuestro país, Guillermo Macpherson, se puede decir que es el primer intento serio de traducción de esta obra. Para su trabajo traductor, Macpherson consulta tanto los *Quartos* de 1608 y 1619 como el *Folio* de 1623; es —por tanto— el primero que traduce directamente del inglés y el primero, también, en adaptarse al verso y prosa del original; su verso siempre es endecasílabo y, en ocasiones, difícil de leer teniendo —por lo general— estos parlamentos en verso, mayor número de líneas que el original que maneja. Sólo cuando Macpherson evita traducir algunos versos —debido a la censura, consecuencia de la Ley de Imprenta— hay coincidencia, en el número de los mismos, en los textos inglés y castellano.

De las traducciones llevadas a cabo en el siglo xx destacaremos en primer lugar la hecha en catalán por Albert Torrellas en 1908. Aunque está toda ella realizada en prosa, el traductor, a modo de prólogo comenta:

> Los diálogos que en el original inglés están escritos en verso, y que forman la mayor parte de esta obra, los hemos traducido en prosa rítmica creyendo, así, poder interpretar mejor las profundas escenas que la inspiración del poeta distinguió con el ritmo[1].

En 1911 Jacinto Benavente hace su traducción en prosa pensando, además de en «la elegancia literaria», en «el diálogo teatral» ya que como él mismo dice:

> Shakespeare era, no sólo autor dramático, sino lo que hoy se llama hombre de teatro[2].

La segunda, y hasta el momento, última traducción catalana de *King Lear,* es la realizada por el también bibliógrafo Anfós Par en 1912. De esta traducción en prosa habría que destacar su magnífica introducción, estudio de las fuentes, críticos ingleses, significación de los personajes, valor estético de la tragedia, etc., amén de un gran acopio de notas, convirtiéndose, por tanto, esta edición en un modelo de lo que podría suponer una traducción filológica, crítica y anotada.

En 1929 Luis Astrana Marín —único autor, hasta el mo-

---

[1] *El rei Lear,* traducción de Albert Torrellas al catalán, Barcelona, Estampa d'E. Domènech, 1908, pág. 7.

[2] *El rey Lear,* traducción de Jacinto Benavente, Madrid, La Lectura, 1911; reed. Barcelona, Éxito, 1960, pág. 362.

mento, que ha traducido la obra completa del dramaturgo inglés en nuestro idioma— publica su traducción de *El rey Lear* dentro de la colección *William Shakespeare. Obras Completas,* entre *La tragedia de Macbeth* y *Timón de Atenas* puesto que las presenta, según afirmación propia, en orden cronológico de creación:

> A nosotros nos ha parecido más racional colocar las obras por el orden en que fueron escritas[3],

haciendo este comentario en razón a que no sigue la tradición inglesa para este tipo de publicaciones, como es el caso del *Folio* de 1623, que divide la producción total shakespeariana en comedias, historias y tragedias.

La traducción de esta obra está en prosa —igual que el resto de sus traducciones, incluidos poemas y sonetos— puesto que él mismo apunta:

> Puede asegurarse que ninguna versión en verso es buena... La razón obedece a que unas veces la métrica y otras la rima impiden permanecer fieles al autor[4].

Sus traducciones tienen gran profusión de notas a pie de página tanto léxicas como de traducción, culturales, etc., haciendo hincapié en las alusiones de Shakespeare a todo lo español, donde —en esta obra— podríamos citar como ejemplo la palabra «carbonado» en II.ii.31-2:

> Draw, you rogue, or I'll so *carbonado* your shanks[5].

En 1967 José M. Valverde publica la producción dramática shakespeariana en *William Shakespeare. Teatro Completo,* colocando esta tragedia de *El rey Lear* entre *Othello, el moro de Venecia* y *Macbeth.* Al igual que Astrana Marín anteriormente, Val-

---

[3] Luis Astrana Marín, *William Shakespeare. Obras Completas,* Madrid, Aguilar, 1929, pág. 17.

[4] *Ibidem,* pág. 20.

[5] *King Lear,* editado por Kenneth Muir para la colección *The New Arden Shakespeare,* Londres, Methuen Co. Ltd., 1975, pág. 66.

verde tampoco sigue la tradición inglesa del *Folio* de 1623 para este tipo de publicaciones, sino que sigue la pauta marcada por el director de la colección *The Penguin Shakespeare,* G. B. Harrison. También Valverde traduce en prosa alegando que:

> ...Poner en verso el teatro completo de Shakespeare requeriría varias décadas de entrega total[6].

Además, cuando habla de la traducción en verso con respecto a la puesta en escena de las obras, comenta que:

> Si se hubiera tratado de traducir alguna obra para su representación teatral, habría considerado inexcusable la versificación —a no ser que previera, con pesimismo, que los actores iban a decir el verso como prosa, en cuyo caso tal trabajo estaría perdido[7]

por lo que deducimos, obviamente, que su trabajo no está pensado para la escena sino para un público lector.

En 1979 se constituye en la Universidad de Valencia, bajo la dirección del profesor Conejero, el Instituto Shakespeare, institución especializada en teatro isabelino y jacobino, teniendo entre uno de sus objetivos la traducción al castellano de las obras dramáticas shakespearianas.

Este mismo año de su fundación, traduce su primera obra: *El rey Lear.* Esta traducción, realizada en equipo, está hecha tanto en prosa como en verso ateniéndose —de esta forma— al original inglés y manteniendo el mismo número de líneas en los parlamentos que están en verso; si bien no nos extendemos más en las características propias de esta traducción, porque ya en otro apartado dentro de este mismo volumen se describen, con amplitud, las particularidades de esta edición. Hemos de resaltar, sin embargo, que al emprender su traducción, el equipo del Instituto Shakespeare siempre tiene en cuenta su «tea-

---

6 José M. Valverde, *William Shakespeare. Teatro Completo,* Barcelona, Planeta, 1967, 2 vols., vol. I, pág. XIII.
7 *Ibidem,* pág. XIII.

tralidad», y buena cuenta de ello es el éxito obtenido en la representación de esta obra, estrenada en el Teatro Principal de Valencia el 19 de noviembre de 1982 y dirigida por Miguel Narros, consiguiendo, como decíamos, una buena aceptación tanto de crítica como de público.

BIBLIOGRAFÍA

I. Ediciones de «King Lear»

a) *Ediciones facsímil*

Edición del *Quarto* de 1608, en la colección *Shakespeare Quarto Facsímiles*, dirigida por W. W. Greg y Charlton Hinman, Oxford, Clarendon Press, 1964.

Edición del *Quarto* de 1619, preparada por P. Daniel, Londres, Charles Praetorius, 1885.

Edición del *Folio* de 1623, en *The Norton Facsimile of the First Folio of Shakespeare*, preparado por C. Hinman, Nueva York, Norton and Company Inc., 1968.

b) *Otras ediciones*

Cambridge Shakespeare, Cambridge, W. G. Clark y W. A. Wright, 1866.

New Variorum, Filadelfia, H. H. Furness, 1880.

Clarendon Shakespeare, Oxford, W. A. Wright, 1886.

Arden Shakespeare, Londres, W. J. Craig, 1901.

New Arden Shakespeare, Londres, K. Muir, 1952; edición corregida y ampliada, 1972.

New Cambridge Shakespeare, Cambridge, G. I. Duthie y J. D. Wilson, 1960.

New Penguin Shakespeare, Harmondsworth, G. K. Hunter, 1972.

II. Fuentes, concordancias y glosarios

Bartlett, J., *A New and Complete Concordance or Verbal Index to ... the Dramatic Works of Shakespeare,* Londres, 1894; reimpresa en 1980.

BULLOUGH, G., *Narrative and Dramatic Sources of Shakespeare*, Londres, 1957-1975, 8 volúmenes.

COLMAN, E. A. M., *The Dramatic Use of Bawdy in Shakespeare*, Londres, 1974.

MUIR, K., *The sources of Shakespeare's Plays*, Londres, 1977.

ONIONS, C. T., *A Shakespeare Glossary*, Londres, 1911; revisada y ampliada en 1938.

PARTRIDGE, E., *Shakespeare's Bawdy*, Londres, 1947; revisada en 1968.

SCHMIDT, A., *Shakespeare-Lexicon*, Berlín y Leipzig, 1923; 3.ª edición revisada y ampliada por Gregor Sarrazin, Nueva York, 1971, 2 volúmenes.

SPEVACK, M., *A Complete and Systematic Concordance to the Works of Shakespeare*, Hildesheim, 1968-1980, 9 volúmenes.

III. ESTUDIOS CRÍTICOS SOBRE LAS TRAGEDIAS DE SHAKESPEARE

BAYLEY, J., *The Characters of Love*, Londres, 1960.

BRADBROOK, M. C., *Themes and Conventions of Elizabethan Tragedy*, Cambridge, 1935.

BRADLEY, A. C., *Shakespearian Tragedy*, Londres, 1904.

CAMPBELL, L. P., *Shakespeare's Tragic Heroes*, Londres, 1930; revisada en 1961.

CHARLTON, H. B., *Shakespearian Tragedy*, Cambridge, 1948.

CLEMEN, W. H., *The Development of Shakespeare's Imagery*, Londres, 1904.

COGHILL, N., *Shakespeare's Professional Skills*, Cambridge, 1964.

COLIE, R. L., *Shakespeare's Living Art*, Princeton, N. Y., 1974.

CONEJERO, M. A., *Eros adolescente. La construcción estética en Shakespeare*, Barcelona, 1982.

— *La escena, el sueño, la palabra. Apunte shakespeariano*, Valencia, 1983; 2.ª edición revisada en 1985.

CRANE, M., *Shakespeare's Prose*, Chicago, 1968.

EDWARDS, P., *Shakespeare and the Confines of Art*, Londres, 1968.

EMPSON, W., *The Structure of Complex Words*, Londres, 1951.

FLATTER, R., *Shakespeare's Producing Hand*, Londres, 1948.

FRYE, N., *Fools of Time*, Londres, 1967.

GRANVILLE-BARKER, H., *Prefaces to Shakespeare*, Londres, 1930; 2 volúmenes.

HAZLITT, W., *Character of Shakespeare's Plays*, Londres, 1980.

HOLLOWAY, J., *The Story of the Night*, Londres, 1962.

KNIGHT, G. W., *The Wheel of Fire*, Londres, 1930; revisada en 1949.

LAWLOR, J., *The Tragic Sense in Shakespeare*, Londres, 1960.
LEAVIS, F. R., *The Common Pursuit*, Londres, 1952.
LERNER, L. (ed.), *Shakespeare's Tragedies*, Harmondsworth, 1974.
MUIR, K., *The Great Tragedies*, Londres, 1961.
— *Shakespeare's Tragic Sequence*, Londres, 1972.
NERO, R., *Tragic Form in Shakespeare*, Princeton, 1972.
PÉREZ GÁLLEGO, C., *Dramática de Shakespeare*, Zaragoza, 1974.
— *El lenguaje escénico de Shakespeare*, Zaragoza, 1982.
RIBNER, I., *Patterns in Shakespearian Tragedy*, Londres, 1960.
SPIVACK, B., *Shakespeare and the Allegory of Evil*, Nueva York, 1958.
STEWART, J. I. M., *Character and Motive in Shakespeare*, Londres, 1949.
STIRLING, B., *Unity in Shakespearian Tragedy*, Nueva York, 1956.
STOLL, E. E., *Art and Artifice in Shakespeare*, Nueva York, 1933.
VICKERS, B., *Shakespeare. The Critical Heritage*, Londres, 1975.
WHITAKER, V. K., *The Mirror up to Nature*, San Marino, California, 1965.
WILSON, H. S., *On the Design of Shakespearian Tragedy*, Toronto, 1957.

IV. ESTUDIOS MONOGRÁFICOS SOBRE «KING LEAR»

ADELMAN, J. (ed.), *Twentieth Century Interpretations of King Lear*, Englewood, N. J., 1978.
BROOKE, N., *Shakespeare: King Lear*, Londres, 1963.
COLIE, R. L., *Some facets of King Lear. Essays in Prismatic Criticism*, Toronto, 1974.
CREIGHTON, C., *An Allegory of King Lear*, Londres, 1913.
DANBY, J. F., *Shakespeare's Doctrine of Nature. A Study of King Lear*, Londres, 1949.
DORAN, M., *The Text of King Lear*, Standford, California, 1931.
— «Command, Question and Assertion in *King Lear*», en *Shakespeare's Art*, Chicago y Londres, M. Crane, 1973.
ECCLES, M., *King Lear. An Outline-Guide to the Play*, Nueva York, 1965.
EGAN, R., *Drama within Drama: Shakespeare's Sense of his Art in «King Lear», «The Winter's Tale» and «The Tempest»*, Nueva York, 1975.
ELTON, W. R., *King Lear and the Gods*, San Marino, California, 1966.
FRASER, R. A., *Shakespeare's Poetics in Relation to King Lear*, Londres, 1962.
GOLDBERG, S. L., *An Essay on King Lear*, Londres, 1974.
GOLDSMITH, R. H., *Wise Fools in Shakespeare*, East Lansing, Mich. and Liverpool, 1955.
HOTSON, L., *Shakespeare's Motley*, Londres, 1952.

JORGENSEN, P., *Lear's Self-Discovery*, Berkeley, 1967.

KERMODE, F. (ed.), *Shakespeare, King Lear. A Casebook*, Londres, 1969.

KOTT, J., *Shakespeare Our Contemporary*, Londres, 1964.

KOZINTSEV, G., *King Lear. The Space of Tragedy*, Londres, 1977.

LOTHIAN, J. M., *King Lear, a Tragic Reading of Life*, Toronto, 1949.

MACK, M., *King Lear in Our Time*, Berkeley, 1972.

MUIR, E., *The Politics of King Lear*, Glasgow, 1947.

MUIR, K., «Madness in *King Lear*», en *Shakespeare Survey*, vol. 13, Cambridge, 1960.

— Y WELLS, S. (eds.), *Aspects of King Lear*, Cambridge, 1982.

NOWOTTNY, W. M. T., «Some Aspects of the Style of *King Lear*», en *Shakespeare Survey*, vol. 13, Cambridge, 1960.

ORWELL, G., «Lear, Tolstoy and the Fool», en *Selected Essays*, Londres, 1957.

PERRET, W., *The Story of King Lear from Geoffrey of Monmouth to Shakespeare*, Weimar, 1903.

REIBETANZ, J., *The Lear World: a study of «King Lear» in its dramatic context*, Toronto, 1977.

ROSENBERG, M., *The Masks of King Lear*, Berkeley, 1972.

SISSON, C. J., *Shakespeare's Tragic Justice*, Toronto, 1962.

SOMERVILLE, H., *Madness in Shakespearian Tragedy*, Londres, 1929.

SPEAIGHT, R., *Nature in Shakespearian Tragedy*, Londres, 1955.

SPENCER, T., *Shakespeare and the Nature of Man*, Cambridge, Mass., 1942.

STAMPFER, J., «The Catharsis of *King Lear*», en *Shakespeare Survey*, volumen 13, Cambridge, 1960.

WALTON, J. K., «Lear's Last Speech», en *Shakespeare Survey*, vol. 13, Cambridge, 1960.

WELSFORD, E., *The Fool*, Londres, 1935.

V. TRADUCCIONES ESPAÑOLAS

El rey Lear, traducción de Francisco Nacente, Barcelona, La enciclopedia ilustrada, 1872.

El rey Lear, traducción de Guillermo Macpherson, Madrid, Luis Navarro, ed., 1873.

El rey Lear, traducción de José M. Quadrado, Palma de Mallorca, «Museo Balear de Historia y Literatura, Ciencias y Artes», 1877.

El rey Lear, traducción de Cipriano Montoliu, Barcelona, Seguí, 1908.

El rei Lear, traducción al catalán de Albert Torrellas, Barcelona, Estampa d'E. Domènech, 1908.

El rey Lear, traducción de Jacinto Benavente, Madrid, La lectura, 1911.

El rei Lear, traducción al catalán de Anfós Par, Barcelona, Associació Wagneriana, 1912.

El rey Lear, traducción de Juan Bautista Enseñat, Barcelona, establecimiento tipográfico de Félix Costa, 1913.

El rey Lear, traducción de Rafael Martínez Lafuente, Valencia, Prometeo, 1915.

El rey Lear, traducción de Celso García Morán, Madrid, Imprenta del Asilo de Huérfanos del Sagrado Corazón de Jesús, 1921.

El rey Lear, traducción de Luis Astrana Marín, Madrid, Aguilar, 1929.

El rey Lear, traducción de Barroso Bonzón, Madrid, Ibéricas, 1934.

El rey Lear, traducción de Fernando Palacios Vera, Barcelona, G. P., 1957.

El rey Lear, traducción de José M. Valverde, Barcelona, Planeta, 1967.

El rey Lear, traducción de Enrique Chueca y Ramiro Pinilla, Bilbao, Moretón, 1973.

El rey Lear, traducción de Lelia Cisternas de Mínguez, Barcelona, Bruguera, 1976.

El rey Lear, traducción de Manuel Ángel Conejero, *et al.,* Valencia, Instituto Shakespeare, 1979.

M. VVilliam Shake-fpeare,

HIS

True Chronicle Hiftory of the life
and death of King *Lear*, and his
three Daughters.

VVith the vnfortunate life of E D G A R,
fonne and heire to the Earle of *Glocefter*, and
his fullen and affumed humour of T O M
of Bedlam .

*As it was plaid before the Kings Maiefty at White-Hall, vp-
pon S. Stephens night, in Chriftmas Hollidaies.*

By his Maiefties Seruants, playing vfually at the
Globe on the *Banck-fide.*

Printed for *Nathaniel Butter.*
1608.

Portada de la primera edición

EL REY LEAR

PERSONAJES

LEAR, el rey
FRANCE, el rey de Francia
BURGUNDY, duque de Borgoña
CORNWALL, esposo de Regan
ALBANY, esposo de Gonerill
KENT, conde
GLOUCESTER, conde
EDGAR, hijo de Gloucester
EDMUND, hijo bastardo de Gloucester
CURAN, un cortesano
OSWALD, mayordomo de Gonerill
VIEJO, criado de Gloucester
DOCTOR
BUFÓN
CAPITÁN, a las órdenes de Edmund
CABALLERO, a las órdenes de Cordelia
HERALDO
GONERILL ⎫
REGAN ⎬ hijas de Lear
CORDELIA ⎭
CABALLEROS, OFICIALES, MENSAJEROS, SOLDADOS Y SIRVIENTES

ACTO I

ESCENA PRIMERA*

(Entran KENT, GLOUCESTER *y* EDMUND.)

KENT

Creí que el rey apreciaba más al duque de Albany que a Cornwall.

GLOUCESTER

Así nos parecía. Pero ahora, con la escisión del reino, no es posible saber a cuál estima más, pues son sus méritos tan similares que ni la más atenta observación podría permitir la elección de uno u otro.

KENT

¿No es éste vuestro hijo, *my lord?*

---

* La escena primera podría dividirse en tres secciones: la primera de ellas (líneas 1-30) sirve de prólogo a la totalidad de la obra, y anuncia la escisión del reino por parte de Lear; en la segunda (líneas 31-277) se definen las tensiones dramáticas que se desarrollan, a lo largo de la tragedia, entre los distintos personajes; por último, en la tercera parte (278-300), las dos hijas, Gonerill y Regan, comienzan a mostrar sus verdaderas intenciones, en clara contradicción con lo expuesto ante el rey anteriormente.

1. *Albany.* Se designa con este nombre la zona que ocupa la parte septentrional de Inglaterra y oriental de Escocia; de ahí que algunos traductores designen a este personaje con el nombre de «Escocia».

[63]

GLOUCESTER

Al menos su crianza siempre estuvo a mi cargo. Me he avergonzado tan a menudo de reconocerle que ya me acostumbré.

KENT

No consigo entenderos.   10

GLOUCESTER

La madre de ese joven sí entendía; abombó su barriga, y antes tuvo, señor, hijo en la cuna que marido en el lecho. ¿Os parece muy mal?

KENT

¡Cómo querer no hecho lo ocurrido, siendo tan bueno el resultado!

GLOUCESTER

Pero tengo otro hijo legítimo y algo mayor que éste, no más querido, sin embargo. Y aunque este bribón viniera al mundo de manera imprevista antes de ser llamado, su madre, ciertamente, era hermosa; y, a fe mía, que holgamos con placer al procrearlo. El bastardo debe ser, pues, reconocido. ¿Conocéis   20
a este noble caballero, Edmund?

10-11. *No consigo entenderos... entendía.* En el original, «I cannot conceive you. GLOUC. Sir, this young fellow's mother could». El juego de palabras del texto inglés *(conceive-could)* se recoge en castellano empleando el verbo «entender» para transmitir el doble significado de «comprender» y «concebir». Este segundo sentido se logra empleando el mismo verbo en sustitución de *could* («podía»), que obliga a una lectura poco inocente del término.

20-1 *¿Conocéis a este noble caballero?* En el original, «Do you know this noble gentleman?» Los trabajos existentes sobre el empleo de «you» y «thou» todavía no han dado como resultado una sistematización clara. Su uso resulta tan indiscriminado en inglés como el «tú» y el «vos» castellanos, con que han sido traducidos con una voluntad estilística. Confiamos en que las nuevas líneas de investigación en curso, que utilizan como útil sistematizador del trabajo el procesador de datos, lleguen a resultados más definitivos.

EDMUND

No, *my lord.*

GLOUCESTER

Es mi señor de Kent. Consideradle, en adelante, mi honorable amigo.

EDMUND

Siempre el servicio de Vuestra Señoría.

KENT

Deberé estimaros y alcanzar a conoceros mejor.

EDMUND

Haré por merecerlo, sire.

GLOUCESTER

Nueve años de ausencia, y ha de partir de nuevo. Viene el rey.

(Trompas. Entran el rey LEAR, CORNWALL, ALBANY, GONERILL, REGAN, CORDELIA *y asistentes.)*

LEAR

Gloucester, atended a los señores de Francia y de Borgoña.

---

22. *my lord.* La traducción castellana recoge este tratamiento por su utilidad como punto de referencia del país donde se desarrolla la acción. Idéntica función tiene el mantenimiento de la forma «sire», próxima a *Sir* (línea 27).

28. *Trompas.* Acotación escénica, traducción del original *(Sennet),* que normalmente anunciaba la entrada o salida del escenario de personajes importantes en rango.

[65]

Sí, Majestad.   30

(Sale[n] [GLOUCESTER *y* EDMUND].)

LEAR

Desvelaremos, entretanto, el más penoso de nuestros proyectos.
Traednos ese mapa. Sabed que hemos dividido
nuestro reino en tres partes; y que es nuestro propósito
firme librarnos en nuestra vejez de toda carga y toda obligación,
y confiarlas a más jóvenes brazos, mientras nos, aliviado,
nos arrastramos a la muerte. Vos, nuestro hijo de Cornwall
y también vos, nuestro no menos querido hijo de Albany,
es nuestra firme voluntad en esta hora dar anuncio a la dote
de mis tres hijas, como prevención de futuras disputas.
Los príncipes de Francia y de Borgoña,   40
rivales en el amor de nuestra hija más pequeña,
han prolongado en nuestra corte su visita amorosa,

---

31. *el más penoso de nuestros proyectos.* En el original «our darker purpose» (lit.: *nuestro propósito más oscuro).* Se anuncia, en este momento, por parte del propio Lear —Gloucester lo había apuntado en las líneas 3-4 de este misma escena— la escisión del reino, que presenta uno de los temas centrales de la tragedia: la idea de renunciar por parte del rey, y, de ahí, la traducción. Véase al respecto, W. Empson, *The Structure of Complex Words,* pág. 127.

32-3. *Sabed... partes.* En el original, «Know that we have divided in three our kingdom». Su posible relación con la cita bíblica «Todo reino en sí dividido será desolado» *(Mateo,* 12, 25) probablemente sirviera de comentario irónico a la tragedia que se iniciaba. No resulta difícil encontrar, a lo largo de esta tragedia, referencias a diversos pasajes de la Biblia en los que se apoya el autor para la elaboración del discurso dramático. Así, en I.i. 245-6 podemos encontrar una referencia a *2 Corintios,* 6, 10; en I.ii. 100-2, otra a *Marcos* 13, 12-3; en I.iv. 258-61, otra a *Deuteronomio,* 28, 15-8, etc.

35-9. *mientras Nos... disputas.* Fragmento omitido en *Folio.*

39. *como prevención de futuras disputas;* en el original, «that future strife may be prevented now». La utilización del sustantivo «prevención», que reproduce fielmente la idea de la forma pasiva, verbo auxiliar y adverbio del original inglés, confiere una mayor naturalidad a la expresión en castellano, además de contribuir a la economía lingüística necesaria en el verso.

40. El ducado de Borgoña era políticamente independiente del reino de Francia.

y han de obtener una respuesta aquí. Decidnos, hijas mías,
cuando nos hemos despojado de nuestro poder,
de nuestras posesiones y las cargas de Estado,
quién nos ama más de vosotras, para que podamos
usar de una más grande generosidad
en quien los méritos con la Naturaleza rivalicen. Gonerill,
primógenita nuestra, hablad primero.

GONERILL

Señor, os amo más de lo que las palabras pueden expresar   50
y más que a vista, espacio, libertad,
más, muchísimo más que lo estimado, lo precioso, lo raro,
no menos que la vida, llena de dignidad, salud, belleza, honor,
tanto como jamás amó un hijo, o un padre fuese amado;
un amor que empobrece el aliento y debilita el habla,
os amo más allá de la forma de decir «muchísimo».

CORDELIA *[Aparte.]*

¿Qué ha de decir Cordelia? Ama y no digas nada.

LEAR

De todos estos confines, de esta línea a aquélla,
llenos de espesos bosques y campiñas,
de ríos caudalosos y praderas extensas   60
os proclamo señora. Y que así sea para los descendientes
de Albany y de vos. ¿Qué dice nuestra segunda hija,
nuestra querida Regan, desposada con Cornwall?

REGAN

Estoy hecha con los mismos metales que mi hermana
y en su medida me valoro. Mi corazón veraz

---

61. *Y que así sea para...;* en el original, «be this perpetual...» (lit.: *Sea esto perpe-
tuo...*). Esta fórmula en castellano recoge el tono solemne de las palabras de Lear
al entregar a sus hijas y descendientes una parte de su reino, al tiempo que comunica la misma idea de duración.

[67]

siente cómo ella expresa mi contrato de amor,
pero de modo leve: me declaro enemiga
de todos los placeres, que, en precioso conjunto,
poseen los sentidos;
tan sólo encuentro la felicidad   70
en el amor a Vuestra Alteza.

CORDELIA *[Aparte.]*

¡Pobre Cordelia, entonces!
Aunque no, ya que segura estoy de que mi amor
sobrepasa mi lengua.

LEAR

Para vos y los vuestros en herencia
quede por siempre este amplio tercio de nuestro hermoso reino,
no inferior en espacio, ni en valor, ni en provecho
al concedido a Gonerill. Y ahora, gozo nuestro,
nuestra última hija y más pequeña, cuyo amor juvenil
enfrenta, interesados, los pastos de Borgoña
y las vides de Francia, ¿qué haréis para obtener   80
un tercio más valioso que el de vuestras hermanas?
¿Qué tenéis que decir?

CORDELIA

Nada, *my lord*.

LEAR

¿Nada?

---

79. *los pastos de Borgoña;* en el original, «the milk of Burgundy» (lit.: *la leche de Borgoña*). El término inglés *milk* sirve para designar la fertilidad de la tierra de Borgoña, famosa por la calidad de su ganado y de *los pastos*. Este efecto no se consigue en castellano con la palabra «leche», especialmente en un texto teatral, y de ahí la traducción.
83-4. Estas dos líneas, que no aparecen en *Quarto,* son de gran importancia, sin embargo, por su efecto dramático.

CORDELIA

Nada.

LEAR

Nada obtendréis de nada. Hablad de nuevo.

CORDELIA

Infeliz como soy, no consigo elevar
mi corazón hasta mis labios. Conforme a nuestro vínculo
os amo, Majestad, no más, no menos.

LEAR

¿Cómo, Cordelia? Cuidad lo que decís,
o arriesgaréis vuestra fortuna.

CORDELIA

                 Mi señor,   90
vos me habéis engendrado, y criado, y amado,
y en la misma medida os correspondo,
os obedezco y amo y, sobre todo, os honro.
¿Por qué se desposaron mis hermanas cuando dicen
que os aman sólo a vos? Si tomara marido
el señor cuya mano asumiese mi emblema llevaría con él
la mitad de mi amor, y deber, y cuidados.

91-2. *engendrado, y criado, y amado.* En el original, «You have begot me, bred me, lov'd me». La repetición de *me*, en inglés, es sustituida en la traducción por la repetición de la conjunción copulativa «y», que produce el mismo efecto de intensidad emotiva, y resulta más natural y breve en la lengua castellana que la repetición del pronombre y del verbo auxiliar en cada caso. En la línea 93 una situación similar se resuelve de forma parecida, y el original, «Obey you, love you, and most honour you», es una sucesión de formas verbales que contiene ecos del «Marriage Service», en el *Prayer Book*— «Wilt thou obey him, love, honour, and keep him...»—, que preparan la comparación con los deberes conyugales.

97. *mi amor, y deber, y cuidados.* En el original, «Half my love with him, half

Cierto es que nunca me desposaré, como mis dos hermanas,
para poder amar solamente a mi padre.

LEAR

¿Es eso lo que dice vuestro corazón?

CORDELIA

Sí, mi señor.   100

LEAR

¿Tan joven y tan dura?

CORDELIA

Tan joven, mi señor, y tan sincera.

LEAR

¡Qué la sinceridad sea, pues, vuestra dote!
Porque, por el sagrado resplandor del sol,
por los misterios de Hécate y la noche,
por toda la influencia de los astros
que nos dan la existencia y nos la quitan
renuncio a todo parentesco, afinidad
de sangre o cualquier otra paterna obligación
y os tendré siempre como extraña   110
para mi corazón y para mí. El bárbaro de Escitia
o aquel que de su prole hace alimento

---

my care and duty». Como en las líneas 91-2, la repetición de la conjunción «y»
sustituye la de otros elementos —*half,* en este caso—, que en castellano resultaría excesivamente artificial.

   99. Este verso está omitido en *Folio.*
   105. Hécate, identificada con la luna, era considerada divinidad infernal y
protectora de brujas. Así aparece, por ejemplo, en *Macbeth,* III.v.
   111. *Escitia* era el nombre que recibía una antigua región que se extendía a
lo largo de gran parte de Europa y la Rusia asiática.

con que saciar su hambre, encontrarán en mí
tanto consuelo, compasión y lástima.
como ahora vos, hija, en otro tiempo mía.

KENT

Majestad...

LEAR

¡Silencio, Kent! No os interpongáis
entre el dragón y su ira.
A nadie quise como a ella, y a sus dulces cuidados
pensaba confiarle mi vejez. ¡Fuera de aquí!
Sea mi paz la tumba, como ahora le niega   120
mi corazón de padre. ¡Llamad a France! ¡Moveos!
¡Llamad a Burgundy! Y vos, Albany, y Cornwall,
unid a la dote de mis hijas mayores la de la tercera.
Que la case el orgullo que ella llama franqueza.
A ambos os invisto de mi autoridad,
de mi poder y de todos aquellos atributos
propios de la realeza. Nos, cada treinta días,
reservándonos a vuestro cargo un centenar de caballeros,
residiremos con vosotros, alternativamente.
Tan sólo retendremos el nombre y todo aquello   130
que comporta el ser rey; las rentas, el poder
y el gobierno de todo lo demás
sean vuestros, hijos míos; y, para confirmarlo,
dividid esta corona entre los dos.

KENT

Mi noble Lear,
a quien siempre he honrado como rey,

113-4. *consuelo, compasión y lástima.* En el original, «Shall to my bosom / Be as
well neighbour'd, pitied and reliev'ticipios ingleses por una serie de sustantivos,
más aptos en castellano para la expresión poética por evitar la monotonía de sus
terminaciones, y permitir una mayor variedad de acentos.

he amado como a un padre, seguí como a señor,
invoqué en mis plegarias como mi gran patrón...

LEAR

El arco está curvado y tenso; rehuid la flecha.

KENT

Pues venga, disparadla, que su punta penetre
por el lugar del corazón. Sea Kent descortés   140
si Lear está loco. ¿Qué vas a hacer, anciano?
¿Piensas acaso que el deber tiene miedo de hablar
cuando el poder se inclina ante la adulación? El honor se
                                   [somete a la sinceridad
cuando la realeza sucumbe a la locura. Mantente en el poder
y a tu más honda consideración somete
este arrebato sin sentido. Respondo de mi juicio con la vida,
tu hija menor no es la que te ama menos,
ni vacíos están los corazones de aquellos que en voz baja
no hacen sonar la hipocresía.

LEAR

¡Basta, Kent, por tu vida!

KENT

Mi vida nunca fue sino un peón   150
jugado en contra de tus enemigos; nunca temí perderla
si era el motivo tu seguridad.

---

141. *¿Qué vas a hacer, anciano?* En el original, «What wouldst thou do old
man?» Véase la nota a la línea 20-1 de esta misma escena, y nótese el empleo de
la forma *thou* —traducida como «tú»—, normalmente reservada para el tratamiento informal, y excepcionalmente insólito, por tanto, para dirigirse a un rey.
En este caso su empleo por parte de Kent parece deliberado para provocar la
reacción del rey, y lograr que vea el alcance de su decisión. Además de estas razones de tipo semántico, se ha tenido en cuenta la naturaleza teatral de la obra,
que determina, igualmente, la elección de palabras y fórmulas escénicamente

LEAR

¡No soporto mirarte!

KENT

Pues mírame bien, Lear, y déjame que sea
el verdadero blanco de tus ojos.

LEAR

¡Por Apolo!

KENT

Por Apolo, rey,
en vano invocas a tus dioses.

LEAR

¡Villano, renegado!

ALBANY y CORNWALL

Conteneos, señor.

KENT

Mata a quienes te curan, y a la podrida enfermedad
paga tributo. Retráctate en tu decisión,
si no, mientras haya un clamor en mi garganta,   160
dirá que haces mal.

---

eficaces. El empleo de «tú» es insustituible para transmitir la emoción dramática
en un pasaje como éste.

152-3. *¡No soporto mirarte!* En el original, «Out of my sight!» (lit.: *¡Fuera de mi
vista!*) Se intenta mantener en la traducción el juego que plantea el original con
sight («vista», «mirada»), *see* («ver», «mirar»), y *blank of thine eye* («blanco de tus
ojos», pero también —en el caso de *blank*— «blanco de la diana»).

157. Esta intervención al unísono de Albany y Cornwall no aparece en
Quarto.

[73]

¡Escucha, renegado,
por la obediencia que me debes, escúchame!
Has intentado que rompiésemos un juramento,
algo que Nos jamás hubiésemos osado,
y tu exceso de orgullo te lleva a interponerte
entre nuestras sentencias y nuestro poder,
lo que ni rango ni naturaleza pueden tolerar;
y en ejercicio de la autoridad toma tu premio:
te concedemos cinco días para prepararte
contra las inclemencias de este mundo,   170
y cuando llegue el sexto vuelve tu odiada espalda a nuestro reino.
Si luego de diez días, en nuestro territorio se encontrase
tu cuerpo desterrado, en ese instante morirás.
¡Márchate ya, por Júpiter! Esto no, nunca se revocará.

Kent

Buena suerte, mi rey, si así quieres mostrarte;
la libertad vive fuera y el destierro aquí.

(A Cordelia.*)*

Que los dioses te tomen bajo su protección, doncella
que piensas en justicia y hablas con verdad,

(A Gonerill *y* Regan.*)*

y que vuestras acciones confirmen cuanto habláis,
que algo bueno resulte de palabras de amor.   180
De esta manera, oh príncipes, Kent os dice hasta nunca;
seguirá en tierra nueva su viejo caminar.

(Sale.)

(Trompas. Entra GLOUCESTER *con* FRANCE, BURGUNDY
y asistentes.)

GLOUCESTER

He aquí al rey de Francia y al duque de Borgoña, mi señor.

LEAR

Mi señor de Borgoña,
a vos nos dirigimos en primer lugar,
ya que con este rey por nuestra hija habéis rivalizado,
¿qué mínima dote, a más de ella, exigiríais ahora?
¿O retiráis vuestra propuesta?

BURGUNDY

Majestad realísima,
no pido más de lo que Vuestra Alteza ya ha ofrecido,
ni creo que vos ofrezcáis menos.

LEAR

Mi muy noble Burgundy,   190
cuando era cara para nos en eso la estimábamos,
ahora su valor ha decaído. Sire, ahí la tenéis;
si algo en esta sustancia pequeña y aparente
o todo en ella, añadiéndole ahora nuestro disfavor,
y nada más, puede adecuadamente conveniros,
ahí la tenéis, es vuestra.

BURGUNDY

No sé qué responder.

---

183. En *Folio*, y en algunas ediciones del siglo XVIII —como las de Rowe y
Pope—, este verso se le asigna a Cornwall.

191. *cuando era cara para nos.* En el original, «when she was dear to us». Es interesante la coincidencia de la doble acepción de los términos *dear* y «cara», en
inglés y en castellano respectivamente, que hacen referencia a algo económica-
mente valioso y afectivamente querido, al mismo tiempo.

Con las imperfecciones que posee, y sin amigos,
recién llegada a nuestro odio, y extrañada
por nuestra expresa voluntad, con nuestra maldición por toda
[dote,
¿queréis tomarla, o la dejáis?

BURGUNDY

Pedonadme, señor,   200
la elección no es posible en tales condiciones.

LEAR

Sire, dejadla entonces; por el poder mismo que me hizo
ya he enumerado todas sus riquezas. En cuanto a vos, gran rey,
nunca traicionaría vuestro amor uniéndoos a quien detesto;
así pues, os suplico desviéis vuestra estima
a un camino más digno que éste, innoble,
que la naturaleza se avergüenza de reconocer
como suyo.

FRANCE

Es extraño
que quien hasta hace poco fuese la preferida,

197-200. *Con las imperfecciones... dejarla?* En el original, «Will you with those
infirmities she owes, / Unfriended, new-adopted to our hate, / Dowered with
our curse and strangered with our oath, / Take her or leave her?» En estos versos, como en otras ocasiones, se ha modificado ligeramente el orden de los elementos para recrear cualidades del texto original, como el paralelismo, motiva-
do por la existencia de verbos cuya traducción castellana exige el empleo de perífrasis. De ahí que el paralelismo que presentan los participios ingleses
unfriended, new-adopted se recree, en castellano, mediante «y sin amigos», «y extrañada», situados al final de dos versos sucesivos. El encabalgamiento que se produce al situar «y extrañada» —que rima con «llegada» en la misma línea—
al final del verso obliga a la transposición de los elementos del verso siguiente.
208. *Es extraño.* En el original, «This is most strange». En castellano, y en el
contexto de este discurso de tono grave, resulta más adecuado emplear el adjeti-

Escena de *Rey Lear* (grabado de J. H. Füssli)

objeto de alabanza y bálsamo de la vejez,
la mejor y más cara, pudiera cometer en un instante
una falta tan grave que se la despojara del favor.
Seguramente su ofensa es a tal punto desnaturalizada
que se convierte en monstruosa,
o el afecto que le declarabais
cae ahora en descrédito. Creer esto de ella
supone tanta fe que mi razón sin un milagro
no lo aceptaría.

CORDELIA

    Sin embargo, aún imploro a Vuestra Majestad
(si carezco del arte untuoso, escurridizo,
de hablar sin un propósito, ya que lo que pretendo   220
lo hago antes de decirlo) que todo el mundo sepa
que no es infame mancha, crimen o maldad,
ni acción impura ni paso deshonroso
lo que me priva de vuestro favor y vuestra gracia;
lo que me hace más rica es, al contrario,
lo que no tengo, una solícita mirada
y una lengua tal que soy feliz de no tenerla, aunque por ello
haya perdido vuestra estimación.

LEAR

    Más te valiera
no haber nacido si no sabes complacerme mejor.

FRANCE

¿Y no es más que esto, un recato instintivo   230
que con frecuencia ni menciona
lo que es de hecho su intención?

---

vo «extraño», desprovisto del adverbio «muy», que debilitaría el tono. Además,
la fórmula elegida contiene el mismo número de sílabas —cuatro— que en
inglés, recayendo el acento sobre la sílaba más importante, la tercera en ambos
casos.

Mi señor de Borgoña, ¿qué decís a la dama?
El amor no es amor cuando se mezcla
con lo que le es ajeno. ¿La queréis?
Ella misma es su dote.

BURGUNDY

Egregio Lear,
dad siquiera la dote que vos habéis propuesto
y de inmediato tomaré la mano de Cordelia,
duquesa de Borgoña.

LEAR

¡Nada! Ya lo he jurado; y soy inamovible.   240

BURGUNDY

Siento que por haber perdido un padre
debáis perder marido.

CORDELIA

¡Quede Burgundy en paz!
Puesto que el rango y la fortuna son su amor,
yo no seré su esposa.

FRANCE

Bella Cordelia, que eres la más rica siendo pobre;
la más valiosa, rechazada; la más amada en menosprecio,
y a ti y a tus virtudes hago mías.
Sea lícito acoger lo que se ha despreciado.
¡Oh, dioses, dioses! Es extraño que del frío desprecio
mi amor se encienda con respeto ardiente.   250
Vuestra desheredada hija, rey, abandonada a mi destino,
es reina nuestra, de los nuestros y de la hermosa Francia.

_____

245-6. Véase la nota a las líneas 32-3 de esta misma escena.

Ni todos los duques de la húmeda Borgoña
podrán comprar a mi doncella, despreciada, preciosa.
Despídete, Cordelia, aunque desnaturalizados sean.
Has perdido un aquí por un dónde mejor.

LEAR

Tomadla, France; es vuestra, puesto que nosotros
no tenemos tal hija, ni hemos de ver
ese rostro de nuevo.
¡Marchaos, pues, sin nuestra gracia, amor ni bendición!   260
Venid, mi noble Burgundy.

(Trompas. Salen LEAR, BURGUNDY, CORNWALL, ALBANY,
GLOUCESTER *y asistentes.)*

FRANCE

Despídete de tus hermanas.

CORDELIA

Joyas de nuestro padre, Cordelia os abandona
lavada por las lágrimas: yo ya sé lo que sois;
y me repugna, como hermana, llamar a esos defectos
por su nombre. ¡Amad a nuestro padre!
A vuestro declarado cariño os lo confío.
Pero, ¡ay!, si yo contara con su amor,
en un mejor cobijo lo tendría.
Así, de ambas me despido.   270

---

254. *despreciada, preciosa;* en el original, «unprized, precious». Se trata de uno
de los casos afortunados en que ha sido posible elegir en castellano dos palabras
que reprodujeran la semejanza fónica y la diferencia semántica del inglés.

255. *desnaturalizados;* en el original, «unkind». Stanton opina que Shakespeare
utilizó el término *unkinn'd,* es decir, «forsaken by thy kindred» *(abandonado por los
de tu especie);* de ahí, la traducción «desnaturalizados», que recoge la idea de rechazo antinatural por parte de los suyos.

REGAN

No nos señales nuestra obligación.

GONERILL

Concentra tus esfuerzos
en darle gusto a tu señor, que te ha acogido
como limosna de fortuna. Has sido de obediencia escasa
y mereces la pérdida de lo que has perdido.

CORDELIA

El tiempo desenmascarará lo que la astucia oculta;
la vergüenza al fin burla a quien faltas encubre.
Que podáis prosperar.

FRANCE

Ven, mi hermosa Cordelia.

(Sale[n] FRANCE y CORDELIA.)

GONERILL

Hermana, no es poco lo que he de decir de lo que a las dos nos
atañe tan de cerca. Creo que nuestro padre se marcha esta
noche.   280

REGAN

Es bien cierto, con vos; conmigo, el mes siguiente.

---

271. En *Quarto*, esta frase de Regan es atribuida a Gonerill y, por tanto, el
siguiente parlamento de ésta se le asigna a Regan.

274. *La pérdida de lo que has perdido;* en el original, «the want that you have
wanted». Se mantiene en la traducción la misma ambigüedad semántica del inglés, conservando la relación morfológica y fonética de los dos términos. La
«pérdida» probablemente haga referencia al afecto paterno y a los bienes que no
ha recibido, y el participio «perdido» a su propio afecto hacia su padre tanto
como a la herencia que éste le ha negado.

GONERILL

Ved cuán llena de capricho está su ancianidad. De ello no es
poca la experiencia que tenemos. Siempre amó más a nuestra
hermana; y el poco juicio con que la ha desterrado ahora resulta demasiado evidente.

REGAN

Ese es un mal de la vejez. Aunque nunca se ha conocido a sí
mismo sino de forma superficial.

GONERILL

Ya la época de su mayor plenitud y fuerza fue también de arrebatos; así pues, hemos de esperar recibir de su vejez no sólo las
imperfecciones de sus hábitos, hace tiempo arraigados, sino 290
también la obstinación desenfrenada que los años de enfermedad y cólera traen consigo.

REGAN

Habremos de esperar de él arranques caprichosos como el destierro de Kent.

GONERILL

Queda todavía su ceremonia de despedida con el rey de Francia; os lo ruego, actuemos de acuerdo; si nuestro padre ejerce
su autoridad en la disposición en que se halla, esta última ce-
sión suya no será sino para nuestra ofensa.

REGAN

Aún habremos de considerarlo.

GONERILL

Debemos hacer algo, y en caliente.   300

(Salen.)

[82]

ESCENA SEGUNDA*

(Entra el bastardo [EDMUND].)

BASTARDO [EDMUND]

¡Naturaleza, eres mi diosa! A tu ley mis servicios
se consagran. ¿Por qué habría yo de soportar el yugo
de la costumbre y permitir que el mundo
con su arbitrariedad me desherede, y sólo por tener
doce o catorce lunas menos que mi hermano?
¿Por qué innoble o bastardo, cuando mis proporciones
son armoniosas, noble mi intención, legítima mi forma
como si fuese el hijo de una mujer honrada?
¿Por qué se nos señala como innobles, o viles?
¿Por qué como bastardos? ¿Por qué como ilegítimos   10
a quienes obtuvimos de la furtiva lascivia de la Naturaleza
mas gallardía e ímpetu que el que en un lecho insípido,
tedioso y duro sirve para procrear
una tribu de necios, engendrados
entre sueño y vigilia? Bien, legítimo Edgar,
poseeré tu patrimonio.

---

* El argumento paralelo *(sub-plot)* de la tragedia aparece expuesto en esta escena en la que destaca el personaje de Edmund, sobre todo por medio de sus monólogos, evidentes por cuanto son los únicos fragmentos en verso de toda la escena, con el valor dramático que esto les confiere.

1. La invocación a la Naturaleza, por parte de Edmund, debe ser contrastada con la consideración que de ella hacen Lear y otros personajes, en la escena precedente; y que suponen uno de los elementos de la dialéctica del drama: Naturaleza, como instinto controlado, frente a Naturaleza, como orden universal predispuesto por Dios (o los dioses).

4. *arbitrariedad;* en el original, «curiosity». Obsérvese cómo, en contextos diferentes, la misma palabra requiere diferentes traducciones, tal y como ya se indicaba en la introducción, en el apartado referido a la traducción. En este caso, *curiosity* es explicada, en los diccionarios y glosarios especializados, como *fastidiousness,* y de ahí su traducción. En I.i.5, sin embargo, esta misma palabra —que significaría en ese contexto *exactness, scrupulousness*— ha sido traducida por «atenta observación»; en I.iv.59 —en el mismo contexto, pero acompañada del adjetivo *jalous*— se ha traducido por «susceptibilidad».

El amor de nuestro padre es del bastardo Edmund
tanto como lo es de su hijo legítimo. ¡Qué graciosa palabra,
                                        [su «legítimo»!
Pues muy bien, mi «legítimo», si esta carta llega
y prospera mi ardid   20
el bastardo Edmund suplantará al legítimo.
Crezco, prospero. ¡Oh, dioses, en pie con los bastardos!

(Entra GLOUCESTER.)

GLOUCESTER

¿Kent al destierro así? ¡Y France partió encolerizado!
¿Y el rey se fue esta noche, renunciando al poder,
relegado a una renta, y todo en un momento?
Bien, Edmund, ¿qué hay de nuevo?

[EDMUND]

Nada, si eso os complace, señoría.

GLOUCESTER

¿Y por qué con tanto empeño ocultas esa carta?

[EDMUND]

No sé de nueva alguna, mi señor.

GLOUCESTER

¿Qué es eso que leíais?   30

[EDMUND]

Nada, *my lord.*

GLOUCESTER

¿No? ¿Y qué era entonces eso que necesitaba ser ocultado tan celosamente en el bolsillo? Lo que es nada no tiene por qué ser ocultado. ¡Veamos! ¡Mostrad! No me harán falta lentes si de nada se trata.

[EDMUND]

Sire, os lo ruego, perdonadme. Es una carta de mi hermano que no he acabado de leer; y, por lo que he apreciado hasta ahora, no creo conveniente que la veáis.

GLOUCESTER

Dadme la carta, sire.

[EDMUND]

Ofenderé tanto si la retengo como si la doy. Lo escrito, a lo 40 que entiendo, es censurable.

GLOUCESTER

¡Venga, pues, y veamos!

[EDMUND]

Espero, por el bien de mi hermano, que escribiera esto como ensayo para comprobación de mi virtud.

GLOUCESTER

(Lee.)

> *Esta política, de respetar la edad, amarga la existencia de nues-*
> *tros mejores años, y nos sustrae de nuestras fortunas hasta que*
> *nuestra vejez no puede disfrutarlas. Empiezo a ver una inútil y*
> *absurda servidumbre en la opresión de la vieja tiranía, que nos*

domina, no porque tenga poder, sino porque la sufrimos. Ven
hasta mí para que pueda hablarte más de esto. Si nuestro padre 50
durmiera hasta que yo lo despertase, disfrutarías para siempre
de la mitad de su renta. Y serías el bien amado de tu hermano.

Edgar.

¡Conspiración! «...durmiera hasta que yo lo despertase», «...dis-
frutarías de la mitad de su renta...» ¡Mi hijo Edgar! ¿Pudo su
mano escribir eso? ¿Concebirlo su corazón y su mente? ¿Cuándo os ha llegado? ¿Quién la trajo?

[EDMUND]

No me ha sido traída, mi señor. He ahí la astucia. La encontré
en la ventana de mi gabinete.

GLOUCESTER

¿Reconocéis la letra como de vuestro hermano?

[EDMUND]

Si el contenido fuese bueno, *my lord*, me atrevería a jurar que lo 60
es; pero visto el mismo me gustaría creer que no lo es.

GLOUCESTER

¡Es suya!

[EDMUND]

Es de su mano, *my lord;* espero que su corazón no esté en su
contenido.

GLOUCESTER

¿Y nunca antes habíais hablado sobre esto?

[86]

[EDMUND] .

Nunca, *my lord*. Mas le he oído a menudo defender que es justo, cuando los hijos maduran y declinan los padres, que el padre debiese ser pupilo de su hijo, y el hijo administrar sus bienes.

GLOUCESTER

¡Ah, malvado, malvado! Lo mismo que en su carta. ¡Malvado 70 repugnante! Desnaturalizado, malvado, detestable y embrutecido. Más que embrutecido. ¡Id, sire! ¡Buscadlo! Haré que lo detengan. Execrable malvado. ¿Dónde anda?

[EDMUND]

No estoy seguro, *my lord*. Si quisierais guardar vuestra indignación contra mi hermano hasta que de él podáis obtener un mejor testimonio de sus intenciones, seguiríais un camino justo; pero si procedéis con violencia contra él, equivocando su intención, se abriría una gran brecha en vuestro propio honor, y haría pedazos en lo más profundo su obediencia. Apostaría mi vida a que esto fue escrito para probar mi afecto hacia vos. 80 Y sin otro propósito de mal.

GLOUCESTER

¿Eso pensáis?

[EDMUND]

Si Vuestra Señoría lo juzga conveniente os situaré donde podáis oírnos conversar sobre ello y vuestros propios oídos os convencerán; y esto, sin más demora, para esta misma tarde.

GLOUCESTER

No puede ser tan monstruoso...

[EDMUND]

Y no lo es, seguro.

GLOUCESTER

...con un padre que lo ama tan tierna y plenamente. Por la tierra y el cielo, Edmund, traédmelo. Sonsacadle, os lo ruego.
Conducid este asunto según vuestro criterio. Renunciaría a mi 90
rango por disipar mis dudas.

[EDMUND]

Sire, lo buscaré de inmediato, llevaré el asunto con la cautela
que los medios permitan, y os lo haré saber.

GLOUCESTER

Estos recientes eclipses en el sol y la luna no nos anuncian
ningún bien. Aunque la sabiduría del instinto pueda razonarlo
de una forma u otra, la naturaleza misma se encuentra azotada
por los efectos que le siguen. El amor se enfría, la amistad
cesa, se enfrentan los hermanos. Motín en las ciudades; en los
campos, discordia; en los palacios, traición; y el vínculo se
rompe entre el hijo y el padre. Ese miserable confirma la pre- 100
dicción: he ahí el hijo contra el padre; el rey se aparta de la vía
natural: he ahí el padre contra el hijo. Hemos visto pasar lo
mejor de los años. Intrigas y traición y todos los desórdenes
perniciosos nos siguen turbulentos hasta nuestra tumba. En-
contrad a ese villano, Edmund; no perderéis nada, hacedlo con
cautela. ¡Y el noble y sincero Kent desterrado! ¡Su culpa, la
honradez! ¡Extraño!

(Sale.)

---

94. Es este uno de los datos que nos permiten aproximarnos a la fecha probable de composición de la tragedia. Gloucester parece referirse a los eclipses
acaecidos en septiembre y octubre de 1605, de luna y sol, respectivamente.
Véase el apartado «Las fuentes de *King Lear*», en la Introducción.
100-4. *Este miserable... nuestra tumba*. Este fragmento no aparece en *Quarto*.
100-2. Véase la nota a I.i.32-3.

[EDMUND]

Es la suprema estupidez del mundo que cuando enfermos de
fortuna, muy a menudo por los excesos de nuestra conducta,
culpemos de nuestras desgracias al sol, la luna y las estrellas; 110
como si fuéramos malvados por necesidad; necios por exigencia de los cielos; truhanes, ladrones y traidores por el influjo de
las esferas; borrachos, embusteros y adúlteros por obediencia
forzosa a la influencia planetaria, y cuanto hay de mal en nosotros fuese una imposición divina. Qué admirable la excusa del
hombre putañero, poner su sátira disposición a cuenta de los
astros. Mi padre holgaba con mi madre bajo la cola del Dragón
y fui a nacer bajo la Osa Mayor, de lo que se deduce que soy
violento y lujurioso, ¡bah! Habría sido lo que soy, aunque la es-
trella más virginal del firmamento hubiera centelleado mien- 120
tras me hacían bastardo. Edgar...

(Entra EDGAR.*)*

...llega oportuno, como la catástrofe en
la comedia antigua. Mi parte es la perversa melancolía, con
suspiros como de Tom de Bedlam. ¡Oh! Los eclipses auguran
estas disonancias: Fa, sol, la, mi.

EDGAR

¿Cómo os va, Edmund, hermano? ¿En qué profunda medita-
ción os encontráis?

---

117. *La cola del dragón.* En astrología, se conoce así a la intersección entre las
órbitas del sol y la luna, considerada como signo infausto, ya que Marte y Venus ejercen su influencia, dando lugar a un temperamento violento y lascivo.
Chaucer, en *A Treatise on the Astrolabe,* II.4, incluía la cola del dragón entre los
que él llamaba *wicked planets* (planetas malignos o dañinos).
123. *Tom de Bedlam;* en el original, «Tom o'Bedlam» (es decir, «Tom of Bethlehem»). Era éste el nombre genérico dado a los locos que pedían limosna, por
cuanto Bethlehem era el nombre del manicomio de Londres. Se alude a *Tom of
Bedlam* —también conocido como *Abraham man*— en Audeley, *Fraternitye of
Vagabondes,* 1565 (ed. 1880, pág. I), y en Jonson, *The Devil is an Ass,* V.ii.35, entre otros.

[EDMUND]

Pensaba, hermano, en una predicción que leí el otro día acerca
de lo que seguiría a estos eclipses.

EDGAR

¿Os ocupáis en esas cosas?

[EDMUND]

Os lo aseguro, los efectos que narra desgraciadamente suce- 130
den: las aberraciones entre padres e hijos; muerte, penuria,
ruptura de viejas amistades; divisiones en el Estado; amenazas
y calumnias contra el rey y sus nobles; sospechas infundadas;
destierro de amigos; disolución de ejércitos; divorcios y no sé
qué más cosas.

EDGAR

¿Desde cuándo sois partidario de la astrología?

[EDMUND]

¿Cuánto visteis a mi padre por última vez?

EDGAR

Ayer noche.

[EDMUND]

¿Hablasteis con él?

131-6. *Las aberraciones... astrología?* Este fragmento aparece omitido en *Folio*.
Ha sido considerado espúreo por cierto sector de la crítica, puesto que sólo aparece en la edición *in Quarto*, y contiene seis palabras que Shakespeare utiliza
únicamente este caso: *unnaturalness* (aberraciones), *menace* (amenazas), *malediction*
(calumnias), *dissipation* (disolución), *cohort* (ejércitos), y *astronomical* (de la astrología).

EDGAR

Sí, dos horas seguidas.   140

[EDMUND]

¿Os separasteis de buen grado? ¿No percibisteis enojo en sus
palabras o ademanes?

EDGAR

No, en absoluto.

[EDMUND]

Considerad, entonces, dónde está vuestra ofensa y os ruego
que evitéis su presencia durante un cierto tiempo, hasta que se
haya mitigado el furor de su enojo, que en este instante tanto
arde que con la violencia hacia vuestra persona no podría cal-
marse.

EDGAR

Algún villano me difama.

[EDMUND]

Eso temo. Os ruego que mantengáis una prudente distancia 150
hasta que el ímpetu de su furor decrezca; y seguid mi consejo:
retiraos a mis aposentos, desde donde, oportunamente, podréis
oír hablar a mi señor. Id, os lo ruego. Tomad la llave. Si hubie-
rais de salir, llevad armas con vos.

EDGAR

¿Armas, hermano?

144-55. *«Os ruego... hermano?»* Este fragmento no aparece en *Quarto*.

[EDMUND]

Hermano, os aconsejo lo mejor. Que no sería yo hombre honrado si no tuviese buenas intenciones hacia vos. Os he dicho lo
que he visto y oído pero someramente, no con su imagen y su
horror. Os lo ruego, marchaos.

EDGAR

¿Sabré pronto de vos?

160

[EDMUND]

Estoy a vuestro lado en este asunto.

(Sale EDGAR.)

Un padre crédulo y un noble hermano,
cuya naturaleza está tan lejos de hacer mal
que no sospecha nada, y sobre cuya necia honestidad
cabalgan mis intrigas libremente. Ya veo la jugada;
obtenga tierras yo por el ingenio, que no por nacimiento;
todo bueno será si puedo conformarlo a mi deseo.

(Sale.)

ESCENA TERCERA*

(Entran GONERILL y mayordomo [OSWALD].)

GONERILL

¿Ha golpeado mi padre a uno de mis caballeros por increpar a
su bufón?

----

* Esta escena que se sitúa en el castillo de Gonerill —que debe alojar a Lear
y a sus seguidores, tras la división del reino— enlazaría dramáticamente con el
final de la escena primera, mostrando las verdaderas intenciones de ambas hermanas.

[92]

Mayordomo [Oswald]

Sí, *madam*.

Gonerill

Me ofende día y noche; a todas horas
viene con un ... otro agravio
que nos enfrenta a todos. No lo toleraré.
Sus caballeros pierden el control y él mismo nos increpa
por cualquier nimiedad. Cuando vuelva de caza no quiero
hablarle. Decid que estoy enferma.
Si abandonáis antiguas consideraciones   10
tanto mejor. De todas esas faltas yo responderé.

[Oswald]

Ahí llega, *madam*. Le oigo.

Gonerill

Vestíos vos y vuestros caballeros cuanta tediosa negligencia
[os plazca
Yo haré que esto se esclarezca.
Y, si no es de su agrado, parta junto a mi hermana.
En esto, bien lo sé, nuestro sentir es uno,
que nadie nos gobierne. ¡Viejo inútil,
que aún quiere usar poderes que había abandonado!
A fe mía que los viejos necios se vuelven como niños
y merecen castigos además de halagos   20
cuando de ellos abusan.
Recordad lo que he dicho.

[Oswald]

Muy bien, *madam*.

16-21. *en esto... abusan.* Este fragmento aparece omitido en *Folio*. También
aparecen omitidas en esta edición las líneas 25-6, *Quisiera... hablar.*

Y que sus caballeros reciban de vosotros las miradas más frías.
No importa lo que ocurra. Advertid a los vuestros.
Quisiera suscitar de ahí ocasión, y así lo haré,
para poder hablar. Escribiré a mi hermana de inmediato,
para que me secunde. Preparad la comida.

(Salen.)

ESCENA CUARTA*

(Entra KENT *[disfrazado].)*

KENT

Si adopto otros acentos además
que puedan encubrir en mis palabras
mis buenas intenciones, alcanzaría el fin
por que troqué mi aspecto. Ahora, Kent desterrado,
si pudieras servir ante quien te condena,
y ojalá que así sea, el señor a quien amas
quizá tu esfuerzo reconozca un día.

(Trompas dentro. Entran LEAR *[caballeros] y sirvientes.)*

LEAR

No me hagáis esperar la cena ni un instante. ¡Id, preparadla!

(Sale un sirviente.)

¿Qué ocurre? ¿Tú, quién eres?

---

* Aunque la división entre esta escena y la siguiente venga marcada en *Folio* —recordemos que el *Quarto* no presenta división en actos y escenas—, podría parecer superfluo dividirlas, puesto que se trata de una acción ininterrumpida dramáticamente, y que se sitúa en el mismo escenario.

Un hombre, señor.

Lear

¿Y cuál es tu trabajo? ¿Qué deseas de Nos?

Kent

Profeso el ser no menos de lo que aparento, y servir lealmente a aquel que ponga en mí su confianza; amar al que es honesto; relacionarme con quien es sabio y habla poco; ser temeroso del divino juicio; luchar cuando no tenga otra elección, y no comer pescado.

Lear

¿Quién eres?

Kent

Persona muy honrada, tan pobre como el rey.

Lear

Si eres tan pobre como súbdito como es él siendo rey, ciertamente eres pobre. ¿Qué quieres?

---

15. *divino juicio;* en el original, «judgement». Se le ha antepuesto el adjetivo «divino» por entender que la palabra *judgement* tiene esta aceptación en este contexto y, por tanto, funciona de forma implícita.

15-6. *no comer pescado;* en el original, «to eat no fish». De entre las diversas interpretaciones que la crítica ha hecho de esta frase, destacamos las que parecen tener mayor aceptación entre los comentaristas: 1) podría tratarse de una alusión sexual, tal y como afirma Partridge, *Shakespeare's Bawdy,* pág. 106; 2) una alusión a la práctica católica de comer pescado los viernes, considerada por los protestantes como una superstición.

KENT

Servir.

LEAR

¿Y a quién quieres servir?

KENT

A vos.

LEAR

¿Me conoces, amigo?

KENT

No, señor, pero algo hay en vuestro porte por lo que gustoso os llamaría señor.

LEAR

¿Qué es ello?

KENT

Autoridad.

LEAR

¿Qué servicios nos puedes prestar?

22-3 *¿Y a quién... vos.* En el original, «Who wouldst thou serve? KENT. You». Se trata de un ejemplo en que se aprecia, por aparecer contrastados, el empleo diferente que se hace de la segunda persona, dependiendo del rango del interlocutor: se utiliza *you* («vos») para dirigirse a un superior, y *thou* («tú») para hablar con una persona de inferior rango. Véase la nota a I.i.20-1.

KENT

Sé guardar un secreto honrado, cabalgar y correr, estropear un 30
buen cuento al contarlo, notificar sin ceremonias un mensaje
sencillo. Estoy capacitado para todo aquello en que son aptos
los hombres ordinarios, y lo mejor de mí es ser diligente.

LEAR

¿Qué edad tienes?

KENT

No tan joven, señor, como para amar a una mujer por su canto, ni tan viejo como para encapricharme de ella sin motivo.
Cuarenta y ocho años llevo a mis espaldas.

LEAR

Sígueme; me servirás a mí; si no me gustas menos cuando acabe la cena, no te dejaré marchar. ¡La cena! ¡Eh! ¡La cena!
¿Dónde está el granuja de mi bufón? Id y traedme a mi bufón.   40

(Sale un sirviente. Entra mayordomo [OSWALD].)

¡Ven! ¡Vos, sire! ¿En dónde está mi hija?

MAYORDOMO [OSWALD]

Con vuestro permiso...

(Sale.)

---

31. *sin ceremonias;* en el original, «bluntly». La elección de esta traducción de
la palabra no es casual, porque contribuye a transmitir mejor la idea de supuesta
torpeza en el dominio del ceremonial propio de la retórica por parte de Kent.

¿Qué es lo que dice este hombre? Traed a ese zoquete.

(Sale un caballero.)

¿Dónde está mi bufón? ¿Está el mundo dormido?

(Vuelve a entrar un caballero.)

¿Bueno? ¿En dónde está ese perro callejero?

CABALLERO

My lord, dice que vuestra hija no está bien.

LEAR

¿Por qué no vino ese villano cuando lo llamé?

CABALLERO

Señor, de una forma rotunda dijo que no quería.

LEAR

¡Que no quería!

CABALLERO

My lord, yo no sé lo que ocurre, pero a mi juicio Vuestra Ma- 50
jestad no es tratado con las atenciones ni la ceremonia acos-
tumbradas. Se aprecia un abandono de la cortesía tanto en
quienes os sirven como en el mismo duque también, y en
vuestra hija.

---

48. En *Quarto* se le atribuye esta frase a Kent.

¿Lo creéis así?

Caballero

Os ruego que me perdonéis, *my lord,* si me equivoco; pero la lealtad no puede silenciarse cuando creo que se ofende a Vuestra Alteza.

Lear

Sólo me recordáis mis sospechas. Últimamente he observado cierta negligencia que preferí atribuir a mi excesiva susceptibilidad más que a intención auténtica y propósito de ya no ser 60 amables. Habré de meditarlo con más detenimiento. ¿Pero dónde está mi bufón? No le he visto en dos días.

Caballero

Majestad, desde que mi señora se fue a Francia el bufón ha decaído mucho.

Lear

¡Basta ya! Lo he notado. Id y decidle a mi hija que quiero hablar con ella.

(Sale un sirviente.)

Y vos, traed aquí al bufón.

(Sale un caballero. Entra mayordomo [Oswald]*.)*

¡Ah!, ¡Vos, señor! ¡Sois vos! Acercaos, señor. ¿Sabéis quién soy?

El padre de *my lady*.

LEAR

«El padre de *my lady*», ¡el bribón de *my lord!* ¡Tú, perro hijo de puta! ¡Tú, villano! ¡Tú, esclavo!

[OSWALD]

No soy nada de eso, *my lord;* ruego que me perdonéis.

LEAR

¿Me desafías con la mirada, desvergonzado?

[OSWALD]

No consentiré que me peguéis, *my lord*.

KENT

¿Ni que tampoco te zancadilleen, rastrero?

LEAR

Te lo agradezco, amigo. Me sirves y yo sabré apreciarlo.

---

76. *rastrero*, en el original, «you base football-player». La traducción recoge la idea que en época isabelina tenía la acepción de *football-player,* es decir, la de persona de baja condición, cuya compañía no era deseable. Si se hubiera traducido por «futbolista» el significado original no se habría recogido, produciéndose un anacronismo por las asociaciones actuales del término.

78-9. *a guardar distancias;* en el original, «I'll teach you differences», que hace referencia al comportamiento distinto que hay que adoptar dependiendo de la extracción social del interlocutor. En este caso una persona más importante obliga a dirigirse a ella con respeto, «guardando las distancias» que una actitud deferente impone.

KENT

¡Venga, sire, levantaos y en marcha! Yo te enseñaré a guardar distancias. ¡Fuera, largo de aquí! Y si quieres medir de nuevo tu estupidez, quédate; pero, ¡fuera, largo! Ten un poco de sen- 80 tido común.

(Sale mayordomo.)

¡Ea! ¡Por fin!

LEAR

Bien, mi fiel servidor, te lo agradezco. Aquí tienes un anticipo por tus servicios.

(Entra el BUFÓN.*)*

BUFÓN

Yo también me lo alquilo. Aquí tenéis mi gorra de bufón.

LEAR

¡Qué hay! ¿Cómo estás, mi pequeño bribón?

BUFÓN

A ti, sire, mi cresta te sentaría mejor.

KENT

¿Por qué, bufón?

---

87. *cresta;* en el origen «coxcomb», cuya traducción literal sería «gorra de bufón», tal y como lo hemos traducido en las líneas 85 y 91.

¿Por qué? Por ponerte de parte de quien ya no goza de favor. Es más, si tú no sabes adaptarte a los vientos que soplan, muy pronto te resfriarás. Toma mi gorra. ¿Ves? Este hombre ha desterrado a dos de sus hijas y dio su bendición a la tercera contra su voluntad. Si le sigues habrás de ponerte mi cresta. ¿Qué te parece, amo? ¡Si yo tuviera dos crestas y dos hijas!

Lear

¿Por qué, muchacho?

Bufón

Si yo les diera toda mi fortuna, me quedaría con mis crestas. Aquí tienes la mía. Mendiga la otra a tus hijas.

Lear

¡Cuidado, sire, con el látigo!

Bufón

La verdad es un perro condenado en su jaula que debe ser sacado a latigazos mientras *madame*, la perra, puede permanecer junto al fuego, aunque apeste.

---

94. *amo;* en el original, «nuncle», abreviatura de *mine uncle*, perteneciente al lenguaje infantil que los bufones adoptan, en ocasiones, para dirigirse a un superior. El castellano carece de esta tradición, y de ahí su traducción por «amo».

100. *madame, la perra.* En el original, «the Lady's Brach». Parece tratarse de una comparación entre la verdad —representada por un perro callejero— y la adulación —un perro de raza—, si además, tenemos en cuenta que Shakespeare suele asociar la figura del adulador con los perros. *Brach* se ha traducido en III .vi.63 por «lebrel». Por otra parte, *Lady* era un nombre muy frecuente para perras, y, dado que en este contexto la palabra «perra» está cargada de connotaciones sexuales, a menudo asociadas al ámbito referencial francés, se ha decidido sustituir *Lady,* más elegante, por *madame,* más pícaro, especialmente si va seguido de la aposición «la perra».

¡Cuánta hiel pestilente!

BUFÓN

Sire, te enseñaré unas rimas.

LEAR

Bien. Adelante.

BUFÓN

¡Atento, amo!
No enseñes todo lo que tienes
ni digas todo cuanto sepas,
prestando menos de lo que posees,
usa el caballo y no las piernas,
no creas todo lo que dicen,   110
tampoco todo lo que veas,
si permaneces en tu casa
no arriesgas todo lo que llevas;
déjate de bebidas y de putas
y tendrás más de veinte por veintena.

KENT

Bufón, eso no es nada.

- 105-15. Aparece aquí la primera de las varias canciones que interpreta el bufón en el drama, y que normalmente sirven de consejo a los demás personajes —Lear, en particular. Son estos los fragmentos cuya traducción ha sido menos literal, manteniendo la idea central y, sobre todo, el aire de canción popular en el lenguaje. Además, el esquema de rimas, propio de este tipo de canciones, se reproduce en castellano, alternándolas, en asonancia, y con algún verso blanco intercalado.

109. *usa el caballo y no las piernas*. En el original, «Ride more than thou goest». La traducción recoge el tono jocoso de la canción, que se perdería si se tradujera por los verbos equivalentes.

BUFÓN

Es como la elocuencia de un abogado que no cobra: pues nada
me pagasteis. Amo, ¿no podríais vos hacer algo con nada?

LEAR

No, muchacho, nada puede hacerse con nada.

BUFÓN *(A* KENT.)

Decídselo, os lo ruego; a eso mismo asciende la renta de sus 120
tierras. A un bufón no creería.

LEAR

¡A un bufón amargo!

BUFÓN

Muchacho, ¿conoces tú la diferencia acaso entre un bufón
amargo y uno dulce?

LEAR

No, amigo mío, mostrádmela.

BUFÓN

Que quien te aconsejó
que entregaras tu hacienda
venga y esté a mi lado
o sé tú quien se venga.
Tendremos de inmediato   130

126-41. *Que quien... arrebatarían.* Este fragmento aparece omitido en *Folio.*
Los diferentes comentaristas opinan que puede tratarse de un fragmento que
hubiera sido censurado por la referencia a los monopolios —véanse, especialmente, las líneas 138-41— que Jacobo I concedía a sus cortesanos, a pesar de la
protesta popular en este sentido.

un dulce y un amargo
bufón, el uno ahí,
otro a cuadros aquí.

LEAR

¿Me estás llamando bufón, muchacho?

BUFÓN

De todos tus otros títulos ya te has desprendido; con éste, sin
embargo, viniste al mundo.

KENT

Este no está del todo loco, *my lord*.

BUFÓN

No, a fe mía, no me lo permitirían los lores y los poderosos. Si
yo tuviese el monopolio, ellos tendrían su parte; y tampoco las
grandes damas dejarían que me guardara toda la locura para 140
mí; me la arrebatarían. Amo, dame un huevo y te daré dos coronas.

LEAR

¿Y cómo habrán de ser esas coronas?

---

133. *a cuadros;* «motley», en el original, era el nombre que recibía el traje del
bufón de corte.
137. *Éste no está del todo loco.* En el original, «This is not altogether Fool». En
varios momentos se juega con la ambivalencia del término *fool* («loco», «bufón»,
etc.). A ello contribuye, fundamentalmente, el hecho de que, en ocasiones, la
inicial de esta palabra vaya en mayúscula —como en este caso—, por lo que es
fácil la referencia tanto a los diferentes significados como al nombre del personaje.

BUFÓN

Las mitades del huevo después de que partido me coma lo de dentro. Cuando partiste tu corona por la mitad y cediste ambas partes, te cargaste el burro a la espalda para cruzar el barro. Poco juicio tuviste bajo tu calva coronilla cuando te desprendiste de la de oro. Y si en esto hablo como lo que soy, que se azote al primero que así lo considere.

> Que nunca un loco lo fue menos,   150
> que siempre el listo es mucho más
> llevando el juicio a sus espaldas
> y como simios a imitar.

LEAR

¿Desde cuándo sois tan pródigo en canciones, sire?

BUFÓN

Lo soy desde que hiciste de tus hijas tus madres, amo, porque cuando les entregaste la vara y te bajaste los calzones he aquí que:

> de alegría lloraban,
> yo de pena cantaba:
> que el buen rey un niño fuera   160
> y tal bufón se hiciera.

Te lo ruego, mi amo, mantén a un maestro que pueda enseñar a mentir a tu bufón; me gustaría aprender a mentir

---

160. *que el rey un niño fuera;* en el original, «that such a king should play bo-peep» (lit.: *que un rey así jugara al escondite).* Como advertíamos, las canciones desenfadadas propias del bufón han sido traducidas con cierta libertad, buscando una equivalencia de efecto. En este caso, «to play bo-peep» es una actividad propia de los niños, y la elección del sustantivo «niño», seguido de la forma verbal «fuera», se realiza también en función del verso siguiente, con el que mantiene cierto paralelismo en la elección de un sustantivo en singular, seguido de la misma forma verbal.

LEAR

Y si mientes, sire, te haremos azotar.

BUFÓN

Me pregunto de qué clase de gente sois tú y tus hijas. Ellas quieren azotarme por decir la verdad, tú quieres azotarme por mentir; y, a veces, se me azota por callarme. Preferiría ser cualquier cosa antes que bufón, y, aun así, no quisiera ser tú, amo. Has podado tu entendimiento por ambos lados sin dejar nada en medio. Mira, ahí llega una de tus ramas. 170

(Entra GONERILL.*)*

LEAR

¿Cómo estáis, hija? ¿A qué viene esa cinta en la frente? Últimamente siempre os veo con ese ceño.

BUFÓN

Eras un hombre de bien cuando no tenías necesidad de preocuparte de su ceño. Ahora eres un cero sin más cifras, y yo soy más que tú; soy un bufón, y tú, nada. Sí, controlaré mi lengua, por supuesto; así lo ordena tu semblante, aunque no digas nada.

¡Chito! ¡Chitón!
Quien hastiado de todo no se guarda
ni corteza ni miga 180
la mendiga.

Ahí tenéis, no el fruto, sino sólo la espiga.

GONERILL

Señor, no sólo este bufón privilegiado, sino otros
de vuestro séquito insolente, a toda hora

[107]

critican y disputan, provocando
riñas intolerables. Mi señor,
haciéndooslo saber creí haber encontrado
solución eficaz, pero empiezo a temer,
por lo que hacéis y decís vos mismo,
que protegéis tal conducta, y la fomenta así   190
vuestro consentimiento. Si así fuera, la falta
no escaparía a la condena ni se haría esperar
la solución, que en aras de la integridad de nuestro Estado
podría, al aplicarse, ser causa de una ofensa,
de otra manera vergonzosa, y a quien necesidad
definiría, sin embargo, como juicioso proceder.

BUFÓN

Pues como ya sabéis, amo,

> por tanto tiempo al cuco nutría el gorrión
> que por las crías su cabeza arrancada acabó.

Extinguida tu vela, nos cubrió la tiniebla.   200

LEAR

¿Sois vos nuestra hija?

GONERILL

Quisiera veros usar vuestro buen juicio
con que me consta estáis dotado, y renunciarais
a esas veleidades que últimamente tanto os alejan
de lo que sois en realidad.

BUFÓN

¿No sabría hasta un burro cuándo es el carro quien tira del ca
ballo?

> ¡Arre, caballo, que te quiero!

[108]

¿Quién de vosotros me conoce? Este no es Lear.
¿Camina Lear así? ¿Habla así? ¿En dónde están sus ojos? 210
Quizá su entendimiento se haya debilitado y su sentido
esté en letargo. ¡Ah! ¿Estoy despierto? No es verdad.
¿Quién sabría decirme quién soy yo?

BUFÓN

La sombra de Lear.

LEAR

Me gustaría saberlo, pues los emblemas de la realcza,
de la razón y del conocimiento quisieran convencerme
erróneamente de que tuve hijas.

BUFÓN

Que harán de ti padre obendiente.

LEAR

¿Cómo os llamáis, hermosa dama?

GONERILL

Señor, ese desvarío trae mucho el recuerdo 220
de esas otras recientes artimañas vuestras.
Os ruego que no malinterpretéis mis propósitos.
Tal viejo venerable deberíais tener más juicio.
Mantenéis aquí un centenar de caballeros
y escuderos; gente insolente, depravada, salvaje;
de modo que esta corte que sus formas pervierten

---

214. En *Quarto*, y en algunas ediciones del siglo XVIII, esta frase es asignada
a Lear.
215-8. *Me gustaría... obediente*. Este fragmento aparece omitido en *Folio*.

más parece posada libertina;
la gula y la lujuria la acercan mucho más
a una taberna y un burdel que a un palacio regio.
La honra pide solución inmediata.   230
Sea pues el deseo de quien de todas formas hará lo que os implora
que reduzcáis un poco vuestro séquito.
Y que aquellos que aún queden a vuestro servicio
sean hombres convenientes para vuestros años,
que se conozcan y os conozcan.

LEAR

                         ¡Infiernos y diablos!
¡Ensillad mis caballos! ¡Reunid mi séquito!
Degenerada bastarda, no te molestaré ya nunca más.
Aún me queda una hija.

GONERILL

Golpeáis a mis hombres y la insolencia de vuestra gentuza
hace sirvientes a sus superiores.   240

(Entra ALBANY.)

LEAR

¡Ay de quien muy tarde se arrepiente! ¡Oh! ¿Vos aquí, señor?
¿Es esta vuestra voluntad? Hablad, señor. Preparad mis caballos.
Ingratitud, demonio con corazón de mármol,
más horrendo que el monstruo marino,
cuando te manifiestas en los hijos.

ALBANY

                         Señor, os ruego que tengáis
                                    [paciencia

LEAR *(A* GONERILL.)

Mentís, buitre maldito.
Mi séquito es de hombres elegidos con singulares méritos;
y que conocen sus obligaciones a la perfección,
que con cuidado escrupuloso
mantienen la honra de su nombre.   250
¡Oh! ¡Cuán pequeña la culpa que en Cordelia horrenda parecía!
Arrancó como una rueda de tormento las fibras de mi ser
de sus propias raíces; sacó el amor que hubo en mi corazón,
y lo colmó de hiel. ¡Oh, Lear, Lear, Lear!
Llama a la puerta que permitió la entrada a tu locura
y escapar a tu juicio. Y vosotros, mi gente, ¡partid!

(Salen KENT *y caballeros.)*

ALBANY

My lord, no soy culpable, pues ignoro
lo que os enoja.

LEAR

Puede que sea así.
Escucha, Naturaleza, diosa venerada, ¡óyeme!
Revoca tu propósito, si era tu intención   260
hacer fecunda a esta criatura.
Llena su útero de esterilidad,
deja yermo su vientre,
que de su cuerpo degradado nunca surja
un fruto que la honre. Y si ha de concebir,
sea un hijo del odio, que viva para ella
como un tormento perverso y desnaturalizado.

---

251. *¡Oh, cuán pequeña... parecía!;* en el original, «O most small fault, how ugly
didst thou in Cordelia show!» En la traducción se modifica la relación sintáctica
de los elementos para poner de relieve la insignificancia de la falta cometida por
Cordelia y el error de evaluación de su padre.
260-3. Véase la nota a I.i.32-3.

Y que su frente joven se le llene de arrugas
y un torrente de lágrimas abra surco en su rostro;
que su dolor y el gozo de ser madre   270
no encuentren sino desdén y escarnio,
que sepa cuánto más amargo es tener hijo ingrato
que mordedura de serpiente. ¡Fuera! ¡Fuera!

(Sale.)

ALBANY

¡Por todos los dioses que adoramos! ¿A qué es debido esto?

GONERILL

No os aflijáis por saber más;
y dejad que su humor obtenga el desahogo
propio de la senilidad.

(Entra LEAR.*)*

LEAR

¡Cómo! ¿Cincuenta de mis caballeros de una vez?
¿Y en quince días?

ALBANY

¿Qué sucede señor?

LEAR

Yo os lo diré. *(A* GONERILL.*)* ¡Vida y muerte! Sí, que me   280
                                                [avergüenza
que tengas el poder que así quebranta mi virilidad;
que estas ardientes lágrimas que a la fuerza me escapan
te hagan digna de ellas. Nieblas y torbellinos te confundan.
Que insondables heridas por esta maldición de padre
se abran en todos tus sentidos. Ojos viejos e ilusos,

[112]

si volvéis a llorar por esta causa, yo os arrancaré
y os tiraré junto a las aguas que vertéis
para ablandar la arcilla. ¿A esto hemos llegado?
Que sea así. Tengo otra hija
de quien estoy seguro, bondadosa y solícita.   290
En cuanto sepa lo que has hecho, tu cara de lobezna
rasgará con sus uñas. Verás cómo recobro
la apariencia a que creías habría renunciado
ya para siempre.

(Sale.)

GONERILL

¿Habéis oído eso?

ALBANY

No me es posible inclinarme de un lado, Gonerill,
por el amor que yo os profeso...

GONERILL

Basta, os lo ruego, ¡Oswald!...
Vos, sire, más bribón que loco, ¡detrás de vuestro amo!

BUFÓN

¡Lear! ¡Mi amo! ¡Espera! Lleva contigo a tu bufón.

A una zorra atrapada   300
y a hijas como vos
a la horca llevara

_____

302. *A la horca llevara;* en el original, «Should sure to the slaughter». El cambio en el orden de los elementos responde a la imposición de la rima con el primer verso: «atrapada». Lo mismo sucede en la línea 303: «si mi gorra la soga comprara» (en el original, «if my cap would buy a halter»).

si mi gorra la soga comprara
y el bufón dice «adiós».

(Sale.)

GONERILL

Muy buenos consejeros ha tenido este hombre. ¡Un centenar
[de caballeros!
¿Es prudente y seguro dejarle mantener cien caballeros?
Sí, para que a cualquier sueño,
cualquier rumor, capricho, queja, o desagrado
le sea posible proteger su demencia senil con sus poderes
y tener nuestras vidas a su merced... ¡Eh, Oswald!   310

ALBANY

Exageráis vuestros temores.

GONERILL

                              Mejor que exagerar la confianza.
Dejad que excluya los peligros que temo,

305-16. *Muy buenos... inconvenientes.* Este fragmento no aparece en *Quarto*.

307-8. *cualquier sueño, cualquier rumor, capricho, queja o desagrado.* En el original,
«every dream, / Each buzz; each fancy, each complaint, dislike». En la traducción castellana se ha resuelto la repetición de *each* por la de «cualquier» en dos
ocasiones, anteponiéndola a los dos primeros elementos, el primero de los cuales está precedido en inglés por *every*. El resto de los elementos en sucesión han
sido separados por comas, dando lugar a un efecto total generalizado de repetición, evitando el resultado artificioso de la repetición acumulativa del término
«cualquier».

311. *Exageráis... confianza.* En el original, «Well you may fear too far. GO-
NERILL. Safer than trust too far». La expresión adverbial *too far* («demasiado
lejos»), que aparece repetida, se ha traducido por el verbo «exagerar»; y los verbos *fear* y *trust* se han sustantivizado, convirtiéndose en «temores» y «confianza». De este modo se evita la repetición monótona de «demasiado», de haber
optado por la traducción más literal.

312-3. *excluya... excluyan.* En el original, «Let me still take away the harms I
fear, / Not fear still to be taken». La traducción castellana reproduce la repetición y el juego existente en inglés entre *fear* y *take*. Este verbo, seguido de *away*

antes que temer siempre que me excluyan. Conozco
su corazón. Lo que ha dicho se lo he escrito a mi hermana;
si ella le acoge a él y a sus cien caballeros
después de haber mostrado los inconvenientes...

(Entra mayordomo [OSWALD].)

                                        ¡Por fin, Oswald!
¡Qué! ¿Habéis escrito ya esa carta a mi hermana?

MAYORDOMO [OSWALD]

Sí, *madam.*

GONERILL

Toma una escolta y la caballo!
Informa con detalle de todos mis temores,   320
y añádele argumentos tuyos
para que el impacto sea mayor. Vete ya;
y apresura el regreso.

(Sale OSWALD.)

         No, *my lord,*
aunque no condeno la blanda indulgencia ni vuestra conducta,
se os censura más por ser necio
de lo que se os alaba por falta de valor.

ALBANY

Hasta dónde penetren vuestros ojos no lo puedo decir;
buscando mejorar, estropeamos a menudo lo que bien está.

---

en el primer caso, se ha traducido por «excluir», y en este sentido se ha aplicado
con cierta libertad al verbo *take* del segundo verso, donde significa «ser apresa-
do», pero, en definitiva, «excluido».

[115]

Y entonces...

ALBANY

Bien, muy bien... A los hechos.   330

(Salen.)

ESCENA QUINTA*

(Entran, LEAR, KENT, CABALLERO y el BUFÓN.)

LEAR

Adelantaos hacia Gloucester con estas cartas. No digáis a mi
hija nada de lo que sabéis, aunque os haga preguntas sugeridas
por la carta. Si no os apresuráis, estaré allí antes que vos.

KENT

No dormiré, *my lord*, hasta haber entregado vuestra carta.

(Sale.)

BUFÓN

Si el cerebro del hombre estuviera en sus pies, ¿no le saldrían
sabañones?

---

* Esta breve escena en prosa es continuación y conclusión de las dos que le
preceden. Sirve, además, para anticipar el tema de la locura de Lear, mostrando
su partida del castillo de Gonerill.

1. *Gloucester*. No el personaje, sino la ciudad de ese nombre cerca de la cual
se hallaba el castillo del duque. J. Dover Wilson, en su edición para *The New
Cambridge Shakespeare*, sustituye por *Cornwall*, basándose en que Lear no podía
saber que su hija estaba en el castillo de Gloucester. Shakespeare, sin embargo,
comete a menudo este tipo de «errores» de anticipación.

LEAR

Sí, muchacho.

BUFÓN

Entonces, te lo ruego, sé feliz. Tu sensatez no necesitará de za-
patillas.

LEAR

¡Ja, ja, ja!   10

BUFÓN

Verás cómo tu otra hija te trata amablemente; pues aunque se
parezca a la de aquí como una poma a una manzana yo digo lo
que digo.

LEAR

¿Y qué dices, muchacho?

BUFÓN

Que su sabor será tan parecido como lo es el de una poma al
de otra poma. ¿Sabríais decirme por qué está la nariz en medio
de la cara?

LEAR

No.

____

12. *poma;* «crab», en el original. Se ha elegido en la traducción un sinónimo
de «manzana», porque una «poma» —tipo de manzana áspera— es tan semejante a una manzana como semejantes son las dos hermanas a que se hace referencia.

Para tener un ojo a cada lado y así poder fisgar lo que escapa al olfato. 20

LEAR

Le hice daño...

BUFÓN

¿Sabrías decirme cómo una ostra hace su concha?

LEAR

No.

BUFÓN

Ni yo tampoco, pero sé por qué la tiene un caracol.

LEAR

¿Por qué?

BUFÓN

Para meter dentro la cabeza, no para dársela a sus hijas, dejando sus cuernos sin cubrir.

LEAR

Quiero olvidar mi naturaleza. ¡Un padre como yo, tan complaciente! ¿Están listos mis caballos?

BUFÓN

En ello están tus asnos. La razón de que las siete estrellas no 30 sean más que siete es muy hermosa.

LEAR

¿Por no ser ocho, acaso?

BUFÓN

Sí, en efecto. Harías bien de bufón.

LEAR

Para recuperarlo por la fuerza. ¡Oh, monstruo ingrato!

BUFÓN

Amo, si fueras mi bufón, haría que te pegaran por haber sido viejo antes de tiempo.

LEAR

¿Cómo es eso?

BUFÓN

No deberías haber envejecido antes de ser sabio.

LEAR

¡No dejéis que enloquezca, loco no, dulces cielos! ¡Conservad mi razón! ¡Yo no quiero estar loco! Bien, ¿están listos mis ca- 40 ballos?

CABALLERO

Preparados, *my lord*.

---

30. *las siete estrellas.* Se trata, probablemente, de las Pléyades, nombre dado en la mitología a las siete hijas de Atlas que, desesperadas por el suplicio de su padre, se mataron y fueron transformadas en estrellas. (María Moliner, *Diccionario de uso del español,* vol. II, pág. 782[1]).

Vamos, muchacho.

BUFÓN

La que ahora es doncella y ríe con mi marcha
no lo será por mucho, si las cosas aguantan.

(Salen.)

ACTO II

ESCENA PRIMERA*

(Entran el bastardo [EDMUND] y CURAN, por lados opuestos.)

BASTARDO [EDMUND]

¡Dios os guarde, Curan!

CURAN

Y a vos, señor. He estado con vuestro padre y le he informado de que el duque de Cornwall y su duquesa Regan estarán esta noche aquí con él.

[EDMUND]

¿Cómo es eso?

CURAN

No lo sé. ¿Habéis escuchado las noticias que circulan —quiero decir los rumores—, que aún no son más que palabras dichas al oído?

---

* Se inicia en este momento la larga secuencia central del drama, que tiene lugar en el castillo de Gloucester o sus alrededores, y se extiende hasta IV.i. inclusive. En esta escena se entrecruzan, por vez primera, los dos argumentos paralelos.

[EDMUND]

Yo no. Os lo ruego, ¿cuáles son?

CURAN

¿No habéis oído que es probable la guerra entre el duque de   10
Cornwall y el de Albany?

[EDMUND]

Ni una palabra.

CURAN

Puede que lo escuchéis en su momento. Adiós, sire.

(Sale.)

[EDMUND]

¡El duque aquí esta noche! ¡Es excelente!
Esto a la perfección encaja con mis planes. Mi padre
ha dispuesto una guardia que prenderá a mi hermano;
y a mí me queda por representar un papel delicado.
¡Rapidez y Fortuna, empezad a actuar!
¡Hermano, una palabra! ¡Bajad! ¡Oíd, hermano!

(Entra EDGAR.)

Mi padre vigila, sire, huid de este lugar;   20
ha corrido la voz de dónde os escondéis.
Ahora tenéis la estimable ventaja de la noche.
¿No habéis hablado en contra del duque de Cornwall?
Viene hacia aquí de noche, rápidamente, ahora,
y con él viene Regan. ¿No habéis dicho
nada sobre sus planes contra el duque de Albany?
Intentad recordarlo.

EDGAR

Estoy seguro. No, ni una palabra.

[EDMUND]

Mi padre llega, perdonadme;
Como un ardid debo sacar la espada contra vos.
Desenvainad; fingid que os defendéis; y hacedlo bien.   30
¡Rendíos! ¡Venid ante mi padre! ¡Luz, aquí!
Huid, hermano. ¡Antorchas! ¡Antorchas! Id en paz.

(Sale EDGAR.)

Algo de sangre derramada hará creer
que me he batido valerosamente, vi borrachos
hacerse más por gusto. ¡Padre! ¡Padre!
¡Alto! ¡Alto! ¿Nadie me ayuda?

(Entran GLOUCESTER y criados con antorchas.)

GLOUCESTER

                    Y bien, Edmund, ¿dónde está
                                        [el villano?

[EDMUND]

Aquí estaba, en lo oscuro, con su afilada espada al aire,
                                        [mascullando
perversos sortilegios, conjurando a la luna,
a que fuera su diosa tutelar.

GLOUCESTER

Pero él, ¿dónde está?

[123]

[EDMUND]

Mirad, señor, que sangro.

GLOUCESTER

¿Y dónde está el villano?   40

[EDMUND]

Huyó hacia allí, señor, cuando no pudo...

GLOUCESTER

Perseguidle, id tras él... «Cuando no pudo», ¿qué?

[EDMUND]

Persuadirme para que asesinara a vuestra señoría;
pero cuando le dije que los dioses
vengadores lanzaban sus rayos contra los parricidas,
y le hablé de cuán múltiple y cuán fuerte
era el lazo que unía al hijo con el padre; en fin, señor,
viendo con cuánta repulsión me oponía
a su propósito antinatural, en un fiero arrebato,
con su espada presta buscó el blanco   50
en mi cuerpo inerme, y me hirió en el brazo;
pero al ver mis espíritus provocados así,
enardecido por lo justo de la lucha, y dispuesto al combate,
o porque se asustara ante el ruido que hice,
rápidamente huyó.

---

50. *buscó el blanco;* «he charges home», en el original. El uso adverbial de *home*
es explicado en diccionarios y glosarios como «indicador de la consecución del
efecto deseado», y en ese sentido se ha traducido. Véase, además, la nota a
III.iii.10.

[124]

GLOUCESTER

Dejadle que huya.
No ha de haber libertad para él en esta tierra;
sino la ejecución si es encontrado. Mi amo, el noble duque,
mi señor y protector, viene esta noche.
Bajo su autoridad proclamaré
que aquel que lo encontrare ganará más favores,   60
conduciendo al tormento al cobarde asesino;
mataré a quien lo oculte.

[EDMUND]

Cuando le disuadía de su intento,
viéndole decidido a realizarlo, con palabras tajantes
le amenacé con descubrirle; él replicó:
«Tú, indigente bastardo, crees que si rebatiera cuanto dices
serían suficientes la verdad,
la virtud o dignidad que haya en ti
para hacer creíbles tus palabras. No, que lo que yo negara
como negaría esto, aunque falsificases   70
mi escritura, lo achacaría todo
a tus incitaciones, tus conjuras, tu artificio maldito;
y tendría que ser idiota todo el mundo
si no pensase que el beneficio de mi muerte
es una incitación muy obvia y poderosa
para hacer que la busques.»

(Trompetas dentro.)

GLOUCESTER

                          ¡Oh, canalla extraño e insensible!
Que negaría su carta, ¿y eso dijo? no fui quien lo engendró.
¡Escucha! ¡Las trompetas del duque! Ignoro por qué viene.
Cerraré los puertos; no escapará el villano;
el duque deberá garantizármelo: enviaré además   80
a todos los lugares su retrato, para que todo el reino
pueda reconocerlo; y de mis tierras,

hijo leal y natural, arbitraré los medios
para hacerte heredero.

(Entran CORNWALL, REGAN *y sirvientes.)*

CORNWALL

Salud, mi noble amigo. Acabo de llegar
y sólo escucho noticias que me preocupan.

REGAN

Si es cierto, no hay venganza posible
para tamaña ofensa. ¿Cómo estáis, *my lord?*

GLOUCESTER

Señora, mi viejo corazón se siente herido, destrozado.

REGAN

¡Cómo! ¿Intentó el ahijado de mi madre arrancaros la vida?   90
¿Él, a quien mi padre puso nombre? ¿Vuestro Edgar?

GLOUCESTER

Señora, por vergüenza debería ocultarse.

REGAN

¿No era él amigo de los pendencieros
que acompañaban a mi padre?

85-6 *Acabo... preocupan;* en el original, «Since I came hither / which I can call
but know, I have heard strange news» (lit.: *Desde que llegué aquí —que no es sino
hace un instante— sólo he escuchado noticias extrañas).* Obsérvese cómo, sin apartarse
demasiado de la literalidad, esta traducción se acerca más al tipo de lenguaje re-
querido por la situación dramática. A Cornwall, que busca el apoyo de Gloucester, le «preocupan las noticias» que pudieran afectar esta alianza.

GLOUCESTER

Lo ignoro, *madam.* ¡Es terrible, terrible!

[EDMUND]

Sí, *madam,* él era de esa gente.

REGAN

No es extraño, pues, que fuera malintencionado.
Ellos le han incitado a matar al anciano, para disfrutar
del gasto y despilfarro de sus rentas.
Esta misma tarde me han hablado de ellos   100
de parte de mi hermana, con advertencias tales
que, si vinieren a albergarse a mi casa,
no me hallarán.

CORNWALL

      Tampoco a mí, os lo aseguro, Regan.
Edmund, he oído que habéis mostrado a vuestro padre
un fervor muy filial.

[EDMUND]

      Es mi deber, sire.

GLOUCESTER

Él descubrió su estratagema, y recibió
esta herida que veis, luchando por prenderle.

CORNWALL

¿Se le persigue?

Sí, *my lord*.

CORNWALL

Cuando se le detenga, nunca más
temeremos su daño. Seguid con vuestros planes,   11(
disponiendo de mí como queráis. Edmund, en cuanto a vos,
cuya virtud y obediencia ahora tanto se valoran,
seréis de los nuestros.
Naturalezas de tan profunda lealtad nos serán necesarias.
Vos sois nuestro elegido.

[EDMUND]

Os serviré, sire,
lealmente, pese a todo.

GLOUCESTER

Doy gracias en su nombre a Vuestra
                                              [Alteza.

CORNWALL

Sabed ahora la razón de nuestra presencia aquí...

REGAN

Sin anunciarnos, atravesando los negros ojos de la noche.
Razones, noble Gloucester, de importancia,
por las que debemos hacer uso de vuestro consejo.   12(

---

117. *Sabed ahora... aquí.* En el original, «You know not why we came to visit
you» (lit.: *Vos no sabéis por qué hemos venido a visitaros*). Se trata de un caso similar
al planteado en la nota anterior. Cornwall cambia, radicalmente, de conversación para pasar a interesarse por los asuntos que realmente le han llevado hasta
Gloucester, y de ahí la traducción.

Nuestro padre ha escrito, y también nuestra hermana,
sobre desavenencias a las que he creído preferible responder
lejos de nuestra casa. Mensajeros de una y otra parte
aguardan desde ahora mi despacho. Viejo amigo,
aliviad nuestra pena y conceded
el consejo preciso para nuestros asuntos,
que necesitan de una inmediata solución.

GLOUCESTER

Lo haré.
Sean bienvenidas Vuestras Altezas.

(Salen. Toque de trompetas.)

ESCENA SEGUNDA*

(Entran KENT *y mayordomo* [OSWALD] *por lados opuestos.)*

MAYORDOMO [OSWALD]

Feliz alba tengáis. ¿Sois de la casa?

KENT

Sí.

[OSWALD]

¿Dónde podemos dejar nuestros caballos?

---

* En esta escena se nos presenta el enfrentamiento entre dos personajes con
funciones dramáticas análogas. Tanto Kent como Oswald actúan de interme-
diarios entre sus respectivos señores y el resto de los personajes.

1. *alba;* en el original, «dawning». Obsérvese, sin embargo, que en la escena
anterior —línea 118— se menciona que es de noche, y en la 25 de esta misma
escena se afirma «pues, aunque sea de noche, la luna brilla aún». Sería otro de
los «errores» de Shakespeare, apenas perceptibles en teatro.

KENT

En el lodazal.

[OSWALD]

Os lo ruego, si en algo me consideráis, decídmelo.

KENT

Yo no os considero.

[OSWALD]

Pues bien, entonces tampoco yo os considero a vos.

KENT

Si te tuviera entre mis garras me considerarías.

[OSWALD]

¿Por qué me tratas así? No te conozco.

KENT

Amigo, yo a ti sí.   10

[OSWALD]

¿Por quién me tomas tú?

---

8. *si te tuviera entre mis garras;* en el original, «If I had thee in Lipsbury pin-fold». *Lipsbury* es un término desconocido, considerado como equivalente de *liptown* («espacio entre los labios»); *pinfold* significa «recinto» —donde se guarda el ganado extraviado. Nares opina que esta expresión significa *between my teeth* («entre mis dientes»), opinión que se ha respetado en la elección de la traducción.

Por un canalla, un truhán, un muerto de hambre, un bellaco
vil y orgulloso, banal, pordiosero, desharrapado, por un caballero de ocho al cuarto, de sucias calzas de lana, por un engo-
rroso bribón, hideputa, sin agallas, chivato, fatuo, petimetre,
lameculos, villano zarrapastroso, uno que vendería hasta las
hembras con tal de hacer méritos, y no es sino una mezcla de
canalla, pordiosero, cobarde, alcahuete e hijo y heredero de
una perra callejera, a quien golpearé hasta que rabie, si niegas
la más mínima sílaba de tus atributos.   20

[OSWALD]

Pero, ¿qué clase de monstruo eres que así insultas a quien no
te conoce, ni conoces?

KENT

¿Qué clase de lacayo eres tú que niegas conocerme? Hace dos
días que te puse la zancadilla y te golpeé ante el rey. ¡Desenvai-

---

12. *un muerto de hambre;* en el original, «an eater of broken meats». La expresión castellana recoge la idea de hombre humilde con elevadas pretensiones,
que transmite el original inglés, ya que *an eater of broken meats* era el criado, al
que se daban los restos de comida.

13. *desharrapado;* en el original, «three— suited» (lit.: *de tres trajes*). Esta traducción conserva el tono de la línea anterior, y reproduce en castellano la descripción de la persona que va mal vestida. La expresión *three-suited* hacía referencia a la situación de los criados, que sólo disponían de tres trajes.

14. *de ocho al cuarto.* En el original, «hundred-pound, filthyworsted-stocking
knave». La expresión «de ocho al cuarto» en castellano se aplica a la persona
que ocupa la escala más baja dentro de un estamento. En época de Jacobo I,
cien libras era la cantidad estipulada para acceder al grado de caballero. La alusión a las medias sucias, de lana, completa la idea, al recordar que los auténticos
caballeros sólo las utilizaban de seda.

15. *sin agallas;* en el original, «lily-livered». Esta expresión inglesa indica un
deficiente riego sanguíneo en el hígado, y, por tanto, daba como resultado, según la teoría de los humores, una personalidad cobarde. La forma castellana
elegida, al ser más coloquial, se aproxima al modelo inglés.

16. *lameculos;* en el original, «super-serviceable». Se trata de una expresión
peyorativa para describir a quien es especialmente solícito para prestar servicios
de todo tipo.

na, bribón! Pues, aunque sea de noche, la luna brilla aún. Haré de ti una sopa de rayos de luna, tú, hideputa, petulante canalla. ¡Desenvaina!

[Oswald]

¡Largo de aquí! Nada tengo que ver contigo.

Kent

¡Desenvaina, canalla! Vienes con unas cartas contra el rey y te pones de parte de la marioneta Vanidad, contra la realeza de su padre. Desenvaina, canalla, o haré con tus dos piernas carbonada. ¡Desenvaina, bribón! ¡En guardia! 30

[Oswald]

¡Socorro! ¡Que me matan! ¡Ah! ¡Socorro!

Kent

¡Ataca, miserable! ¡No huyas, bribón! ¡No huyas, esclavo petulante! ¡Ataca!

[Oswald]

¡Socorro! ¡Que me matan! ¡Que me matan!

---

30. *Vanidad.* Referencia a uno de los personajes representados en las *Moralidades,* en las que normalmente aparecían expuestas las figuras de los vicios y pecados capitales.

31-2. *carbonada;* en el original, «I'll so carbonado your shanks». El término *carbonado,* utilizado como verbo, procede del castellano, y se refiere a alimentos cocidos a la brasa.

33. *¡Que me matan!;* en el original, «Murder!». En la traducción se ha transformado el sustantivo *murder* en una oración con verbo en voz activa y complemento, para indicar que el sujeto que grita está siendo agredido. Si se hubiera traducido por el sustantivo «¡Asesinato!» se habría transmitido la idea de que el autor de los gritos descubría un asesinato.

(Entran el bastardo [EDMUND], CORNWALL, REGAN, GLOUCES-
TER *y criados.)*

BASTARDO [EDMUND]

¡Y bien! ¿Con quién os las habéis? Separaos.

KENT

Contigo, jovenzuelo, si tú quieres. Vamos, te iniciaré en la lucha. ¡Vamos!

GLOUCESTER

¿Espadas? ¿Armas? ¿Qué sucede aquí?   40

CORNWALL

¡Calmaos, por vuestras vidas! El que ataque de nuevo es hombre muerto. ¿Qué sucede?

REGAN

Los mensajeros del rey y nuestra hermana.

CORNWALL

¿Cuál es la causa de vuestro litigio? Hablad.

[OSWALD]

My lord, apenas tengo aliento.

---

38. *jovenzuelo;* «goodman boy», en el original, que se empleaba como fórmula
para dirigirse a un joven petulante. En castellano el sufijo utilizado connota ese
matiz peyorativo.

No es nada extraño, habiendo derrochado tanto vuestro valor. Bribón cobarde, la naturaleza reniega de ti: un sastre debió hacerte.

CORNWALL

Sois una persona extraña. ¿Un sastre hacer un hombre?

KENT

Un sastre, sí, señor. Un pintor o escultor nunca podrían cons- 50 truirlo tan mal, aunque hubieran estado dos años sólo en el oficio.

CORNWALL

Pero hablad. ¿Cómo se originó vuestra disputa?

[OSWALD]

Este viejo rufián, cuya vida en consideración de su barba grisácea he respetado...

KENT

Tú, cero hijo de puta; tú, letra innecesaria. *My lord,* si me lo permitís, a este vulgar malvado convertiré en mortero y enluciré con él la pared de una letrina. ¿Tú, respetar mi barba, libertino?

47-8. *un sastre debió hacerte;* en el original, «A tailor made thee»; es decir, que la indumentaria de Oswald, exclusivamente externa, no refleja su valor o su nobleza de carácter; o bien, está físicamente «mal construido» (línea 51).

53. Este verso atribuido a Gloucester en *Quarto.*

56. *cero;* en el original, «zed» *(zeta).* Esta letra era considerada como algo carente de valor, puesto que normalmente no aparecería en los diccionarios de la época, y de ahí la traducción por «cero» como cifra de valor absoluto nulo.

CORNWALL

¡Silencio, sire!   60
Tú, salvaje bribón, ¿no conoces el respeto?

KENT

Sí, señor, pero la ira tiene privilegio.

CORNWALL

¿Por qué estás irritado?

KENT

¡Que un miserable como este lleve espada
cuando no tiene honestidad! Bribones como este
roen, igual que ratas, hasta la mitad los vínculos sagrados
que son difíciles de desatar; suavizan la pasión
cuando estalla en la razón de sus señores;
son leña para su fuego, nieve para su frialdad,
reniegan, afirman y mueven sus picos de alción   70
con cada ráfaga cambiante de sus amos,
no sabiendo otra cosa que ir detrás como perros.
¡Caiga la peste sobre tu rostro de epiléptico!
¿Ríes de cuanto digo como si yo fuera un bufón?
¡Ah, ganso! Si te tuviese en la llanura de Sarum,
te llevaría cacareando hasta Camelot.

70-1. *mueven... amos.* Esta imagen del alción moviéndose al capricho del viento responde a la creencia generalizada entre los isabelinos de que el alción, o
martín pescador, se movía en la dirección del viento cuando era colgado por el
pico o la cola. Aquí sirve para referirse a cierto tipo de bribones aduladores.

73. *rostro de epiléptico;* en el original, «your epileptic visage». La imagen posiblemente fuera empleada para designar al extraño rostro de Oswald, mezcla de
miedo y de sonrisa.

75-6. *la llanura de Sarum... Camelot.* Se trata de la llanura de Salisbury, y de
Camelot, el legendario castillo del rey Arturo, localizado normalmente en Win-
chester, en el extremo de la mencionada llanura.

Pero, ¿estáis loco, viejo?

GLOUCESTER

¿Por qué os peleabais? Decid.

KENT

No hay contrarios que se tengan
más aversión que yo y este bribón.   80

CORNWALL

¿Por qué decís bribón? ¿Cuál es su ofensa?

KENT

Su aspecto no me gusta.

CORNWALL

Quizá tampoco el mío, ni el de él, ni el de ella.

KENT

Señor, mi oficio es la franqueza.
Mejores rostros vi en toda mi vida
que los que sobresalen en los hombros que ahora veo
ante mí, en este instante.

CORNWALL

                            Este es uno
que, elogiado por su grosería, finge
descarada rudeza, adoptando un estilo
contrario a sus impulsos; no sabe adular, él,   90
alma honesta y sincera, ¡él dice la verdad!

Si se la aceptan, bien; si no, él ha sido sincero.
Ya conozco esta clase de bribones; guardan en su franqueza
más artimañas y más corruptos fines
que veinte aduladores cortesanos,
exagerando meticulosamente sus deberes.

KENT

Señor, de buena fe, con sincera verdad,
bajo la anuencia de vuestra gran figura,
cuya influencia como la corona de radiante fuego
en la frente de Febo centelleante...

CORNWALL

¿Qué pretendéis con esto?   100

KENT

Dejar el habla que os molesta tanto. Sé que no soy ningún adulador; quien con lenguaje llano os engañó era un bribón tan sólo: lo que yo, por mi parte, no seré, aunque me lo pidáis y con ello gane vuestro desfavor.

CORNWALL

¿Qué ofensa le causasteis?

[OSWALD]

Jamás le causé alguna.
Últimamente el rey, su amo, se complace
en golpearme por malentendidos

_____

107-15. *Últimamente el rey... desenvaina.* En el original, «It pleased the King his master very late... tripped... insulted, railed, put upon him,... worthied... got praises... drew». La descripción es tan rica en detalles, y los hechos que narra tan recientes, que se ha optado, en la traducción de los verbos, por la forma de presente histórico.

y él, de acuerdo, y halagando su enfado,
me zancadillea por detrás; ya en el suelo, me insulta y se mofa
[de mí, 110
y hace alardes tales de su hombría
que se enaltece, obtiene alabanzas del rey,
por atacar a quien se rindió ya
y, con la excitación de tan horrible gesta,
de nuevo desenvaina ahora contra mí.

KENT

                            Estos cobardes pícaros
miran a Ajax como a su bufón.

CORNWALL

                    ¡Id a buscar los cepos!
A ti, viejo bribón obstinado, caduco fanfarrón,
te habremos de enseñar.

KENT

                    Señor, para aprender soy demasiado viejo.
No pidáis vuestros cepos contra mí. Yo sirvo al rey,
por cuyo encargo os fui enviado;   120
tendréis poco respeto, mostraréis, en exceso, una malicia osada
contra la gracia y contra la persona de mi amo,
poniéndole los cepos a su mensajero.

CORNWALL

                        ¡Id a traer los cepos!
Por mi vida y honor que ahí permanecerá hasta el mediodía.

REGAN

¿Hasta el mediodía? Hasta la noche, *my lord,* y la noche también.

116-7. *Estos cobardes... bufón.* En *Troilo y Crésida,* Ajax es tratado como bufón
por el cobarde Tersites.

KENT

Pero, señora, si fuese el perro de vuestro padre
no me trataríais así.

REGAN

Siendo su bribón, así lo haré.

(Traen los cepos.)

CORNWALL

Este es un tipo de la misma clase
de los que habla nuestra hermana. ¡Venga, traed los cepos!

GLOUCESTER

Permitidme rogaros: no lo hagáis.   130
Su falta es grave, y el buen rey, su amo, le reprenderá.
Con la ultrajante expiación que habéis impuesto
tan sólo a los canallas más innobles y viles
por hurtos y delitos más comunes
se castiga. El rey tomará a mal,
ya tan menospreciado en la persona de su mensajero,
que así se le confine.

CORNWALL

De eso yo responderé.

REGAN

Mucho peor lo tomaría mi hermana
viendo a su servidor insultado, asaltado
por cuidar sus asuntos. Ponedlos en sus piernas.   140

131-5.   *Su falta... castiga.* Fragmento omitido en *Folio.*
140.   *por... piernas.* Este verso también aparece omitido en *Folio.*

Venid, *my lord*. ¡Marchemos!

(Salen todos menos GLOUCESTER *y* KENT.)

GLOUCESTER

Lo siento por ti, amigo; es deseo del duque,
y todo el mundo sabe sabe que su condición
no admite trabas ni contrariedades. Abogaré por ti.

KENT

No, os lo ruego. Mucho he viajado y sin descanso.
Primero dormiré un poco y luego silbaré.
Que de sus pies acaso pueda venirle a un hombre su fortuna.
Que tengáis un buen día.

GLOUCESTER

De todo esto el duque es responsable.
Será tomado a mal.

(Sale.)

KENT

Buen rey, tú corroboras el dicho popular,   150
tú que abandonas la tranquilidad del cielo
para adentrarte en el ardiente sol.
Acércate, faro del bajo mundo,
que con la ayuda de tus rayos pueda

---

144. *no admite trabas ni contrariedades;* en el original, «will not be rubbed nor stopped». En castellano el matiz del verbo *will* en este contexto, que implica «voluntad firme», queda bien expresado mediante el empleo del verbo «admitir», o sinónimos como «tolerar», seguido de objetos directos; de ahí la sustantivación en el texto castellano, más natural que la forma verbal en pasiva.

[140]

releer esta carta. Sólo vemos milagros desde la desgracia.
Sé que es Cordelia quien la envía,
que, afortunadamente, fue informada
de mi encubierto proceder, y encontrará el momento,
en este estado miserable, de poner un remedio
a las calamidades. ¡Ah, deshecho, cansado de velar!   160
Ojos, aprovechad vuestra fatiga para no mirar
esta morada vergonzosa. Fortuna, buenas noches;
sonríe una vez más, ¡gira tu rueda!

(Se duerme.)

ESCENA TERCERA*

(Entra EDGAR.)

EDGAR

Oí un bando en mi contra
y por un árbol hueco y oportuno
pude escapar del cerco. No hay puerto libre ni lugar
en donde vigilancia y celo desacostumbrados
no acechen mi captura. Mientras consiga huir
podré saberme a salvo; y he pensado
adoptar el aspecto más pobre y el más vil
de cuantos tiene la penuria para, menospreciando al hombre,
acercarlo a las bestias. Recubriré mi cara de inmundicias,
de harapos mi cintura, con nudos mis cabellos enmarañaré,   10
con ostensible desnudez he de afrontar

---

   * En las ediciones originales no se indica cambio de escena en este momento, y aparece claro —a partir de las acotaciones escénicas— que Kent permanece dormido sobre el escenario mientras Edgar recita su breve monólogo, lo que permitiría al espectador percibir la continuidad de la acción dramática entre las escenas segunda y cuarta.
   2. *por un árbol hueco y oportuno;* en el original, «by the happy hollow of a tree». Se ha traducido el sustantivo *hollow* como adjetivo, coordinándolo con *happy*. El resultado, por tanto, en vez de ser «la oportuna oquedad de un árbol», que resultaría excesivamente literal y poco apropiado, es el «árbol hueco y oportuno».

los vientos y las persecuciones de los cielos.
Esta tierra ofrece pruebas y el ejemplo
de los mendigos de Bedlam, que, con voz estruendosa,
clavan en sus pobres brazos, entumecidos y mortificados,
puntas, astillas, alfileres, brotes de romero,
y con este espectáculo, en granjas miserables,
en pobres e insignificantes corrales, pueblos y molinos, fuerzan
[a caridad,
a veces con imprecaciones de lunático, otras veces con ruegos:
«¡Caridad para Turlygod! ¡Caridad para Tom!»   20
Algo sería por lo menos; que Edgar ya no es nada.

(Sale.)

ESCENA CUARTA*

(Entran LEAR, *el* BUFÓN y un caballero.)

LEAR

Es extraño que se marchara de la casa así
sin enviarme el mensajero.

CABALLERO

                        Por lo que yo sé,
anoche no tenían intención
de trasladarse.

---

14. *los mendigos de Bedlam.* Véase la nota a I.ii.123.
20. *Turlygod.* Entre las opiniones expresadas por los diferentes comentaristas, no hay ninguna que permita aclarar el uso de este nombre por parte de Edgar. Podría tratarse de un equivalente de Tom de Bedlam, mencionado a continuación, aunque se ha conjeturado que se podría tratar de una corrupción de «turlupín», secta de vagabundos mentalmente trastornados, en París hacia 1600, que realizaban desnudos sus servicios religiosos. Podría aventurarse esta interpretación a partir de los elementos en común con Tom Pobre *(Poor Tom).*
* Continúa en esta escena la función dramática iniciada en la segunda e interrumpida por el parlamento de Edgar, y se desata el conflicto entre Lear y sus dos hijas. De alguna manera, se refleja un paralelismo entre el estado de ánimo de Lear y los fenómenos de la Naturaleza, expresados por las sucesivas acotaciones escénicas que hablan de «tormenta y tempestad».

KENT

Noble amo, os saludo.

LEAR

¡Ah!
¿Haces de esta vileza pasatiempo?

KENT

No, *my lord.*

BUFÓN

¡Ja! Lleva la liga tosca. Por la cabeza se sujeta al caballo, al perro y oso por el cuello, por la cintura al mono, y al hombre por
la pierna. Cuando a un hombre le baila la pierna se la enfunda
en madera.   10

LEAR

¿Quién es el que ha malentendido tanto tu lugar,
que ahí te ha puesto?

KENT

Él y ella a la vez,
vuestro hijo y vuestra hija.

---

7. *tosca;* «cruel», en el original, reproduciendo el juego con *crewel,* es decir, «de
estambre». El término «tosca» puede servir también para referirse a los
cepos.
9-10. *Cuando a un hombre le baila la pierna se la enfunda en madera;* en el original,
«When a man's over-lusty at legs, then he wears wooden nether-stocks». Es decir, cuando un hombre es un vagabundo «demasiado ligero de piernas» es castigado con los cepos *(wooden nether-stocks).* Este término, ambiguo, adquiere este
último significado al anteponerle el calificativo *wooden* (de madera). Además, el
término *lusty,* por su acepción de «lujurioso», contribuye a apoyar la connota-
ción que la traducción propone.

LEAR

No.

KENT

Sí.

LEAR

Que no, te digo.

KENT

Y yo digo que sí.

LEAR

Que no, no, no podrían.

KENT

Sí que pudieron.

LEAR

¡Por Júpiter! Yo te juro que no.   20

KENT

¡Por Juno! Yo, que sí.

LEAR

          No osarían hacerlo;
no podrían, ni querrían hacerlo;
cometer tal ultraje al honor es peor que matar.

18-9. Ambas líneas omitidas en *Folio*.

Explícame con oportuna diligencia de qué forma, viniendo tú
[de Nos,
pudiste merecer, o imponerte pudieron,
este trato.

KENT

 My, lord, cuando en su casa
les entregué las cartas de Vuestra Majestad
antes de que me levantara del lugar donde mostraba
arrodillado mi respeto, llegó un correo jadeante,
sudando en su premura, casi sin aliento,   30
resollando saludos de su ama Gonerill;
entregó carta, pese a la interrupción,
que al instante leyeron; a causa de su contenido
llamaron a la servidumbre; de inmediato montaron a caballo;
me ordenaron seguirles y esperar el favor
de su respuesta; me lanzaron miradas frías,
y encontrando aquí al otro mensajero,
cuyo recibimiento, vislumbré, había envenenado al mío,
siendo el mismo individuo
que últimamente tanto descaro os muestra, Majestad,   40
habiendo más hombría que razón en mí, desenvainé.
Despertó a la casa con fuertes y cobardes gritos,
y vuestro hijo e hija hallaron esta ofensa
digna de la vergüenza que aquí sufro.

BUFÓN

Aún perdura el invierno mientras los gansos salvajes vuelan
por ahí.

 Los harapos del padre
 vuelven ciego a su hijo,

45-54. Este fragmento no aparece en *Quarto*.
45-6. *Aún perdura el invierno.* En el original, «Winter's not gone yet if the wild geese fly that way». Lo más crudo del invierno sólo llegará cuando los gansos salvajes hayan concluido su emigración. Este comentario viene a indicar que aún sufrirá tiempos peores.

si el padre tiene bolsa
se convierte en su amigo;
Fortuna, mala furcia,
no estás con el mendigo.

Por eso te harás rico en dolores a causa de tus hijas tanto
como te sea posible contar en todo un año.

LEAR

¡Oh, cómo crece hacia mi corazón esta especie de cáncer!
¡Hysterica passio! Baja, tú, amargura que asciendes.
Tu lugar está abajo. ¿En dónde está esa hija?

KENT

Con el conde, señor, ahí dentro.

LEAR

No me sigáis, quedaos ahí.

(Sale.)

CABALLERO

¿No cometisteis ninguna ofensa sino la que habéis dicho?   60

---

53. *dolores;* «dolours», en el original. Es un juego de palabras basado en la ho-
mofonía entre esta palabra y *dollars,* nombre dado, en la época, a los pesos espa-
ñoles y a los táleros alemanes.

55-6. *esta especie de cáncer;* en el original, «this mother». Recibía el nombre de
«mal de la madre» una sensación de angustia y sofoco sufrida por las mujeres,
que se extendía progresivamente, pareciendo formarse en el útero *(mother,* en
inglés, e *hystera* en griego); de ahí «Hysterica passio», en el verso siguiente,
abundando en el mismo sentido. La palabra «cáncer» no se emplea en su sentido estricto, sino en el más amplio de enfermedad molesta que se extiende. El
movimiento que seguía la *Hysterica passio* era ascendente —partiendo del vientre
hasta llegar al corazón—, de ahí que Lear le imprepue a permanecer abajo. En
una posible segunda lectura simbólica, Lear instaría a sus hijas —la peor de las
enfermedades— a que se mantuvieran «abajo», es decir, sometidas a su autoridad, en vez de intentar suplantarlo y ahogarlo en su movimiento ascendente.

KENT

Ninguna.
Pero, ¿cómo el rey viene con tan poco séquito?

BUFÓN

Si te hubieran puesto los cepos por esa pregunta, bien te lo habrías merecido.

KENT

¿Por qué, bufón?

BUFÓN

Te enviaremos a la escuela con la hormiga y que ella te enseñe que no se trabaja en invierno. Todos cuantos siguen sus narices se guían por los ojos, a excepción de los ciegos; y no hay una nariz entre veinte que no pueda oler a quien apesta. Cuando do una rueda grande vaya montaña abajo, déjala ir; no sea que te rompas el cuello por seguirla. Pero si una grande va hacia arriba, déjate llevar. Cuando un sabio te dé mejor consejo, devuélveme el mío; me gustaría que nadie lo siguiera salvo los bribones; pues es un loco el que lo da. 70

> El que te sirve y busca beneficios,
> y te secunda sólo en apariencia
> hará equipaje al empezar la lluvia
> y sabrá abandonarte en la tormenta;
> mas yo me quedaré, el bufón se queda
> dejando que alce el vuelo la cordura.
> Si un truhán lo hace se convierte en loco,
> mas no en truhán el bufón, ni su locura. 80

(Entran LEAR *y* GLOUCESTER.*)*

KENT

¿En dónde has aprendido todo eso, bufón?

[147]

Bufón, no fue en los cepos.

LEAR

¿Que se niegan a hablarme? ¿Que están enfermos y agotados?
¿Que han viajado toda la noche? Excusas,
simples imágenes de rebelión, de huida.
Trae mejor respuesta.

GLOUCESTER

Mi querido señor,
vos conocéis el carácter colérico del duque;
lo terco e inflexible que es en su proceder.   90

LEAR

¡Venganza! ¡Peste! ¡Muerte! ¡Confusión!
¿«Colérico»? ¿«Carácter»? Gloucester, Gloucester,
quiero hablar con el duque de Cornwall y su esposa.

GLOUCESTER

Bien, *my lord,* así les he informado.

LEAR

¡Que les has «informado»! ¿No me entiendes, acaso?

GLOUCESTER

Sí, mi señor.

94-5. Estas líneas, así como la 99, no aparecen en *Quarto.*

LEAR

El rey desearía hablar con Cornwall, y el amado padre con su hija
también quisiera hablar, para exigirles obediencia.
¿Están ya «informados» de esto? ¡Mi hálito y mi sangre!
¿«Colérico»? ¡Que es «colérico» el duque! Dile a ese brusco
[duque que... 100
pero no, aún no; puede que no esté bien:
la enfermedad siempre descuida las obligaciones
a las que nos sujeta el estar sanos. No,
ya no somos los mismos cuando, oprimida, la Naturaleza
obliga a que la mente sufra con el cuerpo. Habré de contenerme
Me irrita este deseo impetuoso de tomar
por hombre sano al enfermizo. ¡Abajo mi poder!
¿Por qué amarrado así? Este hecho me convence
de que el traslado de ella y el del duque
es solamente una estrategia. Dadme a mi servidor.   110
Id a decir al duque y a su esposa que quiero hablar con ellos,
¡y que inmediatamente! Ordenadles que vengan y me escuchen
o que a la misma puerta de su cámara golpearé el tambor
hasta que con el ruido le dé muerte a su sueño.

GLOUCESTER

Quisiera que todo entre vosotros fuera bien.

(Sale.)

LEAR

¡Ay de mí, mi corazón se inflama! Pero, ¡calma!

BUFÓN

Grítale, amo, como la cocinera gritaba a las anguilas cuando
las metía vivas en la pasta. Les golpeaba la cresta con un palo

---

116. *mi corazón se inflama*. En el original, «my heart, my rising heart». Se trata
de un estadio de la *Hysterica passio*. Véase la nota a las líneas 55-6.

y les gritaba: «Calma, golfillas, calma.» Era su hermano quien,
por puro afecto a su caballo, untó su heno con manteca.   1

(Entran CORNWALL, REGAN, GLOUCESTER *y sirvientes.)*

LEAR

Buenos días a ambos.

CORNWALL

Saludo a Vuestra Gracia.

*(*KENT *es puesto en libertad.)*

REGAN

Me alegra ver a Vuestra Alteza.

LEAR

Regan, te creo. Sé la razón que tengo para pensar así,
pues si no te alegraras, me divorciaría
del sepulcro mismo de tu madre
por ser el de una adúltera... ¿Estás libre?
Ya hablaremos de eso... Amada Regan,
que ya tu hermana no lo es. ¡Oh, Regan! Ha clavado
el afilado pico de la ingratitud, como un buitre, aquí,
y apenas me es posible hablar contigo; no querrías creer   13
con qué manera tan perversa... ¡Oh Regan!

119-20. *untó su heno con manteca.* En el original, «'Twas her brother that in
pure kindness to his horse buttered his hay». Esta acción se realizaba frecuentemente por ciertos posaderos para que los caballos no comieran el heno; en este
caso es realizada por «su hermano» por error o ignorancia.

REGAN

Os lo ruego, señor, tened paciencia. Espero
que vos sepáis valorar su mérito
menos que ella faltar a su deber.

LEAR

¿Cómo? ¿Qué dices?

REGAN

Yo no puedo creer que mi hermana
haya faltado a su deber. Señor, si por ventura
ha refrenado los excesos de vuestros seguidores
es por un fin y una causa tan buenos
que la eximen de culpa.

LEAR

¡Yo la maldigo!

REGAN

¡Oh, señor! Sois anciano;   140
la Naturaleza en vos bordea el límite de su confín,
deberíais ser guiado y dirigido
con la prudencia del que comprende vuestro estado
mejor que vos. Por ello os ruego
que volváis con mi hermana y le digáis
que habéis sido injusto.

LEAR

¿Yo, pedirle perdón?
Piensa lo que esto supondría para mi linaje.
«Querida hija, confieso que soy viejo;

_____

134-9. *¿Cómo... de culpa.* Este fragmento no aparece en *Quarto.*

que la vejez no es útil; de rodillas te imploro,
dame vestido, cama y alimento.»

15

REGAN

¡Buen señor, basta ya! Son éstas feas artimañas.
Regresad con mi hermana.

LEAR

Nunca, Regan.
Ella que me ha quitado la mitad de mi séquito;
que me ha mirado con hostilidad; que me ha herido,
con lengua de serpiente, el mismo corazón.
¡Que sobre su cabeza ingrata caiga la ira del cielo
y tú, aire maligno, los huesos de sus descendientes
castígalos con la cojera!

CORNWALL

¡Basta ya, señor, basta!

LEAR

¡Veloces rayos, dirigid vuestras llamas cegadoras
hacia sus ojos despreciables! Infectad su belleza,
brumas que el poderoso sol arranca del pantano,
caed y hacedle ampollas.

16

REGAN

¡Dioses, dioses!
¡Lo mismo me desearéis cuando la cólera os posea!

LEAR

No, Regan, a ti nunca te maldeciré;
tu tierna y femenina condición nunca te hará caer
en la rudeza. Son sus ojos feroces; y los tuyos

confortan y no queman. Ya no serías tú
si escatimaras mis placeres, recortaras mi séquito,
dieras réplicas duras, si redujeras mis prerrogativas
e impidieras mi entrada, finalmente,   170
con cerrojos. Tú conoces mejor
a qué te obliga tu naturaleza;
los vínculos filiales; los signos de la cortesía;
los compromisos de la gratitud. No has olvidado
que la mitad del reino fue mi dote.

REGAN

A nuestro asunto.

(Trompetas dentro.)

LEAR

¿Quién puso argollas a mi servidor?

(Entra mayordomo [OSWALD].)

CORNWALL

¿Qué trompeta es esa?

REGAN

Es mi hermana, la conozco. Confirma así la carta
donde anunciaba su venida. ¿Llegó vuestra señora?

LEAR

Este es el miserable cuyo orgullo prestado
vive en la veleidosa cortesía de aquella a la que sigue.   180
¡Fuera, lacayo, fuera de mi vista!

CORNWALL

¿Qué dice Vuestra Gracia?

(*Entra* GONERILL.)

LEAR

¿Quién puso argollas a mi servidor? Regan, espero
que tú no lo supieras. ¿Quién llega? ¡Oh cielos!
¡Si de verdad amáis a los ancianos, si vuestra dulce norma
aprueba la obediencia, si sois viejos también,
haced de ésta vuestra causa! ¡Bajad, poneos de parte mía!
¿Puedes mirar mi barba sin avergonzarte?
¡Oh, Regan! ¿Vas a cogerla de la mano?

GONERILL

¿Por qué no de la mano? ¿En qué he ofendido?
No todo cuanto la indiscreción percibe es una ofensa,   1
aunque así lo califique la vejez.

LEAR

                                ¡Oh, pecho mío! Eres muy fuerte.
¿Todavía resistes?... ¿Cómo mi servidor fue a parar a los cepos?

CORNWALL

Allí lo puse yo, señor, pero su proceder
merecía mucha menos consideración.

LEAR

¿Vos? ¿Que vos lo hicisteis?

---

182. *¿Quién... servidor?* En *Quarto* este parlamento es asignado a Gonerill.

[154]

Regan

Padre, os lo ruego, aceptad vuestra debilidad.
Hasta que acabe el mes estipulado,
volved a residir junto a mi hermana,
despedid la mitad de vuestro séquito, luego venid conmigo.
Ahora estoy lejos de casa, y sin los medios   200
que serían precisos para vuestro acomodo.

Lear

¿Volver con ella y con cincuenta caballeros menos?
No, antes renunciaría a todo abrigo;
prefiero combatir la hostilidad del aire,
ser amigo del lobo y la lechuza,
del afilado diente de la necesidad. ¿Volver con ella?
Hacia el apasionado France, que sin dote tomó
a nuestra más pequeña, también podría ir
y arrodillarme ante su trono y, servilmente, mendigar pensión
para una vida innoble. ¿Regresar con ella?   210
Convénceme de que prefiera ser esclavo o arriero
antes que este lacayo detestable.

Gonerill

Como elijáis, señor.

Lear

Te lo ruego, hija mía, no me trastornes más.
Adiós, pequeña mía, no te molestaré.
No habremos de encontrarnos más, ni volver a vernos.
Pero eres de mi carne, de mi sangre, hija mía;
o mejor, un mal, que hay en mi carne,

---

212. *este lacayo detestable;* en el original, «this detested groom». Puede referirse
al propio Lear —que se sentiría como un lacayo servil, de obedecer a sus hijas— o, como algunos editores indican —por medio de la acotación escénica
pertinente— a Oswald.

y que estoy obligado a llamar mío. Eres como un tumor,
una úlcera infecta, un absceso de pus
en mi sangre corrupta. No te reprenderé;
que la vergüenza venga cuando quiera; yo no la invoco;
no le ordeno al señor del trueno que dispare,
ni le cuento hazañas sobre ti al supremo juez Júpiter.
Enmiéndate cuando puedas; mejora si te place;
puedo esperar y quedarme con Regan,
yo y mis cien caballeros.

REGAN

No diría yo tanto;
aún no os esperaba ni estoy preparada
para una adecuada bienvenida. Escuchad a mi hermana;
aquellos que confunden razón con vehemencia
deben contentarse con pensar que sois viejo,
y así... pero ella sabe lo que hace.

LEAR

¿Es cierto lo que escucho?

REGAN

Señor, me atrevo a mantenerlo. ¿Qué? ¿Cincuenta sirvientes?
¿No está bien? ¿Y qué necesidad tenéis de más?
¿O de tantos, si el gasto y el peligro
hablan en contra de tamaño número? ¿Cómo, en una casa,
podría tanta gente bajo dos gobiernos mantenerse en concordia?
Difícil es; casi imposible.

GONERILL

¿Y no podríais, *my lord,* ser atendido
por los que ella llama sus criados, o quizás por los míos?

¿Por qué no, mi señor? Si por casualidad os descuidasen,   240
podríamos reprenderles. Si venís conmigo,
pues entreveo un peligro, os ruego que traigáis
tan sólo veinticinco; a nadie más
daré mi sitio y mi permiso.

LEAR

Os lo di todo...

REGAN

Y en buena hora lo disteis.

LEAR

Os hice mis tutoras; os di mi confianza,
pero con una condición, que me siguiera
un número determinado. ¡Y bien! ¿Debo ir a ti
con veinticinco? Regan, ¿es eso lo que dices?

REGAN

Y lo vuelvo a decir, conmigo ni uno más, *my lord*.   250

LEAR

¡Ah, malvadas criaturas! Parecen bien dotadas
porque hay otras más perversas; no siendo las peores
aún son dignas de elogio. Iré contigo.
Tus cincuenta siquiera son el doble de sus veinticinco,
y tu amor dobla el suyo.

GONERILL

Oíd, *my lord*.
¿Y qué necesidad tenéis de veinticinco, diez o cinco,

para que os acompañen a una casa donde el doble de ellos
tiene la orden de serviros?

REGAN

¿Y por qué uno siquiera?

LEAR

¡Oh! No razonéis la necesidad; los más bajos mendigos
tienen en lo más pobre algo superfluo.   26•
No permitáis a la Naturaleza más de lo que la Naturaleza necesita
y la vida del hombre será tan insignificante como lo es la de
                                                        [las bestias.
Sois una dama; si solamente al ir caliente fueseis suntuosa...
Pero Naturaleza no necesita lo que te vistes de suntuosidad
puesto que apenas te calienta. Aunque, por una auténtica exi-
                                                        [gencia...
¡Vamos, cielos, dadme esa paciencia, la paciencia de que nece-
                                                        [sito!...
Aquí me veis, oh dioses, sólo un viejo,
con tantas penas como años y mísero en los dos.
Si sois vosotros quienes movéis los corazones de estas hijas
contra su padre, no me enloquezcáis   27•
hasta el extremo de que impasible lo soporte; ¡dadme la noble
                                                        [ira,
y no dejéis que el arma femenina, el agua
goteante, mancille mis mejillas de hombre! No, brujas desnatu-
                                                        [ralizadas,
tomaré tal venganza contra vosotras dos
que todo el mundo... He de hacer tales cosas...
las que serán aún no lo sé; pero sí que serán
el terror de la tierra. Pensáis que lloraré;
pero no lloraré.
Tengo razones suficientes para llorar, pero este corazón

(Tormenta y tempestad.)

estallará antes en cien mil pedazos   28•
que yo derrame lágrimas. ¡Bufón, me vuelvo loco!

(Salen [LEAR, GLOUCESTER, KENT, *el* BUFÓN *y un caballero].)*

CORNWALL

Retirémonos. Va a haber una tormenta.

REGAN

Esta casa es pequeña; el anciano y su gente
no pueden ser acomodados.

GONERILL

Es culpa suya; él mismo se ha privado de reposo,
y tiene que probar forzosamente su locura.

REGAN

A él en persona lo recibiré con gusto,
pero ni a uno sólo de sus seguidores.

GONERILL

                           También es ése mi propósito.
¿Dónde está *my lord* de Gloucester?

(Entra GLOUCESTER.)

CORNWALL

Ha ido tras el viejo. Ahí viene.   290

GLOUCESTER

El rey está muy irritado.

288-9. *También... Gloucester?,* asignado al duque (Cornwall) en *Quarto*. En esta
misma edición los versos 290 y 293 le son asignados a Regan.

CORNWALL

¿Adónde se dirige?

GLOUCESTER

Ha ordenado montar, pero no sé hacia dónde.

CORNWALL

Lo mejor es dejarle ir, sabe guiarse.

GONERILL

My lord, en modo alguno le roguéis que se quede.

GLOUCESTER

¡Ay! Cae la noche, y los rudos vientos rugen con fiereza.
Apenas hay, en muchas millas,
un arbusto.

REGAN

Señor, para los hombres testarudos,
los daños que ellos mismos se procuran
han de ser sus maestros. Atrancad las puertas.
Le acompaña una escolta de desesperados,
y a lo que puedan instigarle, siendo tan fácil de engañar,
el buen sentido recomienda temer.

CORNWALL

Cerrad puertas, *my lord.* La noche es despiadada.
Regan nos aconseja bien. Protejámonos de la tormenta.

(Salen.)

[160]

ACTO III

ESCENA PRIMERA*

(Sigue la tormenta. Entran KENT *y un caballero, por separado.)*

KENT

¿Quién va con este tiempo de tormenta?

CABALLERO

Alguien, atormentado como el tiempo.

KENT

Os conozco. ¿Dónde se encuentra el rey?

CABALLERO

En lucha con la ira de los elementos;
ordena al viento que arrastre al mar la tierra
o que la tierra invada el encrespado mar

---

* Breve escena de transición cuya función dramática es puramente informativa, lo que explicaría la cantidad de omisiones en los textos originales, *Quarto* y *Folio.*

2. *alguien, atormentado como el tiempo;* en el original, «one minded like the weather, most unquietly». En la traducción el participio «atormentado» incorpora los significados del verbo *minded* y del adverbio *most unquietly*, como descripción de un tiempo desapacible, de tormenta.

y cambie o muera todo. Mesa su blanco pelo,
que impetuosas ráfagas, ciegas de ira atrapan,
enfurecidas, con desprecio.
Lucha en su reducido mundo por vencer   10
el conflictivo ir y venir de la lluvia y el viento.
Esta noche en que la osa que cría yace en su cubil
y el león y el lobo hambriento
guardan seco el pelaje, sin cubrirse, corre
conjurando a quien con todo acabará.

KENT

¿Y quién está con él?

CABALLERO

Sólo el bufón, esforzándose por aliviar
su corazón herido.

KENT

Sire, yo os conozco
y es garantía suficiente para que me atreva
a encomendaros algo de importancia. Hay discordia
—pese a que ésta se oculta tras el rostro   20
del engaño— entre Albany y Cornwall
que tienen (y quién no, si Fortuna
les ha encumbrado y dado trono en lo alto)
sirvientes que aunque así lo parecen son espías de France
e informadores de nuestra situación. Lo que se ha visto,

7-15. *Mesa... acabará.* Fragmento omitido en *Folio.*

10. *su reducido mundo;* en el original, «his little world of man». Se trata de una alusión a la teoría de la correspondencia existente entre el microcosmos, representado por el cuerpo humano, y el macrocosmos o universo entero.

22-9. *Que tienen... profundo.* Este fragmento no aparece en *Quarto.*

23. *les ha encumbrado y dado trono en lo alto;* en el original, «throned and set high». Tanto *throned* como *set* están modificados por *high*. En la traducción *set high* se ha sustituido por un verbo equivalente, «encumbrar», y *high* se ha colocado a continuación de «dado trono».

intrigas y disputas entre duques,
o bien las tensas riendas que ambos han colocado
al viejo y generoso rey, no son sino, quizás,
signos externos de algo más profundo.
Lo cierto es que de Francia a este reino disperso   30
un ejército viene y, sabedor
de nuestra negligencia, ha llegado en secreto
a los mejores puertos, y está a punto
de izar sus estandartes. Y ahora a vos:
si confiando en mí os atrevierais a ganar
Dover a toda prisa, encontraréis allí
a quienes agradezcan vuestro fiel testimonio
del pesar ingrato y enloquecedor
del que se duele el rey con motivo.
Soy gentilhombre por crianza y sangre,   40
con esa seguridad y conocimiento
os ofrezco ese encargo.

CABALLERO

Quisiera hablaros más.

KENT

                    No, os lo ruego
como confirmación de que soy mucho más
que mi apariencia, abrid esta bolsa, y tomad
su contenido. Si vierais a Cordelia,
y estoy seguro de que la veréis, enseñadle este anillo,
y ella os dirá quién es aquel
que aún no conocéis. ¡Maldita tempestad!
Marcho en busca del rey.   50

CABALLERO

Dadme la mano. ¿Nada más tenéis que decir?

30-42. *Lo cierto... encargo.* Fragmento omitido en *Folio.*

Pocas palabras, mas de mayor efecto;
cuando al rey encontremos, vos por ese camino, yo por éste,
quien primero lo vea llame al otro.

(Salen.)

ESCENA SEGUNDA*

(Sigue la tormenta. Entran LEAR *y el* BUFÓN.)

LEAR

¡Soplad, vientos, que estalle vuestro rostro! ¡Soplad! ¡Enfureceos!
¡Diluvios y huracanes, desencadenaos
hasta inundar las torres y ahogar los gallos!
¡Llamas de azufre, raudas como el pensamiento,
avanzad rayos que dividen el roble,
chamuscad mi cabeza encanecida! ¡Y tú, trueno, que todo
haces temblar, aplasta la redondez del mundo!
¡Rompe los moldes de la Naturaleza, derrama la simiente
que engendra al hombre ingrato!

BUFÓN

¡Oh, amo! El agua bendita de la corte en casa seca es preferible 10
a ésta de lluvia a la intemperie. Buen amo, entra y pide a tus
hijas su bendición. Esta noche no tiene piedad de sabios ni de
locos.

---

* Es esta la escena central del drama, en la que se enuncia el tema fundamental de la tragedia de forma vigorosa: el enfrentamiento entre el hombre y la
naturaleza, con sus aspectos positivos y negativos.

1. *¡Soplad, vientos, que estalle vuestro rostro!* En el original, «Blow, winds, and
crack your cheeks». Esta imagen tiene su origen en la representación que se hacía de los vientos en las esquinas de los mapas como rostros con las mejillas
hinchadas, soplando.

3. *gallos.* Traducción del original *cocks,* equivalente a *weathercocks* («veletas»).

LEAR

¡Haz que truene tu vientre! ¡Escupe, fuego! ¡Y vomita tú, lluvia!
Ya que ni lluvia, viento, trueno o fuego son mis hijas.
No os acuso, elementos, de ingratos,
jamás un reino os di, ni os llamé hijos.
No me debéis obediencia; descargad, pues,
vuestro horrible deseo; soy aquí vuestro esclavo,
un pobre viejo, enfermo, despreciado y débil.   20
Pero a pesar de todo os llamaré lacayos,
puesto que habéis unido a mis degeneradas hijas
un batallón creado en lo más alto contra una cabeza
tan vieja y blanca como ésta. ¡Oh, qué infamia!

BUFÓN

Quien tiene casa en que meter cabeza, mantiene la cabeza en
buen lugar.

> Quien calienta la funda
> sin calentar el rabo
> se llena tan de tiña
> como un pobre de harapos.   30
> Quien usa el dedo gordo
> y el corazón olvida
> verá cómo los callos
> hasta el sueño le quitan,

pues nunca hubo mujer bella que hiciera muecas al espejo.

(Entra KENT.)

LEAR

No, seré un modelo de paciencia.
Nada diré.

KENT

¿Quién va?

[165]

La gracia y quien la enfunda, es decir, un cuerdo y un loco.

Señor, ¿estáis ahí? Quienes aman la noche   40
no aman noches como ésta. Los airados cielos
aterran a los nómadas de la oscuridad
y a sus cavernas los reducen. Desde que soy hombre,
tal cortina de fuego y estallido de truenos,
tales gemidos de rugiente viento y lluvia, no
recuerdo haber oído. La naturaleza humana no puede soportar
ni la aflicción ni el miedo.

                    Que los grandes dioses,
que sostienen este horrible tumulto sobre vuestras cabezas,
encuentren a sus enemigos. Tiembla, miserable,
tú que tienes en ti crímenes ignorados,   50
sin el castigo de justicia. Ocúltate, tú, sangrienta mano,
tú, perjuro, y tú, simulador de la virtud,
incestuoso. Mezquino, rómpete en pedazos,
tú, que, bajo apariencia oculta y conveniente,
has intrigado contra la vida humana. Culpas
secretas, vuestros escondites romped, e implorad gracia
a estos ministros de venganza. Soy un hombre
más ofendido que ofensor.

---

39. *quien la enfunda.* En el original, «grace and a cod-piece, that's a wise man and a fool». *Cod-piece,* sustantivo concreto («funda») empleado metonímicamente, ha sido desarrollado a nivel sintáctico, manteniendo el doble nivel de la alusión del original, en «quien la enfunda», es decir, una acepción genérica, referida a cualquier persona que concede primacía a los aspectos físico y sensorial, y específicamente alusivo al bufón, cuyo atuendo se caracterizaba por ir adornado con una funda de proporciones exageradas, y cuyo comportamiento, en general, estaba de acuerdo con su indumentaria. Finalmente, «quien la enfunda» puede modificar también a «la gracia», es decir, a quien la oculta por su actitud contraria a ella. En esta frase se hace referencia al rey —noble, espiritual, oficialmente cuerdo— y al bufón —bajo, material, asociado a la locura.

¡Cómo! ¡Vos sin cubrir!
Noble señor, cerca de aquí existe una cabaña;
algún cobijo os podrá dar contra la tempestad.   60
Reposad ahí; yo regresaré a esa casa tan dura,
más dura que la piedra con que se erigió,
donde hace un instante, al preguntar por vos,
se me negó la entrada... y forzaré
su avara cortesía.

Lear

Mi cabeza comienza a desvariar.
Vamos, muchacho. ¿Cómo estás? ¿Tienes frío?
Yo también tengo frío. Amigo, ¿dónde está esa cabaña?
Es extraño el arte de la necesidad
que hace precioso lo que es vil. Venga, a tu cabaña,
pobre granuja loco, parte de mi corazón   70
todavía se entristece por ti.

Bufón

El que tenga muy poco, poquito entendimiento
diga, ¡hey! con la lluvia, diga ¡ho! con el viento,
y Fortuna le alegre muy poquito, y más no,
que la lluvia es diaria; diga ¡hey!, diga ¡ho!

Lear

Cierto, muchacho. Llevadnos, pues, a la cabaña.

(Sale[n] Lear y Kent.)

72-5. *El que tenga... diga ¡ho!* Se trata de una estrofa de canción popular anónima que Shakespeare utiliza también en *Twelfth Night*, V.i.

Propicia es esta noche, que enfría hasta las furcias.
Os diré una profecía antes de partir:
Cuando los curas hagan algo mejor que hablar;
y ya no ponga el tabernero agua en la bebida;   80
cuando el noble enseñe a su sastre a coser;
cuando no quemen al hereje sino al buscaputas;
cuando la corte haga justicia,
y no haya escudero con deudas, ni caballero pobre;
cuando en la lengua muera la calumnia;
cuando no haya rateros en la multitud;
y en la era su oro cuente el usurero;
y putas y alcahuetes construyan las iglesias;
entonces, sólo entonces, el gran reino de Albión
caerá confundido: 90
y el tiempo ha de venir, quien viva para verlo,
en el que usemos para andar los pies.
Esta profecía hará Merlín allá,
que yo tan sólo existo en el tiempo de acá.

(Sale.)

ESCENA TERCERA*

(Entran GLOUCESTER *y* EDMUND.)

GLOUCESTER

¡Ay! ¡Edmund! No me gusta este proceder contra natura.
Cuando les supliqué que me dejaran compadecerlo, me priva-

77-94. *Propicia... de acá.* Fragmento que no aparece en *Quarto*. Shakespeare
aprovecha esta «profecía», atribuida al legendario Merlín, para describir, por
medio del bufón, una serie de abusos comunes cometidos en su tiempo. Algunos comentaristas opinan que las líneas 89-91 deberían ir situadas tras la 82,
pues, mientras el contenido de las líneas 79-82 se refiere a la situación real de la
época, las 83-88 hablan de utopías.

* Esta breve escena sirve para recordarnos el argumento paralelo del drama,
trasladando la acción, de nuevo, al castillo de Gloucester.

ron del uso de mi propia casa; me negaron, bajo pena de per-
petua desgracia, que intercediera, le hablara o apoyara en forma alguna.

BASTARDO [EDMUND]

¡Es brutal e inhumano!

GLOUCESTER

¡Basta! No digas nada. Hay discordia entre los duques, y lo que
es peor: he recibido esta noche una carta; es peligroso hablar.
Se encuentra en mi escritorio bajo llave. Estas injurias que el
rey soporta hoy serán vengadas. Ya ha desembarcado parte de   10
un ejército y tenemos que estar al lado del rey. Iré en su busca
y le ofreceré mi ayuda en secreto. Ve y entretén al duque con
tu conversación, y de ese modo mi ayuda pasará inadvertida
para él. Si por mí preguntasen, estoy enfermo, en cama. Y aun
a costa de mi muerte —que así me amenazaron— he de ayudar al rey, mi señor. Cosas extraordinarias han de acontecer,
Edmund. Te lo ruego, sé cauto.

(Sale.)

[EDMUND]

De vuestro gesto prohibido sabrá al instante el duque;
y también de la carta. Me parece
que es éste un buen servicio, que valdrá para mí   20
lo que mi padre pierda: todo, ni más ni menos.
Que los jóvenes suben cuando los viejos se derrumban.

(Sale.)

---

10. *vengadas;* «revenged home», en el original. Literalmente, «totalmente vengadas», pero véase la nota a II.i.50.

[169]

ESCENA CUARTA*

(Entran, Lear, Kent y el Bufón.)

Kent

Aquí es, *my lord*. ¡Entrad, mi buen señor!
La crueldad de esta noche al desnudo
es demasiado dura para el hombre.

(Sigue la tormenta.)

Lear

Dejadme solo.

Kent

Mi buen señor, entrad.

Lear

¿Queréis romperme el corazón?

Kent

Antes rompería el mío. Mi buen señor, entrad.

Lear

Pensáis que es excesivo que esta furiosa tempestad
nos penetre hasta el hueso; así es para vos.

---

* Es esta una de las escenas fundamentales de la tragedia en la que, de nuevo, vemos la relación entre lo que sucede en la mente de Lear y los fenómenos naturales de «tormenta y tempestad». Es de destacar, además, la referencia al orden social en este momento en que nadie es lo que debería ser, según el orden impuesto en una estructura rigurosamente jerárquica. Lear, Edgar y Kent han perdido, o al menos no actúan según, su rango original.

Pero allá donde el mal inexorable habita
el leve no se siente. Huyes del oso,
pero, si al mar enfurecido te conduce la fuga, regresas a las   10
fauces de la bestia. Que es vulnerable el cuerpo
cuando la mente es libre. Esta tormenta del espíritu
me quita todo sentimiento
salvo el que late aquí... ¡Ingratitud filial!
¿No es como si esta boca arrancara la mano
que le tiende alimento? Sentirán mi castigo.
No, no he de llorar más. ¡Cerrar la puerta
en una noche así! ¡Qué diluvie! Lo resistiré.
¡En una noche así! ¡Regan, Goncrill!
¡Ah, vuestro viejo padre, generoso, que os lo dio todo de
                                                [corazón! 20
Este es camino de locura. ¡Evitémoslo!
¡Basta ya! ¡Basta ya!

KENT

Mi buen señor, entrad.

LEAR

Entrad vos, os lo ruego. Procuraos refugio.
Esta tormenta no dejará que me obsesione
con lo que más me hace sufrir. Sí, entraré.
Entrad muchacho, id delante. ¡Ah, miseria sin techo!

(Sale [el BUFÓN].)

¡Venga! ¡Entrad! Yo rezaré primero y luego dormiré.
Pobres desnudos miserables, donde quiera que estéis

17-8. «*Cerrar... resistiré*. Este fragmento no aparece en *Quarto*.
20. *que os lo dio todo de corazón;* en el original, «whose frank heart gave all». En
la traducción se ha cambiado el sujeto, función que ha pasado a desempeñar
Lear (viejo padre), ya que en esta situación el tono resulta más sincero si se en-
laza con un pronombre de relativo. *Frank heart*, por lo tanto, pasa a desempeñar
la función de complemento, adoptando una expresión castellana equivalente,
que recoge la idea de sinceridad y buena fe: «de todo corazón», empleando incluso el sustitivo «corazón», como en el original.
26-7. Estas líneas no aparecen en *Quarto*.

sufrís el azote de esta tormenta sin piedad.
¿Cómo podrán defenderos vuestras testas sin techo,   30
vuestro vientre vacío, vuestros andrajos llenos de agujeros
de un tiempo así? Qué poca ha sido mi preocupación.
Magnificencia, aquí está tu remedio:
disponte a sufrir tú como los miserables,
aprende a arrojarles lo superfluo,
y que así los cielos les parezcan más justos.

EDGAR *(Dentro.)*

¡Braza y media, braza y media! ¡Pobre de Tom!

BUFÓN *(Dentro.)*

No entres, amo. No. Hay un espíritu. ¡Ayuda! ¡Ayuda! ¡A mí!

KENT

Dame tu mano. ¿Quién va?

BUFÓN *(Dentro.)*

¡Un espíritu! ¡Un espíritu! Dice que se llama «Tom Pobre».   40

KENT

¿Qué eres, que te revuelves en la paja?
¡Sal de ahí!

(Entran EDGAR *y el* BUFÓN.*)*

---

31. *vuestros andrajos llenos de agujeros;* en el original, «your looped and windowed raggedness». La traducción se sirve de un sustantivo concreto («andrajos») al carecer del término abstracto equivalente a *raggedness.* Los participios coordinados *looped* y *windowed* carecen, igualmente, de un término equivalente. Dado que su función es acumulativa, ya que ambos elementos hacen alusión al mismo hecho —las ropas están agujereadas—, se ha traducido la idea de intensidad mediante «Llenos de», y se ha sustituido la forma de participio, que sería «agujereado» por el sustantivo «agujeros», más breve y frecuente.

EDGAR

¡Atrás! El demonio maldito me persigue. A través del espino sopla el gélido viento. ¡Uuhhhh! Gana la cama y entrarás en calor.

LEAR

¿Cómo has llegado a esto? ¿Dando todo a tus hijas?

EDGAR

¿Quién le da una limosna a este pobre de Tom?... A quien ha asediado el demonio maligno con el fuego y la llama; con el vado y el remolino, sobre pantano y ciénaga; y le ha tentado con el cuchillo en la almohada y con la soga en el reclinatorio; 50 que le ha puesto veneno en la mesa; y le ha hecho soberbio de corazón, hasta el punto de montar un corcel bayo que trota sobre puentes de cuatro pulgadas e ir tras su propia sombra por traidora. ¡Dios bendiga tus cinco sentidos! Tom tiene frío. ¡oh, tt, tt, tt, tt, tt, tt! ¡Que el cielo te guarde de huracanes, estrellas nefastas y maleficios! Caridad para el pobre de Tom que el maldito demonio atormenta. ¡Ah, si pudiera asediarlo, ahora, aquí y allí, y allí...!

(Sigue la tormenta.)

LEAR

¿Y es esto a lo que sus hijas le han llevado?
¿Nada pudiste salvar? ¿Les diste todo?   60

BUFÓN

No, se guardó una manta; tendríamos si no que avergonzarnos.

---

54. *cinco sentidos;* es decir, las cinco facultades mentales: sentido común, fantasía, imaginación, juicio y memoria.
54-5. *¡Oh, tt, ... tt!* Sonido producido por los dientes al castañetear a causa del frío.

LEAR

¡Que todas las fatales amenazas que se ciernen
sobre la culpa humana, caigan sobre tus hijas!

KENT

Señor, no tiene hijas.

LEAR

¡Muere, traidor! Tan sólo hijas ingratas
someterían la Naturaleza a tal humillación.
¿Es que es costumbre acaso que padres repudiados
no compadezcan a su carne?
¡Sabio castigo! Esta es la carne que engendró   70
las crías de pelícano.

EDGAR

Al sentarse en sus colinas empinóse Pillicock.
¡Aúu, Aúu, Aúu!

---

71. *Las crías de pelícano;* en el original, «those pelican daughters». En castellano la traducción de los elementos que aparecen en el texto original no es posible sin recurrir a una perífrasis, por ejemplo, «hijas que se comportan como pe-
lícanos», ya que no se les puede yuxtaponer el sustantivo «pelícano» con función adjetival, ni tampoco existe un adjetivo derivado de esta palabra. Se ha optado, por lo tanto, por sustituir la comparación por una identificación, permiti-
da semánticamente por el empleo del demostrativo *those,* para lo cual sí existe
una solución sencilla, la anteposición de la preposición «de». Una vez realizada
esta opción, ha sido necesario adaptar el sustantivo *daughters* al contexto animal,
sustituyéndolo por «crías», femenino en castellano, y que enfatiza el significado
de brutalidad que se quiere comunicar. Existen numerosas alusiones en la época
al sacrificio realizado por la madre de las crías, que se hacía sangre para darles
calor y sustento. En *King Lear* se avanza un paso más, ya que son las propias
crías quienes se procuran el alimento y calor.

72. *Pillicock.* La afinidad fónica con *pelican,* del verso anterior, le sugiere al
bufón este verso, procedente de una canción obscena, por cuanto que *pillicok* es
un término utilizado para designar el órgano genital masculino.

Esta gélida noche a todos nos ha de volver locos y nos trastornará.

Teme al demonio maligno, honra a tus padres. No jures en vano, no blasfemes y no forniques con la esposa legítima de otro. No codicies. No vistas con lujo... Tom tiene frío.

¿Qué fuiste?

Un siervo orgulloso de corazón y espíritu; tenía el pelo rizado; 80
llevaba el guante de mi amada en el sombrero, y para servir a
su lascivo corazón, con ella me entregaba al acto de la oscuridad. Profería tantos votos como dije palabras, que luego rom-
pía ante la sagrada faz del cielo. Acariciaba en sueños la lujuria
para satisfacerla al despertar. Apasionadamente amaba el vino
y los dados y superaba al gran turco en mujeres. De corazón
falso, ligero oído y manos sanguinarias; como el cerdo, perezoso; astuto, como el zorro; voraz, como el lobo; rabioso, como
el perro; como el león, con su presa. Ni el crujir de suelas ni el
roce de la seda descubran tu pobre corazón a la mujer. No 90
pongas pie en burdeles, ni tu mano en la enagua, ni tu nombre

---

87-9. *como el cerdo... con su presa;* en el original, «hog in sloth, fox in stealth,
wolf in greediness, dog in madness, lion in prey» Se ha buscado en castellano
una equivalencia, transformando los sustantivos abstractos en adjetivos, y rela-
cionándolos con el animal prototipo de esas características mediante una comparación expresada por «como». El orden de los elementos, que en inglés sigue
el mismo esquema (sustantivo concreto + *in* + sustantivo abstracto) en una serie
de intensidad creciente, necesita de la introducción de variaciones en castellano,
porque las palabras contienen más sílabas, y el ritmo así lo exige, pero el resultado en ambos casos es la culminación del proceso ascendente marcado por la
sucesión de elementos.

90-1. *No pongas pie en burdeles.* En el original, «Keep thy feet out of brothels, en libros de usureros. Y desafía al demonio. Todavía sopla el gélido viento a través del espino. Uuh, uuh, uh, Delfín, pequeño mío, detente, déjalo trotar.

(Sigue la tormenta.)

LEAR

Mejor en la tumba que enfrentar tu cuerpo desnudo al furor del cielo. ¿Es que el hombre es sólo esto? Considéralo mejor. No le debes la seda al gusano, ni la piel a la bestia, ni la lana a la oveja, ni el perfume al gato. ¡Ah! He aquí tres que están adulterados. Tú eres el ser mismo; el hombre puro no es más que un pobre animal, desnudo y erguido como tú. ¡Fuera, harapos! Ven, desnúdame.

(Entra GLOUCESTER con una antorcha.)

BUFÓN

Os lo suplico, amo, conteneos; es mala noche para andar. Un pequeño fuego en campo salvaje sería ahora como el corazón de un viejo lascivo; sólo una chispa; frío el resto del cuerpo. ¡Mira! Ahí llega un fuego que camina.

---

thy hand out of plackets, thy pen from lender's books, and defy the foul friend». Se ha traducido *Keep thy foot out of* por «No pongas pie en», donde la partícula negativa «no» recoge el sentido de *out of*, porque de este modo los elementos coordinados que dependen del verbo se suceden con mayor facilidad en castellano, introducidos por «ni... en», más breve y aceptable que la repetición de «fuera de» o «lejos de». En castellano se ha indicado una pausa más larga mediante el punto situado después de «usureros». La razón de esta señalización de pausa más larga, donde en inglés aparece una coma, es la mayor longitud de los elementos en castellano.

93-4. *Delfín, pequeño mío, detente.* «Dolphin my boy, boy; sessa», en el original. Se trata de una frase muy discutida y prácticamente incomprensible. Puede tratarse del nombre de una caballo —o un grito de reclamo, según otros comentaristas—, mientras que *sessa* parece provenir del francés *cessez.*

EDGAR

Es el demonio Flibbertigibbet, el abominable; llega con el cre-
púsculo y se va con el canto del gallo; es el que nubla el ojo, el
que lo pone bizco y hace el labio leporino; es el que corrompe
el trigo maduro, y atormenta a la pobre criatura en la tierra.

> Fue a pie por los valles tres veces San Withold   110
> y en pesadilla nueve secuaces encontró.
> Le dijo: «A tierra, atrás,
> semilla del diablo, jura tu fe y atrás.»

KENT

¿Cómo estáis, Majestad?

LEAR

¿Quién es éste?

KENT

¿Quién va ahí? ¿Qué buscáis?

GLOUCESTER

¿Quiénes sois vosotros? ¿Vuestros nombres?

EDGAR

Tom Pobre, que come ranas, sapos, renacuajos, lagartos, sala-
mandras; que, con rabia en el corazón, cuando el demonio se
enfurece, come estiércol de vaca por ensalada, se traga viejas 120

---

106. *Flibbertigibbet*. Este nombre, junto a los de los otros diablos mencionados en el drama, aparecen en la sátira de S. Harsnett, *A Declaration of Egregious
Popish Impostures*, y, sin duda, de ahí los obtuvo Shakespeare.
110-13. No se conoce el origen de estos cuatro versos, que parecen cons-
truidos como un «conjuro» contra las pesadillas nocturnas. San Withold aparece
en otros textos como protector contra el mal.

ratas y carroña de perro, bebe agua verde del estanque, y es fustigado de parroquia en parroquia, puesto en cepos, encarcelado y castigado; el que tuvo tres capas para su espalda y seis camisas para el cuerpo.

> para la guerra, espada, y un caballo bravío
> para montar, y rata, ratón y cervatillo
> durante siete años su comida han sido.

Cuidado con quien me sigue. ¡Atrás Smulkin, atrás demonio!

GLOUCESTER

¿Cómo? ¿No tendría Vuestra Gracia compañía mejor?

EDGAR

El príncipe de las tinieblas es un caballero. Modo, le llaman; y 130
Mahu...

GLOUCESTER

Nuestra carne, *my lord,* y nuestra sangre
llegan a ser tan viles que odian a quien las engendró.

EDGAR

Tom Pobre tiene frío...

GLOUCESTER

Venid conmigo. No puede inclinarse mi deber
a las crueles órdenes de vuestras hijas;
su orden fue cerrar mis puertas y dejar que la noche

---

128. *Smulkin.* Véase la nota a la línea 106, de esta escena.
130-1. En el libro de Harsnett, mencionado en la nota a la línea 106, *Modo* y *Mahu* son los nombres que reciben los comandantes de las legiones infernales.

cruel tomara posesión de vos. Me he arriesgado
a buscaros para conduciros
hasta donde la comida y el calor os esperan.   140

LEAR

Dejadme hablar primero con este filósofo.
¿Qué es lo que causa el trueno?

KENT

                    Mi señor,
aceptad su petición; entrad en casa.

LEAR

Unas palabras antes con el docto tebano.
¿En qué os ocupáis?

EDGAR

En evitar al diablo y en matar alimañas.

LEAR

·Permitidme unas palabras en privado.

KENT

Insistid una vez más en que os siga, *my lord*.
Su juicio empieza a desvariar.

(Sigue la tormenta.)

GLOUCESTER

                    ¿Podéis culparlo?
Sus hijas le desean la muerte. ¡Ah, el buen Kent!   150
Así predijo que sería, ¡pobre desterrado!

[179]

Decís que el rey se vuelve loco; amigo, yo os diré,
yo mismo, al borde estoy también de la locura. Tuve un hijo,
proscrito ahora de mi sangre; ha querido mi muerte
hace poco, muy poco; le amé, amigo,
como nunca un padre amó a un hijo. Y, si he de ser sincero,
el dolor me ha trastornado el juicio. ¡Triste noche!
Ruego a Vuestra Gracia...

LEAR

                    ¡Oh! ¡Disculpadme, sire!
Noble filósofo, tu compañía.

EDGAR

Tom tiene frío...

GLOUCESTER

Amigo, entrad en la cabaña; calentaos.

LEAR

¡Vamos! ¡Entremos todos!

KENT

                    Por aquí, *my lord*.

LEAR

                              ¡Con él!
Pues quiero a este filósofo conmigo.

KENT

Complacedle, *my lord*. Dejadle entrar.

[180]

Ocupaos de él.

KENT

¡Venga! ¡Vamos! ¡Seguidnos!

LEAR

Vamos, buen ateniense.

GLOUCESTER

¡Ni una palabra! ¡Chsss!

EDGAR

Roldán, el caballero, vino a la torre oscura
y sus palabras eran: «Fin, fon, fan, aún perdura   170
olor de sangre inglesa sobre mi empuñadura.»

(Salen.)

ESCENA QUINTA*

(Entran CORNWALL *y* EDMUND.)

CORNWALL

Me he de vengar antes de partir.

170-1. Se trata, en este caso, de la adaptación de una balada perteneciente a
las leyendas de Carlomagno, en la que aparece el personaje de Roldán, sobrino
suyo y héroe de famosas gestas.
* De nuevo, una breve escena en prosa que se desarrolla en el interior del
castillo de Gloucester, y que sirve de preparación para la tortura de Gloucester
—paralela a la de Lear— que tendrá lugar en la escena séptima.

Bastardo [Edmund]

Me preocupa, *my lord,* pensar que se me pueda criticar, pues mi
naturaleza cede ante mi lealtad.

Cornwall

Comprendo ahora que no fuera sólo la inclinación perversa de
vuestro hermano lo que le hizo desear su muerte; sino un orgullo insultante, planeado por su reprobable maldad.

[Edmund]

¡Qué fortuna maligna, que me hace arrepentirme de ser justo!
Esta es la carta de la que habló, que prueba que es espía al servicio de France. ¡Cielos! ¡Ojalá que esto no hubiera sido traición ni yo su delator!

10

Cornwall

¡Acompañadme ante la duquesa!

[Edmund]

Si el contenido de este papel es cierto, ante un asunto grave os
encontráis.

Cornwall

Cierto o falso, os ha hecho conde de Gloucester. Buscad a
vuestro padre, que esté preparado para su detención.

[Edmund]

Si lo encuentra ayudando al rey aumentará la sospecha... Se-
guiré el camino de la lealtad aunque cruel sea el conflicto entre
ella y mi sangre.

---

14. Por traidor, Gloucester es desposeído de su título que pasa a Edmund, al
haber sido desheredado Edgar por su padre previamente.

CORNWALL

Pongo mi confianza en vos; tenéis en mí un padre más querido. 20

(Salen.)

ESCENA SEXTA*

(Entran KENT y GLOUCESTER.)

GLOUCESTER

Mejor aquí que al aire libre. Aceptadlo con agrado. Trataré de hacer si puedo más confortable este sitio. No he de estar mucho tiempo lejos de vosotros.

(Sale.)

KENT

Toda la fuerza de su juicio ha cedido a su cólera. ¡Que los dioses recompensen vuestra bondad!

(Entran LEAR, EDGAR y el BUFÓN.)

EDGAR

Frateretto me llama, y me dice que Nerón es pescador en el lago de las Tinieblas. Ruega, inocente, y guárdate del mal espíritu.

---

* Se desarrolla esta escena en el interior de un granero o edificio similar, cerca del castillo de Gloucester. Es interesante resaltar que en la edición *in Folio* está omitida la parte central, referente al imaginario juicio contra las hijas de Lear, que, si bien no contribuye al desarrollo argumental, está cargada de intensidad dramática y profundidad en la esencia de la tragedia de Lear.

6. *Frateretto.* Véase la nota a III.iv.106.

[183]

BUFÓN

Te lo ruego, amo, dime si un loco es noble o plebeyo.

LEAR

¡Es un rey, es un rey!   10

BUFÓN

No; es un plebeyo que tiene por hijo a un caballero... Que loco es el plebeyo que hace noble a su hijo antes de serlo él.

LEAR

Que un millar de tridentes, llameando su fuego, caigan silbando sobre sus cabezas.

EDGAR

El diablo maligno me muerde la espalda.

BUFÓN

Loco aquel que confía en la docilidad del lobo, la salud de un caballo, el amor de un joven o el juramento de una puta.

LEAR

Así se hará, a juicio he de llevarlas ahora mismo.
Sabio juez, venid, sentaos aquí.
Y aquí, sentaos vos, sabio señor. Y ahora, vosotras, zorras...   20

10-1. Estas líneas no aparecen en *Quarto*.
15.21. Como apuntábamos al principio de la escena, este fragmento no aparece en *Folio*.

EDGAR

¡Miradlo ahí con los ojos encendidos! ¿No queréis ojos,
madam, en vuestro juicio?

Pasa el arroyo, Bessy, ven a mí...

BUFÓN

Que hay una brecha en su barcaza,
que tiene miedo de acercarse a ti,
que está callada.

EDGAR

El diablo maligno acecha a Tom Pobre con voz de ruiseñor.
Hoppedance pide a gritos dos arenques para el vientre de
Tom. No graznes, ángel negro; no tengo comida para ti.

KENT

¿Cómo estáis, señor? No os quedéis ahí, asombrado.   30
¿Por qué no reposáis sobre estas almohadas?

LEAR

Antes veré su juicio. Presentad su evidencia.
Vos, entogado juez, ocupad vuestro sitio.
Y vos, su compañero en equidad,
sentaos a su lado. Y vos, también del tribunal,
tomad asiento.

EDGAR

Procedamos con justicia.

---

28. *Hoppedance*. Véase la nota a III.iv.106. El nombre que utiliza Harsnett es,
sin embargo, *Hoberdidance*, y así ha sido enmendado por algunos editores. En
IV.i.59 aparece como *Hobbididence*.

¿Duermes o velas, pastor mío?
pastan ovejas en el campo,
que basta un soplo de tu dulce boca   40
para dejarle a salvo.

¡Purr!, el gato es gris.

LEAR

Que comparezca ella primero. Es Gonerill. Juro aquí ante este
honorable tribunal que echó a patadas al pobre rey, su padre.

BUFÓN

Acercaos, señora. ¿Es vuestro nombre Gonerill?

LEAR

No puede negarlo.

BUFÓN

Perdonad, os confundí con un asiento.

LEAR

He aquí otra, cuyos perversos ojos nos proclaman
de qué materia es su corazón. ¡Detenedla!
¡Hierro y fuego! ¡A las armas! ¡Ah, también corrupción!   50
Falso juez, ¿por qué la dejas escapar?

EDGAR

¡Benditos sean tus cinco sentidos!

---

42. *Purr.* Probablemente se trate del nombre de uno de los diablos mencionados por Harsnett, a los que hemos hecho referencia en notas anteriores. Algunos comentaristas optan, sin embargo, por considerar que se refiere al sonido
producido por un gato cuya forma hubiera asumido algún diablo, y, de ahí, la
traducción.

[186]

Kent

¡Tened piedad, señor! ¿Dónde está ahora la paciencia de la que
tanto presumíais?

Edgar *(Aparte.)*

Tanto empiezan a sufrir mis lágrimas por él
que estropean mi disfraz.

Lear

Hasta los mismos perros,
Tray, Blanch y Sweetheart, vedlo, me ladran.

Edgar

Tom les embestirá. ¡Atrás perros!

> Sea su boca blanca o negra   60
> diente que muerde envenena,
> mastín, braguete, bastardo,
> dogo, español, lebrel, galgo,
> rabilargo o rabicorto
> gemirán de cualquier modo
> pues si embisto de cabeza
> todos huyen como bestias.

¡Do, de, de, de. Sese! ¡Adelante! ¡A fiestas, ferias y mercados!
Tom Pobre, tu cuerno está vacío.

Lear

¡Que se despedace a Regan, para que veamos qué es lo que ali- 70
menta su corazón! Vos, sire, os tomo como uno de mis cien

---

68. *¡Do, de, de, de, Sese!* Se trata, posiblemente, del sonido que producen los
dientes al castañetear a causa del frío. Véase la nota a III.iv.54-5. Para *Sese*, véase la nota a III.iv.93-4.

caballeros; si bien no me complace de qué guisa vais. Vos diréis que es persa; sin embargo, cambiáosla.

(*Entra* GLOUCESTER.)

KENT

Mi buen señor, yaced aquí y descansad un poco.

LEAR

¡Silencio! ¡No hagáis ruido! ¡Corred las cortinas: así, eso! Cenaremos por la mañana.

BUFÓN

Sí. Y yo me acostaré a mediodía.

GLOUCESTER

Acercaos, amigo. ¿Dónde está el rey, mi dueño?

KENT

Aquí, señor. Mas no le molestéis; le ha abandonado el juicio.

GLOUCESTER

Amigo, yo os lo ruego, tomadlo en vuestros brazos.   80
He oído que hay un complot de muerte contra él.
Hay preparada una litera; colocadle en ella,

---

77. *Sí. Yo me acostaré al mediodía;* en el original, «And I'll go to bed at noon». Entre los comentaristas se dan hasta siete posibles significados de esta frase del bufón —la última que este personaje pronuncia en la tragedia—, y aparece omitida en *Quarto*. Podría interpretarse como un anuncio de su muerte prematura, o que se trate de una respuesta «natural» a Lear que, cuando dice «cenaremos al mediodía» rompe el ritmo natural de la cotidianidad. Quizá anuncia su despedida del escenario porque Lear ha perdido el juicio por completo y ya no necesita de otro loco. Se daría así la intención evidente de usar lo más absurdo que, al mismo tiempo, es lo más poético.

y dirigíos a Dover, amigo, donde encontraréis
asilo y protección. Tomad a vuestro dueño.
Si tardáis media hora, vuestra vida, la suya
y la de todo aquel que piensa en defenderle
están perdidas ciertamente. Tomadle,
y seguidme, que yo os conduciré, pronto, a un lugar
para aprovisionaros.

KENT

                    Oprimida la Naturaleza duerme.
Este reposo podría servir de bálsamo para los nervios rotos   90
que, si no se presentan mejores circunstancias,
tendrán difícil cura... Ven, ayúdame
a llevar a tu amo. No te quedes atrás.

GLOUCESTER

                              ¡Vamos, en marcha!

(Salen LEAR, KENT, GLOUCESTER *y el* BUFÓN.*)*

EDGAR

Cuando vemos a nuestros superiores llevar nuestro dolor,
apenas si pensamos que nuestras miserias sean nuestros
                                                    [enemigos.
Quien sufre solo, sufre más en la mente
renunciando a libertad y a imágenes felices;
pero la mente descuida un sufrimiento tal
cuando la pena tiene compañero, y el sufrimiento compañía.
¡Qué ligero y soportable mi dolor parece ahora,   100
cuando lo que a mí me doblega hace al rey inclinarse!
¡Tuvo hijos como yo tuve padre! ¡Fuera, Tom!
Atención a los ruidos, y quítate el disfraz

89-107. Todo este fragmento, excepto la frase de Gloucester «¡Vamos, en
marcha!», no aparece en *Quarto*.

cuando los falsos juicios que te ensucian con pensamiento
[errado
sean revocados en prueba de justicia y se te reconcilie.
¡Aunque ocurra algo más esta noche, quede el rey a salvo!
¡Cuidado, ocúltate!

(Sale.)

ESCENA SÉPTIMA*

(Entran CORNWALL, REGAN, GONERILL, *el bastardo* [EDMUND]
y sirvientes.)

CORNWALL

Acudid pronto a *my lord,* vuestro esposo; enseñadle esta carta:
el ejército de Francia ha llegado. Buscad al traidor Gloucester.

REGAN

¡Ahorcadlo en seguida!

GONERILL

¡Que le saquen los ojos!

CORNWALL

¡Dejadlo a mi cuidado! Edmund, acompañad a nuestra hermana. La venganza que tomaremos contra el traidor de vuestro
padre no es apropiada para vuestros ojos. Avisad al duque, ya
que allí os dirigís, para que haga rápidos preparativos; que nosotros haremos otro tanto. Nuestros mensajeros serán veloces
y eficaces entre nosotros. Adiós, querida hermana; adiós, *my* 10
lord de Gloucester.

---

* Se desencadena la violencia física en la persona de Gloucester, estableciendo así un paralelismo entre la tortura física que éste sufre, y la tortura mental de
Lear, de la escena inmediatamente anterior.

(Entra mayordomo [Oswald].)

¡Y bien! ¿Dónde está el rey?

MAYORDOMO [OSWALD]

Mi señor de Gloucester se lo llevó de aquí.
Una treintena de sus caballeros
que, ansiosos, lo buscaban, lo hallaron en la puerta,
y, con otros servidores suyos,
han partido hacia Dover, donde presumen de tener amigos
bien armados.

CORNWALL

Preparad los caballos para vuestra señora.

GONERILL

Adiós, noble señor, hermana, adiós.

(Salen GONERILL y OSWALD.)

CORNWALL

Adiós, Edmund.

(Sale EDMUND.)

      ¡Id a buscar al traidor Gloucester!   20
¡Atrapadle como a un ladrón, traedle ante nosotros!
Aunque no sea posible disponer de su vida sin proceso,
nuestro poder habrá de someterse a nuestra ira,
lo que podrán los hombres censurar,

---

14. *una treintena de sus caballeros;* en el original, «some five or six-and-thirty of his knights». Se ha elegido en la traducción una expresión equivalente al número indeterminado próximo a treinta: «treintena», en lugar del «treinta y cinco o treinta y seis» del original.

(Entran Gloucester *y sirvientes.)*

mas no impedir. ¿Quién va? ¿El traidor?

Regan

¡Él es! ¡Ingrato zorro!

Cornwall

¡Atadle con fuerza esos brazos acartonados!

Gloucester

¿Qué intentan Vuestras Gracias? Amigos míos, pensad
que sois mis invitados. No me hagáis juego sucio.

Cornwall

¡Os digo que lo atéis!

Regan

¡Apretad fuerte! ¡Repugnante traidor!   30

Gloucester

Despiadada mujer, vos lo sois, yo no.

Cornwall

¡Atadlo a esta silla! Villano, ahora sabrás lo que...

Gloucester

¡Por los nobles dioses! Que es innoble acto
arrancarme la barba.

REGAN

¡Tan blanca y de un traidor así!

GLOUCESTER

Perversa dama,
los pelos que me arrancáis de la cara
se habrán de alzar para acusaros. Yo soy vuestro anfitrión.
Con manos de ladrón, mi gesto de hospitalidad
no deberíais violentar. ¿Qué os proponéis?

CORNWALL

¡Vamos, señor! ¿Qué nuevas acabáis de recibir de Francia?   40

REGAN

Contestad sin rodeos. Sabemos la verdad.

CORNWALL

¿Qué confabulación tenéis con los traidores
que acaban de desembarcar en el reino?

REGAN

¿En qué manos
habéis puesto al lunático rey? Hablad.

GLOUCESTER

Tengo una carta escrita con sólo conjeturas,

___

37. *se habrán de alzar para acusaros;* en el original, «will quicken and accuse
thee». Al tratarse del final de una amenaza, se perdería la gravedad si se emplea-
ran dos verbos en futuro unidos por la conjunción «y», y el resultado adoptaría
un tono casi infantil, distinto del que se desprende del original. La idea de continuidad temporal y de su consecuencia lógica está implícita en *and* y explícita
en «para».

que me llegó de alguien de corazón neutral,
y no de un enemigo.

CORNWALL

¡Astuto!

REGAN

¡Y falso!

CORNWALL

¿Adónde habéis mandado al rey?

GLOUCESTER

A Dover.

REGAN

¿Y por qué a Dover? ¿no se os advirtió, bajo amenaza...?

CORNWALL

¿Y por qué a Dover? Que responda a esto.   50

GLOUCESTER

Me encuentro atado, y debo soportar la arremetida.

REGAN

¿Por qué a Dover?

GLOUCESTER

Porque no quiero ver cómo vuestras crueles garras
le arrancan sus cansados ojos de anciano; ni a vuestra feroz
                                                    [hermana

hundir sus colmillos de jabalí en su carne ungida.
El mar —con una tormenta como la que su cabeza soportó
                                                    [desnuda
en una noche, oscura como el mismo infierno— se habría
                                                    [levantado
hasta apagar los fuegos estelares.
Aun así, ¡pobre y anciano corazón!, ayudó a los cielos a llover.
Si los lobos hubiesen aullado a tu puerta en esta hora terrible   60
habrías dicho: «Abre, buen guardián,
ya es suficiente crueldad.» Mas he de ver
las alas de la venganza caer sobre esas hijas.

CORNWALL

Nunca lo habréis de ver. Vosotros, sujetad la silla.
Sobre estos ojos tuyos mi pie colocaré.

GLOUCESTER

Que todo el que desee llegar a la vejez
me ayude. ¡Qué cruel! ¡Oh, dioses!

REGAN

Un lado a solas haría burla del otro. ¡Que sean los dos!

CORNWALL

Si veis la venganza...

SIRVIENTE [1.ᵉʳ SIRVIENTE]

¡Deteneos, *my lord!*
Os he servido desde niño,   70

---

57. *en una noche oscura como el mismo infierno;* en el original, «in hell-black
night». La construcción inglesa en que *hell,* yuxtapuesto a *black,* lo modifica, de-
terminando su cualidad, se ha traducido en castellano mediante una perífrasis
explicativa, introducida por «como». Se ha añadido el elemento «mismo» para
enfatizar la oscuridad de la noche.

pero nunca os presté un servicio mejor
que ahora, al pedir que os detengáis.

REGAN

¿Cómo, perro?

[1.er SIRVIENTE]

Si tuvierais pelo en la barbilla,
yo os lo arrancaría en la disputa.

REGAN

¿Qué pretendéis hacer?

CORNWALL

¡Uno de mis servidores!

[1.er SIRVIENTE.]

¡Sea! ¡En guardia! ¡Aceptad el riesgo de la cólera!

REGAN

Dame tu espada. ¡Un siervo rebelarse así!

(Lo mata.)

[1.er SIRVIENTE]

¡Oh, muerto soy! *My lord,* os queda un ojo
para mirar el mal que yo le he hecho. ¡Ah!

CORNWALL

Impidamos que siga viendo. ¡Fuera, vil gelatina!   80
¿Dónde tu brillo ahora?

[196]

GLOUCESTER

Oscuro todo y desolado. ¿Dónde está mi hijo Edmund?
Edmund, aviva todas las chispas de la Naturaleza
para vengar este acto horrendo.

REGAN

                              ¡Fuera, traidor villano!
Llamáis a aquél que os odia.
Él fue quien denunció vuestras traiciones;
y es demasido bueno para tener piedad de vos.

GLOUCESTER

¡Oh, locura mía! Edgar fue calumniado.
¡Oh, dioses! ¡Perdonadme y protegedle a él!

REGAN

¡Id! ¡Arrojadlo fuera, y que olfatee   90
su camino hacia Dover!

                    (Sale [alguien] con GLOUCESTER.)

                    ¿Qué os ocurre, *my lord*? ¿Qué mirada es esa?

CORNWALL

Me han herido. Seguidme, mi señora.
expulsad a ese canalla sin ojos; echad a este rufián
al vertedero. Regan, sangro mucho.
En mala hora viene esta herida. Dadme vuestro brazo.

                    (Salen.)

96-104. Fragmento omitido en *Folio*.

SIRVIENTE [2.º SIRVIENTE]

No me importará hacer maldad alguna
con tal de que este hombre acabe bien.

2.º SIRVIENTE [3.er SIRVIENTE]

                                    Si ella vive bastante,
que al fin encuentre muerte natural,
toda mujer se habrá de volver monstruo.

1.er SIRVIENTE [2.º SIRVIENTE]

Sigamos al viejo conde, busquemos al de Bedlam   100
para guiarlo adonde quiera; su nómada locura
se presta a cualquier cosa.

2.º SIRVIENTE [3.er SIRVIENTE]

Ve tú; yo iré por vendas y por claras de huevo
para poner en su sangrante cara. ¡Cielos, ayudadle!

(Sale[n].)

ACTO IV

ESCENA PRIMERA*

(Entra Edgar.*)*

Edgar

Mejor estar así, despreciado y saberlo,
que no adulado en el desprecio. Eso es peor,
la fortuna más baja y humillante
persiste aún en la esperanza, no vive en el temor:
qué lamentable el cambio cuando se tiene el bien,
que el mal en risa se convierte. ¡Bienvenido, pues,
tú, aire sin materia que yo abrazo!
El pobre al que has lanzado a lo peor
nada debe a tus ráfagas.

(Entran Gloucester *y un* Viejo.*)*

¿Quién viene?
¡Mi padre conducido por un pobre! ¡Oh mundo, mundo,

[mundo! 10

---

* Con esta escena concluye la gran secuencia central de la tragedia. Edgar,
que durante la tormenta se había convertido en reflejo de la locura de Lear,
vuelve ahora junto a su padre para cumplir la función de lazarillo.

6-9. *¡Bienvenido... ráfagas.* Estas líneas no aparecen en *Quarto.*

10. *¡Mi padre conducido por un pobre!* En el original, «My father, poorly led!» Es
esta la lectura que encontramos en *Folio,* mientras que en *Quarto* se puede leer
parti-eyed (cuya traducción literal sería «con ojos de múltiples colores», puesto

Si por tus extraños cambios no te odiáramos
la vida no se resignaría a la vejez.

Viejo

¡Mi buen señor!
Yo fui vuestro vasallo y el de vuestro padre
durante ochenta años.

Gloucester

¡Marchaos! ¡Buen amigo, alejaos!
Vuestros consuelos no me hacen bien alguno
y os hacen daño a vos.

Viejo

No podéis ver vuestro camino.

Gloucester

Yo no tengo camino, no necesito ojos, por lo tanto;
cuando veía, tropecé. Ocurre con frecuencia
que nuestros medios nos hacen confiados; y nuestros defectos   20
confirman las ventajas. ¡Querido hijo Edgar,
pasto para la ira de tu padre engañado!
Si pudiera vivir para mirarte al tacto
diría que de nuevo tengo ojos.

Viejo

¿Cómo? ¿Quién anda ahí?

---

que *parti* equivaldría a los prefijos «multi» o «poli», para designar cosas com-
puestas de colores o materiales heterogéneos). Opinamos que, desde un punto
de vista teatral, Edgar notaría antes el hecho de que su padre era «conducido
por un pobre», quedando, de alguna manera, implícito el hecho de que ha de ser
guiado puesto que ha quedado ciego.

¡Oh, dioses! Nadie puede decir: «Estoy en lo peor»,
peor estoy que nunca.

VIEJO

Es Tom, el pobre loco.

EDGAR *[Aparte.]*

Y aún puedo estar peor. No es lo peor
mientras pueda decir: «Es lo peor.»

VIEJO

Amigo, ¿adónde vais?

GLOUCESTER

¿Es un mendigo?

VIEJO

Mendigo y también loco.   30

GLOUCESTER

Algo de juicio tiene o no sabría mendigar.
Yo vi anoche, durante la tormenta, a un hombre así
que me hizo pensar que es un gusano el hombre.
Mi hijo vino entonces a mi mente; aunque mi mente
le era entonces poco amiga. Después aprendí más:
somos para los dioses lo que las moscas son para los niños,
nos matan para su diversión.

EDGAR *[Aparte.]*

¿Cómo es posible?

[201]

Malo es el oficio de hacer de loco ante el dolor,
con rabia para él mismo y los demás... Dios te bendiga, amo.

GLOUCESTER

¿Es el hombre desnudo?

VIEJO

Sí, *my lord.*   40

GLOUCESTER

Os lo ruego, alejaos. Si en atención a mí
quisierais alcanzarnos a una milla o dos de este lugar,
en el camino a Dover, hacedlo en nombre del antiguo afecto
y traed algo con que cubrir esta alma desnuda,
a la que rogaré me guíe.

VIEJO

Pero, sire, está loco.

GLOUCESTER

Es el mal de estos tiempos, los locos guían a los ciegos.
Haced lo que os ordeno, o mejor, haced lo que os plazca,
y, ante todo, marchaos.

VIEJO

Le llevaré el mejor traje que tenga,
ocurra lo que ocurra.

(Sale.)

GLOUCESTER

¡Eh, vos, hombre desnudo...!   50

[202]

EDGAR

¡Tom Pobre tiene frío!... No puedo fingir más.

GLOUCESTER

¡Acercaos, amigo!

EDGAR *[Aparte.]*

Pero debo... Benditos dulces ojos: cómo sangran.

GLOUCESTER

¿Conocéis el camino hacia Dover?

EDGAR

Sí, con puertas y postigos, el de a caballo y el de a pie. A Tom Pobre le han espantado su buen juicio. Dios os guarde, hijo de un hombre bueno, del diablo maligno. Cinco diablos han estado a la vez dentro de Tom Pobre: Obidicut, el de la lujuria; Hobbididence, príncipe del mutismo; Mahu, del robo; Modo, del asesinato, y Flibbertigibbet, de gestos y muecas, que hace 60 tiempo que posee a sirvientas y doncellas. ¡Guardaos entonces, amo!

GLOUCESTER

Toma, coge esta bolsa. Tú a quien han humillado con sus golpes
las plagas de los cielos. El que yo sea desgraciado
te haga a ti más feliz. ¡Cielos, obrad así!
¡Que el hombre superfluo y alimentado con lujuria
que hace esclavas vuestras leyes, que al no sentir no ve,
sufra vuestro poder rápidamente!

57-62. *Cinco diablos... amo!* Este fragmento aparece omitido en *Folio*.
58-60. *Obidicut... Flibbertigibbet.* Véase la nota a III.iv.106.

Así, el reparto deshaga todo exceso
y cada hombre tenga suficiente. ¿Conoces Dover?

EDGAR

Sí, amo.

GLOUCESTER

Hay un acantilado cuya alta cima colgante
se mira horrorizada en el profundo límite.
Llévame al mismo borde.
Y la miseria que soportas, allí repararé
con algo muy precioso que hay en mí. Desde ese lugar
no necesitaré ya de tu guía.

EDGAR

Dadme el brazo.
Tom Pobre os guiará.

(Salen.)

ESCENA SEGUNDA*

(Entran GONERILL, *el bastardo* [EDMUND] *y mayordomo*
[OSWALD]*.)*

GONERILL

Bienvenido, *my lord;* me extraña que no venga a nuestro encuentro nuestro apacible esposo. ¿Dónde está vuestro amo?

---

* Se inicia con esta escena una nueva secuencia dramática en la que se vis-
lumbran las relaciones entre Edmund y las dos hijas de Lear, así como entre éstos y los demás personajes —Albany, en particular—, en el escenario del castillo de Gonerill, que sirve de puente entre las escenas anteriores, en Gloucester,
y las siguientes que suceden en Dover, lugar que adquiere el valor simbólico de
escenario de la catarsis trágica.

Mayordomo [Oswald]

Dentro, *madam;* pero jamás un hombre cambió tanto.
Le hablé del ejército que había desembarcado
y sonrió. Le dije que veníais vos,
y su respuesta fue: «¡Tanto peor!»
Cuando de la traición de Gloucester,
y del leal servicio de su hijo le informé, me llamó idiota
y me dijo que había vuelto del revés el derecho.
Lo que más le debiera disgustar parece que le agrada;   10
lo que es grato, le ofende.

Gonerill *(A* Edmund.)

                    No es necesario ir más allá.
Es el miedo cobarde de un espíritu
que no se atreve a emprender nada; no escucha los ultrajes
que obligan a respuesta. Los planes hechos durante el camino
pueden tener efecto. Regresad, Edmund, al lado de mi hermano;
pasad revista rápido y conducid sus fuerzas.
Debo cambiar las armas en la casa, y colocar la rueca
en manos de mi esposo. Este sirviente fiel
nos servirá de intermediario. Es probable que oigáis, dentro
                                                [de poco,
si osáis arriesgaros por vuestro propio bien,   20
órdenes de una dama. Llevad esto; no habléis;
acercad la cabeza. Este beso, si se atreviera a hablar,
elevaría vuestra alma por el aire.
Imaginadlo e id con Dios.

Bastardo [Edmund]

Vuestro hasta en las filas de la muerte.

(Sale.)

GONERILL

¡Mi bien amado Gloucester!
¡Oh! ¡Qué diferente un hombre de otro hombre!
Tú eres quien merece favores de mujer.
Un imbécil ha usurpado mi cama.

[OSWALD]

Señora, aquí viene *my lord*.

([Sale]. Entra ALBANY.)

GONERILL

En otro tiempo se me valoraba.

ALBANY

¡Oh, Gonerill!
Ya no vales ni el polvo que los ásperos vientos   30
arrojan a tu cara. Me da miedo tu instinto.
Una naturaleza que desprecia su origen
no posee en sí misma límites seguros.
Quien a sí misma se desgaja del tronco
que le daba su savia, forzosamente habrá de marchitarse
y encontrará en la muerte su destino.

GONERILL

¡Basta ya! ¡El sermón es ridículo!

---

26. Este verso no aparece en *Quarto*.
29. *En otro tiempo se me valoraba;* en el original, «I have been worth the
whistle» (lit.: *He merecido el silbido*). Es una alusión irónica al proverbio *It is a
poor dog that is not worth the whistle* («No vale nada el perro al que nadie se molesta
en llamar con un silbido»).
31-50. *Me da miedo... profundidades.* Fragmento omitido en *Folio*.

Sabiduría y bondad parecen viles al villano.
Lo sucio sólo place a lo que es sucio. ¿Qué habéis hecho?
Tigres, ya que no hijas, ¿cómo habéis actuado?   40
Un padre, un digno anciano
a quien, con reverencia, hasta el oso enfurecido lamería.
¡Salvajes y degeneradas! Le habéis hecho enloquecer.
¿Pudo mi buen hermano consentir que obrarais así?
¡Un hombre, un príncipe a quien él tanto protegió!
Si los cielos no envían sus visibles espíritus
rápidamente para que pongan fin a esas ofensas viles, ocurrirá
que a sí misma, a la fuerza, la humanidad habrá de devorarse
como los monstruos de las profundidades.

GONERILL

                              ¡Hombre con hígado de leche! 50
Que ofreces a los golpes tu mejilla y tu cabeza a los errores,
que no tienes debajo de las cejas un ojo que distinga
tu honor de tu vergüenza; que no sabes que tan sólo los locos
tienen piedad de los villanos a los que se castiga
antes que hayan hecho daño. ¿Dónde está tu tambor?
France despliega estandartes en esta tierra de silencio
y con yelmo de plumas amenaza tu estado,
mientras tú, idiota moralizador, sigues sentado y gritas:
«¡Oh! ¿Por qué lo hace?»

---

42. *el oso enfurecido;* en el original, «the head-lugged bear», que se traduciría, literalmente, como «el oso al que se ha reducido poniéndole una correa o argolla
alrededor del cuello», y que, por tanto, reacciona con furia. El verbo más próximo, aplicable a caballos o toros, de que disponemos sería «encabestrar», que
contiene, asimismo, un doble nivel de significado, literal y metafórico. Dada la
frecuencia con que los osos eran utilizados en espectáculos durante el periodo
isabelino, existía un vocabulario referente a estas actividades, vocabulario del
que carecemos en castellano. De ahí la traducción más libre del significado de la
imagen, excesivamente distanciada para una comprensión contemporánea.

50. *hígado de leche;* en el original, «milk-livered». Compárase con II.ii.15., en
que *lily-livered* se ha traducido por «sin agallas».

ALBANY

¡Mírate, diablo!
Una misma deformidad no nos parece tan horrible   60
en el demonio como en la mujer.

GONERILL

¡Necio estúpido!

ALBANY

Cosa encubierta y deformada, no cambies nunca, por vergüenza,
tu cara en monstruo. Si me fuera posible
el dejar que estas manos obedecieran a mi sangre
estarían dispuestas para arrancar y dislocar
tus huesos y tu carne. A ti, sin embargo, te protege tu forma
                                                    [de mujer 70
por demonio que seas.

GONERILL

¡Oh! ¡Vuestra virilidad! ¡Miau!

(Entra un mensajero.)

ALBANY

¿Qué noticias traéis?

MENSAJERO

¡Oh! ¡Mi buen señor, el duque de Cornwall ha muerto!
Lo mató su sirviente cuando iba a arrancar
el otro ojo a Gloucester.

_____

62-9. De nuevo, fragmento omitido en *Folio*.

Albany

¿El otro ojo a Gloucester?

Mensajero

Un sirviente al que crió, movido por el remordimiento
se le opuso en tal acto, dirigiendo su espada
contra su gran señor que, exasperado,
se lanzó sobre él, y entre ellos lo mataron,
pero no sin haber recibido ese golpe fatal   80
que le hizo sucumbir después.

Albany

        Esto prueba que arriba
estáis vosotros, jueces, y podéis vengar estos crímenes nuestros
con rápidez. Pero, ¡oh, pobre Gloucester!
¿Perdió su otro ojo?

Mensajero

        Los dos, *my lord,* los dos.
Esta carta, señora, exige rápida respuesta;
la envía vuestra hermana.

Gonerill *[Aparte.]*

        Por un lado, me gusta.
Pero siendo viuda, y mi Gloucester con ella,
puede que mi imaginación se desmorone
sobre mi vida odiosa; por el otro
no es tan amarga la noticia... Voy a leerla y la contestaré.   90

(Sale.)

Albany

¿Dónde estaba su hijo cuando los ojos le quitaban?

[209]

Mensajero

Venía hacia aquí con mi señora.

Albany

No está aquí.

Mensajero

No, *my lord;* lo encontré de nuevo regresando.

Albany

¿Conoce tal infamia?

Mensajero

Sí, *my lord;* fue él quien lo culpó.
Y, con ese propósito, abandonó la casa, para que su castigo
pudiera darse en plena libertad.

Albany

Vivo, Gloucester,
para daros las gracias por el amor que mostrasteis al rey,
también para vengar a vuestros ojos. Acercaos, amigo,
decid qué más sabéis.   10

(Salen.)

ESCENA TERCERA*

(Entran KENT *y un caballero.)*

KENT

¿Conocéis la razón por la que el rey de Francia marchó tan
pronto?

CABALLERO

Algo que dejaría a medias en su país
y en lo que pensaba desde que vino;
algo que para su Estado puede significar
temor y riesgo tales que su marcha
fue inevitable.

KENT

¿Y a quién ha dejado como general?

CABALLERO

A *monsieur* La Far, mariscal de Francia.

KENT

¿Provocaron vuestras cartas en la reina algún signo de dolor?   10

---

* Nos encontramos ante una escena esencialmente informativa, lo que podría explicar su omisión en el texto del *Folio*. En este sentido, cabría relacionar
esta escena con la primera del acto III.

3.10. *Algo... dolor?* Estas líneas aparecen en *Quarto* —recordemos su omisión en el *Folio*— transcritas como prosa. Todas las ediciones y traducciones
contemporáneas así lo consideran también, pero no las pertenecientes al siglo XVIII —Pope, Theobald, Capell, etc.— que opinan, y en ellos nos apoya-
mos, que se trata de verso, aunque con un mínimo grado de irregularidad. Obsérvese, además, que el resto de la escena es verso, y, de ahí, la intención de re-
tomar la tradición del XVIII, y unificar toda la escena.

Sí, mi señor; las tomó en mi presencia y las leyó;
de cuando en cuando, surcaba su mejilla
delicada una lágrima. Parecía ser dueña
de su propia emoción, que, no obstante, buscaba,
rebelde, gobernarla.

Kent

¿Creéis, entonces, que se conmovió?

Caballero

Sin llegar a la cólera; la paciencia y el dolor disputaban por ser
la mejor expresión de su belleza. Habéis visto
sol y lluvia a la vez; eso mismo eran sus lágrimas y sus sonrisas,
pero mejor aún; esa alegre sonrisa que jugaba
en su maduro labio parecía ignorar qué extraños huéspedes   2(
habitaban sus ojos, de los que se escapaban
como perlas que salen de diamantes.
Pronto, como rareza, se apreciaría el pesar
si supiéramos todos soportarlo.

Kent

¿No hizo pregunta alguna?

Caballero

De hecho, una o dos veces pronunció el nombre de «padre»,
y suspiraba como si le oprimiera el corazón.
Gritó: «¡Hermanas! ¡Hermanas! ¡Vergüenza de mujeres!
                                                [¡Hermanas!
¡Kent! ¡Padre! ¡Oh, hermanas! ¿Cómo? ¿Con tormenta? ¿De
                                                [noche?
¡Que nadie crea en la piedad!» Sacudió entonces
el agua bendita desde sus ojos celestiales,   30
y humedeció su queja; después se retiró
para estar sola con su dolor.

[212]

KENT

Son las estrellas,
que están sobre nosotros, las que rigen nuestra naturaleza;
si no, hombre y mujer nunca podrían engendrar
hijos tan diferentes. ¿No le hablasteis después?

CABALLERO

No.

KENT

¿Sucedió esto antes que el rey marchara?

CABALLERO

No, después.

KENT

Pues bien, señor, el desdichado Lear está aquí, en la ciudad.
A veces, en sus momentos lúcidos, recuerda
lo que nos ha traído, pero no accederá en modo alguno,   40
no irá a ver a su hija.

CABALLERO

¿Por qué, mi buen señor?

KENT

Una inmensa vergüenza lo retiene; su propia crueldad
que la desposeyó de bendiciones, la expulsó
a suertes extranjeras, entregó lo que a ella le pertenecía
a sus otras dos hijas con corazón de perro; todo esto remuerde
                                                    [su conciencia

con tanto odio que el fuego de su vergüenza
lo mantiene apartado de Cordelia.

CABALLERO

¡Pobre caballero!

KENT

¿No habéis oído nada de las fuerzas de Albany y de Cornwall?

CABALLERO

Sí, que están en marcha.

KENT

Bien, sire, os llevaré hasta Lear, nuestro amo,   50
y os dejaré para que lo asistáis. Una causa importante
hace que todavía siga encubierto por un tiempo;
cuando me dé otra vez a conocer no lamentaréis
el haberme ofrecido vuestra amistad. Os lo ruego,
venid conmigo.

(Sale[n].)

---

46. *el fuego de su vergüenza;* en el original, «burning shame». En castellano el
calificativo «ardiente» no se puede aplicar al sustantivo «vergüenza», porque tiene connotaciones positivas y de actividad. Sin embargo, la sustitución por el
sustantivo «fuego» permite la expresión de la intensidad del sentimiento y del
efecto inmovilizador que produce.

ESCENA CUARTA*

(Entran con tambores y estandartes CORDELIA, [DOCTOR], *caballeros y soldados.)*

CORDELIA

Sí, es él. Lo hallaron no hace mucho
tan loco como el mar enfurecido; cantando a gritos,
coronado de flores y de malas hierbas,
con bardanas, cicuta, ortigas, cardaminas, cizaña
y todos los hierbajos estériles que crecen
entre los trigos que nos alimentan. Mandad una centuria,
rastread cada acre de altas hierbas;
traedlo ante mis ojos. ¿Qué puede la sabiduría
del hombre para restaurar los sentidos de los que fue privado?
Daré cuanto poseo a quien lo cure.   10

CABALLERO [DOCTOR]

Hay un remedio, *madam*.
La nodriza de la Naturaleza es el reposo,
del que él carece; para provocarlo
existen muchas hierbas eficaces, cuyo poder sabrá
cerrar los ojos de su angustia.

CORDELIA

                                        ¡Ah, secretos benditos,
vosotros, y toda desconocida virtud sobre la tierra,
surgid junto a mis lágrimas! ¡Dad ayuda y remedio

---

    * Esta breve escena en la que aparece de nuevo Cordelia, la hija menor de
Lear, sirve de anuncio a la séptima de este mismo acto en la que se produce el
reencuentro con su padre.
    14. *hierbas;* en el original, «simples». Se trata del término medicinal que dis-
tingue los elementos simples (hierbas medicinales) de los compuestos.

a la desgracia de un buen hombre! ¡Buscad! ¡Buscadle
antes que su furia ingobernada le destruya la vida;
pues necesita medios que la guíen!

(Entra un mensajero.)

MENSAJERO

¡Nuevas, *madam!*   20
Fuerzas británicas avanzan hacia aquí.

CORDELIA

Ya lo sabíamos. Y preparados
aquí aguardamos su llegada. ¡Oh, padre querido!
Tú eres lo que me preocupa.
Por ello el magnánimo France tuvo piedad
de las lágrimas solícitas de mi dolor.
A nuestras armas no las anima una hueca ambición
sino el amor, el afecto y los derechos de mi anciano padre.
¡Pronto he de verlo y escucharlo!

(Salen.)

ESCENA QUINTA*

(Entran REGAN *y mayordomo* [OSWALD].)

REGAN

¿Se han puesto en marcha los hombres de mi hermana?

25-8. Cordelia subraya —ante un público que sería particularmente sensible
a las cuestiones de interferencias extranjeras— que la intervención de Francia
en Inglaterra no tiene motivos políticos, sino puramente humanitarios.

* De nuevo nos encontramos ante una breve escena de transición. Se nos
presenta a Regan, estableciendo un paralelismo con la escena segunda de este
mismo acto, en la que predominaba el personaje de Gonerill. De esta forma se
completa el triángulo formado por ambas hermanas y Edmund, con Oswald
como intermediario.

Mayordomo [Oswald]

Sí, *madam*.

Regan

¿También él en persona?

[Oswald]

Muy a disgusto, *madam*.
Vuestra hermana es el mejor soldado.

Regan

¿No habló lord Edmund, en casa, con vuestro señor?

[Oswald]

No, *madam*.

Regan

¿Qué puede contener la carta de mi hermana?

[Oswald]

Lo ignoro, *madam*.

Regan

Se marchó a toda prisa por un asunto grave.
Gran error fue tras sacarle los ojos
dejar vivir a Gloucester; allá donde va mueve   10
a todo corazón en contra nuestra. Pienso que Edmund se ha ido
apenado por su miseria, a concluir
su vida de tinieblas, además de espiar
a los ejércitos del enemigo.

[OSWALD]

Es preciso, *madam*, que yo le alcance con mi carta.

REGAN

Nuestras tropas parten mañana; quedaos aquí;
son peligrosos los caminos.

[OSWALD]

No me es posible, *madam*;
le prometí a mi ama llevar a cabo esta misión.

REGAN

¿Por qué le escribe a Edmund? ¿No podíais
comunicar sus nuevas de palabra? Es muy probable...
algo... no sé qué cosa. Yo sabré
agradecéroslo... Dejadme abrir la carta.

20

[OSWALD]

Madam, preferiría...

REGAN

Sé que vuestra señora no ama a su marido,
de eso estoy segura; la última vez que estuvo aquí
lanzaba extrañas y elocuentes miradas amorosas
al noble Edmund. Sé que tenéis su confianza.

[OSWALD]

¿Yo, *madam*?

---

25. *extrañas y elocuentes miradas amorosas;* en el original, «strange oeilliads and most speaking looks». Según el *Oxford English Dictionary*, que cita este fragmento, *oeilliads*, proveniente del francés, significa «miradas amorosas». La traducción evita, de alguna manera, la redundancia entre esta palabra y *looks*.

REGAN

Hablo estando segura; la tenéis, lo sé.
Por eso os aconsejo que toméis buena nota:
mi señor ha muerto; Edmund y yo hemos conversado;   30
más conveniente es él para mi mano
que para la mano de vuestra señora. El resto lo podéis deducir.
Si lo encontráis, os ruego que le deis esto,
y cuando vuestra señora lo oiga todo de vos
os ruego que le llaméis a razón.
Así que partid presto.
Si por casualidad sabéis algo de ese ciego traidor,
mis favores serán para aquel que lo mate.

[OSWALD]

Si lo encontrara, *madam*, os demostraría
de qué parte estoy.

REGAN

¡Id con Dios!   40

(Salen.)

ESCENA SEXTA*

(Entran GLOUCESTER y EDGAR.)

GLOUCESTER

La cima de esa colina, ¿cuándo la alcanzaré?

---

* De acuerdo con la crítica, es esta la escena más grande del teatro trágico shakespeariano. Articulada en tres partes, nos presenta la llegada de Gloucester a Dover, acompañado de su hijo Edgar, donde piensa poner fin a su vida. En segundo lugar, su encuentro con Lear, que señala el punto de fusión entre los dos dramas paralelos; y, por último, la intervención y muerte de Oswald a manos de Edgar, que abandona así su disfraz de Tom de Bedlam.

EDGAR

Ya estáis subiendo; fijaos cómo nos cuesta.

GLOUCESTER

El suelo se me antoja llano.

EDGAR

Es mucha la pendiente.
¡Escuchad! ¿No oís el mar?

GLOUCESTER

No oigo nada.

EDGAR

Entonces es que vuestros sentidos se alteraron
por el tormento de los ojos.

GLOUCESTER

Debe de ser así.
Tu voz parece haber cambiado, y hablas
mejor que antes y con más sentido.

EDGAR

Os engañáis; yo no he cambiado
más que en mis ropas.

GLOUCESTER

No lo creo, ahora hablas mejor.   10

EDGAR

Vamos, sire: este es el lugar. ¡No os mováis! ¡Qué terrible
y aturdidor mirar hacia el vacío!
Los cuervos, las cornejas vuelan a media altura
y parecen apenas del grosor de los escarabajos; a mitad del camino
cuelga alguien que recoge hinojos, oficio peligroso.
No parece mayor que su cabeza.
Los pescadores que caminan por la playa
se me antojan ratones, y allí debajo una gran nave anclada
apenas si se ve del tamaño de un bote, y éste del de una boya   20
demasiado pequeña para los ojos. El murmullo del mar,
que rompe contra los innúmeros guijarros insignificantes,
no puede oírse desde aquí. No me atrevo a mirar.
Temo que me dé vueltas la cabeza, y, perdida la vista,
me precipite en el vacío.

GLOUCESTER

Llévame adonde estás.

EDGAR

Dadme vuestra mano; ahora estáis a un pie
del borde. Ni por todo lo que hay bajo la luna
me atrevería a dar un salto.

GLOUCESTER

Suelta mi mano.
Ten, amigo, esta otra bolsa; en ella hay una joya
que muy bien vale que la acepte un pobre. ¡Que las hadas

[y dioses

hagan que prosperes! Aléjate;   30
dime adiós y que te oiga marchar.

EDGAR

Y ahora quedad en paz, mi buen señor.

[221]

GLOUCESTER

Adiós, de todo corazón.

EDGAR

Juego así yo con su desesperanza
sólo porque se cure.

GLOUCESTER

(Se arrodilla.)

¡Oh, dioses poderosos!
A este mundo renuncio, y en vuestra presencia
me despojo de mi tristeza con serenidad.
Si aún pudiera soportarla, y no caer en lucha
con vuestra voluntad inexorable,
la mecha de mi naturaleza aborrecida se consumiría.
Si Edgar viviera, ¡oh, bendecidlo!
Ahora, amigo, adiós.

EDGAR

Ya me voy, sire, adiós...

[GLOUCESTER se arroja al suelo.]

Pero no sé cómo la imaginación puede robar
el tesoro de la vida cuando la vida misma
en el robo consiente; si él hubiera estado donde lo pensó
ya no tendría pensamientos... ¿Vivo o muerto?...
¡Vos, señor! ¡Amigo! ¿Me oís, señor? ¡Hablad!...
Podría haber muerto de verdad, sin embargo revive...
¿Quién sois, señor?

---

45. Evidentemente, Edgar finge ser otra persona distinta de Tom, que habría quedado «arriba del acantilado».

[222]

Marchaos y dejadme morir.

EDGAR

Aunque estuvierais hecho con tela de una araña, con plumas
[o con aire,
al caer vuestro cuerpo desde tanta altura   50
os habríais estrellado como un huevo; pero respiráis,
sois de sustancia dura, no sangráis, habláis, estáis sano.
Diez mástiles, uno sobre otro, no forman la distancia
de la que habéis caído en perpendicular.
Vuestra vida es milagro. Hablad de nuevo.

GLOUCESTER

Pero, ¿he caído o no?

EDGAR

Desde la horrible cima del límite calizo.
Mirad hacia lo alto; la estridente alondra, de tan lejos,
no puede ver ni oír. Pero, mirad hacia lo alto.

GLOUCESTER

¡Ay, ay! No tengo ojos.   60
¿No tiene la desgracia el beneficio
de terminarse con la muerte? Hubo un tiempo en que los
[miserables
tenían el consuelo de engañar la ira del tirano,
frustrando su orgullosa voluntad.

EDGAR

                              Dadme el brazo. Así, arriba.
¿Cómo estáis? ¿No sentís vuestras piernas? Os sostenéis de pie.

[223]

GLOUCESTER

Muy bien, bastante bien.

EDGAR

Es de lo más extraño.
En la cresta del acantilado, ¿qué cosa era lo que se
separaba de vos?

GLOUCESTER

Un pobre mendigo desgraciado.

EDGAR

Desde aquí abajo sus ojos se le aparecían
como dos lunas llenas; tenía mil narices,
cuernos torcidos y ondulados como escrespado mar.
Era un demonio. Así, pues, vos, padre afortunado,
pensad en que los dioses más puros, que se hacen honrar
con lo que es imposible para el hombre, os han guardado.

GLOUCESTER

Ahora lo recuerdo. De ahora en adelante habré de soportar
la aflicción hasta que ella misma me grite:
«¡Basta, basta!» y muera. A ese ser de que habláis
yo tomé por un hombre; a menudo, decía:
«¡El demonio, el demonio!» Él me condujo a ese lugar.

EDGAR

Sean tus pensamientos libres y pacientes.

(Entra LEAR.*)*

Pero, ¿quién llega?   80

[224]

El más cabal sentido nunca vestiría
a su señor así.

LEAR

No, no pueden acusarme de acuñar moneda. Soy el rey.

EDGAR

¡Oh! ¡Visión desgarradora!

LEAR

La Naturaleza está por encima del arte, en este aspecto. Ahí
tienes tu soldada. Ése de ahí maneja el arco como un espanta-
pájaros. ¡Tensádmelo una yarda! ¡Mirad, mirad, un ratón!
¡Quietos, quietos! Este pedazo de queso tostado servirá. ¡Aquí
está mi guantelete: lo arrojaré contra un gigante! ¡Traed las
alabardas! ¡Oh, pájaro, buen vuelo! ¡En el blanco, en el blanco! 90
¡Chsss! ¡Decid el santo y seña!

EDGAR

Dulce mejorana.

LEAR

Pasad.

GLOUCESTER

Yo conozco esa voz.

LEAR

¡Ah! ¡Gonerill, con barba blanca! Me adulaban como a un pe-

_____

87. *yarda;* en el original, «clothiers's yard» (lit.: *yarda de tejedor).* La longitud
de la flecha inglesa correspondía a la de la yarda, utilizada en sastrería *(cloth-
yard)* como medida para los tejidos.

rro, y me decían que tuve pelos blancos en la barba antes que
los hubiera negros. ¡Decir «sí» y «no» a todo lo que decía yo!
Ni «sí» ni «no» eran buena teología. Una vez que la lluvia llegó
a mojarme y el viento me hizo tiritar; cuando el trueno no quiso callarse a mi mandato, las descubrí y conocí por el olor. Va-   100
mos, no son hombres de palabra: me dijeron que yo lo era
todo. ¡Mentira! No estoy hecho a prueba de fiebre.

GLOUCESTER

Recuerdo bien ese timbre de voz.
¿No es el rey?

LEAR

   Sí, rey pulgada a pulgada.
Cuando miro fijamente, ¡ved cómo tiembla el súbdito!
Yo perdono la vida de ese hombre. ¿Cuál era tu delito?
¿Adulterio?
No morirás; ¿morir por adulterio? No.
El reyezuelo lo hace y la mosca dorada
copula en mi presencia.   110
¡Que la fornicación prospere! Pues el bastardo hijo de Gloucester
fue más benévolo con su padre que mis hijas
engendradas en sábanas legítimas. ¡Adelante, lujuria,
            [indiscriminadamente,
pues me faltan soldados! Contempla a esa dama burlona,
cuya cara, entre sus muslos, es presagio de nieve,
que hace remilgos de su virtud y que sacude la cabeza
al oír el nombre del placer.
Ni la puta ni el fogoso caballo van a ello
con apetito más desenfrenado.
De cintura para abajo son centauros,   120
aunque mujeres por arriba.
El talle es patrimonio de los dioses;
el resto, del demonio. He ahí el infierno, he ahí la oscuridad,
he ahí el abismo del azufre, escaldadura, quemazón,
hedor, consunción; ¡asco, asco, asco! ¡Pfff! ¡Pfff!
Dadme una onza de almizcle, boticario,

[226]

para que endulce mi imaginación.
He aquí tu dinero.

GLOUCESTER

¡Oh! Dejad que bese vuestra mano.

LEAR

Dejad primero que la limpie; apesta a muerto.

GLOUCESTER

¡Oh! ¡Arruinada obra de la Naturaleza! Así este gran mundo   130
se hundirá en la nada. ¿Me conocéis, acaso?

LEAR

Recuerdo bien tus ojos. ¿Bizqueas al mirarme? No, ciego Cupi-
do, hagas lo que hagas, no volveré a amar. Lee este desafío. Fí-
jate sólo en el estilo.

GLOUCESTER

Aunque fueran soles todas las letras, yo no podría verlas.

EDGAR

No lo creería si me lo contaran,
pero es verdad y se me rompe el corazón.

LEAR

¡Leed!

GLOUCESTER

¿Cómo? ¿Con el pozo de mis ojos?

[227]

¡Oh! ¿Conque ése es vuestro tono? ¿Sin ojos en la cara, ni dine- 140
ro en la bolsa? Vuestros ojos se encuentran en un oscuro
pozo y vuestra bolsa expuesta a la luz; aun así veis cómo va el
mundo.

GLOUCESTER

Lo veo a tientas.

LEAR

¡Cómo! ¿Estáis loco? Un hombre puede ver sin ojos cómo va
el mundo. Mirad con vuestros oídos: ved cómo aquel juez insulta al ladrón humilde. Poned el oído: cambiadlos de sitio y
iale-hop! ¿Quién es el juez, quién el ladrón? ¿Habéis visto al perro de un labriego que le ladre a un mendigo?

GLOUCESTER

¡Claro, señor!   150

LEAR

¿Y a la criatura huir del perro? Ahí pudiste ver
el gran emblema de la autoridad:
a un perro en su cargo se le obedece siempre.
¡Tú, guardia villano, detén tu mano ensangrentada!
¿Por qué azotas a esa puta? Descúbrete la espalda,
pues deseas usarla con ardor en aquello
por lo que la fustigas. El usurero cuelga al que es ratero.
A través de las telas harapientas se ven los grandes vicios;
las togas y ropajes de piel todo lo ocultan. El pecado con oro
                                                [se recubre,
y la fuerte lanza de la justicia se rompe inofensiva.   160
Vestidlo con harapos y el dardo de un pigmeo lo atravesará.

_____

159-64. *El pecado... que acusa.* Este fragmento no aparece en *Quarto*.

[228]

Nadie es culpable, nadie, os digo, nadie; yo los absuelvo.
Hacedme caso, amigo mío, pues yo tengo el poder
de sellarle los labios al que acusa. Procúrate unos ojos de cristal,
y como un intrigante rastrero finge ver
las cosas que no ves... Y bien, muy bien, muy bien.
¡Quitadme las botas! Más fuerte, más, así.

EDGAR

¡Oh, mezcla de claridad y sinsentido,
razón de la locura!

LEAR

Si queréis llorar por mi fortuna, tomad mis ojos.   170
Os conozco muy bien. Gloucester es vuestro nombre.
Debéis tener paciencia. Aquí vinimos sollozando;
sabéis que cuando olemos el aire por primera vez
gemimos y lloramos. Quisiera platicaros: escuchad.

GLOUCESTER

¡Ah, maldito! ¡Maldito sea aquel día!

LEAR

Al nacer lamentamos haber venido a este gran escenario
de locos. ¡Este es un buen sombrero!
Qué fina estratagema sería herrar con fieltro
toda una escuadra de caballos. Yo lo intentaré,
y cuando llegue sigilosamente hasta mis hijos,   180
entonces, ¡mata, mata, mata, mata!

(Entra un caballero.)

CABALLERO

¡Ah, ahí está! ¡Detenedlo! Señor,
vuestra hija más querida...

LEAR

¿Ningún rescate? ¡Qué! ¿Yo prisionero?
Soy por naturaleza bufón de la Fortuna. Tratadme bien;
cobraréis el rescate. ¡Traedme cirujanos!
Tengo herido el cerebro.

CABALLERO

Tendréis cualquier cosa.

LEAR

¿Nadie conmigo? ¿Solo?
Razón hay para hacer de sal a un hombre,
y usar sus ojos como regaderas de jardín,   190
y abatir el polvo del otoño. Moriré con valor
como un esposo acicalado. ¡Qué! Quiero estar alegre.
Venga, pues; soy el rey, señores, ¿lo sabéis?

CABALLERO

Sois rey y os obedeceremos.

LEAR

Entonces queda vida todavía. Venid y lo conseguiréis.
Lo conseguiréis corriendo... ¡Ja! ¡Ja! ¡Ja! ¡Ja!

(Sale.)

CABALLERO

Espectáculo tan lamentable en un desventurado,
excede las palabras en un rey. Tenéis una hija,
que, de la maldición universal que os impusieron
las otras dos, redime a la Naturaleza.   200

EDGAR

Salud, noble señor.

CABALLERO

Deprisa, sire, ¿qué queréis?

EDGAR

¿Habéis oído algo sobre una próxima batalla, sire?

CABALLERO

En efecto, señor. Todos lo saben; quien puede distinguir algún
[sonido
lo ha oído comentar.

EDGAR

Pero, hacedme el favor,
¿a qué distancia se encuentra el otro ejército?

CABALLERO

Cerca, y avanza rápido; se espera de un momento a otro divisar
el grueso de sus fuerzas.

EDGAR

Os lo agradezco, sirc; es todo.

---

203. *En efecto, señor. Todos lo saben;* en el original, «Most sure and vulgar». Probablemente la fórmula castellana más utilizada para responder afirmativa y enfáticamente a una pregunta es «en efecto», que recoge la idea de *most sure*. *Vulgar* significa «conocido por todos». En esta respuesta breve, condensada y directa se ha utilizado la forma activa: «todos lo saben», más adecuada que la pasiva.

CABALLERO

Aunque la reina por motivos especiales esté aquí
su ejército está en marcha.

EDGAR

(Sale.)

Os lo agradezco, sire.

GLOUCESTER

¡Oh, dioses misericordiosos, quitadme el aliento!

210

¡No dejéis que me tiente de nuevo mi espíritu maligno
a morir antes que os plazca!

EDGAR

Padre, rogáis bien.

GLOUCESTER

Decidme, buen señor, y vos, ¿quién sois?

EDGAR

Un pobre hombre, amansado por golpes de fortuna,
que, a través de los dolores que sintió y conocía,
es ya sensible a la piedad. Dadme vuestra mano.
Yo os conduciré a algún refugio.

GLOUCESTER

Gracias de todo corazón.
¡Que el premio de los cielos y su bendición
os sean dados una y otra vez!

(Entra mayordomo [OSWALD].)

Mayordomo [Oswald]

¡La recompensa que se ofrece! ¡Qué fortuna!   220
Esa cabeza tuya sin ojos fue primero encarnada
para hacer mi riqueza. Tú, traidor viejo y desgraciado,
piensa ya en lo que eres; está pronta la espada
que habrá de destruirte.

Gloucester

                    Poned en vuestra mano amiga
la fuerza suficiente para hacerlo.

[Edgar se interpone.]

[Oswald]

                    ¿Cómo te atreves, campesino,
a ayudar a un público traidor?
Vete, si no el contagio de su suerte
caerá sobre ti. ¡Suéltale el brazo!

Edgar

No h'de soltarlo, sire, si no hay 'uena razón.

[Oswald]

¡Suéltame, infame, o morirás!   230

Edgar

'uen ca'allero, seguir 'uestro camino y dejar a'ste pobr'ombre
en paz. Si la fanfarronería me quitara la vida, ya m'abría ido al

---

229-38. El habla que se utiliza en el original es una especie de dialecto, utilizado convencionalmente en el teatro de la época, que se aproxima al dialecto de
Somersetshire. Se ha intentado reproducir, en castellano, la pronunciación de
una persona de escasa educación que, como en el original, se caracteriza fundamentalmente por elisiones y confusiones de sonido.

[233]

otro mundo. No, n'os acerquéis al viejo; alejaros, os l' advierto,
o probaré qué's lo más duro: vuestro melón o mi garrote. Lo
digo 'n serio.

[Oswald]

¡Fuera, estercolero!

Edgar

Vo' yarrancaros los dientes, sire. ¡Venir! No m 'importan
vuestros estoques.

[Oswald]

Maldito, me has matado. Siervo, toma mi bolsa.
Si quieres prosperar, dale tierra a mi cuerpo,   240
y entrega la carta que encontrarás aquí
a Edmund, conde de Gloucester. Búscalo
en el campamento inglés. ¡Oh, muerte intempestiva!
¡Muero!

Edgar

Te conozco bien, rufián rastrero,
tan obediente a los vicios de tu señora
como lo exige la maldad.

Gloucester

¡Qué! ¿Está muerto?

Edgar

Sentaos, padre; descansad.
Veamos sus bolsillos; la carta de la que habló
podría serme favorable. Está muerto; sólo siento   250
que no tuviera otro verdugo. Veamos.
Cede, suave cera; y escrúpulos, no nos culpéis;

si para conocer las mentes de nuestros enemigos les arranca-
[mos el corazón,
más legal hacerlo con sus cartas.

(Lee la carta.)

Recordemos nuestras mutuas promesas. Tenéis muchas oportuni-
dades para eliminarlo; si no os falta voluntad, el tiempo y el lu-
gar os serán favorables. Nada se logrará si él vuelve vencedor;
entonces seré prisionera y su lecho mi prisión; libradme de su
odioso calor, y ocupad su lugar por vuestro esfuerzo.

Vuestra —preferiría decir esposa— afectuosa servidora, Go 260
nerill.

¡Oh, espacio incalculable el del deseo de una mujer!
¡Conspirar contra la vida de un marido virtuoso,
y poner a mi hermano en su lugar! Aquí, sobre la arena,
te cubriré, impío mensajero
de lujuriosos asesinos; y cuando la ocasión sea propicia
mostraré este papel infame ante los ojos
del duque, cuya muerte se tramaba. Ha de ser bueno para él
que de tu muerte y de tu encargo pueda hablarle.

GLOUCESTER

El rey está loco. ¡Qué terco es mi vil juicio,   270
que aún sigo en pie, y siento, muy consciente,
mis enormes dolores! Mejor si enloqueciera
para que mi dolor se viese separado de mi pensamiento
y confundido en mi imaginación perdieran mis horrores,
la conciencia de sí.

(Tambor a lo lejos.)

EDGAR

Dadme la mano.
Me parece escuchar un tambor a lo lejos.
Venid, padre, os encomendaré a un buen amigo.

(Salen.)

[235]

ESCENA SÉPTIMA*

(Entran CORDELIA, KENT [DOCTOR] *y un caballero.)*

CORDELIA

¡Oh, mi buen Kent! ¿Cómo he de obrar y de vivir,
para igualaros en bondad? No viviré los años suficientes
ni encontraré la forma de medirla.

KENT

Madam, el reconocimiento supera cualquier otra recompensa.
Mis informes son sólo la verdad modesta,
no más, no menos, sino así.

CORDELIA

Poneos ropa más digna;
esa ropa es recuerdo de aquellas malas horas;
quitáosla, os lo ruego.

KENT

Perdonadme, señora:
pero ser reconocido acortaría los planes que ya he hecho;
me permito rogaros que no sepáis quién soy   10
hasta que el tiempo y yo creamos oportuno.

CORDELIA

Que sea así, mi buen señor... ¿Cómo se encuentra el rey?

---

* Se inicia con esta escena la secuencia final de la tragedia, y cabría destacar
en ella los símbolos que aparecen. Por una parte, la música como oposición al
fragor de la tormenta que había dominado la parte central de la obra; y, por
otra, la «ropa nueva» de Lear, símbolo del hombre nuevo, después de salir de su
estado de locura.

CABALLERO [DOCTOR]

Madam, duerme todavía.

CORDELIA

¡Oh, vosotros, benévolos dioses,
curad la gran herida de su naturaleza maltratada!
¡Oh, ajustad los sentidos desafinados y estridentes
de este padre convertido en niño!

[DOCTOR]

Si place a Vuestra Majestad,
despertemos al rey. Ha dormido ya mucho.

CORDELIA

Dejaos guiar por el conocimiento, y proceded
según ordene vuestra voluntad. ¿Está vestido?   20

(Entra LEAR, *en una silla llevada por sirvientes.)*

[DOCTOR]

Sí, señora; aprovechando su profundo sueño
se le vistió con ropa nueva.
Estad presente, *madam,* cuando le despertemos;
no dudo de que se hallará recuperado.

CORDELIA

Muy bien, muy bien.

[DOCTOR]

Os lo ruego, acercaos. Haced sonar más fuerte esa música, más.

CORDELIA

¡Oh, padre querido! Que la curación deje en mis labios
vuestra medicina, y permita a este beso
reparar las violentas heridas que mis dos hermanas
han cometido contra Vuestra Gracia.

KENT

¡Princesa tierna y cariñosa!

CORDELIA

Si no fuerais su padre, ese cabello blanqueado   30
exigiría su piedad ¿Fue este un rostro para estar
a la merced de los furiosos vientos?
¿Para oponerse al trueno profundo y fulminante,
en el golpe terrible súbito del veloz relámpago?
¿Para velar, oh pobre centinela,
con este débil casco? Hasta los perros de mis enemigos,
aun habiéndome mordido, habrían pasado aquella noche
junto a mi fuego; ¿y os visteis obligado, pobre padre,
a refugiaros con los cerdos y desesperados,
en la escasa y podrida paja? ¡Oh, Dios!   40
Me sorprende que vuestro juicio y vuestra vida
no se hayan terminado de una vez. Ya despierta. ¡Habladle!

[DOCTOR]

Madam, hacedlo vos; es lo mejor.

CORDELIA

¿Cómo está mi noble señor? ¿Cómo se encuentra Vuestra
[Majestad?

33-6. *¿Para oponerse... casco?* Fragmento omitido en *Folio.*

35. *Oh, pobre centinela;* en el original, «poor perdu». Procede esta palabra del
francés *sentinelle perdue,* término con el que se designaba al soldado que se aden-
traba —en descubierta— en el territorio enemigo.

Sois injusta al sacarme de mi tumba;
vos, alma inocente; pero me encuentro atado
a una rueda de fuego; y mis lágrimas caen
como plomo fundido.

CORDELIA

Señor, ¿me conocéis?

LEAR

Eres un espíritu, lo sé; ¿dónde ocurrió tu muerte?

CORDELIA

¡Lejos, aún, muy lejos!   50

[DOCTOR]

Está medio dormido; dejadlo solo unos instantes.

LEAR

¿Dónde he estado? ¿Dónde estoy? ¿Un día luminoso?
Me encuentro muy confuso. Me moriría de piedad
al ver a otro en este estado. Y no sé qué decir.
No juraría que mis manos son éstas.
Veamos; siento el pinchazo de esta aguja.
Quisiera estar seguro de mi situación.

CORDELIA

Mirad, señor,
y elevad vuestras manos para la bendición.
No, señor, no os arrodilléis.

                              Os lo ruego, no os burléis de mí;   60
soy un anciano, necio y ya senil,
los ochenta cumplidos, ni hora más ni hora menos;
y, para ser sincero,
me temo que no tengo todos mis sentidos en su lugar.
Creo que debería conoceros y también a este hombre;
pero dudo; porque desconozco qué lugar es este,
y no alcanza toda mi sabiduría
a recordar mis vestiduras; ni dónde me hospedé
la última noche. No os riáis de mí,
pues, como que soy hombre, creo que esta dama
es mi hija Cordelia.

CORDELIA

                    Y lo soy: soy yo.   70

LEAR

¿Húmedas vuestras lágrimas? Sí, por mi fe. No lloréis, os lo
                                                      [ruego.
Si tenéis veneno para mí, lo tomaré.
Ya sé que no me amáis, pues vuestras hermanas,
y así lo recuerdo, me han hecho mucho mal,
y vos tenéis motivos; ellas, no.

CORDELIA

                         Ningún motivo, ninguno.

LEAR

¿Estoy en Francia?

─────────

61. *los ochenta cumplidos;* en el original, «four score and upward». La veintena
es una unidad de frecuente uso en inglés. A las «cuatro veintenas y más» del
original correspondería la forma más familiar y expresiva en castellano «los
ochenta cumplidos».

KENT

En vuestro propio reino, señor.

LEAR

No abuséis de mi fe.

[DOCTOR]

Tranquilizaos, señora; la furia mayor,
como veis, en él ha muerto; aún es peligroso
hacerle ver los huecos del tiempo que perdió.   80
Rogadle que entre y no le molestéis
hasta que esté tranquilo.

CORDELIA

¿Desea Vuestra Alteza caminar?

LEAR

Tened paciencia conmigo. Os lo ruego, olvidad y perdonad;
soy viejo y algo estúpido.

*(Salen [*LEAR, CORDELIA, DOCTOR *y sirvientes].)*

CABALLERO

¿Es cierto, sire, que el duque de Cornwall fue asesinado así?

KENT

Más que cierto, sire.

85-95. Este fragmento, omitido en *Folio*, tiene las mismas características, de
texto puramente informativo, que veíamos en III.i y IV.iii, lo cual explicaría
esta omisión.

CABALLERO

¿Quién guía a sus gentes?

KENT

Según dicen, el hijo bastardo de Gloucester.

CABALLERO

Parece que Edgar, su hijo desterrado, se encuentra en Alemania
con el conde de Kent.   90

KENT

Las noticias son confusas. Conviene estar en guardia; los
                                                          [ejércitos
del reino se acercan con rapidez.

CABALLERO

El resultado habrá de ser sangriento. Id con Dios, sire.

KENT

Mi propósito y fin se habrán cumplido,
para bien o para mal, según se luche hoy en la batalla.

Sale [n].

ACTO V

ESCENA PRIMERA*

(Entran, con tambores y estandartes. EDMUND, REGAN, *caballeros y soldados.)*

BASTARDO [EDMUND]

Que os informe el duque si mantiene su última decisión
o si después, por algo, ha sido aconsejado
de que cambie sus planes... Está lleno de escrúpulos
y de dudas... Traedme su voluntad precisa.

REGAN

Algo le ha sucedido al mensajero de nuestra hermana, estoy
[segura.

[EDMUND]

Es de temer, *madam*.

REGAN

Bien, mi noble señor,
ya conocéis el bien que para vos deseo;

---

* Se inician en esta escena los preparativos finales de la batalla que servirá de conclusión a la tragedia, y se nos hace evidente el conflicto entre Gonerill y Regan por la persona de Edmund.

[243]

decid, sinceramente —pero decidme sólo la verdad—
¿no amáis vos a mi hermana?

[EDMUND]

Con un amor respetuoso.

REGAN

¿Y nunca habéis abierto brecha prohibida   10
en el camino de mi hermano?

[EDMUND]

Tal pensamiento os engaña.

REGAN

Me pregunto si os habéis ayuntado, penetrándola en su
                                                    [intimidad;
si podemos decir que es realmente suya.

[EDMUND]

No, *madam*, por mi honor.

REGAN

Jamás se lo consentiré; mi querido señor,
nunca lleguéis a intimidad con ella.

[EDMUND]

No temáis.
¡Hela ahí con el duque, su marido!

10-1. *brecha prohibida en el camino de mi hermano?;* en el original, «my brother's
way to the forfended place?» (lit.: *el camino de mi hermano hacia el lugar prohibido?),*
con matices obviamente sexuales que se amplían en los versos 12 y 16.

11-3. *Tal pensamiento... suya.* Fragmento omitido en *Folio,* así como los versos
18 y 19, 23 a 28, y 33.

(Entran con tambores y estandartes ALBANY, GONERILL
y soldados.)

GONERILL

Antes preferiría perder yo la batalla
que ver cómo mi hermana me desliga de él.

ALBANY

Queridísima hermana, sed bienvenida.   20
He oído, señor, que el rey se ha reunido con su hija
y con otros a quienes el rigor de nuestro Estado
ha inducido a rebelión. Nunca he sido valiente
donde no pude ser honrado. Con respecto a este asunto,
nos concierne porque Francia invade nuestras tierras;
no por su apoyo al rey y a otros, inducidos
a combatir, me temo, por causa justa y grave.

[EDMUND]

Señor, decís muy bien.

REGAN

¿Por qué discutir esto?

GONERILL

Uníos contra el enemigo.
Pues estas discusiones domésticas y sus pormenores   30
están fuera de cuestión.

ALBANY

Determínese entonces
con los más forjados en la guerra la estrategia a seguir.

[EDMUND]

Me reuniré con vos al instante en vuestra tienda.

REGAN

Hermana, ¿os unís a nosotros?

GONERILL

No.

REGAN

Sería conveniente. Os lo ruego, venid.

GONERILL

¡Ajah! Empiezo a comprender... Ya lo creo que iré.

(Salen ambos ejércitos. Entra EDGAR.)

EDGAR

Si alguna vez se dignó hablar vuestra gracia con un hombre
                                                    tan pobre,
escuchadme un instante.

ALBANY

Os daré alcance. Hablad.

EDGAR

Antes de entrar en la batalla, dad lectura a esta carta.   40
Si lográis la victoria, que suene la trompeta
para el que os la entregó. Que aun pareciendo miserable,
yo puedo ser el caballero que deberá probar
lo que en ella se afirma. Si perdéis,

vuestros asuntos en este mundo tendrán así su fin,
y cesará la intriga. Que la fortuna os acompañe.

ALBANY

Esperad a que haya leído la carta.

EDGAR

Se me ha prohibido.
Cuando llegue el momento, basta que el heraldo llame,
y, de nuevo, me presentaré.

(Sale.)

ALBANY

Id, pues, con Dios.
Leeré este pliego.   50

(Entra EDMUND.*)*

BASTARDO [EDMUND]

El enemigo está a la vista; preparad las tropas.
He aquí el cálculo de su verdadero número y efectivos
según escrupuloso reconocimiento;
urge ahora que os apresuréis.

ALBANY

Estaremos preparados.

(Sale.)

[EDMUND]

He jurado amor a cada una de estas dos hermanas;
entre sí desconfían, como quien de una víbora

sufrió la mordedura. ¿A cuál de ellas tomaré?
¿A las dos? ¿A una? ¿O a ninguna? De ninguna puedo gozar
si ambas con vida permanecen. Tomar a la viuda
es irritar y volver loca a su hermana Gonerill;   60
y difícilmente alcanzaré mi meta,
estando vivo su marido. Utilizaré, por el momento,
su autoridad en la batalla, que cuando concluya
ella será, pues desea librarse de él, la que conciba
su pronta eliminación. En cuanto a la gracia
que él pretende para Cordelia y Lear,
finalizada la batalla, y ambos en nuestro poder,
no verán su perdón; corresponde a mi rango
mandar, no discutir.

(Sale.)

ESCENA SEGUNDA*

(Trompas dentro. Entran, con tambores y estandartes,
LEAR, CORDELIA *y soldados. Cruzan el escenario y salen.)*

(Entran EDGARD *y* GLOUCESTER.)

EDGAR

Venid, padre, aceptad la sombra de este árbol
como a vuestro anfitrión. Rogad porque triunfe la justicia.
Si vuelvo junto a vos alguna vez
os traeré consuelo.

GLOUCESTER

¡Señor, la gracia os acompañe!

*(Sale [*EDGAR*].)*

---

* La función de esta breve escena es la de sintetizar la suerte de la batalla
por medio de las palabras de Edgar, debido a la dificultad de representar aquélla
sobre el escenario.

(Trompas y toque de retirada dentro. Entra EDGAR.)

EDGAR

¡Huyamos, anciano! ¡Dadme la mano: huyamos!
El rey Lear ha sido derrotado; él y su hija, presos.
¡Vuestra mano; moveos!

GLOUCESTER

No, ni un paso, señor, basta un lugar así para pudrirse.

EDGAR

¡Cómo! ¿De nuevo pensamientos lúgubres?
Tanto ha de sufrir un hombre su partida como su llegada;   10
es necesario madurar. En marcha.

GLOUCESTER

                              Así es; en verdad.

(Salen.)

ESCENA TERCERA*

(Entran victoriosos, con tambores y estandartes, EDMUND; LEAR *y*
CORDELIA, *prisioneros; soldados y* CAPITÁN.)

BASTARDO [EDMUND]

¡Que algunos oficiales se los lleven y los vigilen con severidad
hasta que sea conocida la voluntad suprema
de los que han de juzgarlos!

---

11. *Es necesario madurar;* en el original, «Ripeness is all». Alusión al concepto
cristiano de estar preparado para la muerte, al tiempo que se señala uno de los
«mensajes» de la tragedia: la importancia de la experiencia.

* Sin duda la escena más articulada de la tragedia en la que participan todos

CORDELIA

No somos los primeros
en soportar el mal, aun manteniendo recto proceder.
Por vos, rey maltratado, abatida me siento,
y no por mí, que, con mi ceño, retaría al de la hipócrita fortuna.
¿Es que no veremos a estas hijas y hermanas?

LEAR

¡No, no, no! ¡A la prisión! ¡Ven! ¡Vamos!
Allí cantaremos solos como pájaros enjaulados.
Cuando pidas que te bendiga, arrodillado,   10
imploraré tu perdón; y así, viviremos,
y cantaremos, y rezaremos, y contaremos viejos cuentos,
y nos reiremos de las mariposas de colores, y oiremos a los
                                                        [infelices
referir las nuevas de la corte; y hablaremos con ellos,
quién pierde, quién gana, quién asciende o quién cae;
y poseeremos el misterio de las cosas,
como si fuésemos espías de los dioses; y sobreviviremos
entre los muros de nuestra prisión a las sectas y los poderosos
que a merced de la luna surgen y sucumben.

[EDMUND]

Lleváoslos.

LEAR

Sobre tales sacrificios, Cordelia, hija mía,   20
los mismos dioses arrojan su incienso. ¿Te he recuperado?
Quien quiera separarnos traiga una brasa del cielo
para espantarnos con fuego como a zorros. Seca tus lágrimas,

---

los protagonistas —que habían aparecido en la primera escena de la obra—, y
en la que se indican, en una serie de acciones violentas, los resultados de los
mecanismos que los personajes habían puesto en movimiento en aquella primera escena.

que antes la abundancia les devorará hueso y carne que tengan
nuestro llanto. Primero hemos de ver cómo mueren de hambre.
¡Ven!

(Sale[n LEAR *y* CORDELIA].)

[EDMUND]

Venid aquí, capitán. Escuchadme.
Tomad esta orden y seguidles hasta la prisión.
Os he ascendido un grado; si actuáis
como aquí se os indica, os abriréis camino   30
hacia un destino noble. Habéis de saber
que los hombres son como su tiempo; la ternura
no es propia de una espada; vuestro importante cometido
no admite discusión; o aceptáis hacerlo
o buscáis la fortuna en otro sitio.

CAPITÁN

Lo haré, *my lord.*

[EDMUND]

En marcha; y consideraos afortunado cuando hayáis cumplido.
Advertid que os he dicho «al instante»; llevadlo, pues, a cabo
tal como lo he escrito.

CAPITÁN

No puedo tirar de un carro, ni comer avena seca;
lo haré si un hombre puede hacerlo.   40

(Sale el CAPITÁN.)

---

24. *hueso y carne;* en el original, «flesh and fell» (lit.: *carne y piel»),* que comunica una idea de totalidad, y a la que corresponde la expresión castellana «carne y hueso».

39-40. Ambos versos omitidos en *Folio,* así como el fragmento que va desde la línea 55 a la 60.

(Trompas. Entran ALBANY, GONERILL, REGAN *y soldados.)*

ALBANY

Habéis mostrado hoy, sire, vuestra valentía,
y la fortuna os ha guiado bien. Tenéis prisioneros
a quienes en la lucha de hoy eran nuestros adversarios;
yo os los reclamo, para que sean tratados
como sus méritos y nuestra seguridad
aconsejen hacerlo.

[EDMUND]

           Señor, consideré oportuno
asignar al viejo y miserable rey
una prisión y una guardia especial;
su vejez tiene hechizo, y, más aún, su rango,
para poner de su parte el afecto del pueblo   50
y hacer volver las lanzas mercenarias contra nuestros ojos,
que son los que les guían. Con él envié a la reina,
siendo el motivo el mismo; y ambos están dispuestos
para comparecer mañana, u otro día
adonde el tribunal sea convocado. Ahora estamos cubiertos
de sudor y de sangre, el amigo ha perdido a su amigo,
y las mejores causas con ira se maldicen
por quienes sienten su rigor.
El asunto de Cordelia y su padre
requiere un lugar más apropiado.

ALBANY

                    Con vuestra licencia, sire,   60
os considero sólo un inferior en esta guerra,
no como a hermano.

REGAN

Eso depende del favor que deseemos concederle.
Vos debíais haber consultado nuestro parecer,

[252]

antes de hablar así. Él guió nuestras fuerzas;
ha revestido con autoridad mi nombre y mi persona,
hasta el punto que orgulloso puede
llamarse vuestro hermano.

GONERILL

¡Detened vuestro ímpetu!
Más destaca por su propio valor
que por lo que vos le habéis dado.

REGAN

Investido por mí   70
con mis derechos, se iguala a los mejores.

ALBANY

No alcanzaría más, si con vos se casara.

REGAN

Las burlas a menudo resultan profecías.

GONERILL

¡Hola, hola!
Que es bizco el ojo que de ese modo te informó.

REGAN

Me siento mal, señora; de lo contrario os contestaría
con vómitos de ira. General,
tomad a mis soldados, a mis prisioneros, y mi patrimonio,
y disponed de ellos, de mí misma; los muros

---

71. En *Quarto* este verso le es atribuido a Gonerill, mientras que el verso 77
no aparece en esa edición. El parlamento de Edmund, en la línea 82, le es atribuido a Regan, en ese mismo texto.

son vuestros. Sea testigo el mundo de que aquí os nombro
mi señor y mi dueño.

GONERILL

¿Pretendéis gozarlo?   80

ALBANY

No está en vos el negaros.

[EDMUND]

Ni en vos, mi señoría.

ALBANY

Lo está, bastardo infame.

REGAN

Haced que suenen los tambores y se demuestre así que son
                                                [vuestros mis títulos.

ALBANY

Esperad, atended a razones. Edmund, os arresto
por alta traición y, por la misma causa,
a esta serpiente de oro. Y vuestra pretensión, querida hermana,
en interés de mi esposa la descarto.
Es ella quien está prometida en secreto a este señor,
y yo, su marido, veto vuestras amonestaciones.
Si deseáis casaros, hacedme a mí la corte,   90
que mi señora ya está comprometida.

GONERILL

                              ¡Magnífica la farsa!

[254]

Estáis armado, Gloucester; que suenen las trompetas.
Si nadie comparece para probar contra vuestra persona
vuestras infames y manifiestas traiciones,
he aquí un desafío. Dejaré prueba en vuestro corazón,
o nunca tomaré alimento, de que no sois otra cosa
que lo que de vos he proclamado.

REGAN

¡Mal, me siento mal!

GONERILL

Si así fuera, nunca confiaría en cierta medicina.

[EDMUND]

Mi guante es mi respuesta. Quienquiera, en este mundo,
que me llame traidor, miente como un villano.   100
¡Que suenen las trompetas! Y comparezca quien se atreva;
sostendré contra él, contra vos, o quien sea,
con firmeza, mi honor y mi verdad.

(Entra un HERALDO.)

ALBANY

¡Un heraldo!
Confía sólo en tu valor, pues tus soldados,
reclutados todos en mi nombre, han sido
del mismo modo licenciados.

REGAN

Se apodera de mí la enfermedad.

ALBANY

No se encuentra muy bien, conducidla a mi tienda.

[Sale REGAN, acompañada.]

Aproximaos, heraldo; que suene la trompeta.
Leed esto en voz alta.

(Suena una trompeta.)

HERALDO *(Lee.)*

Si hay en las filas de este ejército algún hombre de carácter o rango que 11
quiera probar contra Edmund, supuesto conde de Gloucester, que es un
obstinado traidor, que aparezca cuando la trompeta haya sonado por
tercera vez. Él está dispuesto a su defensa.

(Primera trompeta.)

¡Otra vez!

(Segunda trompeta.)

¡De nuevo!

(Tercera trompeta.)

(Una trompeta responde dentro. Entra EDGAR, armado.)

ALBANY

Preguntadle lo que se propone, y por qué comparece
a la llamada de trompeta.

HERALDO

¿Quién sois vos?
Vuestro nombre y rango y por qué contestáis
a esta llamada.

[256]

Sabed, mi nombre está perdido,
mordido por gusanos, roído por el diente de la traición;   120
soy, sin embargo, tan noble como el adversario
al que vengo a enfrentarme.

ALBANY

¿Quién es ese adversario?

EDGAR

¿Quién, aquí, responde por Edmund, conde de Gloucester?

[EDMUND]

Él mismo. ¿Qué tenéis que decirle?

EDGAR

Desenvainad la espada,
y que os haga justicia vuestro brazo,
si mi palabra ofende a un noble corazón. He aquí la mía.
Sabedlo: es privilegio de mi honor,
mi voto y juramento. Yo declaro
a pesar de vuestra fortaleza, posición, juventud y grandeza,
a pesar de vuestra espada vencedora y ostentosa fortuna,   130
de vuestro valor y de vuestro coraje, que sois un traidor
infiel a vuestros dioses, a vuestro hermano y a vuestro mismo
                                       [padre:
conspirador contra este noble príncipe ilustre;
y que sois, desde el punto más alto de vuestra cabeza
a la suela, e incluso al polvo bajo los pies,
un traidor con piel de sapo. Decid «no»,

---

129. *a pesar de;* en el original, «Maugre». Término francés típico del lenguaje caballeresco utilizado en este parlamento.

y esta espada, este brazo, y mi más firme voluntad
se plegarán para probar en vuestro corazón, al que le hablo,
que mentís.

[EDMUND]

Debería, por derecho, preguntar vuestro nombre,
pero ya que vuestro aspecto es tan noble y guerrero   140
y vuestra lengua exhala pruebas de estirpe superior,
desdeño y rechazo lo que podría no aceptar
de buen grado y con seguridad, según la ley de la caballería.
Devuelvo contra vuestra cabeza estas traiciones;
que esta mentira diabólica abrume vuestro corazón;
pero ya que sólo rozan y no hieren,
esta espada les abrirá camino de inmediato
hacia donde descansarán eternamente. ¡Hablad, trompetas!

(Llamada a las armas. Luchan.)

ALBANY

¡Perdonad! ¡Perdonadle!

GONERILL

¡Gloucester, esto es traición!
Por las leyes de las armas no estabais obligado a responder   150
a un adversario que no conocéis. No habéis sido vencido,
sino engañado y traicionado.

ALBANY

¡Cerrad la boca, señora,
o con este papel os la cerraré yo! ¡Deteneos, sire!
Tú, peor que palabra alguna, lee tu propia infamia.
¡No lo rompáis, señora! Veo que lo conocéis.

---

141. Este verso no aparece en *Quarto*.

¿Y si así fuera? Son mías las leyes, y no vuestras.
¿Quién puede denunciarme por ello?

ALBANY

¡Monstruoso ser!
¿Conocéis vos este papel?

GONERILL

No me preguntéis lo que conozco.

(Sale GONERILL.)

ALBANY

¡Seguidla! Está desesperada. ¡Controladla!

[EDMUND]

De cuanto me acusáis, soy responsable,   160
y más, de mucho más; el tiempo lo revelará.
Ya ha pasado, también yo. ¿Pero quién sois vos
que así me aventajáis en fortuna? Si sois noble
os perdono.

EDGAR

Vaya mi caridad por la que me ofrecéis.
En sangre no soy menos que vos, Edmund;

---

158. En *Folio*, la frase de Gonerill le es atribuida a Edmund, por cuanto, en
aquella edición, Gonerill sale del escenario tras decir la línea 157: *¿Quién... ello?*
165. *Vaya mi caridad por la que me ofrecéis;* en el original, «Let's exchange cha-
rity». Se recoge en castellano la idea del original inglés, adaptándolo a sus claves
escénicas. Una traducción literal, donde apareciera el verbo «intercambiar» con
«caridad» como objeto directo resultaría cómica por el carácter abstracto de este
último elemento. Sin embargo, al desarrollar el verbo en los dos elementos del

y si más, más daño me habéis hecho.
Mi nombre es Edgar, hijo de vuestro padre.
Los dioses son justos, y hacen de nuestros vicios placenteros
un instrumento de tortura.
El lugar oscuro de pecado donde él os engendró   170
le ha costado los ojos.

[EDMUND]

Habláis en justicia. Es cierto.
La rueda ha completado su vuelta. Heme aquí.

ALBANY

Me pareció que vuestra misma figura ya auguraba
una real nobleza. He de abrazaros.
Que la aflicción parta mi corazón si alguna vez
os odié a vos o a vuestro padre.

EDGAR

Noble príncipe,
lo sé.

ALBANY

¿En dónde estabais escondido?
¿Cómo habéis sabido de las miserias de vuestro padre?

EDGAR

Al velar por ellas, *my lord*. Escuchad este corto relato,
y cuando esté contado que mi corazón estalle.   180
Para escapar del bando sanguinario
que tan de cerca me seguía —¡oh, dulzura de nuestra vida

---

intercambio, tomando la clave de obras dramáticas españolas del Siglo de Oro,
que se hacen eco del código del honor, la traducción queda resuelta más satis-
factoriamente.

[260]

que nos induce a preferir la muerte cada instante
antes que muerte súbita!— decidí disfrazarme
con andrajos de loco, y asumí una apariencia
que hasta los mismos perros despreciaban, y vestido así
encontré a mi padre, que de sus anillos sangrantes
acababa de perder sus piedras preciosas; me hice su guía,
le acompañé, mendigué para él, salvándole de la desesperación,
sin que jamás —y esa es mi culpa— me revelara a él   190
hasta hace media hora, cuando estaba armado;
no estando muy seguro de la victoria, aunque lo deseaba,
pedí su bendición, y de principio al fin
conté mis sufrimientos; mas su agobiado corazón,
¡ay!, demasiado débil ya para la lucha,
entre los dos extremos de la pasión, alegría y dolor,
se quebró sonriendo.

[EDMUND]

                Esta historia vuestra me conmueve,
y quizá me haga bien. Pero, continuad,
parece que tengáis algo más que decir.

ALBANY

Si se trata de cosas aún más tristes, calladlas,   200
porque estoy a punto de llorar
oyéndoos.

EDGAR

                Éste debiera parecer el límite
a quien no goza del dolor; hay otros, sin embargo,
que haciéndolo más grande, irían más allá
hasta llegar al fondo.
Mientras clamaba, un hombre se acercó
y, al verme en ese estado lamentable,
quiso evitar mi abominable compañía; pero viendo quién era
el que sufría de ese modo, con sus brazos robustos
rodeó mi cuello, y sus gritos sonaron,   210

[261]

haciendo estallar los cielos; se desplomó sobre mi padre,
y contó de sí mismo y de Lear la historia más penosa
que oído alguno haya escuchado; según la relataba
crecía su dolor, comenzando a romperse
los hilos de la vida; por segunda vez, entonces, las trompetas
                                                    [sonaron,
y allí quedó, agonizando.

ALBANY

¿Y quién era ese hombre?

EDGAR

Kent, sire, el desterrado Kent, que, oculto en su disfraz,
siguió a su enemistado rey, y le prestó servicios
impropios de un esclavo.

(Entra un CABALLERO.)

CABALLERO

¡A mí! ¡Ayuda! ¡Auxilio!

EDGAR

Auxilio, ¿para qué?

ALBANY

¡Hablad, señor!   220

EDGAR

¿Qué significa este puñal ensangrentado?

221-19. Este fragmento aparece omitido en *Folio*, mientras que la línea 221,
¿Qué... ensangrentado?, le es atribuida a Albany en la edición *in Quarto*.

CABALLERO

Está caliente. Y aún humea.
Estaba hace un instante en el pecho de... ¡Y ahora, está muerta!

ALBANY

¿Muerta, quién? Pero, hablad.

CABALLERO

Vuestra esposa, sire, vuestra esposa. Y su hermana
por ella envenenada; así lo ha confesado.

[EDMUND]

A ambas estaba prometido. Ahora, los tres, por fin,
nos unimos en nupcias... y en un instante.

EDGAR

Viene Kent.

(Entra KENT.*)*

ALBANY

Que se traigan los cuerpos, estén o no con vida.

(Se traen los cuerpos de GONERILL *y* REGAN.*)*

Este juicio de los cielos, que nos hace temblar,
no mueve a compasión. ¿Es ese el hombre?   230
No permite esta hora el homenaje
que las formas requieren.

KENT

He venido
para desear, por última vez, a mi rey y señor las buenas noches.
¿No está aquí?

ALBANY

Grandeza tal y la hemos olvidado.
Hablad, Edmund, ¿dónde está el rey? ¿Y dónde está Cordelia?
¿Veis esta escena, Kent?

KENT

¡Dios! ¿Por qué una cosa así?

[EDMUND]

Al menos Edmund fue amado.
Una envenenó a otra por mi causa,
y luego se quitó la vida.

ALBANY

Ya es igual. Que se les cubra el rostro.   240

[EDMUND]

Aún me queda un aliento; quiero hacer algún bien
pese a mi propia naturaleza. Enviad a alguien
—daos prisa— al castillo; pues mi orden escrita
es de muerte contra Lear y Cordelia.
¡Vamos, llegad a tiempo!

ALBANY

¡Corred, corred, corred!

[264]

¿Adónde, *my lord*? ¿Quién tiene vuestro escrito?
Mandad una señal de contraorden.

[EDMUND]

Bien pensado; tomad mi espada,
dádsela al capitán.

EDGAR

Apresuraos, por vuestra vida.

[EDMUND]

Vuestra esposa y yo le dimos orden   250
de ahorcar a Cordelia en su propia celda
culpándola de estar desesperada,
fingiendo su suicidio.

ALBANY

¡Que los dioses la protejan! Lleváoslo de aquí al instante.

(Entra LEAR, *con* CORDELIA *en sus brazos.)*

LEAR

¡Aullad! ¡Aullad! Vosotros que sois hombres de piedra.
Si tuviera vuestras lenguas y ojos los usaría de forma
que haría estallar la bóveda del cielo. Se ha ido para siempre.
Sé cuándo alguien ha muerto y cuándo vive;
está ya muerta como la misma tierra. ¡Dadme un espejo!
Si el aliento empaña o mancha su cristal,   260
¡entonces, es que vive!

---

249. *Apresuraos, por vuestra vida,* le es atribuido a Albany en *Quarto.*

KENT

¿Es este el fin predicho?

EDGAR

¿O imagen de ese horror?

ALBANY

¡Que todo se derrumbe y todo acabe!

LEAR

Hace temblar la pluma... ¡Vive aún!... Si así fuese
me redimiría de todas las tristezas
que haya sentido siempre.

KENT

¡Oh, mi buen señor!

LEAR

Os lo ruego, ¡alejaos!

EDGAR

Este es el noble Kent, vuestro amigo.

LEAR

¡Caiga la peste sobre todos vosotros, asesinos, traidores!
Podría haberla salvado; ahora se ha ido para siempre.

---

262. *¡Que todo se derrumbe y todo acabe!* En el original, «Fall and cease!» En la traducción castellana ha sido necesario introducir elementos —implícitos en inglés— para garantizar la corrección gramatical de la exclamación. La elección de «todo» como sujeto viene dictada por el contexto de tragedia de grandes dimensiones, donde se alude, incluso, al fin del mundo (línea 261).

¡Cordelia! ¡Cordelia! Quédate aún. Espera.
¿Qué es eso que decías? Su voz fue siempre suave,
dulce y leve, adorno propio de mujer.
Ya he matado al esclavo que te llevó a la horca.

CABALLERO

Doy fe de que sucedió así.

LEAR

        ¿No es cierto, amigo?
Tiempo hubo en que mi contundente espada
le habría hecho saltar. Soy viejo ahora
y estos mismos pesares me derrotan. ¿Quién sois vos?
Mis ojos ya no son de los mejores... Os lo diré enseguida.

KENT

Si alguna vez Fortuna se enorgulleció de haber amado y odiado
                                    [a dos seres,
ésos somos nosotros.

LEAR

Tengo la vista oscurecida. ¿No sois Kent?

---

279. *esos somos nosotros*. En el original, «If Fortune brag of two she lov'd and
hated, / One of them we behold». «Esos somos nosotros», en una primera lectura, resulta extraño, como traducción de *one of them we behold*, que parece significar «contemplamos a uno de ellos», lo cual no tiene mucho sentido si se sitúa
después de *two*, y ambos seres sujetos a los caprichos de la Fortuna están presen-
tes. Debe leerse, por tanto, en relación a las palabras anteriores de Kent, y en-
tenderlo, visualizándolo, como aplicable a ambos, ya que los dos tienen ante sí a
un ser amado y odiado por la Fortuna. Al traducirlo hemos elegido una forma
que haga posible que esa ambigüedad, inoperante en el nivel poético, quede su-
primida, y donde una expresión igualmente breve desempeñe una función equivalente.

Sí, el mismo,   280
vuestro servidor Kent. ¿Dónde está Cayo, vuestro siervo?

LEAR

Es un buen hombre, os lo aseguro.
Sabe batirse, y además muy rápido. Está muerto y podrido.

KENT

No, mi buen señor; yo soy el hombre...

LEAR

Me ocuparé de eso de inmediato.

KENT

...que desde el instante mismo de vuestra desgracia y vuestra
caída ha seguido vuestros tristes pasos...

LEAR

Sed bienvenido, pues.

---

280. *Tengo la vista oscurecida;* en el original, «This is a dull sight». Como en la
nota anterior, la aparente ambigüedad de estas palabras —aplicables al espectáculo sombrío o a la vista débil de Lear— se resuelve con la frase que Lear
pronuncia acto seguido, preguntándose sobre la identidad de su interlocutor:
Are you not Kent? Por tanto, contextualizándolo, sólo existe una posible lectura,
que hemos traducido sin posibilidad de confusión, convirtiendo el pronombre
demostrativo que denota proximidad, *this,* seguido del verbo *to be,* en la primera
persona del presente de indicativo del verbo «tener».
281. *Cayo.* Se menciona, por vez primera, el nombre utilizado por Kent en
su disfraz de servidor de Lear.

KENT

...Ese hombre, y no otro. Todo es tristeza, muerte, oscuridad.
Vuestras hijas mayores han buscado su propia destrucción,
y ahora están muertas en la desesperanza.

LEAR

En eso está mi pensamiento. 290

ALBANY

No sabe lo que dice, y es inútil
que nos presentemos ante él.

(Entra un mensajero.)

EDGAR

Del todo inútil.

MENSAJERO

My lord, Edmund ha muerto.

ALBANY

Y ahora ya, ¡qué importa!
Y vos, nobles amigos y señores, sabed nuestra intención:

---

288. *Todo es tristeza, muerte, oscuridad;* en el original, «All's cheerless, dark and deadly». Se han traducido los tres adjetivos, que hacen referencia a una situación de muerte y fin, por sustantivos equivalentes, que confieren mayor fuerza al convertir una situación temporal (todo está triste) en un estado permanente («todo es tristeza»). En inglés habría resultado artificial, excesivamente largo y cacofónico, el empleo de tres sustantivos, que habrían tenido que recurrir al empleo del sufijo *-ness* en los tres casos *(cheerlessness, darkness and deadliness).* Sin embargo, en castellano existen estos tres sustantivos abstractos con mayor variedad formal, uno de ellos sin sufijo en su formación, y los otros dos con variación en la terminación: tristeza y oscuridad.

294 y 296. *Sabed nuestra intención.* En el original, «Know our intent»; y *«en*

Cuanto consuelo llegue será dado
a esta gran ruina. En cuanto a Nos, restituiremos,
mientras el viejo rey esté con vida,
el poder absoluto. Vosotros, recobrad vuestros derechos,
con las ventajas y la dignidad que vuestro honor
tan justamente ha merecido. Todos nuestros amigos obtendrán   300
la recompensa a su virtud, y nuestros enemigos
el cáliz que merecen. ¡Oh! ¡Mirad, mirad!

LEAR

Y a mi pobre bufón lo han ahorcado... ¡No, no, más vida no!
¿Por qué un perro, un caballo, una rata han de tener vida,
y tú ya ni el aliento? Nunca más volverás,
¡nunca, nunca, nunca, nunca, nunca!...
Os lo ruego, soltadme este botón. Gracias, sire.
¿Veis esto? ¡Miradla! ¡Mirad sus labios!
¡Mirad! ¡Mirad!

(Muere.)

EDGAR

¡Se va! *¡My lord! ¡My lord!*

KENT

¡Rómpete, corazón! Te lo suplico, ¡rómpete!

---

cuanto a Nos, restituiremos...; en el original, «For us, we will resign...». Nótese la
forma de plural mayestático, propio del soberano, que ya empieza a emplear Albany para comunicar sus decisiones.
    303. *bufón;* «fool», en el original. Utilizado probablemente como apelativo ca-
riñoso hacia Cordelia. Algunos comentaristas han pensado que se trata de una
identificación, en la mente de Lear, con el personaje del bufón, reforzada por la
idea de que ambos personajes podrían haber sido representados por el mismo
actor.
    308-9. *¿Véis... Mirad!* Este fragmento no aparece en *Quarto.* La frase de Kent,
en la línea 310, le es atribuida a Lear en esa misma edición.

[270]

EDGAR

¡My lord! ¡Abrid los ojos!

KENT

Dejad en paz su espíritu. Permitidle marchar.
Él odiaría a quien quisiera sobre la dura rueda de este mundo
prolongar su tortura.

EDGAR

Definitivamente, lo ha dejado.

KENT

Milagro es que haya resistido tanto tiempo
cuando no hizo sino usurpar su vida.

ALBANY

Lleváoslos de aquí. Nuestro deber ahora
es cubrirnos de luto. Vosotros dos, mis amigos sinceros,
gobernad ese reino y curad este Estado malherido.

KENT

Dentro de poco, sire, yo tendré que partir.
Me llama mi señor, y no puedo negarme.

320

EDGAR

Nosotros llevaremos todo el peso de estos tiempos tan tristes
diremos lo que nos dicte el corazón, no lo que deberíamos decir.

321-4. El parlamento de Edgar aparece atribuido en *Quarto* a Albany, probablemente por la convención teatral de que el último parlamento habría de ser
dicho por la persona de rango más elevado sobre el escenario. El hecho de que
estas palabras estén, sin embargo, puestas en boca de Edgar recuerda que esta
tragedia pone los conflictos personales por encima de los generales, y, aunque
se reinstaura el orden social, como sucede generalmente en las tragedias shakes-

[271]

Los más viejos han soportado más. Nosotros que poseemos
[juventud,
nunca veremos tanto, ni viviremos tanto tiempo.

(Salen con una marcha fúnebre.)

---

pearianas, la última voz que escuchamos tiene los ecos de la tragedia privada
que se inició en la primera escena cuando las hijas mayores de Lear emplearon
una retórica de adulación que desencadenó una tragedia desestabilizadora del
equilibrio de todo el reino. Son los comportamientos individuales los que deter-
minan el rumbo del Estado, y Edgar manifiesta su deseo de que la sinceridad
sustituya, como principio rector, a la hipocresía.

ÍNDICE

Colección Letras Universales

II

DE PRÓXIMA APARICIÓN